OCTOBER NIGHTS

KEVIN LUCIA

Crystal Lake Publishing
www.CrystalLakePub.com

WELCOME
TO ANOTHER

CRYSTAL LAKE PUBLISHING
CREATION

WELCOME TO ANOTHER CRYSTAL LAKE PUBLISHING CREATION.

Thank you for supporting independent publishing and small presses. You rock, and hopefully you'll quickly realize why we've become one of the world's leading publishers of Dark Fiction and Horror. We have some of the world's best fans for a reason, and hopefully we'll be able to add you to that list really soon.

To follow us behind the scenes (while supporting independent publishing and our authors), be sure to join our interactive community of authors and readers on Patreon (https://www.patreon.com/CLP) for exclusive content. You can even subscribe to all our future releases. Otherwise drop by our website and online store (www.crystallakepub.com/). We'd love to have you.

Welcome to Crystal Lake Publishing—Tales from the Darkest Depths.

CAMEO

When it's time
Say goodbye to warm
blood,
Shut the window,
And lean into the shadow.
See what happens
just after Midnight.

—Jessica McHugh

"Notice where we are?"
"A bridge?"
"Not just *any* bridge."
"Ah. The bridge over Cocytus."
"Where the veils are thin, and once we
cross, we leave the mortal realm."
"And into the world of enchantment, where we
see things as they really are."
"Where dreams are true."
"*Stories*, too."

—Boys in the Trees, 2016

OCTOBER.

Red-orange sunsets bleed into purple-bruised skies shot through with yellow streaks. Crisp air nips at noses and earlobes. Trees wave red, orange, yellow and burnt umber tapestries, and withered leaves crackle across sidewalks. Jack-o'-lanterns grin joyful fire from porches. In front lawns skeletons, witches, ghosts, zombies, and other monsters sway and gibber. Everywhere, anticipation awaits the dark, magical birth of mystery on the last night of the month.

October.

My favorite time of year.

And, as it happened this October, I was in-between projects. I'd just completed the final edits for my novella *The Night Road* and sent them to my publisher. Two other manuscripts were with beta readers, so I had some free time. Seeing as how my best friends Chris Baker (the town Sheriff) and Father Ward (Headmaster of All Saints School) were out of town, this meant lounging on a late October Saturday morning at Bassler Memorial Library. Skimming books on folklore and mythology, as well as town history, looking for a spark to light the flame of a new story.

In many ways, I enjoy this process as much as the writing itself. So early on in a project, *ideas* were all that mattered. Gut instinct. Atmosphere. Sitting at a table tucked in a quiet corner of the library, books spread before me, notepad and pen to the side, I didn't worry about character motivations and whether they made sense. Plausibility was of no concern. I wasn't getting a headache from rooting out overwrought metaphors. I didn't care if plots seemed too convenient.

At this moment, nothing mattered but the sparks. As I

browsed legends and sifted through our town's history, I reveled in a very Bradbury-esque "tingling of the ganglion and detonation of the dendrites." If a folktale caught my fancy, I jotted down the free-association ideas it generated. When odd historical occurrences gave me pause, I scribbled existential questions about their probable (and maybe supernatural) catalysts.

I'd spend an hour or so (three, if my synapses were really humming) filling up a composition notebook with ideas, questions, quick descriptions and plot sketches, and sometimes even badly rendered pictures which looked like they were drawn by a two-year-old. Of course, several days later, after the glow of my mania faded, I'd flip through the notebook with a cooler eye, looking for concepts "with legs", as they say. But at that moment, only *ideas* mattered.

I'd decided to write something Halloween-themed, possibly for release next year. I'd gathered several books about autumn myths and legends from different cultures. I skimmed the town history books specifically for strange events occurring around October. By fortune's gracious whims, I'd also found a slim volume of poetry which included a long poem called *Halloween, A Romaunt with Lays Meditative and Devotional*, by Arthur Cleveland Coxe. Several stanzas were thought-provoking, so I jotted them down into my notebook.

I hadn't yet formed an outline for the collection, but I was well on my way. My "ganglion tingling and my dendrites detonating." So absorbing was the work, I didn't notice anyone standing next to me until I heard a gentle cough.

I looked up and saw a smiling Kevin Ellison standing at my elbow. Kevin owned Clifton Height's only used bookstore, Arcane Delights. The same store his father owned before he passed away from Alzheimer-related complications six years ago. Like his father, Kevin had retired from teaching English to run the store.

He nodded at the pile of books before me. "Must be engrossing."

I smiled sheepishly. "Sorry about that. How long have you been standing there?"

Kevin chuckled softly. "Not long. No worries. I know how you get. Any good ideas?"

I gestured at my notebook, which was already filled with several pages of notations. "I do. The hard work will come later, when I have to figure what's really good and what's not."

"Ah, yes. 'Kill your darlings.' The hardest part about writing. Well, I'm only here to complicate matters, I'm afraid."

I affected a stone-face and lifted an eyebrow, doing a very poor imitation of Mr. Spock. "Fascinating," I smiled. "Whaddya got? You know me. I'll take ideas from anywhere. Beg, borrow, even steal."

Oddly enough, Kevin didn't smile at my self-deprecation. "Remember when I re-opened Arcane Delights? When someone left us that box of . . . odd donations?"

I leaned back, interested. "Of course. That journal you found, containing stories someone wrote about Clifton Heights. They inspired *Through a Mirror, Darkly*." I offered him a wry smile. "I still think you should've let me credit you as co-author."

He shook his head, smiling . . . but an odd uneasiness lingered in his eyes. "Thanks, but no. *Through a Mirror* is all yours. Anyway."

He paused, smile fading. For a moment he looked deeply conflicted, as if he wasn't sure what to say next.

"Kevin. What?"

"We got another donation this morning. A box of books someone left outside the front door, before we opened."

I looked at him for several seconds, my ganglion tingling and my dendrites fairly exploding. "What are you saying?"

5

For the first time, I saw the black leatherbound book he carried under his arm. I recognized it, of course. I had one just like it in my office. The one Kevin found in a box of donations when he first opened Arcane Delights. The one containing stories which helped me write *Through a Mirror, Darkly*.

I gestured at the book. "Is . . . that what I think it is?"

He nodded, almost regretfully.

"I dunno, Kevin. Maybe you should use it this time. Write your own collection and take full credit."

Kevin shook his head. Shifted the black leatherbound book into his hand and held it out to me. "Nah. These aren't . . . my kind of stories. They're your kind. Plus, they're the kind you could probably use, right now."

My mouth fell open. I probably gaped like a fish for several minutes before I summoned the wherewithal to stammer, "They're Halloween stories? From Clifton Heights?"

He didn't say anything. Just shrugged, and held the book out to me. Barely restraining my eagerness, I took it—but didn't open it right away. I set it down on the table and glanced back at Kevin, feeling slightly shocked at the glimmer in his eyes. I saw what I took to be guilty regret. Even a little sadness.

I grinned. "It's fine, Kevin. Really. It's just a book, right?" I patted it with a forced nonchalance. "What's the worst that could happen?"

He offered me a small smile, turned and left. He didn't say anything, of course, because he knew better.

So did I.

Which of course didn't stop me from opening the book and reading.

'Tis the night—the night
Of the grave's delight,
And the warlocks are at their play!
Ye think that without,
The wild winds shout,
But no, it is they—it is *they*!

*Halloween, A Romaunt with Lays Meditative and
Devotional,*
by Arthur Cleveland Coxe

THE RAGE OF ACHILLES

I.

Halloween
8 PM
All Saint's Church

THE CONFESSIONAL DOOR creaked shut and someone sat on the bench. Father Ward straightened from a state of quiet meditation and listened.

Only silence.

Father Ward wasn't expecting visitors. Normally All Saints was closed on Halloween but, as a new priest freshly home, he wanted to serve his community as best as was possible. He loved hearing confession and offering what comfort he could—and for some reason he couldn't put his finger on, tonight of all nights, he felt called to the confessional booth. Whether or not anyone actually came was secondary. He was here, ready to listen to whatever troubles anyone needed to share.

Hoping to set his visitor at ease, he bent close to the grate. "Welcome to All Saints," he said. "How can I help you?"

A cough. Then, "I . . . I need to talk to someone."

"How long since your last confession?"

The man coughed again. "I honestly can't remember."

"What matters is you're here now. What's on your heart?"

A deep sigh. "I've been away, but I've come back. I need to do something, but I don't . . . don't know if I can . . . "

***

I got back in town a few hours ago, Father. First thing I did was walk around. It was quiet, but of course things usually are, here. Clifton Heights is a rarity. Our worst offenses—at least, when I lived here—usually amounted to petty larceny and low-grade vandalism. At any moment, I knew a patrol car would roll by.

Yellow lights glowed from living room windows. On each porch were jack-o'-lanterns of all kinds. Here a round Jack, carved with the classic triangle nose and eyes and a buck-toothed grin. There a taller pumpkin, eyes more rounded, with a serpentine smile. Over there, one whose grin threatened to eat the world. All of them lit by blazing candles, throwing orange flickers on front walks.

I walked on, smelling the dust of autumn leaves and the faint scent of cooking pumpkin. It reminded me, too well, of one kind of Jack-o'-lantern in particular.

The kind Evan loved making.

The kind he'd never make again.

2.

All Saints Church

"I'M SORRY FOR your loss."

A rasping sigh. "Thank you. Evan was gentle and mostly soft-spoken, unless in the midst of an . . . episode."

"What kind? If you don't mind my asking."

"Evan had difficulty controlling his emotions, and he was large for his age. He suffered from poor coordination. Often bumped into kids without meaning to. But he never intentionally hurt others. When he got angry, he just wasn't rational."

"He loved Halloween, I take it?"

Father Ward heard the man's smile. "Yes. He adored it. Over the years he dressed up as superheroes, cowboys, knights, astronauts. He loved dressing up."

"And he loved carving jack-o'-lanterns?"

"Yes. He preferred friendly jacks, though. Cross-eyed with gap-toothed grins. He wanted a funny face on our doorstep, inviting all the kids to our house. That was the interesting thing about Evan, Father. He didn't want to go trick-or-treating. He wanted kids to visit our house, so he could give them candy. But every year he was disappointed. No kids showed up. I don't know why, exactly, though I can guess. No one in school ever bullied Evan directly, Father . . . but you remember how kids are. They dislike what they don't understand.

"He didn't have many friends. Didn't participate in any school functions, except the year he was a bat boy for the varsity baseball team. That ended in disaster, when one of their best players shoved Evan to the ground because he got in the way at the plate. He wouldn't go back after that.

"His outbursts in school earned him a reputation. Kids and even their parents were always looking at him oddly. As if expecting him to do something strange, at any moment. That didn't stop Evan from believing trick or treaters would come, though. Every Halloween, he'd sit in a chair next to the door, a bowl of candy in his lap, dressed in his chosen costume, rocking back and forth, waiting.

"No one ever came."

Emotion tightened Father Ward's throat. "Must've been hard."

"He always hid his disappointment well. Always smiled and nodded, with only a small glimmer in his eye as he said, 'It's okay. They'll come next year. I know it.' But they never came. And now . . . none ever will."

"Again, my condolences. Outliving your child is a horrible burden."

"It's worse. I blame myself for allowing Evan to . . . " A sniff. "If I had never . . . "

A gasp, which dissolved into quiet sobs. Father Ward waited, his heart twisted by the pain he felt radiating through the grate. Finally, the man swallowed and continued.

"Linda felt the same way. That it was my fault. Why shouldn't she? I made a decision without her input. Anyway. Several weeks after, she packed her things and left. Three days later I got a call from a divorce lawyer in Utica."

***

Night was falling, the sky darkening. I was walking, not sure where I was headed, but I felt pulled somewhere regardless. Though I imagined the houses on both sides were filled with laughter and giggles of excitement over the night ahead, silence surged around me, the only sound my shoes scraping asphalt, crisp autumn leaves skittering along the sidewalk, and the breeze ruffling the trees.

When I reached Main Street, I saw it was lit in yellow and orange. Storefront and restaurant windows were strung with harvest-colored lights. On doorframes, orange and black streamers fluttered. The windows of several shops were populated by cardboard cutouts of ghosts, goblins, vampires, werewolves and Frankenstein monsters. They passed by in a blur, until I found myself standing before Handy's Pawn and Thrift, on Acer Street.

Don't know if you've been there, but Evan and I visited Handy's regularly. After a bad day of school one September, when Evan was eight, I picked him up early and was driving around town while he sobbed *'It's not fair!'* over and over. He said a boy had stolen his box of crayons during Art class. He'd responded the way he always did when angry. He slammed the table with both fists as hard as he could and screeched at the top of his lungs. The boy called him a retard. Evan threw himself on the floor, kicking and screaming.

I believed Evan's story. I figured his teachers did too. As usual, however, *Evan* was the one sent home. I didn't fight it. You get used to it, after a while.

Anyway, I'd turned onto Acer Street and was heading toward the Salvation Army when Evan shouted, "There!"

I stopped the car and found myself before Handy's. I'd heard of the store but had never driven by it before, much less gone inside. From what I saw, couldn't figure why I'd want to. The front windows on either side of the door offered nothing but old shoes, stacks of dusty board games, and piles of rusted tools.

I'm not sure what caught Evan's eye. It didn't matter, however. Evan had switched from sobbing to bouncing with excitement, so I didn't care what he saw in Handy's.

"What's up, bud? Want to check it out?"

As an eight-year-old, Evan acted younger. It's part of his condition. A developmental delay, they called it. I remember him pressing his face against the rear passenger window, breath fogging the glass. "Yeah."

"Okay. We'll stay ten minutes. Then we leave. Deal?"

Linda and I had learned early on Evan needed specific timeframes to help him transition from one activity to another.

"Deal." A pause, and then, "If I see something I like, can we get it, Daddy? Please?"

I didn't answer right away. Whatever I bought would become Evan's obsession for the next few weeks. He would carry it everywhere. Home, on the bus, at school, in the car, to church. He'd sleep with it. bathe with it, bring it to dinner. It would consume him, and drive us insane.

But.

I couldn't deny Evan this small comfort. Especially after the day he'd suffered. It would drive us crazy and I'd catch hell from Linda, but even so.

"Sure, Evan. If it's small. Okay?"

I glanced in the rearview mirror, and Evan's delighted grin nearly broke my heart.

"Okay!"

3.

All Saints

"HOW LONG HAVE you been gone from Clifton Heights?"

"A year. A week or so after Linda's divorce lawyer called, I left town. Went to stay with some friends down in Cortland. Stupid to skip out, but I just couldn't stay around anymore."

"Why have you come back?"

A pause.

Feet shuffling.

A deep breath, and then, "To make things right."

***

Handy's was the junk shop I'd taken it for. Tins full of screws and marbles, old tools, cameras, and jumbled piles of toys. I figured it wouldn't be long until Evan grew bored.

Surprisingly, he made a bee-line to some ceramic figurines cluttering a nearby shelf. He didn't hesitate and picked up a bird. A grayish-blue one with black wing tips. "This one, Daddy." Evan held it up, beaming. "I want this one."

I was impressed. Initially the figurines had appeared chipped and yellowed with age. In Evan's hands, however, the ceramic bird looked painstakingly crafted and life-like. Honestly, I could almost imagine it taking flight.

"Nice. What is it . . . a barn swallow?"

"It's a mockingbird. I take it you're not a birdwatcher."

I turned to see the shopkeeper standing behind us. He was tall, with a neatly-trimmed white beard and hair. His face was almost stern, but warm green eyes glimmered. He smiled gently.

"Not a birdwatcher, no," I admitted. "Not like my dad, anyway. He knew every bird around here by sight. Had most of the trees memorized, too. Me, I know a birch tree when I see one, can pick out a maple leaf . . . "

The shopkeeper nodded. "We all have our callings." He regarded Evan, who still cradled the ceramic mockingbird. "You've got something more special to mind."

Most folks looked at me with pity. In the shopkeeper's eyes I saw only admiration.

"He's not like the rest of us, is he?"

Something in his tone struck me. "No. He's not. He's different."

"Not different." The shopkeeper folded his arms and regarded Evan warmly as the boy continued to examine the mockingbird from every angle. "He's better. Better than us, anyway. And the mockingbird suits him." He paused, then said, "Mockingbirds don't do one thing but make music for us to enjoy . . . they don't harm anyone, but sing their hearts out for us. That's why it's a sin to kill a mockingbird."

I swallowed, my throat suddenly tight. I knew the quote, of course. We read *To Kill a Mockingbird* in high school. But as much as the shopkeeper's quote moved me, it hurt, too. "I appreciate the sentiment. At times, maybe you're right. Maybe he is like a mockingbird, and his uniqueness is music."

I gazed at Evan holding the mockingbird, and thought of his irrational rages over a picture he'd drawn wrong or a toy not working the way he wanted. I thought about how the slightest change in routine could send him into earthshaking meltdowns. "Too often, though, the sounds Evan makes are not musical."

"'O sing gods, the rage of Achilles,'" the shopkeeper whispered.

I sighed. "Not so romantic. He's not Achilles, or the gods, I'm afraid."

The shopkeeper nodded, instantly apologetic. "It is, of course, none of my business. I can't imagine the daily toll."

His curious spell over me faded. I glanced at my watch. "Wow. Almost four. Linda's going to think we disappeared."

The shopkeeper nodded. "By all means. The mockingbird is twenty-five cents. Feel free to bring Evan back. I have many more figurines in stock. Don't expect to have a demand for them anytime soon."

I nodded. "Sure. Evan, would you like to come in next week?"

Evan had wandered down the aisle as he'd examined the ceramic mockingbird. He glanced up, blinking slowly, looking more peaceful than I'd ever seen him. "Sure, Dad. Sounds great."

I shrugged. "Looks like we've got a deal."

The shopkeeper waved toward the sales counter. "A pleasure to serve you. If you'll follow me?"

***

Oddly enough, Evan didn't obsess over the figurines he would go on to collect like I'd feared he would. He did love them, however. We often came across Evan in his room, gazing at them on the narrow wooden shelf I mounted the day after purchasing the mockingbird. He sat on the edge of the bed, hands folded in his lap, rocking gently, humming to himself.

Evan's collection grew. He added more birds, along with owls, hawks, eagles, foxes, raccoons, and deer. In the five years Evan collected them, never once did the shopkeeper indicate they were in danger of running out. Up until the last day, the shelves stretched around his bedroom.

After it happened, I sat on his bed, staring at the figurines. They glared at me, their eyes accusing me for my failure to protect him. I sat there for hours, taking their judgment.

Two weeks later, Linda left while I sat there. I didn't hear her leave. Didn't hear if she said goodbye.

I never spoke to her again.

4.

All Saints

FATHER WARD RUBBED his mouth, thinking. He felt compelled to keep the man talking as long as possible. Why, he didn't know. "If you don't mind my asking . . . what was your son's diagnosis?"

"Autism. High-functioning. Intelligent, but as I said, he couldn't handle complex situations. Would get confused and irrational. Also, he had to be taught things repeatedly. Things other kids picked up on their own." The man chuckled slightly. "We brushed our teeth, combed our hair and put on deodorant together every day. He learned best by mimicking others. Got to be our morning routine. He looked forward to it. Needed it."

"Routine was important to him."

"Yes. Everything had to be just so. For a while, Linda and I worried his intelligence would be wasted because of it. He made progress, though. Developed a charming personality, got better at socializing. He still needed his routines, but he became more flexible, sometimes initiating change himself. See, he wanted to do something different. Wanted to do something on his own. And I let him. I . . . " His voice dissolved into wracking sobs.

Father Ward remained silent, waiting until the man pulled himself together, which he did after several minutes. "What happened?"

A deep sigh. "It was a week before Halloween. Friday. We always went to Handy's for a figurine on Fridays. He also had library books to return. He loved reading. We thought after high school maybe he could take a few classes at Webb Community. Maybe someday work a job. Something to give him purpose." A harsh sob.

Silence, until the man continued.

***

A week before Halloween, Evan was excited as usual. He wanted to see the decorations on Main Street, and that night we were going to carve our jack. He couldn't wait.

Anyway, we visited Handy's first. He took longer than usual because he wanted to see their Halloween toys and costumes. I often wonder if we'd gotten out of there earlier, could we have avoided what happened?

He bought a cardinal. I'll never forget it. A bright red cardinal, perched on a branch. He brought it to the counter himself, paid for it with the allowance he earned doing simple chores around the house. The shopkeeper asked how school was going. Evan told him in exhaustive detail. The routine completed, we were on the sidewalk, at the car when he asked, "Dad . . . I want to do it myself this time."

I stopped, car door open. "Do what?"

Evan took a deep breath—eyes shining, as if he was excited—and said, "I want to return my books alone."

"Sure, Ev. I'll wait in the lobby—"

He shook his head, determined. "No. I want to cross the street by myself. Go in, return my books, get new ones, and cross the street, by myself. You can wait on the sidewalk."

This caught me off guard, though I suppose it shouldn't have. He'd been asking to do more things on his own. But cross the street by himself—twice? Go in and out—by himself?

"I dunno. Not sure if you're ready."

"You're not ready. I am."

He was right. It wasn't just about me worrying that he wasn't ready. It was about me not being ready to accept that he might be.

"You can stand on the sidewalk and watch me, Dad," he said, still serious. "You can see me the whole way."

I should've said no.

God, I should've said no. Or at least called Linda first. But I was so tired. You love your kid, want to accept him as he is, protect him . . . But you want him to be at least a *little* normal. To fit in. Especially when, even though he's never said it, you know he wants to fit in, too. And all I could think about, standing there, was him waiting on our front porch every Halloween for kids who never came. I could at least give him this.

Why didn't I call Linda?

Here's the worst part.

I knew she'd say no. She'd want me to play it safe.

I was tired of safe.

***

Bassler Memorial Library is around the corner from Handy's, on the opposite side of Main Street, right before Black Creek Bridge. I'd forgotten how wide Main Street was at the crosswalk. For a moment I thought about backing out and walking Evan into the library as usual.

But I knew such a change wouldn't be well received. Evan had improved at dealing with the unexpected, but when you told him something was going to happen in a certain way, it *had* to happen that way. Evan would accept no alternatives. He was thirteen, and if you met him in passing, he seemed normal enough. But he could pitch a fit with the best of them. It was too late to renege on our deal. Especially if I didn't want him screaming and crying and, believe it or not, throwing himself to the ground.

We reached the crosswalk. He pressed the button for the 'walk' sign on the telephone pole and waited patiently for it to click over. Humming, gently working his new cardinal figurine in his hands. The light on the other side of the street finally showed a walking green figure. He smiled and said, "Don't worry, Dad. I'll be fine."

Those were his last words.

But at the time, I felt okay. There wasn't any traffic, and

my unease had receded. I thought it was a big opportunity, y'know? For him and me. So much so, on a whim, I dug into my pocket and pulled out my iPhone, tapped the camera app and told Evan, "Smile big. Mom'll be proud."

He stopped and smiled over his shoulder.

I snapped the picture.

Without another word, he continued across Main Street.

Here's another mistake. I should've watched him the whole way and back. But he was *doing* it. I was proud of him and wanted to share. So, as he was crossing the street, because there were no cars, I texted the picture of him to Linda, with the caption: Our boy's growing up!

She called right away. Her response was *not* excited at all.

"What the hell is he doing?"

I cringed at her tone. I was hoping she would see this as a good sign, but I guess deep down I'd known she'd be upset. Here's the thing: though I'd mostly accepted Evan's autism, I wanted him to grow. Be more independent. Try new things. Hell, I didn't care if he *never* went to college. He could live with us for as long as he needed. I wasn't in a hurry for him to get out. I just wanted him to live. Linda did too. But mothers always want to protect their babies, don't they? Evan was her baby. She wanted to protect him. Maybe too much. I'm not going to lie. We fought about that, occasionally.

Well, maybe more than occasionally. Loudly, too.

The worst part?

Sometimes, in my lowest moments . . . I wonder if I sent that picture to agitate her.

"Well," I said into the phone, "Evan asked to cross the street by himself. He had a good day at school, so I thought, 'Why not?' We've been talking about giving him more freedom, so . . . "

"So you're letting him cross Main Street by himself? Are you crazy?"

I tried to force my anger down. I heard 'Are you crazy?' a lot. Too much.

"C'mon, Linda."

Evan had reached the median. He stopped, looked both ways and continued. "He's halfway across. There aren't any cars. Hardly ever are in this part of town."

"You should've called me. You can't make snap decisions like this. It's not safe! You can't treat Evan normally!"

My control slipped. "Right." Evan reached the other side and entered the library. "Because it's better to treat him like a freak."

"You know that's not what I mean. We have to be careful. You're too reckless!"

"He'll be fine. I know we have to be careful, but we can't keep him locked away from the world—"

"You're such an ass. Of course I don't want that. But I wouldn't let him cross a street by himself on a whim, without running it by you first! I'll bet you didn't even remind him not to wear his earbuds!"

It hit me, hard.

She was right.

See, Evan had an iPod loaded with his favorite music. Music calmed him. He took his iPod everywhere.

I was going to reply—can't remember with what, now—something spiteful and petty, I'm sure.

Evan's condition was hard on our marriage. After he was diagnosed, his autism dominated our lives. Did you know two-thirds of marriages with special needs children end in divorce? I know why. All your energy is focused on dealing with the rages. The screaming, kicking, throwing things. Maintaining irrational routines. Evan hardly slept at all because his mind never stopped. Ever. We were walking zombies half the time. Stumbling through life on three to four hours of sleep a night. Tough situations bring out the best or the worst in people. I'm afraid it brought out the worst in us. Linda and I had been worn down to the nubs, with nothing left for each other.

I took a deep breath and saw Evan standing on the opposite sidewalk, having apparently returned his books and gotten new ones. When the green walking figure flashed, he started across the street toward me.

"He's fine. He's already on his way back. You're right, maybe I should've called you first, and I will next time—"

A snort. *"Sure."*

I ignored her and continued. "But he's fine, so stop worrying . . . "

There's an intersection past Bassler Library, where Acer Street cuts across Main. I don't know how I didn't see the battered green truck idling there at the stoplight, or hear it. I don't know how long it sat there before turning right onto Main Street. All I know is I didn't notice it until the driver got impatient waiting for the light to change.

***

With a coughing grumble, the green truck turned right onto Main. Fear lanced through my heart, freezing it, but I saw Evan had cleared the truck's lane. If he kept going the truck would miss him. He'd be safe and it'd be an insane close-call story I could tell Linda and she'd rip me a new one, but he'd be safe . . .

It happened, in flickers. The truck, accelerating. Evan, a step and a half clear of its path. He dropped something which hit the street and shattered. I can still hear it shattering, today.

He turned, saw what remained of his newly purchased cardinal. Closed his hands into fists, and screamed. He couldn't hear me shouting. Couldn't hear the truck. The slender white wires of his earbuds trailing from his ears to his iPod in his right coat pocket. Just like Linda said, I'd forgotten to tell Evan not to listen to his music when crossing the street.

Evan turned, reaching for the cardinal, screaming,

bending over into the truck's path. *I* screamed. The truck growled, but if Evan's iPod was turned up as high as usual . . .

His hand touched the cardinal's bright red shards.

The truck hit him.

I can't give you a play-by-play. It's all a jumbled blur. I didn't hear a sickening crunch, or a wet thump. The truck hit my son's head, flipping him away, onto his back. I didn't hear the back of his head strike asphalt, only my ragged breath thundering in my ears as I ran toward him.

Lying on his back.

Head surrounded by a widening pool of blood.

Staring sightlessly at the sky, library books scattered around him, pieces of the cardinal clutched in his fist.

The truck sped away.

I raised my iPhone—from which my wife was screaming—and took a picture of the license plate.

5.

All Saints

GRIEF CLENCHED FATHER Ward's heart. He'd seen some terrible things as an Army Chaplain in Afghanistan. But to see this happen to someone you love, before your eyes . . .

"Did they find the truck?"

An emotion-choked pause. "Yes. With my picture of the license, it was easy. Judd Kirsch is a forty-two-year-old bachelor who works days at the lumbermill. He lives in the Commons Trailer Park. Lot 34. He struggled with a mild drinking problem he readily admitted to, but the day he took my son away had been an especially hard one at the mill. He'd downed a few more beers than usual over dinner at The Stumble Inn. Was on his way home to sleep it off when he turned right onto Main Street. He swerved slightly when he reached down to grab what he says was a can of Pepsi from the cooler in the passenger seat. He says he wanted to get some caffeine in his system to 'even out.' When his truck clipped my son in the head, he swore it was a pothole, and if he'd known he'd hit someone, he would've stopped.

"He couldn't stop crying at the pre-trial hearing. Was put on suicide watch in jail. Guess he tried to hang himself with his belt, which put the trial off, because he was remanded downstate to Riverdale Psychiatric for evaluation.

"But that doesn't matter. He took my son away. Evan's gone and he's never coming back. And what did they finally decide to do? Take his driver's license away for three years, slap him with civil fines, make him take AA. Sure, my lawyer says me leaving during the trial screwed things up, because it left things in Linda's hands, and she got spineless and didn't push for a harsher sentence. But I'm back now. Because Evan won't stop. He never stops. He wants me to do something about it. Make it right, finally.

"Make Kirsch pay."

***

Before I came here to confess, Father, I walked around and ended up at Handy's, like I said. It was the same as the last time I'd been there, decorated for the season. Strings of yellow and orange lights ran along the shelves. A whole wall had been given over to Halloween-themed trinkets. Plastic jack-o'-lanterns and skeletons, pumpkin flashlights, trick or treat buckets, wax vampire teeth, face paints, rows of Halloween costumes on hangers, and masks.

"May I help you?"

I faced the shopkeeper. His eyes widened slightly. "Mr. Carrington. I would say it's good to see you, but I know the memories this place must hold. It's been some time since we last spoke."

I nodded. "Yes."

"I can't express how sorry I am. Any condolences I could offer would feel meaningless, I'm sure. What happened was a tragedy, for everyone involved, but of course for Evan . . . for someone so vibrant and alive . . . "

I never understood the shopkeeper's odd, awe-struck reverence of Evan. Linda and I had endured too many of his meltdowns and draining obsessions to feel the same, but I appreciated the gesture anyway.

"Thank you. You were always kind to Evan. It meant a lot. I wanted to say thank you, and . . . "

I shrugged and tried to leave, realizing I'd done what I'd come to do. "Anyway. Thank you. Evan loved this store. Coming here meant a lot, and . . . "

"I know why you're here."

The words startled me, halting me mid-step. They also

sparked an unreasoning anger in me, of all things. Along with guilt.

I know why you're here.

"The past can't be changed," the shopkeeper said gently. "Nothing you do tonight will restore Evan."

I turned to the shopkeeper and something flipped inside me. I don't know how else to describe it. I went from feeling aggravated at him—all right, pissed off—to feeling empty.

I shook my head. "Don't know what you're talking about."

The shopkeeper stepped forward and gripped my elbow firmly. "Don't do what you came to do."

He drew me closer, and something in his eyes drilled me to my core. "You need to let go, Peter."

His words touched me. I almost gave in, right then and there. Almost let go of the pain and anger.

But I couldn't forget Evan's sightless gaze.

The shopkeeper, maybe feeling the tension in my arm, said again, "You don't have to do this."

I pulled myself from him and walked away, heading to the door. "Happy Halloween," I said quietly. "Maybe I'll stop by again next year."

The bell rang as I pushed through the front door. Something held me up, though. I paused in the doorway, suddenly wishing to feel the shopkeeper's firm hand clasp my shoulder, along with his voice softly rasping, "This is your last chance."

But there was nothing.

When I looked over my shoulder, the shopkeeper was gone. Slipped quietly away, into the back room maybe. I waited for a minute, half-expecting him to magically reappear next to me, gently pushing the door closed, not letting me leave.

Nothing.

I turned away and left.

6.

All Saints

"SO HERE I AM. That's what brought me here; what the shopkeeper said. How can I let go of what happened to Evan?"

Father Ward sat forward, hands clasped before him. He couldn't quiet an odd feeling about this man's story. More worrisome, however, was the man—Peter's—assertion he was here to do something for his son. To make this Judd Kirsch pay.

"Sir—Peter, if I may—please understand, I don't want to trivialize your experience. I can see how you feel as if your son is with you. The memories of our lost loved ones are never gone. They're always with us. But we also can't underestimate the role guilt plays in the grieving process. I'm not trying to diminish your pain, but—"

"No!"

Father Ward jerked back from the confessional grate, not only because of the anger in Peter's tone, but also because of an icy menace he felt seeping into his booth.

"It's my son. Yes, I feel guilt, for letting him cross the street alone. For running away during the trial. For not being around to make sure that *shit* who took my son got punished right. That shit who is now 'sober' and attending AA once a week and feels terrible about what he did, but really he's probably sitting in his shit-ass trailer right now, lot 34, sucking down a cold one and laughing his ass off at how he dodged jail. Evan wants me to make right, he . . . "

A wrenching sob.

The confessional door slammed open, and the man—Peter—stumbled down the aisle, crying "Evan! Oh, God Evan!" over and over.

Father Ward sat frozen.

All Saint's front doors opened and slammed shut.

Shivering, gripped by a sudden cold which chilled him to the bone, Father Ward slowly stood and pushed open the door of his booth. The church appeared as it always had. A simple Adirondack Catholic Church, not baroque nor Gothic, sanctuary paneled with earth-toned wood, polished and gleaming oak pews, the Stations of the Cross in stained glass windows all around. The lights were dim. The flickering votive candles near the exit cast an air of peaceful reverence.

The church was empty.

He sagged against the confessional, gripped by conflict. He knew it was impossible to help everyone. But every time he couldn't help, when someone's pain burned too greatly for comfort . . .

lot 34
he's there right now
laughing
make it right
Evan wants me to make it right

. . . he was reminded of his own failures. How he'd let others down. Especially overseas on his tour.

He closed his eyes and prayed. *Please, God. This man— Peter—he can't be serious, can't be planning to do . . . what?*

Acid churned in his stomach. He couldn't call the police. He'd be violating The Sacrament of Confession. And for what? It wasn't a crime to express anger or the desire for revenge. He had no proof this man was going to do anything . . .

lot 34
he's there right now

Father Ward gripped the confessional door-frame, resolution flooding through him, strengthening his legs. He couldn't call the police based on a confession. He had no real evidence, and he'd be breaking a sacrament. But he didn't have to sit here. He hadn't been a soldier; he'd been an Army Chaplain. Had never held a gun in combat, but he'd served in Afghanistan. He'd seen good men die, seen innocent bystanders suffer, and he'd seen other things rational thought couldn't explain. He wasn't going to sit and wait.

He just wasn't the type.

7.

DESPITE A MOUNTING URGENCY, Father Ward drove the speed limit through town. At only quarter to nine, the sidewalks were teeming with hordes of goblins, princesses, ghosts, superheroes and monsters, and their parents, big brothers and sisters. A lover of Halloween since childhood, the sight usually warmed him. Tonight, however, he could only think of:

lot 34
Evan wants
make it right

Within ten minutes he turned onto Bassler Road, leaving town. Five minutes later, he turned right into the Commons Trailer Park. A wave of nostalgia crested inside, surprising in its strength. He remembered playing basketball on the Commons asphalt court with his friends. Buying trinkets at the Commons Community yard sales. He hadn't been here in more than ten years, but it looked mostly the same. He drove slowly, even though every nerve in his body screamed *HURRY!* as he scoured the lot numbers for . . .

34.

He braked and put his car into park. Slowly, he opened the door and got out. He stood and stared, gripped by worry.

The trailer on lot 34 sat dark and silent. The screen door hung open, swinging in the slight breeze, banging against the siding. No other cars—certainly not a green pick-up truck—sat in the short gravel drive. The trailer appeared empty, as if no one was home.

Even so, the urgent feeling that he must *do something* strengthened, along with the looming sense of the awful, the tragic, the unavoidable, and even worse: the inevitable.

"You son of a bitch!"

"No, God . . . no! I never meant to—"

A sharp crack and a flash of light came from within the trailer.

"No!" Father Ward stumbled forward, but before he could make it to the front steps he thought he heard, floating on the breeze, *"Evan . . . I'm sorry."*

Another crack, a flash of light, and a heavy thump, like a body falling.

He cried out again, all his emotions concentrated to a point. He lurched forward, reaching out to grab the small porch's railing to haul himself up the steps and into the trailer, knowing it would be worse than anything he'd seen overseas.

His hand closed on air.

His right foot descended through empty space. He stumbled and fell to one knee, barely avoiding falling flat on his face. He rested there for a moment, mind blank, and sucked several deep breaths before he stood on shaking legs.

He was standing in an empty rectangular patch of knee-high grass, in an empty lot where the trailer had once been.

Questions swirled around him.

He shoved them aside.

Father Ward stumble-walked back to his car. He turned and regarded the now leaning, rotted lot sign in the car's headlights. He could barely make out the faded 34.

He stared at the sign.

Pushing away his questions.

He shook his head, got into his car and pulled away.

***

A bell jingled when Father Ward opened and closed Handy's door. He'd driven straight from the Commons, mind still blank. On some level he was surprised Handy's was open after eight on Halloween night, but on a deeper level, he wasn't surprised at all.

He glanced around as he walked down the middle aisle. Everything was as Peter had described, decorated for

Halloween. Even in his confusion, Father Ward felt vaguely pleased at how Handy's looked—it was still the same as when he and his friends frequented its cluttered shelves, buying odds and ends with their lawn-mowing money. He even fancied he recognized a few items. An old Magic Eight Ball, and a Louisville Slugger.

"Father Ward. So good to see you."

He glanced up to see the shopkeeper standing behind the sales counter. He had to blink a few times, experiencing a curious folding of time. The shopkeeper looked like he hadn't aged a day.

Father Ward smiled. "You know me? Are you a parishioner of All Saints?"

The shopkeeper chuckled, waving. "Afraid not, Father. I've become a bit agnostic in my old age. No, word traveled fast when you returned from Afghanistan. The people here love and respect you, son." The shopkeeper's expression sobered a bit, eyes bright and penetrating. "I hope you know this."

Father Ward shrugged. The last thing he wanted to talk about was his military service. "I suppose," he said lightly, in an attempt to brush off the shopkeeper's oddly weighted comment.

"What can I do for you?"

There it was. Father Ward breathed deep, pulled back the wall he'd erected at the Commons, and finally let his questions free. "This is going to sound odd. Maybe even crazy. And I can't tell you much, because it involves the Sacrament of Confession . . . "

The shopkeeper nodded. "Of course. Even an agnostic grump like myself understands the importance of the sacraments. Go on, and don't worry about sounding crazy. You grew up here. You know Clifton Heights is a . . . unique town."

"Yes. Anyway, out of curiosity . . . you do much business tonight? It's Halloween, so . . . "

The shopkeeper nodded. "Some business, yes." He gestured at a large glass bowl of Snickers candy bars on the counter. "Mostly for the little ones who've visited. Mr. Handy loves children and Halloween. So do I. We make a point of staying open late on Halloween. We've become a regular stop on the children's rounds the past few years."

Father Ward swallowed down the uneasy feelings in his gut. "Any other visitors? Say . . . a regular who hasn't visited in a while, maybe because they've been out of town for about a year?"

Understanding dawned in the shopkeeper's eyes. He folded his arms and regarded Father Ward closely. "Well. Clifton Heights has certainly welcomed you home with open arms, hasn't it? I take it you were hearing confessions tonight at All Saints?"

Father Ward nodded.

"Did Father Thomas say anything in particular about hearing confessions on Halloween night?"

Father Ward shook his head. "He doesn't hear confessions on Halloween."

The shopkeeper nodded gravely. "Not anymore, anyway. And you can bet there's a reason." He regarded Father Ward closely. "Why were you?"

Father Ward shrugged. "I'm new. I volunteered. Don't know why. Just . . . wanted to. Felt like I . . . I would be needed, tonight."

The shopkeeper sighed. "I know because of the sacrament you can't say much, so I'll put it simply: Yes, someone visited tonight. A former regular. Peter Carrington. He used to visit every Friday to buy a ceramic figurine for his son Evan. Wonderful boy. He had many special needs, but was still a bright light. A tragedy, what happened to him."

Father Ward felt himself nod unconsciously, even though he wasn't supposed to confirm any of this. "What happened?"

The shopkeeper continued. "Hit and run around the corner. A local man—Judd Kirsch—turned too quickly and hit Evan as he was crossing the street, coming back from the library. Apparently Evan dropped something, bent over to pick it up. Kirsch claimed he never saw the boy and kept driving, thinking he'd hit a pothole. Unfortunately, Kirsch had a bit of a drinking problem. He hit Evan and went home to his trailer in the Commons, unaware."

Father Ward licked his lips. "I came from there, and . . . I'm not sure what I saw."

The shopkeeper's eyes widened. "So you tried to actually stop it? Fascinating." He offered Father Ward an enigmatic grin. "You've come home for real."

"I didn't . . . I thought . . . " Father Ward swallowed, forcing himself to breathe slowly. "There wasn't anything there. No trailer on lot 34, but I thought . . . I saw muzzle flashes . . . but it was gone. There wasn't anything there but weeds."

"Of course not. Hasn't been for eight years. Even after hauling off Kirsch's old trailer and putting a new one there, Phil Seward couldn't get anyone to stay there past Halloween, as I'm sure you know why."

Father Ward rubbed the back of his neck. Puzzle-pieces fit together in his head, but the picture forming . . . could he believe it?

"At the risk of asking you to violate your vows . . . I assume you don't need to hear the whole story. You've already heard it."

Father Ward nodded. "I'll hear it again next year . . . won't I? If I hear confessions on Halloween night."

A slow nod. "I imagine, yes."

"How long ago did this happen?"

"The accident, eleven years ago. Peter killing Kirsch and himself, ten."

"So he keeps coming back," Father Ward whispered. "Why? Because of his guilt, his pain, he can't get over Evan's death . . . ?"

Evan wants me to make it right

The shopkeeper shook his head. "It's worse, I think," he said softly. "Evan's not dead."

Father Ward stared. "What?"

"Evan survived the accident. He suffered severe cerebral hemorrhaging, but he didn't die."

"He's alive?" Father Ward rasped. "He's alive, and every year . . . "

he won't stop
he never stops
when he gets angry
he isn't rational

"He's in a vegetative state, kept alive by machines, with no brain activity detected since the accident," the shopkeeper said, his voice oddly flat. "His mother refuses to cease life support. She left Peter, but still lives in town."

he won't stop
he never stops

"'O sing, gods,'" Father Ward whispered, "'the rage of Achilles.'"

"Indeed."

Silence fell between them. There was nothing more to say, nothing more Father Ward could say, given his vows.

"Does Mrs. Carrington . . . allow visitors for Evan?"

The shopkeeper nodded slowly. "It is my understanding, yes. And, for the record: far as I know, Father Thomas has never visited Evan. Nor have I spoken to him on Halloween night, as I am with you now."

"He's busy," Father Ward said automatically, speaking by rote. "Running All Saints Academy and the church, and being the chairman of the board for the Boys' Home."

"Indeed he is. But if there's anyone who can someday offer Peter Tomas . . . or Evan . . . absolution, I believe it's the man who rushes off to prevent something awful from happening without regard to his own safety, the man who has an open mind about . . . certain things."

Father Ward nodded, his head finally empty again, his heart heavy. As he turned to leave, the shopkeeper said, "Happy Halloween, Father Ward. Don't be a stranger."

Father Ward regarded the shopkeeper, again struck by the illusion that the man was ageless. "Thank you. I will."

He turned and pushed through the door, and stepped out into the cool October night.

I heard the sound of coming wings;
'Twas dark as the second death,
But I could see a thousand things,
For I heard a being's breath:
A whisper—a sigh—was here—was there,
For darkness is Fancy's light:
And horrible phantoms were filling the air,
For I heard the low stroke of their flight.
Oh should they touch me!
Or oh should they clutch me!
How shrunk my poor soul in its fright!

*Halloween, A Romaunt with Lays Meditative and
Devotional,*
by Arthur Cleveland Coxe

LONG NIGHT
IN THE VALLEY

I.

October 31ˢᵗ
The Stumble Inn

"WHAT THE HELL'S wrong with you guys? Get your asses in gear!"

Bobby Malfi rapped the mahogany bar in muted anger. He was a short man with narrow shoulders, arthritic knuckles and a weathered face. An avid sports fan who hadn't played a single game of any kind in his life, he held strong opinions about how every sport *should* be played. Everyone loved the old coot, though. He attended every Clifton Heights home sporting event without fail, and over the years, his presence became talismanic. Bobby's attendance most likely meant victory, but his absence brought ill tidings of doom for the home team.

At the moment, Bobby's main concern was professional basketball. He rapped the bar again. "Damn it. Got money on this game. The Knicks're playing like a bunch of junior high brats. Running around like chickens with their heads cut off!"

He waved at the small television mounted on the wall at the end of the bar. "Down twenty-five. So much for this 'championship' season the papers been talking about."

Bobby scowled at the five harried blue figures racing around as five white figures efficiently and calmly played tight, aggressive defense. One of the Knicks' guards (a blue figure) launched an off-balance three-point shot. Bobby tracked it hopefully, squeezing his hand into a fist . . .

The basketball ricocheted off the rim.

Tinny applause roared from the television as a player in white grabbed the rebound and dribbled up the court.

"Damn!" Bobby pounded the bar. "Last year, the Knicks averaged nearly a hundred points a game," he complained to the bartender, Gus Ambrose, who watched the game from the other side of the bar. "It's the middle of the third quarter and they've barely cracked sixty. What the hell?"

Gus shrugged his broad shoulders. "It's pre-season, Bobby," he said as he wiped down the bar absentmindedly. "Why in the world would you bet on a pre-season game?"

"Because my brother Buster had a line on these guys. Said they were going to wipe the floor with the Spurs tonight. Got all these off-season trades which made them contenders."

Another distant roar from the television as the home crowd—San Antonio—voiced their appreciation. Bobby scowled and waved again. "This sure ain't the look of a contender!"

Gus flipped the towel onto his left shoulder, crossed his arms and shrugged. "Guess maybe Buster should stick with running his cab business instead of trying to be a bookie."

Bobby grabbed his nearly empty mug of beer. "Ain't *that* the God's honest truth." He tossed back his drink, thumped it back down on the bar and slid it toward Gus. Without taking his eyes off the television, Gus grabbed the mug. He took it over to the Saranack Black & Tan tap, and began filling it. "Shouldn't you be out trick or treating with the grandkids?"

"Their grandmother's taking them out with my daughter. She loves that stuff. Me? After working all day at the quarry? Fuck no. Besides," he gestured at the television, "*this* is enough of a horror show, for fuck's sake." Another burst of applause. "C'mon! Stop throwing away the damn ball!"

Sitting on the opposite end of the bar, Micah Cassidy stared into the mirror behind rows of liquor bottles, nursing his beer. He was trying to ignore the conversation between Bobby and Gus, though it was nearly impossible, as they were the only other ones there. Also, they were talking basketball—a subject Micah couldn't ignore, no matter how much he wanted to. Which didn't make sense, of course. After everything that had happened, he should hate the game. He didn't watch it on television anymore, and didn't read the sports page every day, either. However, despite his best intentions, when basketball was mentioned within earshot, he always listened. He couldn't help it.

Micah sighed as his gaze traveled the length of the bar. It was Halloween night, part of the reason why The Inn was empty. Most of the regulars were either out trick-or-treating with their families or standing watch over their homes in their annual—but vain—attempt to ward off legions of Clifton Heights teens armed with eggs, soap and toilet paper.

He and Amy had no kids, and he didn't care what the teens did tonight. He'd clean it up tomorrow. Besides, they didn't see many teens where they lived, out on Gato Road. Not even on Halloween night. Too far out of town. Worst they'd suffered last year was a smashed jack-o'-lantern.

Gus had made a half-hearted attempt to decorate the bar for the season. Orange lights circled the mirror behind the bar. Sitting at regular intervals among the liquor bottles were plastic, electric light-up jack-o'-lanterns. Probably everyone's favorite decoration was the life-sized cardboard cutout of Elvira mounted to the wall next to the men's restroom. It always gathered jokes and comments, and even one or two drunken marriage proposals every October.

"Dammit," Bobby spat, apparently disgusted by another Knicks mistake. "Haven't you guys ever heard of ball movement? Work the ball around the perimeter, for God's sake! At least *try* to find the open man!"

Micah grunted, knowing he should keep quiet. Take the path of least resistance, as always. It's what he'd done for the past twenty-eight years, after all. How he'd managed to survive, emotionally. Keep quiet to himself at all times. Sometimes he couldn't, however, much as he wanted to.

"It's San Antonio's man-to-man defense," he said, staring into the plastic leer of a jack-o'-lantern on the other side of the bar. "Their switches are so tight most teams turn the ball over after two or three passes. Forces run-and-gun teams to play a half-court offense. Slows them down. Forces them out of their fast break."

Micah could almost feel Bobby turning a skeptical gaze on him, but he didn't look up. He continued, staring into the plastic jack-o'-lantern's black, triangle eyes. "The Knicks are a fast break team. Half-court offense isn't their strength. So San Antonio tightens the screws on defense, switching on every screen or pick and roll. Forces the Knicks to grind out the clock, which they don't like to do. They like to score quick and hard. Usually off the second pass, to keep other teams off-balance. The more they have to pass the ball around, the sloppier they get."

Cheers exploded again from the television. Bobby thumped the bar. "Sumbitch. Another turnover, and San Antonio scores again."

Micah looked up and met Bobby's rueful grimace. "Looks like you're right," Bobby growled. "Knicks can't make more than three passes before they cough up the damn ball."

Micah shrugged, offering a small smile, nothing more. He shouldn't have spoken. If he stopped now and didn't say anything more, maybe the old guy would forget about him and turn his focus back to the game, instead of . . .

"This guy knows his ball," Bobby said to Gus Ambrose. "He play somewhere?"

Too late.

Gus smiled as he picked up a glass mug and started toweling it off. He was primed to tell the story, like always. Micah looked down into his beer and cursed silently. He didn't blame Gus. He meant well. It was his own fault. He should've kept quiet.

"C'mon, Bobby. You've never heard of Micah Cassidy, from Old Forge High?"

Bobby shook his head. "I'm a loyal Clifton Heights fan, Gus. You know that. If it ain't happening in the 'Heights, it ain't happening."

"Well then." Gus waved in his direction. "This is Micah Cassidy. He's . . . oh, hell. Micah, do you mind if . . . ?"

To his credit, Gus looked embarrassed at nearly rambling into his story without asking permission first. Micah supposed if he'd stopped Gus the first time he'd told his tale to a Stumble Inn patron years ago, the bartender wouldn't have kept repeating it over and over. It was too late now. Besides, Micah knew if he *did* complain, Gus would feel bad for a night or two, then retell the whole story to someone else without hesitation.

He waved, giving Gus permission to continue.

Besides, after tonight he'd never have to hear Gus tell that story ever again.

"This is Micah Cassidy," Gus continued, "one of the best shooting guards ever to play in Webb County. Four-year varsity starter at Old Forge High. Scored over 3,000 points in his career. Twenty-eight years later he still holds the number one spot in most points scored in Section Two, Class C Division. Scouts from all over were calling him. Lots of scouts thought he could go pro. If not the NBA, then overseas in Europe."

Micah looked away, back into those black triangle eyes on the other side of the bar, feeling Bobby Malfi stare at him, like everyone did when Gus spun his tale. "DI or *pro* ball, huh? Don't look like much. Not very tall, is he?" A pause. Then, directed at him, "No offense, course."

Micah shrugged as Gus defended his size, like so many times before.

"Maybe not, but Micah was quick as a jackrabbit. He dribbled that basketball like it was a yo-yo on a string. Was a hawk on defense. Led the conference in steals two years running. And his jump shot, friend. Man alive. Like a *machine*. Precision, every single time. He still holds the record for highest career field-goal percentage. I swear he shot better the harder defenses guarded him. Plus, he could jump outta the gym. I can't count how many times he drove the lane and dunked over players twice his size. Micah landed a full-ride to Syracuse. Would've blown it up there. I know it."

Micah's cue. He knew it well. Much as he hated the attention, he couldn't blow off Gus. The guy would be crushed, in his own way, because then he wouldn't be able to vigorously defend Micah's greatness. "C'mon, Gus," he protested weakly. "Lot of great players on Syracuse's squad that year." He looked away from the plastic jack-o'-lantern and offered Gus and Bobby a weak grin. "I would've been lucky to play twenty minutes a game."

Gus beamed, delighted Micah was playing along. "No way. You were exactly what they needed. A marksman from beyond the three-point arc who was also a playmaker off the dribble. You would've started freshman year. I'm sure of it."

Micah shrugged. Playing the role Gus wanted him to. He knew from experience if he did, the whole spiel would end sooner. "Doesn't matter now."

Gus folded his arms, somber expression darkening his face as he turned and gazed out the front window. "Yeah. Damn shame."

He said nothing for several seconds. Staring into the middle distance, blithely ignoring Bobby, who in turn was staring at Gus, eyes wide and curious. Gus loved to put on a show. He'd keep staring silently out the front window until . . .

"Well?" Bobby blurted, face drawn tight in anticipation. "Are you gonna finish the story, or ain't ya?"

Gus nodded slowly. Smiling a little now. Satisfied at the suspense he'd created. "That young man," Gus said as he pointed at Micah, "sacrificed his career trying to save a boy's life."

This part Micah hated. For some reason, tonight it felt worse than usual. A black pit opened inside him. He turned away and mumbled, "I *didn't* save him, Gus."

Usually, he feigned speechlessness to get things over with. Tonight, however, fresh guilt stabbed his guts anew.

"Don't matter," Gus said, voice full of pride. Which should've been one consolation, at least. Gus retold the story because he was proud of him. Micah tried to take comfort from that.

But he couldn't.

Because it was a lie.

All of it.

"C'mon now," Bobby said, the Knicks/San Antonio game forgotten. "You ain't any closer to telling me the story. If you're gonna tell it, let's get on with it."

"Well, it's a helluva tale. Happened at Blackfoot Valley Sports Camp. Twenty years ago. After Micah's senior year," he nodded at him. "Micah's future was signed and sealed, but he sacrificed it trying to save a kid's life."

Bobby frowned. "Blackfoot Valley. That's outside town somewhere, right?"

"Yep. On Kipp Hill Road. A big complex for all sorts of summer sports camps. Basketball, football, baseball, soccer, and cheerleading. Though what the hell they did at cheerleading camp is beyond me. Maybe pom-pom waving drills."

Gus continued. "They had two sports fields and a dozen outdoor asphalt basketball courts, with twenty cabins for the kids to sleep in. Some of Webb County's best basketball players—hell, some of the best in Northern New York—cut their teeth as campers, and then as counselors. The counselors kept order in the cabins, refereed the games, sometimes coached."

"But it ain't running no more, is it?"

Gus shook his head. "Not for a while. Folks these days hire personal trainers because everyone's kid is a superstar and deserves individual training, right? Going to a camp where they whip your ass into shape ain't the 'in' thing these days, so Blackfoot Valley had been hurtin' for a while. But," Gus sighed, "I'd be lying if I said what happened with Micah didn't put the nails in the coffin."

Bobby motioned with his hand, an impatient *let's get on with it* gesture. "So what happened?"

"There's a deep gorge in the woods behind the camp. Blackfoot Valley itself. One of the kids went wandering into the woods at night. A kid from Micah's cabin. Now, Micah was on rounds when he checked his cabin and found the kid gone. He searched all over the camp. Couldn't find the kid, so he ducked into the woods behind. Finally, he spotted this kid lying at the bottom of the gorge. Micah tried to reach him, thinking it wasn't that far down . . . when he slipped. Rolled halfway down and tore ligaments and cartilage in his knee. Cracked the kneecap, tore up some muscle."

"Hell." Bobby looked Micah up and down. Micah saw his gaze linger on the metal-hinged brace he wore over his pants on his right knee. "Lucky you can walk at all."

Micah swallowed and managed a reply. "I couldn't for a while. It took a few surgeries and lots of therapy. I still have to wear this brace, though. I get around okay, but . . . "

"Parents probably screamed holy hell."

Gus nodded. "Sure enough. Luckily another counselor noticed Micah missing after a while, so he went to the caretaker's house to raise the alarm. They found Micah and the kid—think his last name was Phelps—out there in the gorge. The shit hit the fan the next day. Not sure if the camp ever got sued, but I know the whole thing hurt its image, bad."

As if he'd memorized every step in a carefully choreographed dance, Gus nodded somberly at Micah. "Helluva thing Micah did. With a big future waiting for him. College education paid for. Him risking everything to try and save that kid."

Guilt soured the beer in Micah's stomach, as the past whispered to him . . .

don't be a hero, Micah
you're no hero
you're a special kind of stupid
that's what you are

With great effort, he pushed the ghostly words away. "I didn't do anything. Never got near to saving him." Micah choked down a surge of self-loathing as he mumbled into his beer, "I'm no hero."

"Hell. You coulda been playing poker or hoops like the other counselors, but you were doing your job. Makes you a hero in *my* book."

A hot flash pulsed through Micah, unexpected in its intensity. He was supposed to keep his peace. Mumble another feeble protest, against which Gus would insist on his hero-status. For some reason, however, he couldn't do it. Not tonight. He knew deviating from the script meant attracting unwanted attention, and a part of him wanted to carry on as usual. Stay quiet. Avoid making waves.

But tonight he couldn't play the role of the small-town hero in Gus' little passion-play, no matter how good the bartender's intentions. He snapped his head up and pinned Gus with a hot stare.

The bartender paused, mouth gaping at this unexpected change.

"What happened to Phelps, Gus?" Micah's chest felt tight. "Tony Phelps. Know what happened to him? Do you?"

Gus stared at him, hands lying limp on the bar, unable to cope with Micah's sudden digression from their well-practiced script. Micah focused on Bobby instead. "Want to know what happened to this kid I *saved*? The kid I threw away my basketball career for? Huh?" Without waiting for an answer, Micah plunged ahead. "He broke his skull. Bled all over his brain. Never woke up. He died a week later. So, yeah. I *saved* him. Saved him so he could lie in the hospital like a vegetable for a week before croaking. That's what I sacrificed my career for. One more week for a vegetable to breathe."

An oppressive silence fell over the bar. Broken only by the tinny screams from the small television mounted on the wall, now long forgotten.

Micah covered his face with a hand and rubbed his temples with his fingertips at the sudden ache there. He felt ashamed. Gus never meant any harm in telling his story. In his own way, the amiable bartender was proud of Micah. But for some reason, Micah couldn't handle the same old story tonight. He didn't know why.

yes you do

"Ah, hell. I'm sorry, Gus. I didn't mean . . . " He rubbed his face and waved limply. "It's not you. Not feeling so good tonight."

A few more minutes of silence. When Gus spoke, his voice was gruff yet apologetic. "S'all right, Micah. I tell the damn story too much, anyway. I should've given it a rest for once."

Micah shrugged, feeling tired. "It's okay, Gus. Don't know what my problem is."

"Well, maybe this'll make you feel better. Heard tell Nuemann Development is gonna bulldoze Blackfoot Valley under tomorrow. Close the final chapter in that wretched book, finally."

Shock rippled through Micah. He looked at Gus. "They're tearing it down?"

Gus shrugged. "So I hear. Nuemann Development found a buyer for the land."

A cold sensation blossomed in Micah's chest. He stood abruptly. "I gotta go. See ya, Gus."

Sensing both men's stares, Micah limped out of the bar, the hinge on his knee brace clicking.

2.

DESPITE THE STRANGE compulsion which had driven him from The Stumble Inn, Micah found himself stuck on the sidewalk, unable to take another step. Across the street, his pickup truck waited in the bar's parking lot. Even though his mind urged him to cross the street, get into his truck and drive away, he couldn't make himself do it.

gonna bulldoze Blackfoot Valley under tomorrow

Micah closed his eyes and rubbed his face with hands that ached from handling scrap metal all day. Conflicting thoughts raged in his head. Cross the street to his truck and drive home to Amy. Go back inside and apologize to Gus for being an ass. Or, drive to the edge of town and do what he'd planned on doing all day.

He didn't know what to do. What he *should* do, or even what he *wanted* to do.

Jubilant cries from across the street startled him. He dropped his hands and opened his eyes to see five people walking on the opposite sidewalk, headed in the other direction. In street clothes, wearing masks or painted faces.

A couple—a man and woman—walked hand-in-hand, their painted Calavera skull-masks gleaming white under the streetlamps, grinning death-head grins. Their cohorts loped ahead of them on the sidewalk, wearing cheap plastic masks. Frankenstein's monster, a Jason Vorhees hockey mask, and Michael Myers. The latter looked surprisingly unsettling, in its inhuman blankness.

They continued on their way. The three ahead shouted and hollered. The grinning-skull couple brought up the rear, at ease, like the king and queen of Halloween, following their capricious court jesters.

They paid him no mind.

Not even the slightest glance in his direction as they passed.

Of course, why should they? Halloween was for the young. Or at the very least, young at heart. He was neither.

Micah stood on the sidewalk, watching the troupe as they stopped at the far corner of Ford and Main. He wondered what he'd been doing on Halloween as a teenager, twenty years ago. More than likely shooting endless jump shots in a gym somewhere, perfecting his form while other kids his age had fun. Or, maybe he'd been engaging in the *other* activity besides basketball which had taken up his senior year. The activity which had led to . . .

His thoughts trailed off.

The group of fright-faced folk had congregated at the corner. The three wearing monster masks gesticulating animatedly, apparently conflicted over where they should go next. The couple had separated. The woman stood with her back to him, hands stuffed into her pockets. The man cupped a cigarette to his mouth, flicked a lighter, and looked at Micah. Looking like a painted Day of the Dead James Dean, sporting a styled pompadour above his skull-face, he lit his cigarette. A practiced flick of the wrist snapped the lighter shut. He stuffed the lighter into his pants pocket. Took a deep drag. And—still staring with deep, bottomless skull eyes—casually blew out smoke as if he hadn't a care in the world.

The King of Halloween.

A ridiculous thought, but a notion Micah couldn't shake. The young man smoking and staring at him with his painted skull-black eyes was the King of Halloween. Touring the night with his Queen and their loyal subjects. Micah hadn't been a great student (too busy breaking scoring records and doing other things he shouldn't have been doing), but he thought his old high school English teacher at Webb County High, Mr. Slocum, might be impressed with the metaphor.

They were probably deciding which part of Clifton Heights to terrorize next. Of course, "terrorize" wasn't the correct word. Sheriff Baker didn't mess around on

Halloween night. All the cops would be patrolling. Especially along the residential streets, where most kids would be trick-or-treating. Worst these guys would get up to was a few smashed pumpkins, nothing more.

Even so, the King (as Micah kept thinking of him), stared. Despite how ridiculous it seemed, the longer he stared, the more uneasy Micah felt. It was the optical effect of the black paint around the man's eyes, of course. They looked like bottomless eye sockets, spilling out a blackness which seeped into Micah's bones.

The man took another drag on his cigarette.

Blew out smoke.

Raised his other hand and offered Micah a solemn two fingered salute.

Cold, unreasoning fear curdled Micah's thoughts. He turned, and instead of crossing the street to his truck, limped down the sidewalk, trying to put as much distance between him and the people on the corner. He had no destination in mind, and though he knew his sudden fear was irrational, he heeded it anyway.

***

His iPhone rang. At the corner of Main and Acer, Micah stopped on the sidewalk, pulled it out of his pocket and saw his home number flashing. He tapped the pulsing green icon and held it up to his ear. "Hey."

"Hey," came Amy's unassuming voice. *"Hate to nag, but you still at The Inn?"*

"Yeah," Micah lied, "but I'm about to head home."

"Okay. Could you swing by the Mobilmart on the way? I'm out of eggs for breakfast tomorrow."

"Sure. No problem."

"Thanks." A pause, then, *"You okay?"*

Micah swallowed. Amy was perceptive by nature. Naturally empathetic, she could sense anyone's emotional state instantly. She always knew his mood.

Amy was a good woman. A loving wife and a gentle soul.

She alone had made the last twenty-eight years passable. Even happy, on occasion.

She hadn't been his girlfriend when he'd lost everything. That was Stacy Pollamus. A cheerleader with spritz-frozen hair, painted-on face and breasts the size of soccer balls. She didn't stick around long. She'd wanted to date a Division I basketball player at Syracuse University, not a truck driver for Greene's Scrap Metal who limped around on a bad knee.

He and Amy met at Greene's. She'd worked as a cashier when he'd first been hired. Now she worked in the main office, handling Greene's business accounts. She'd grown from a shy young girl into a quietly strong, kind woman. Amy had made life worth living.

But she hadn't made the guilt go away.

"Yeah, I'm fine. Tired is all."

"Knee hurting? Long day on the road today."

Unconsciously, Micah gingerly flexed his knee, the metal hinges clicking. He'd only been standing still for a few minutes, but stiffness was already creeping into the joint.

She was right. Today's gig had run long. Greene's had been contracted to clean out a series of old storage units over in Woodgate. He'd left work at 8:00 AM this morning with Scott Greely—a friendly guy with biceps the size of Micah's head. After driving two hours into the middle of nowhere, he'd helped Scott (what little he could manage with his knee) until they'd filled the truck's oversized bed with scrap metal. They returned to Greene's, weighed and dumped their load, drove back to Woodgate, and did it all again. Though he'd only helped carry small pieces, his right knee now throbbed.

"It's a little sore," he lied again, reaching down and gently massaging his swollen kneecap through his jeans. "Think I need to see Dr. Martin. This brace's hinges are getting loose. Need a new one."

At least that last part was true.

Of course, if Amy knew he'd helped Scott load the truck

by carrying anything heavier than an alternator, she'd give him hell. In her quiet way.

Amy wasn't stupid. *"You also helped Scott load the truck today, didn't you?"*

He sighed. "A little. Maybe."

"Scott's got arms the size of tree trunks. Can do it himself just fine."

"I know. Long trips get boring, sitting in the truck the whole time. And Scott's not invincible, y'know? Needs help like the rest of us."

"Sure he does. I bet you bribed him with a round of free drinks to let you help without him tattling to me."

Despite the weird compulsion which had driven him out of The Inn and the lingering unease he still felt over Skull Face's stare, Micah laughed outright. "You got me. Don't be too hard on Scott. It took a bribe of drinks *and* wings, this time. Poor guy's too nice to say no."

The phone crackled with Amy's chuckle. *"I bet."* She sobered slightly, however, adding, *"Seriously, Micah. I don't mean to nag. You know your limits best. But you also know how much you pay for it the next day. You need to be careful. Okay?"*

"I know. Be home soon."

liar

"Kay. Love you."

"You too."

She hung up. Micah switched his phone off and put it away. He should go home. Swallow the past like he always did. Go home, sleep next to his waiting wife, pull her warm body close to him for comfort, and hope he didn't wake up screaming—again—from nightmares of his last night at Blackfoot Valley Sports Camp.

And his plans for tonight?

He'd always felt grateful to Greene's for hiring him. Never mind all the other drivers being in their mid-fifties. Never mind Micah knowing full well he'd kept the job this long only because Amy was Old Man Greene's favorite niece, and because Old Man Greene was also a rabid basketball fan.

Never mind it all. He felt thankful for a job he could manage despite his knee. An occasionally interesting job with decent pay and solid benefits. He felt thankful for everything.

Any real man, any *good* man, would dismiss tonight's plans without hesitation. But the weight of them wouldn't go away, like the weight hanging over his soul. He didn't know how to make it go away, unless he . . .

Hell with this.

He pivoted, about to head back to his truck, when another ridiculous thought occurred to him. What if Skull Face and his entourage hadn't left the corner? What if he was there, smoking casually while his crew argued about where to go next, his woman looking on. Still smoking, still staring?

So what?

He lived in Clifton Heights. The Adirondacks. Not New York City, or Syracuse, or even Utica. No gangs roamed its streets, rife with thugs prone to mugging people on Main Street at night. It wasn't as if Skull Face and his crew had baseball bats and switchblades at the ready. They were bored small town folks stuck in a boring town on Halloween night, out to smash some pumpkins, and that's all.

Even so, he was afraid to look over his shoulder. Skull Face might still be there at the corner, smoking and staring at him. Or even worse, standing behind him. Sure, his eye sockets had been painted black. However, standing under the street lamp, his *eyes* had looked black. That blackness had dug into Micah, boring into deep, secret parts inside . . .

A bell jingled, down Acer Street.

A door opened.

Micah looked around the corner down Acer Street and caught a door closing. The bell jingled as it did. Bright yellow light shone on the sidewalk. Light from a store still open, or perhaps just closed. Either way, if he could get to the store, he'd be safe, protected from . . .

Protected?

From *what*?

A bunch of punks?

Almost in response, his knee throbbed. A reality he hadn't wanted to think about occurred to him. If those punks wanted trouble, he'd be ill-equipped to stop them, even with the thing in his left jacket pocket. He was outnumbered. His knee would hinder any escape. In fact, just the right blow to his knee would effectively cripple him. Then he'd be at their mercy . . .

Which would be for the best, maybe. Then you wouldn't have to use what's in your pocket.

Micah closed his eyes and rubbed his face, hating the helplessness churning in his belly. It took him back to the days right after the accident, and the blinding pain which had made walking seem like a dim fantasy. Then the surgeries and therapy had stopped because his mother's money ran out, and insurance wouldn't cover the costs anymore . . .

Stop it.

He took a breath and wiped his face once more. Opened his eyes, and limped to the door which had just closed. Bright light still spilled from it onto the sidewalk.

At the door, he raised a hand to knock—but was arrested by a sign in the window. Gold letters on a maroon background read:

HANDY'S PAWN AND THRIFT
WE HAVE
THINGS YOU NEED

He stood still for several seconds. Hand raised in the air, repeating the last two lines in his head: *we have, things you need.* A catchy phrase to draw customers inside, for sure. Especially considering that it was a junk shop. Based on what he glimpsed through the windows, it most likely didn't have anything *anyone* needed. Unless they needed old toys, rusty tools, moldy books, and other useless odds and ends.

For some reason, however, those last three words—*things you need*—felt important. Something inside him hummed in resonance with their implications.

things you need

He shook off the feeling and knocked on the door. No one answered, so he knocked again.

The door opened.

Apparently, it hadn't latched tightly. That didn't seem quite right; however. Micah felt sure he'd heard the door close before he approached it. Of course he remembered how, growing up, the latch would never catch when he closed the screen door on their trailer. How he'd always sworn to his mother he'd closed it, but ten minutes later it'd be wide open. That was a trailer's battered screen door, however. This was a solid wooden door on a store. You'd think it would close better, but Micah supposed if the latch on a trailer screen door could go bad, it could go bad on a door like this one, too.

Right?

He pushed the door open and stepped inside. "Hello? Anyone here?"

No answer.

Micah reached behind him, compelled for some reason to push the door closed and hold it there until it latched. Once he'd done so, he wandered up the store's middle aisle. He looked around, taking in its wares. Like he'd thought, Handy's was nothing more than the local thrift junk store. There'd been two in Old Forge when he was a kid. He'd never been in this particular store, but it didn't look much different. Aisles full of everything. Fifty-year old ice skates, old tools, lamps, sewing machines, broken toys, yellowed boxes of board games, and rows of old-fashioned soda bottles.

Things you need.

Sure.

Like I need anything in here.

"Hello! I'm so sorry I didn't hear you. Was out back sorting through some recent acquisitions."

Micah turned to the voice, slightly startled, but for some reason not really scared. Something in that voice set him at ease. Made him feel protected.

From *what?*

A tall man with white, closely-trimmed hair and a beard stood behind the sales counter in the rear of the store, seemingly out of nowhere. Micah couldn't tell how old the man was, really. The white hair and beard indicated at least several years past middle age, but the man's face bore no wrinkles past faint crow's feet and laugh lines. His eyes, however, burned a bright blue, full of a youthful energy.

A sudden thought occurred to him. As sudden as his intuition about Skull Face. The tall, trim but sturdy-looking shopkeeper standing behind the sales counter was ageless. He'd always looked that way, and would always look that way.

It was a ridiculous notion. As ridiculous as that of Skull Face, the King of Halloween. Micah brushed it off, though with some difficulty and a faint sense of unease.

The shopkeeper offered him a congenial smile. "Anything in particular you're looking for?"

"No. I'm good," Micah said, trying his best to sound casual, maybe even bored. "Was at The Inn having a few beers after work, and now I'm . . . "

running away from Skull Face, the King of Halloween

" . . . just killing some time before going home, is all."

"Ah. Indeed." The shopkeeper's eyes twinkled as he placed his hands flat on the sales counter. "Such an odd expression, when you think about it. 'Killing time.' As if Time were a mere animal which could be hunted down and killed."

Micah shrugged, his gaze wandering cluttered shelves filled with the kinds of things left over after a garage sale had ended.

"In reality Time, I think, is something which can't be killed. It's always happening. It's all one thing. You know, there are some who believe there's no past, no present, or future. Just an eternally overlapping *now*. Like a sphere, on which linear progression is merely an illusion."

Micah stopped, turned and actually smiled at the shopkeeper. "Okay. I don't know anything about all that. But I watch a *lot* of movies. Doc Brown from *Back to the Future*, right? When he told Marty time was like an orange, and the past and present were together at the same time? That if we only understood how, we could travel in any direction on the skin of that orange?"

The shopkeeper held up a finger. "Yes! A fine film. And Christopher Lloyd's performance as Doctor Emmett Brown is *completely* unsung, in my humble opinion. Should've won an Oscar for it. But, it's also an old spiritualist belief. Buddhist or something, I can't exactly remember. But the gist is this: The past, present and future all occur at once. To travel either to the past or future, one needs only the right cosmic conditions and the will to do so."

Micah shook his head, his amusement evaporating, suddenly ill at ease with the conversation's direction. "Yeah. I suppose."

The shopkeeper chuckled. "Well, I'm sure that's enough metaphysical rambling for one night. Though it's Halloween, of course. The perfect night for such matters, when the veil between worlds is thin. The right cosmic conditions, if you will."

Micah shrugged again, examining the sales counter the shopkeeper stood behind. To the right stood several jewelry cases, the kind which spin on a base. To the left, he saw a seasonal display of Halloween decorations. Plastic pumpkins and jack-o'-lanterns, jack-o'-and lantern flashlights. Foam tombstones and skulls, plastic skeletons which could be hung from the ceiling. A small bin of plastic masks, and several organized racks of costumes.

"If you're here at this hour I take it you're not married, or don't have children?"

Micah approached the sales counter, unsure as to why he was lingering. Surely Skull Face and his crew had gone their way by now. Even so, he didn't want to leave quite yet. He felt another stab of helplessness, but he shoved the feeling down.

"It's the second, actually. Amy—my wife—and I have tried several times, but no luck so far." The shopkeeper's face fell. He looked genuinely sorry. "That's a shame. I apologize if I dredged up some painful memories with such an insensitive question."

Micah waved and shook his head. "No worries. We've taken all the tests. Doctors can't find anything wrong with either of us. We just can't get pregnant. Just weren't meant to, I guess."

His gaze was meandering to his right, toward the jewelry boxes, when he saw it. Sitting on a wire shelf attached to the front counter. A shelf filled with old footballs, soccer balls, a few baseballs, and in the middle, nestled among them . . .

A blue and gold basketball.

With *Blackfoot Valley* emblazoned on it.

Micah's throat tightened. He had difficulty breathing. He also felt faint. His fists clenched, fingernails digging in his palms. His heart started pounding so hard he swore the shopkeeper must be able to hear it.

The shopkeeper must have sensed the change in Micah's demeanor and mistaken it for excitement—because he smiled wider. "An official Blackfoot Valley Sports Camp basketball," he said. "When the camp was in its heyday, every basketball player in Webb County dribbled one down their sidewalk or shot one in their driveway. Or desperately wanted to. A cheap rubber basketball mass-produced for use at Blackfoot Valley Basketball Camp, given to every camper at the camp's end. Owning one meant you'd trained at the Adirondacks' premier sports camp."

Micah licked his lips and said nothing, staring at the basketball. It looked brand new. Straight from the box. Its blue and gold vibrant and fresh. It looked almost *wet,* as if it had just been colored. At one time, Micah had owned several of these. No longer, of course. He'd gotten rid of them—along with all his plaques, trophies, and his scrapbook—after he'd ruined his knee.

The shopkeeper continued. Either not noticing Micah's discomfort, or ignoring it. "These basketballs were so coveted that in the brief overlap of the camp's existence and the internet age, Blackfoot Valley sold them online, so you no longer had to attend camp to own one." He sobered, frowning slightly. "Unfortunately, many saw that as a marketing ploy to make up for the camp's declining enrollment."

Micah swallowed once more. Cracked his neck and flexed his fingers, trying to force himself to relax. First, his strange anger at Gus' routine story. Then, the startling news that Blackfoot Valley was scheduled for bulldozing *tomorrow.* Skull Face and his Halloween Gang. Now *this*?

What the hell was going on?

it's Halloween, of course

the perfect night for such matters

"Did you play basketball in high school? Watch it on television, much?"

Micah cleared his throat and smiled, dragging his eyes away from the basketball to meet the shopkeeper's kindly gaze. "No," he lied. "Not at all."

The shopkeeper looked like he was about to reply, but

Micah finally shook off his paralysis. "Thanks for letting me come in and warm up. Think it's time to get going. My wife'll wonder if I got kidnapped."

The shopkeeper nodded. "Of course. As I said, it is Halloween, after all. Spirits are abounding tonight. Looking for lost souls to carry off. Or so various legends say, anyway. Before you leave, however . . . a parting gift."

The shopkeeper reached under the counter and pulled out a small orange gift bag with a black, cheerfully smiling jack-o'-lantern on it. "Sadly, I haven't had many trick-or-treaters out this way for many years, though I'm always prepared for them. In any case, I'm going to have a lot of these left over at the night's end, and though I love giving out candy, I don't have much of a sweet tooth, myself."

Micah instinctively reached for the proffered bag, but an odd wariness stayed his hand. Urban legends of poison-laced chocolate bars and apples rigged with razor blades flitted through his mind. That, and for some reason, he couldn't help conjuring up the classic scene from Disney's *Snow White and the Seven Dwarfs,* of the old woman offering Snow White her poisoned apple.

However, common sense came to the rescue. He'd only moved here when he'd married Amy, but she'd lived in Clifton Heights her entire life. As had her family, and extended family. If the shopkeeper of the town pawnshop was a psycho suspected of handing out bags of poisoned candy, she would've heard about it.

Micah shoved his paranoia aside and accepted the bag. He quickly peered into it, glimpsing the usual Halloween fare. Mini Milky Way and Three Musketeers bars, a single Reese's Peanut Butter Cup, a package of Smarties, a small box of Milk Duds, and several other treats.

He held the bag up. "Thanks. My wife likes chocolate. She'll be happy."

The shopkeeper inclined his head. "Well, I'm sure you're

familiar with the old saying. 'Happy wife; happy life.' Words to live by."

Micah felt a genuine smile. "That's the truth. Are you married?"

The shopkeeper shook his head regretfully. "I was, but she passed a long time ago."

"My condolences." Micah found that he meant it. The shopkeeper seemed a little aloof and odd, maybe even eccentric, but essentially harmless and with a kind air.

"Appreciated, but it was a long time ago. I've made my peace with it."

"Right. Anyway. Thanks again."

He turned to leave, made it as far as the door, but stopped with his hand on the doorknob when the shopkeeper said, "Mr. Cassidy?"

Micah faced him. "Yeah?"

"Clifton Heights is a small town. Filled mostly with good-natured folks. However, it's also Halloween night. A night on which some folks simply . . . do not act themselves."

The shopkeeper folded his hands on the sales counter, smiling slightly. "Legend says that's because the walls between realms are thin, allowing beings from beyond to penetrate into our world and roam, looking for lost souls to devour. Myself? I believe over the years Halloween has simply become synonymous with 'mischief'. Sometimes that mischief is more consequential than egged cars or smashed pumpkins. I trust you're going straight home?"

Micah paused, then lied for the second time in twenty minutes. "Yes."

The shopkeeper's smile spread. "Then a happy All Hallows' Eve to you. I hope Amy enjoys the candy."

Micah nodded, turned the doorknob and pushed out into the night.

3.

AS MICAH'S TRUCK idled at the intersection of Levingston and Main, waiting for the red light to turn green (which seemed to be taking an oddly long time), he reached into the Halloween bag the shopkeeper had given him. He didn't really like chocolate all that much, but he had seen a package of Smarties Sweet'n Tart candies in there, and he wouldn't mind those.

As he rifled through the bag, keeping one eye on the red light, his mind worked over something which had been bugging him since he'd walked back to his truck. He hadn't been able to put his finger on it, but it was something the shopkeeper had said . . .

Cassidy

Mr. Cassidy

That was it. The shopkeeper (whose name he'd never managed to get) had called him *Mr. Cassidy* before he left. Micah glanced down at the breast of his work shirt, but he wasn't wearing the one with his name stitched on it. Even if he had been, it only had his first name, not his last. That only left one possibility; the shopkeeper had known who Micah was the whole time.

Any sense of goodwill Micah felt toward the shopkeeper evaporated. The questions he'd asked Micah about playing or watching basketball seemed manipulative, now. Even a little cruel. If he'd known who Micah really was, he would've also known what happened to his career, and what happened to his knee. That the shopkeeper had never once mentioned Micah's knee-brace or the way he limped didn't matter. He'd been playing with Micah the whole time.

Micah's taste for Smarties faded. He pulled his hand out of the bag. As he did so, his fingers brushed something cold and metallic. Not a razor blade, but something textured with what felt like a design. As he worked his fingers through the candy, he thought maybe he felt links in a chain . . .

Micah withdrew his hand from the bag and saw he'd been correct. It was a necklace of some sort, with an odd-looking charm on it.

He stared at the charm, not sure what to think. Had the shopkeeper put it inside his bag on purpose?

He couldn't have. Micah hadn't been watching him *that* closely, but the shopkeeper had reached under the counter, pulled out the orange candy bag, and handed it to him. Maybe he'd had the necklace already in his hand, and slipped it into the bag when he reached under the counter. That would imply, however, that he'd been prepared to do so.

Why?

Maybe the shopkeeper put something in every bag? A cheap item from his shelves, for free? A Halloween gift? That made more sense. It certainly didn't look very valuable. It was probably cheap pewter. The kind carnival jewelry was made from.

Micah shook his head and stuffed the charm and its necklace into his right pocket (not his left pocket, of course). Oddly, he felt a weird sense of peace. He no longer felt so bad about the shopkeeper knowing his name, or that he might've been playing a cruel game with him. Having the necklace in his pocket made him feel *good*, for some reason. Almost good enough to forget about what was in his left pocket.

Almost.

Micah looked up and was about to check the traffic signal when bright light filled his truck's cab, almost blinding him. He squinted into his rearview mirror. A car was pulling up behind him, its headlights on high. Micah shielded his eyes and looked again as the car stopped. It looked long and low to the ground. Midnight black finish glittered.

Whoever sat behind the car's steering wheel gunned the engine once, twice, then a third time. Micah wasn't a car expert, but the engine sounded big, like it belonged to an older car, restored and maybe even souped-up.

The driver gunned the engine again.

Micah looked closer. He saw silhouettes of several heads. Immediately, unbidden, the image came of Skull Face smoking on the corner of Main and Ford. Staring at him before offering a casual, almost knowing two-fingered salute. As if to say: *See you around.*

There was no reason for Micah to think Skull Face—the King of Halloween—was driving the car behind him. None at all. Yet the thought wouldn't go away.

Micah looked forward into the night, hands tightening on the steering wheel as his heart pounded. His rationalizations felt empty and meaningless.

The driver gunned his engine again, this time adding a double-tap on the horn. The sound startled Micah out of his daze. When he glanced up, he saw the light was green.

Micah released the brake, stepped on the gas, and slowly drove through the intersection. When he glanced in the rearview, he saw the car sitting there at the light, motionless. Even though its headlights dwindled and then disappeared when Micah turned into a curve, Micah still felt uneasy.

Micah shook it off, wondering just what the hell he was doing and why he wasn't heading home. Of course, in his heart, he knew exactly where he was headed. He knew what he was intending to do. He refused to admit it, however. He drove on into the night.

***

Ten minutes later, Micah parked his truck before Blackfoot Valley Sports Camp. In his headlights, on a chain-link fence running across the drive, a white sign read:

NUEMANN DEVELOPMENT

close a chapter, finally

On scrap runs for Greene's, he did his best to avoid Kipp Hill. When he couldn't, he drove past the old camp, staring straight ahead in white-knuckled silence. He *should* feel happy. Someone was finally tearing it down. Even so, he didn't know how to feel, which scared him.

He sat there, staring at the white sign glaring in his headlights. He couldn't see much past it in the dark, but with a little effort he could imagine the asphalt drive winding away from the road to the front parking lot. Directly beyond sat the dining hall. To the right, set on a knoll, was the recreation building.

This is stupid.

Go home. Go home to Amy, forget about this, and let them bulldoze the fucking place down.

Forget about it.

Micah grunted. He grabbed his heavy Maglite off the passenger seat and shut the truck's engine off. He opened the door and swung his legs out, wincing at the ever-present pain arcing across his kneecap as he eased out onto the asphalt drive of what remained of Blackfoot Valley Sports Camp.

***

The asphalt was heaved and cracked in places where the ground had settled over the years. The grass and weeds were slowly but inevitably working to reclaim the space, pushing up through the cracks. Micah moved carefully, worried about his knee buckling as he navigated his way to the fence blocking the camp's entrance. The fence was about six or seven feet high. It stretched past the reach of his flashlight's beam in either direction. He assumed it ran around the camp's perimeter and through the woodland area behind.

As he limped, pain throbbed in his knee to the tune of his heartbeat. He wondered what the hell he was doing. He found no answer. No rational reason for coming here, so late at night, on Halloween no less. No explanation for the sudden urge to revisit the place where his life had changed so drastically.

Yet he couldn't deny the pull in his gut toward Blackfoot Valley. If he were honest with himself, he'd felt it since the moment Gus said it was being torn down.

Micah stopped at the gate.

A sliver of doubt blunted his compulsion. It was padlocked shut, so he couldn't get in. Which was a good thing. He could go home to Amy and forget this crazy idea of wandering all over the camp's ruins. He didn't need to hurt his knee any worse than it already was.

As he thought this, however, he stepped closer to the gate, shining his flashlight on the chains looped around its latch. He grabbed the fence and tugged. He was rewarded with the sight of the chains loosening. He bent over and examined them closer. Sure enough, maybe because of the camp's scheduled destruction the next day, the gate wasn't padlocked after all. The chain was merely looped around the latch in several lazy passes, secured with a standard hardware store spring-loaded clasp. One finger-flick and the clasp unhooked.

Micah pulled the chain free. It fell into a pile on the

cracked asphalt, ringing against the night. It lay in his flashlight's beam. For a moment, Micah couldn't repress the macabre notion it was entrails or a freshly killed snake piled at his feet. He shook off the weird image and pushed the gate open. It gaped smoothly and silently, as if freshly oiled. Micah briefly thought about getting back into his truck and driving it into the parking lot, but panning his flashlight back and forth, he saw several downed trees blocking the way. He could step around them, but not drive around them.

He paused, thinking one last time about going home.

Then, without further hesitation, Micah entered Blackfoot Valley Sports Camp for the last time.

4.

AFTER SLOWLY SKIRTING the felled trees, Micah proceeded up the path, his knee brace clicking in the quiet. The camp appeared eerily preserved in the shadows. Directly ahead sat the L-shaped dining hall. He remembered slipping into it with other counselors late at night to snack on leftover desserts.

Good times.

Full of promise and potential. Moments now gone forever.

Careful, he told himself as his mind skittered around memories.

Directly ahead and to the left he saw the two-story house which had served as the main office. Also, the home of the camp's year-round caretaker, Sam Bagely. Micah remembered him dimly. A short, athletic young man in his twenties with a perpetually smiling face and twinkling blue eyes, framed by a head of tight brown curls.

He hadn't been smiling the morning after, when talking to the cops. Not at all. His eyes hadn't twinkled, either. More like glittered with an icy, furious gleam.

Careful.

Looking around, Micah thought something was missing. He didn't know what, so he continued between the dining hall and the main house. Up close he saw the evidence of decay. Peeling and cracked paint, warped siding. All the windows on both buildings were boarded up. Under the pale gleam of his flashlight, both buildings looked faded.

On the main house's leaning front porch were piles of trash. Its roof sagged in several places. One of its peeked gables had collapsed. Swinging his flashlight ahead, he again noticed how heaved the pavement was. The lawn had gone to weed long ago.

He shined the flashlight behind the main house at the two shotgun-shack coaches' dorms. During his last summer here (a week before it all came crashing down) Micah had coached a team in the junior high division. He'd got to bunk in the coaches' dorm that week instead of babysitting campers. Now, the roof of both dorms sagged in the middle, near collapse.

Micah aimed his flashlight up the hill, his resolve faltering. The asphalt pathway looked worse, split and cracked by time. If he tripped on a rut and twisted his knee, how would he explain it to Amy? Worse, if he twisted his knee so badly he couldn't make it back to his truck, what then? If he needed to call 911, how would he explain his presence here?

This is stupid.

Why am I here?

He panned his flashlight along the row of cabins on the left side of the path. In them, the years appeared most evident. They'd fallen apart far worse than the other buildings. No one had bothered boarding up these windows. As his flashlight's beam passed, shards of broken glass glittered. All the cabins (the ones he could see, anyway) had caved in, the roofs long ago succumbing to years of snow build-up. Several cabins had collapsed entirely.

Bunk beds had been dragged outside. They either leaned upright against the cabins or lay tipped over onto their sides. Their mattresses looked oddly bloated. Like weird egg sacs ready to burst. A few mattresses lay in the grass; white islands in a sea of weeds.

The cabins were surely trashed inside. Micah figured his imagination would have to do, because he wasn't investigating them. Brushing a doorframe could bring the cabin down on him. So he conjured up images of them cluttered with beer cans and bottles. Campfire remains, bunk beds tipped over onto each other, mattresses stacked on the floors or leaning against the walls, and piles of old clothes on heaving concrete floors. He'd heard enough rumors over the years of kids sneaking onto the grounds to party after dark for the images to be believable.

Micah stood still, panning his flashlight back and forth up the hill. Night in the Adirondacks always fell with an oppressive totality. Tonight, this far from town, the darkness was absolute. Outside his flashlight's beam he could hardly see anything. The air felt dense. It was oddly quiet, also.

Why am I here?

Micah turned in frustration, panning his flashlight back toward the entrance. From his new angle he realized what was missing.

The Recreation Hall.

A two-story building formerly set into the hill alongside the dining hall, where most of the campers spent their free time. On the first floor was the snack bar/lounge area, with a ping-pong and a pool table, and several arcade games. In the lounge's corner had been a circle of old recliners. As a counselor, he and others played countless rounds of penny poker there into the early morning hours.

The second floor was an open area used to show movies. During the day, instructional videos. During the evening, entertainment. He remembered watching *Karate Kid II* on the second floor the summer after his seventh grade year.

The Recreation Hall was gone. Timbers jutted skyward from a foundation crumbled and charred in his flashlight's beam. A fire, maybe, though he didn't remember hearing about one.

Micah stared at the Rec Hall's ruins. With each passing moment, a sensation of foreboding built inside. Something felt wrong, but he couldn't make himself leave. Rather, he felt compelled to travel deeper into the ruined camp's darkness. He turned up the trail that wound through camp. As his flashlight's beam swung along the ground, he idly noted graffiti spray-painted on the cracked asphalt path. Standard slogans, the usual.

Call Jenny T for a good time.
Lynn rox my sox.
Bobby T sux ass.

Pentagrams and other odd designs filled in the spaces between slogans, including one which looked like the strange pewter medallion the shopkeeper had, for whatever reason, slipped into the orange bag of Halloween candy he'd given Micah.

A noise interrupted his thoughts. A scraping. Tires rolling over asphalt.

The entrance.

Micah turned awkwardly. Pain flashed through his knee. Instinct told him to switch the flashlight off. Facing the parking lot, he saw a long black car, low to the ground, pulling in next to his truck. Its headlights lit up the parking lot like prison searchlights tracking escapees.

Skull Face and his troupe.

The King of Halloween and his court.

Micah had no way of telling for sure—he couldn't see who rode in the midnight-black car (which looked like a restored Monte Carlo from the late seventies). He *felt* the truth of it, however, deep in his gut. Skull Face was driving, lady-friend by his side, the court jesters jittering in the backseat, ready to sow chaos. Though he had no way of knowing this either, he felt sure it had been them sitting behind him at the traffic light. Skull Face at the wheel, gunning the engine.

It didn't mean anything. The ruins of Blackfoot Valley were a likely place to visit on Halloween night. If Gus Ambrose knew the camp was scheduled for demolition then others probably knew, also. It was easy to imagine. The Halloween Jesters debating where to go next. Should they smash pumpkins out on McDonough Avenue? Menace residential areas and spook little kids until the cops showed up? Maybe go to All Saints Church, First Methodist, or Clifton Heights Baptist and spray paint pentagrams and inverted crosses all over the parking lots? Go to Bassler House and see if anyone was throwing a kegger?

Skull Face would say, very quietly, his face lit by the glow of his cigarette, "I hear they're tearing down Blackfoot Valley. Could have some fun there, before it's gone."

They weren't here for him. It was a ridiculous coincidence . . .

like that basketball at Handy's?

. . . on a night of ridiculous coincidences. Skull Face and his troupe were *not* hunting him. They *weren't*.

But he couldn't banish the memory of Skull Face staring at him.

Smoking leisurely, then offering him a casual two-fingered salute. As if to say: *See you soon.*

Unbidden, the shopkeeper's last words came back to him.

the walls between realms are thin

allowing beings from beyond to penetrate into our world

A sharp report made him jump. A dark, lithe form stood next to the car, having just shut its driver side door. Several other reports followed, as the passengers disembarked and clustered behind the driver.

It had to be his imagination. He was too far away, but Micah swore he heard a lighter *click* open. A small flame illuminated the driver's face as he lit another cigarette. In the brief flare, Micah couldn't see much—but he saw enough.

Painted white face.

The corner of a painted death-head grin.

Black, bottomless eye sockets.

Another *click* and the flame disappeared, leaving only the orange tip of the cigarette. Even though Micah could no longer see, especially because Skull Face and his crew were standing behind the car's headlights, he knew they were looking straight at him. He could imagine the jesters whispering to their king, *Where is he? He's here somewhere, I know it* . . .

Micah turned and limped up the path into the darkness, away from Skull Face and his crew. Whatever they were up to, it was no good. Micah didn't want to encounter them here in the ruins of Blackfoot Valley, alone.

Again, he chided himself. This wasn't the big city. They certainly weren't hardened criminals, and were most likely interested in mischief, nothing more. They wouldn't do anything violent to him, they *wouldn't* hurt him, like . . .

The Longtrees.

Flushed with adrenaline at the memory, Micah moved faster despite the pain blossoming under his kneecap. He was dreadfully aware of his brace clicking and his boots scraping asphalt, sure the sounds would draw attention as he limped up the moon-splashed path ahead . . .

A white sneaker flashed around the far corner of the bathroom, a rectangular concrete building in the middle of the courtyard. A breathless panic gripped his heart. Micah stumbled. Something twisted inside his head. Vertigo struck him. He wobbled, his bad knee buckling, almost giving out as he got dizzier. Despite the threat of pursuit, he stopped, closed his eyes, and breathed deep.

The throbbing in his knee subsided.

The dizziness passed, quickly replaced by annoyance. It was Phelps, dammit. He knew it. Maybe it was just some kid fucking around after lights out, but he didn't think so. He knew, he felt it in his bones. It was Phelps, trying to back out of the deal.

Micah straightened and marched up the path toward the bathrooms. His knee twinged slightly (must've strained it playing ball with the other counselors last night), but he brushed the pain aside. The Longtrees were coming. If he didn't get Phelps to square things before then, what they'd to do to him would hurt far worse than a sore knee.

As he approached the bath area, a weird visual quirk

made it look like the path was covered in spray-painted graffiti. He blinked and saw nothing but smooth black asphalt. His tired eyes were obviously playing tricks on him.

Nearing the bath area, he thought it odd his knee wasn't hurting, especially considering how fast he was walking uphill. However, that itself was an odd notion. Sure, it felt sore from weeks of playing basketball on asphalt—but there wasn't anything wrong with his knee.

Was there?

Rounding the corner of the bath area, he dismissed the thought. He needed to get this shit wrapped up, fast. The camp director, Jerry Rueben, was gone for the night. Bags hated being disturbed after lights out. He was usually "entertaining" college girls home on break. No way he wanted to piss Bags off by intruding. There'd be hell to pay when it was time to clean up Friday after the campers left.

Finding nothing around the corner of the bath area, Micah slammed the door open, hoping to scare Phelps if the fucker was hiding inside. "Hey! Phelps! Get your ass out here!"

Nothing but silence in the thick darkness, which seemed odd. The counselors always left the bathroom lights on overnight. Couldn't have ten-year-old kids stumbling around in the dark at two in the morning. This convinced Micah that Phelps was hiding inside, probably in one of the stalls. He reached out to flick the lights on.

Nothing.

An empty click, and darkness.

Why should there be any lights? Blackfoot Valley had been shut down for twenty years. It was scheduled for demolition tomorrow morning. There wouldn't be any electricity. Why'd he think there would be? More importantly, why turn on the lights when he was trying to hide from Skull Face and his crew? And the damnedest thing was, after limping up the hill so fast, his knee should be throbbing in pain. Yet, it wasn't. It felt a little sore, nothing worse.

A dream-like haze settled over Micah. It made no sense that his knee didn't hurt after climbing a cracked, heaved asphalt path. Of course, it made about as much sense as him coming out here tonight, on Halloween, or Skull Face and his crew following him here. No use denying it any longer. Skull Face and his crew had followed him. Why, he had no idea. But that was why they were here.

Paralyzed by uncertainty, he panned his flashlight around the bath area. His nostrils twitched at the clinging stench of stagnant water. As his flashlight passed over rows of toilet stalls against the far wall (some doors gone or hanging on one hinge) the smell intensified. He gagged.

He turned to leave, flashlight panning the wall of sinks and mirrors. Most of the mirrors were broken. Several sinks had been ripped out, leaving nothing but pipes sticking up from cracked cement. On some of the mirrors he saw more graffiti and symbols. One in particular, a circle with spiral hooks in the center. Next to it, on the walls: *The Yellow King Rulz.*

Micah released a heavy breath. Confusion, and, yes, *fear* muddied his thoughts. He didn't understand why he'd come here, or why those punks had followed him. He didn't understand why he'd limped *here* to hide, of all places. It didn't feel real. More like a nightmare, or the kind of hallucination that comes with a high fever, or . . .

"It's *not* a fever, bucko. *That* I can tell you for sure."

5.

MICAH LOOKED OVER his shoulder in the direction of the voice, back toward the bathroom stalls. Cold fingers strummed his spine. His guts clenched, his heart trip-hammering against his rib cage.

"It's real," the voice said casually, as if pronouncing the weather.

Micah heard it. The metallic *click* of a lighter and the faint *hiss* and crackle of a cigarette tip crisping in a flame. Another *click*, and the lighter flicked shut.

"But I can tell you this," the voice paused as its owner took a quick puff and release, "you're definitely in a nightmare. No two ways about that. And the more you run, the worse it's going to get."

Micah's throat clenched with fear. All the years since his knee injury, he'd done his best to never feel helpless. He could either crawl in a hole and die, or continue living as best he could. He'd chosen the latter. Found his job at Greene's, met Amy, and survived.

Now, knowing he couldn't run away—that the best he'd manage was a lame shamble as Skull Face approached, smoking casually, staring at him like a hawk does a rodent . . . he trembled with fear. He hated it, but couldn't deny it.

"What . . . " his voice rasped, caught in his throat, and he had to cough to dislodge it. "What do you want? Why are you following me?"

Skull Face smiled. Took an exaggerated puff of his cigarette, and exhaled. Made a show of inspecting his fingernails, flicked ash off his cigarette, and said in a contemplative voice, "I don't know if I'd say I . . . followed you, really."

He looked up at Micah, black eyes burning into his. "Saw you outside that bar, of course. But I *felt* you, first. More like smelled, really. Your sadness. Regret. Despair."

Skull Face smiled, his painted skull-grin looking impossibly wide. "It's what I like best."

Micah gripped the flashlight so hard his knuckles ached. He raised it slightly, thinking maybe if he swung hard, he might be able to knock Skull Face down long enough to hobble away. But a crushing sense of futility descended. Even if he could knock Skull Face down, he wouldn't get far. Then it dawned upon him. How had Skull Face gotten here first? He'd just seen him down in the parking lot.

"Who . . . who are you? *What* are you?"

Skull Face took another drag. The end of his cigarette glowed. He exhaled and said, "I'm a thing that needs what you have. And I can't have you getting rid of that thing, can I?"

Micah shook his head. "I don't understand."

Skull Face took a step closer, grin fading. As he drew near, Micah saw a dim red light in his cave-black eye sockets. "Well, this is where it happened, right? Where you lost everything? That's why you're here, tonight. Yes?"

Micah tried but couldn't speak. The longer he stared into Skull Face's pitch-black eye sockets, the more a creeping, icy numbness spread through him.

Skull Face shook his head and clucked his tongue. "You have no idea why you wanted to come here, do you? Not even the slightest."

Skull Face raised his cigarette to his lips, grinning. "You're a special kind of stupid, Micah . . . "

you're a special kind of stupid
that's what you are

Anger pulsed through Micah, hot and burning. He clenched the flashlight, the muscles in his forearm and bicep trembling.

" . . . and I'd say you got what you deserved. So did that little fucker, Tony Phelps."

At the mention of Tony's name, Micah swung the flashlight at Skull Face's head, hard as he could. The impact felt immensely satisfying, shivering all the way up his arm to his shoulder. Unbelievably enough, Skull Face *did* go down, though he toppled sideways without a sound. Not even a grunt.

Micah didn't stop to wonder why. He turned and, ignoring the fiery pain in his knee, lurched toward the bathroom door. He slammed his shoulder against it, pushed it open . . .

The bathroom was a bust. Phelps wasn't in there. Micah glanced toward the dome, which covered two indoor courts. Yellow-orange light spilled from its entrance along with the sounds of feet scuffing asphalt, a basketball banging off the rim and guys yelling *"I got ball!"* and *"Screen! Switch!"* There wasn't anywhere for Tony to hide in there. Nothing but a wide-open space full of counselors playing basketball and watching. Even so, he'd check. Maybe Tony stopped in there long enough to get chased back to the cabins by one of the counselors while he'd been exploring the bathroom.

The instant Micah lurched into the dome's remains a musty odor of age and disuse hit him. Though not as powerful as the stench in the old bath area, this musk was worse in its own way. The air smelled thick with dust. His nostrils twitched. The back of his throat itched as he panted, out of breath from fleeing Skull Face. A coughing fit loomed.

Micah shined his flashlight around, looking in vain, he knew, for somewhere to hide. The court on which he'd once spent hours honing his skills was now littered with beer bottles, cans and campfire remains. The wooden benches lining the court were rotten and decayed. He saw mounds of clothes and blankets, a few mattresses from the cabins. He limped forward, panning the flashlight around the court's perimeter, knee throbbing, brace clicking. Only one basket remained of the six he remembered. It stood on the far end, and was sagging, its rim bent and dangling. The other baskets lay in heaps around the court. Despite his near panic, a deep sadness rose inside. It was all gone.

Destroyed by time. Torn down by vandals caring no more for the game than a rat cares for art. All the hours he'd spent here over the summer. Pushing himself through conditioning, ball-handling, and shooting drills? All ground into dust, as his dreams were.

He was to blame. Whatever Skull Face and his friends had planned for him . . . maybe he deserved it.

Limping to the far exit, he scuttled to a clicking stop as Skull Face's queen stepped into his path.

6.

PAIN RADIATED FROM Micah's knee down through his shin as he stopped too fast. He gasped as Skull Face's Queen sauntered toward him. She kept her hands in her pockets. Her elfin face was painted in delicate lines and feminine accents. Her expression was inquisitive as she frowned, forehead wrinkling in confusion. "How are you slipping back and forth?" she said. "You shouldn't be able to do that."

Micah had no idea what she was talking about and was about to say so, but before he could, he heard: "It's that damn shopkeeper. He's always meddling."

Micah cast a terrified glance over his shoulder to see Skull Face striding purposefully after him, casual cigarette smoking demeanor gone, all business now. Skull Face's temple was torn up where he'd struck it with his flashlight. Through the bloodless, gaping wound, white bone gleamed.

Desperate fear thrumming in his heart, Micah turned and swung the heavy flashlight at Skull Face's queen, who had closed the distance between them faster than seemed possible. She blocked the flashlight with her forearm. Even though Micah swore he heard something *crack*, her painted-on skull face remained blank. Her right hand darted in and grabbed his neck, squeezing it in a vice-like grip.

Micah gasped, his airway cut off. He tried to swing the flashlight again, and the queen laughed, painted death-head grin snarling as she batted it away.

She squeezed tighter.

He clawed weakly at her unrelenting grip. She heaved him into the air. As he hung, dangling, darkness crept in at the edges of his vision. Over the pounding of his heart in his ears, he barely heard Skull Face say, "Easy, love. Not quite finished with him yet, are we? Still need to feed the boys."

still need to feed the boys

White-hot panic surged through him. He flailed and kicked harder, but the queen squeezed tighter, laughing in manic delight, her eyes bright and mad at the back of her black eye sockets. A numbing fog crept over his mind . . .

His pocket.

In his left jacket pocket.

With a desperate burst of energy, Micah stuck his left hand into his jacket pocket and pulled out the .38 he'd meant to kill himself with. He pointed it in the queen's face and pulled the trigger three times in quick succession. Her face exploded into a spray of parchment-like tatters and bone fragments. She didn't cry out in pain, more like howled in rage.

She staggered back and dropped him.

When Micah fell, somehow he absorbed most of the impact with his good leg and kept his footing, though his knee screamed in agony. He ignored it, limping as fast he could toward the dome's exit and then outside, even as he heard things made of bone scrabbling on asphalt after him.

Micah's stride quickened as he left the guys waiting for next game, his agitation swelling into an unfocused, almost irrational fear. Neither Sam Greene nor Kevin Ellison had seen Tony in the dome, so Micah figured his target must've ducked around the side. Maybe he was heading for the far courts, or the cabins on the hill.

Micah wasn't having it. Phelps needed to face what was coming to him. Micah would make damn sure of it, except . . .

Micah slowed and stopped. He looked around, gripped by a strange sensation. Something felt wrong. Out of place. Like he'd forgotten something he desperately needed to remember. Something his life depended on, and not only that . . .

He felt like someone was chasing him.

He looked over his shoulder and saw nothing but the yellow-orange rectangle of the door leading back into the dome, and the darting figures of counselors playing basketball. He turned away from the dome and panned his flashlight in a full circle.

In addition to the court under the dome, Blackfoot Valley had nine asphalt outdoor basketball courts. The three on the far right were smooth and green, the courts used for tennis during tennis camp. The three ahead were regular asphalt. The green courts were secured by high chain-link fencing which was padlocked every night. Phelps was likely heading for the cabins on the hill.

As Micah turned in that direction, a flash of white disappeared into the tree line, confirming his suspicions. Enrollment was low this week, so the hillside cabins were empty. Phelps was obviously planning on hiding out there, hoping to dodge tonight's gig.

No way *that* was happening. Phelps had begged Micah for a piece of the action from the first night of camp. He'd gotten his piece of action, all right. No way he was backing out now. Especially considering Micah himself was already in dutch with the Longtrees.

Micah stepped toward the tree line, but once again a nagging sensation that he'd forgotten something checked him. It was like a sliver stuck under his fingernail. Not really painful, but when he moved just right, it bothered him.

Determined, Micah shoved the feeling aside and strode across the basketball courts to the tree line, where he was sure he'd seen Phelps disappear. If he didn't get the kid to man-up and do his part, Micah would have more important things to worry about than weird feelings.

In retrospect, he should've figured Phelps would get cold feet. By Tuesday he could barely look Micah in the eye. He shouldn't be surprised Phelps was flaking. The signs had all been there.

Didn't matter. Micah's ass was on the line. He'd been dealing (discreetly of course, never during basketball season) for the Longtrees for about two years. Normally he was careful and didn't take chances. Most importantly, he didn't use himself. The extra cash helped pay for individualized college conditioning programs in the off-season. The kind usually reserved for athletes from rich families. Not to mention it helped put food on the table and pay his own car insurance, so Mom could work fewer hours and fewer nights.

However, he'd made a few uncharacteristic mistakes this summer. Misjudged other kids, like he'd apparently misjudged Phelps. One kid—Benny Thompson from Indian Lake—went home after camp, first week of July, and OD'd on the product he was supposed to be selling in his town. Afraid of the Longtrees himself, Thompson lied to the police, saying he got the stuff from guys working out of Utica. Nobody came sniffing around Micah then, but he could tell the Longtrees hadn't been pleased.

Next came Lonny Sanders, who'd gotten strung out three weeks ago. Again, on product he was supposed to take back to Eagle Bay and sell. His fellow cabin-mates pulled Micah from a game in the dome. By the time Micah got to the kid's cabin, Sanders was rolling around in his bunk, naked, singing New Kids on the Block songs. Micah sat up with him all night.

The next day he managed to pass Lonny off as sick so he didn't have to play any games or run drills. Another close call, and even though the Sanders kid was able to pay for the product he used, Micah could tell the Longtrees hadn't been happy about that little adventure at all, either. Now Phelps was running around camp, hiding from Micah. If he didn't get shit locked down now and the Longtrees arrived to *another* fuck up, Micah was finished.

A grim determination filled him as he crested the path leading up to the cabins on the hill behind the courts. He wasn't going to let Phelps fuck things up. He'd wanted in with the Longtrees; Micah had dealt him in. Now he was going to sing the song and dance the dance he'd signed up for.

Or else.

Of course, Micah didn't know what "or else" meant. He'd never laid a hand on anyone his whole life. Maybe he didn't need to, though. Maybe all he needed was to lean on Phelps. Threaten the kid. He'd come around. Once Phelps finished his deal, he'd start dealing with the Longtrees directly, and Micah would be out. If Phelps backed out and left Micah hanging . . .

Micah reached the middle cabin, dismissing his concerns for the moment. He paused outside the door, then in one movement grabbed the handle and slammed it open. "Phelps! Get your ass out here, now! No way you're backing out on me."

A pause.

Micah panned his flashlight back and forth across the empty cabin (for a weird moment it looked trashed, with graffiti covering the walls), then toward the bathroom in back, where he thought he heard the squeak of a sneaker on floor tile. Sounded like someone hiding behind a door . . .

Micah whirled clumsily on his bad knee, but it was too late. The bathroom door slammed open and one of the King's court jesters—the one in the terrifyingly blank Michael Myers mask—leaped toward him, hooting at the top of his lungs in manic glee.

7.

MICAH TRIED TO RUN, but his knee buckled. He stumbled, left foot catching over the right. He crashed to the ground on one shoulder and cried out.

Mike Myers dove for him, hands outstretched, still cackling. Micah flung himself onto his back, raised the .38, and shot Myers three times in the chest to no effect, save exaggerated twitches with each bullet, as if the jester were a cartoon character struck by imaginary slugs, nothing more.

Micah pulled the trigger again, only to hear the gun *click.*

Mike Myers threw his hands into the air and screamed triumphantly. "Yeah, man! *Fuck* yeah! You hardcore mother*fucker!*"

With a sweeping blow, Myers knocked the .38 out of Micah's hand, sending it clattering into the shadows. Even though the gun was empty, the dismissive gesture only made Micah feel even more helpless. He screamed in rage and fear as he swung his flashlight and struck Myers in the temple, harder than he'd hit Skull Face.

Something cracked loudly. Myers' head flopped onto his right shoulder. A ragged, bloodless stump poked up from between his shoulders as leathery-dry skin flapped from where his head had torn away.

"Hey! You motherfucker!" Myers fell to one knee, his head dangling by the thinnest shred of tissue.

It was a comic sight strangely incongruent with the terror pumping in his heart. Mike Myers kneeling, one hand grabbing his hair and the other groping for his neck stump as he tried to jam his head back into place, missing each time as he muttered, "Goddamn motherfucking son of a *bitch*, I'm gonna rip your fucking *heart* out . . . "

Micah rolled over, scrambled to his feet and lurched toward the cabin's door, barely able to put any weight on his bad knee at all.

When he stepped outside, Micah closed his eyes and sighed, wondering where the hell Phelps was. The cabin was empty, which meant Phelps was either hiding in one of these other two cabins, or he'd taken the trail winding into the woods toward Blackfoot Valley itself. Kid would probably kill himself. Wouldn't *that* end up in a nice little shit show?

To make matters worse, Micah felt lightheaded. A dull headache was pounding behind his eyes. He was having trouble seeing. Everything seemed out of focus, warped, like he was looking through a pair of glasses with the wrong prescription. That, and, oddly enough, his right knee *really* bothered him.

He pinched his nose and rubbed it, whispering, "Dammit. What the hell is wrong with me?"

A soft squeak sent cold fingers playing along his shoulders, and he tensed until he heard someone whisper, "Micah?"

Micah opened his eyes and looked toward the direction of the voice, to the far cabin on the left. A shivering, lanky kid in a white shirt, yellow shorts and white sneakers stepped out.

Annoyed relief filled Micah. Phelps had led him all over camp, wasting his time, and the Longtrees were going to be here any minute, expecting cash from Phelps' deal. Micah wasn't normally violent, but right now he felt like he could smack the shit out of Phelps, who obviously didn't have a clue how much trouble he'd gotten into.

"Get the hell over here," he rasped. "What do you think you're doing? Running all over camp? Lucky I saw your ass. The Longtrees are gonna be here any minute. You do the deal?"

Tony Phelps, a sophomore from Booneville, approached

Micah, wringing his hands like an old lady, looking like he was about to burst into tears. He was skinny and shaking like a junkie desperate for a fix. His face glowed in Micah's flashlight beam, eyes wide and trembling.

"I said," Micah repeated through gritted teeth, "did you deal to Cabin 2 like you were supposed to?"

Phelps licked his lips and swallowed. "Uh . . . no. I can't, Micah. I can't. It's . . . man. I don't wanna get busted, and . . . "

Uncharacteristic anger surged through Micah. His hand snapped out and grabbed a fistful of Phelp's white t-shirt. Phelps yelped. Micah felt sure if he checked, he'd smell piss all over the kid.

He yanked Phelps's face inches from his own. "Listen to me very carefully. You *begged* to be in this. And you sure enjoyed the sample you got Sunday night. Said it made you play like Michael Fucking Jordan. Couldn't miss a shot, could you? But you haven't done jack-shit since. It's Thursday night. Camp ends tomorrow. Everyone's going home. You were supposed to have dealt to those assholes in Cabin 2 by tonight. Why the hell hasn't that happened?" He shook Phelps. The kid's head bobbled back and forth on his skinny neck. "Why?"

"I don't wanna get busted, Micah. I . . . thought I could do it, but . . . I can't. What if they didn't want to buy? Or told someone I was selling . . . "

Micah closed his eyes for a second, forcing himself not to smack Phelps upside the head. When he felt more under control, he opened his eyes and pinned Phelps with a hot glare. "Those assholes in Cabin 2 are from Livingston Manor. They fucking eat smack for breakfast and wash it down with Old English. They wouldn't squeal. Selling to them should've been easy. They're pros. They'd cut their grandmothers' throats for a hit."

"I . . . I can't do it, man. What if I get caught, or . . . "

Micah shook him again, bobbling the kid's head some more. "So you weren't gonna say anything? Just cut and run on me and the Longtrees? Those boys don't like that." Not to mention, of course, the shit Micah would've been in had the Longtrees showed up to find Phelps missing.

A blubbering sob burst past Phelps' lips. Tears leaked down his face. "S-shit, man. What am I gonna do?"

"I'll tell you what you're gonna do. You're gonna suck it up, stop bawling and hustle your ass down to Cabin 2 to deal before the Longtrees get here. Because it's not only your ass on the line. You begged, and stupid-fucking-me, I felt bad for you and backed you up. Now *I'm* in the shit. These guys like their baseball bats, Phelps. But they don't exactly like baseball. Get me?"

Phelps wiped his eyes with the back of his hand, sucking in deep gasps of air in an effort not to cry, nodding so hard Micah wouldn't be surprised if his head bobbed off at the neck. "O-okay. I'll t-try."

"No, you'll *do*. The Longtrees'll be here soon. They're gonna want their cash. They don't get it; things are going bad for both of us."

He released Phelps' shirt and smoothed it down. Doing so, he noticed the necklace Phelps wore. He slid his hand under it and drew it out. Held up his flashlight and examined the silver pendent hanging from it. A pattern made up of interweaving threads with no end and no beginning.

"Cool necklace. What is it?"

Calmer, Phelps sniffled and said, "My Uncle Ian sent it to me from Ireland last year. Supposed to be a Celtic infinity knot."

"Infinity knot, huh? Cool."

An idea struck him. The pendant's chain felt delicate, easy to break. Without warning he yanked, jerking Phelps' head forward. The kid yelped, but Micah was rewarded with the barely audible *snap* of the chain breaking.

"Ow!" Phelps' face screwed up, as if he was about to cry again. Rubbing the back of his neck, he muttered, "What the hell, man?"

Micah ignored Phelps' complaints and held the chain up, dangling the pendent before him.

"Here's the deal. I'm going to hold onto this until you get down to Cabin 2 and deal. Once you do what you're supposed to, you get this back. Sound fair?"

"My Uncle gave it to me for my birthday, man."

"Well, now you got some more motivation. In addition to the Longtrees coming to kick your ass if the job ain't done. Let's go, Nancy."

He gestured toward the path with his flashlight. Phelps slouched forward, shoulders sagging. The kid was acting like he was heading to his own funeral (which wasn't far from the truth, if the Longtrees didn't get paid), but Micah didn't care. If they hustled, maybe the dumbass could deal before the Longtrees showed up, and save them both a beating.

His relief fled, however, when he saw the Longtrees standing in the path leading back down to the courts. Waiting for them, baseball bats in hand.

8.

MICAH SLID TO a halt, flashlight suddenly heavy in his hand as a deep sense of pointlessness washed over him. There, standing in the middle of the path leading down to the ruins of Blackfoot Valley Sports Camp, was Skull Face. Next to him, his queen, her skull face pieced back together into a hideous jig-saw puzzle. Jason Vorhees and Frankenstein's monster stood behind them.

A bone-cold hand grabbed the back of his neck. Mike Myers—holding Micah by the neck, other hand holding his own head in place—peered over his shoulder. "What the *hell* man? You keep slipping back and forth. How are you doing that? It's against the rules!"

Myers shook him by the scruff of his neck. Micah couldn't form a coherent thought. From the moment he'd seen Skull Face and his crew roll into the ruined parking lot of Blackfoot Valley, he'd operated on fear-laced adrenaline. Now that adrenaline had faded, his instinct told him this mad chase had neared its conclusion.

"It's gotta be the shopkeeper," said a gruff voice Micah hadn't heard yet. He saw Frankenstein's monster gesturing, and assumed it was him who had spoken. "Like Jimmy said, that guy's always messin' with our shit."

Skull Face—Jimmy, apparently—flashed his death's-head grin as he ambled up the path. "The funny thing is, I don't think Micah even knows what he's doing, or how," he said. "He's just running scared. Like a rabbit or squirrel dodging blindly through bushes until it pops out into a clearing, and *bam!*" Jimmy snapped his fingers. "A hawk swoops down and bites its head off." Jimmy stopped within five feet of Micah and stuck one hand into his jeans pocket. His queen by his side, Jason Vorhees and Frankenstein's monster bringing up the rear. "Poor Micah," Jimmy said with a reasonable facsimile of genuine sympathy. "He doesn't know. Tonight's the night. The night of the grave's delight. The night he's supposed to . . . "

Jimmy pointed his finger at his ruined temple, miming a gun and pulling the trigger. "Blammo. You knew it deep down, though. That's why you had the gun on you, but you didn't *want* to know. Did you?"

Micah swallowed, sour defeat churning in his stomach. All he could do was shake his head, what little Mike Myers would allow with his icy grip still clamped to his neck.

"Sad thing is, I could've been the answer to it all." Jimmy took another step closer, red glimmering in the back of his black eye sockets. "I wasn't planning on harvesting *you* tonight, in particular. But like I said, I smelled you, Micah, the second you left that bar. Don't know why I've never smelled you before. Maybe you just weren't quite ready."

He held up a finger. "But tonight? I smelled it on you. And was ready to make it quick and painless. But you reneged. And yeah, the shopkeeper *had* to have something to do with it. There's no way you could've dodged all over this place without his help. But that wouldn't have worked unless you *wanted* that help."

Jimmy stepped closer. His forehead gash was still bloodless, but under the moonlight, Micah saw white things squirming there. A foul odor—of damp decay and rot— washed over him. He tried to twist away, but Michael Myers squeezed the back of his neck and held him fast.

"You called to me, Micah. Whether you know it or not. Whether you want to admit it, or not. You did. And I heard it. Smelled it. I came for you. At the stoplight, I came for you, and you were supposed to have come with me. But you didn't."

Jimmy took one more step, bringing them almost nose to nose. Only abject fear kept Micah from gagging openly at the awful stench wafting over him. "I let it go. Figured you needed some time. Figured we'd catch up here, and then you'd be ready."

Skull Face snarled. "But you ran. And kept running. You *struck* me. Which of course didn't actually do anything, but it's the principle of the thing. No one strikes me. *No one.*"

Jimmy stepped back, a distant calm settling over him. He withdrew his other hand from his pocket, and cracked his knuckles. "We were going to make this easy. It's not going to be easy now, Micah. It's going to hurt. A lot. And we're going to enjoy every minute of it."

9.

"WE WERE GOING to make this easy. It's not going to be easy now, Micah. It's going to hurt. A *lot*."

Micah stared at Bobby and Billy Longtree. Both of them were tall and skinny, their greasy hair pulled back into ponytails, narrow and thin faces blank. Black eyes glittered in the moonlight, reminding him, as always, of snakes. As he'd warned Tony, both of them brandished baseball bats, each holding theirs loosely by their sides.

For a moment, Micah experienced a weird kind of double-vision. Imagining both of them wearing masks, for some reason. His stomach surging, he shook the mirage off. They were too late to seal the deal. They were fucked.

Royally.

He squeezed the infinity pendant he'd taken from Phelps. Its points dug into the flesh of his palm. It was oddly warm against his skin. "Bobby. Billy," he said. "Little early, aren't you?"

no they're not
they're dead
have been for years

Micah frowned at the strange thoughts flitting through his head. What the hell was wrong with him? Was he losing it?

Bobby Longtree smiled; revealing stained yellow teeth. "Late? You must not be wearing a watch, Micah. It's past midnight. Course, maybe you lost track of time. Looks like you been busy," he pointed his bat at Phelps, "chasing down strays."

Billy, nearly identical to Bobby except for a craggier face, added in a soft but menacing voice, "Hope there hasn't been any trouble. Especially after the last few . . . incidents."

Micah did his best not to cringe at the Longtrees' desire

to avoid "trouble." He'd seen them use their bats all too gleefully in the past.

He squeezed the pendent harder. Strangely enough, it felt warmer, to the point of real heat, now.

He swallowed, faking an ease he didn't feel. "No problems. Tony here was having some . . . confidence issues." He gestured over his shoulder. Didn't dare look away from the Longtrees, as if it signaled weakness. "We've got things sorted out. Maybe you could head over to your other jobs, swing back here in an hour or two? Things'll be settled by then."

Bobby's sick smile spreading wider. His face looked like a skull, his smile a death-head grin. He twirled his bat by its handle and slapped its head into his open palm with a loud smack. "Nope. Other jobs are out in Eagle Bay, and we're spending the night there. Don't wanna come back this way tonight."

The pendant burned in Micah's hand. He licked his lips, desperation cracking his already weak facade. "Listen. Maybe you could head into town. Have a few drinks, then come back. This won't take long, I promise."

Billy shook his head sadly. Micah knew his reluctance was feigned. Billy would be all too happy to administer his efficient brand of discipline when the time came. "I'm disappointed in you, Micah. This is strike three, man. We were hoping you'd make things right after those last two clusterfucks."

"C'mon," Micah protested weakly. The pendant was burning his skin, but for some reason he couldn't let it go. "The kid's a little jumpy is all. I talked him off the ledge, and we're heading down to Cabin 2 right now."

"Uh-uh. Too late. We checked on the way up. Saw you hadn't hit it and did our own deal. We did *your* job, Micah. You know how we feel about that."

Micah's mouth went dry, and his bladder twitched. Also, a strange heaviness throbbed in his right knee, though he didn't know why. It ached with a strange, phantom pain. "Guys. We can figure something out. I've had shitty luck this summer, but we've worked together for a while now. We've got a solid thing. Let's not throw it away."

Bobby stepped forward, smiling. "*Had* a solid thing, Micah. Had. Like Billy said, this is strike three. Your little buddy was desperate to get into the action. Wanted to work with us. Be a big man. But here's something we know you don't. Little fucker there, who begged you to hook him up? He split the shit we gave him with the kids in his cabin, first night of camp. One of his buddies went and squealed to Bags. Bags called us. All on your watch, Micah. Which makes you responsible for *another* mess."

Angry shock rippled through Micah. He glared over his shoulder at Phelps, who stood wide-eyed and pale in the night. "You fucking son of a bitch."

Phelps didn't respond or move. He looked frozen, as if stuck in a bubble where time didn't exist.

"So we gotta take care of this, see? It looks bad. Not only did you bring us someone who ain't got the stones to deal, you brought us someone who screwed us over and stole from us. A serious lapse in judgment, Micah. Another one." Billy shook his head. "Sloppy. You've gotten fucking sloppy. Must be that scholarship's gone to your head."

Micah faced the Longtrees, the pendent blazing in his hand. "Listen. We can still fix this. We can roll the kids he gave it to. Get cash from them. We can come up with the money, somehow. He can come up with the money. And how's this gonna look, tomorrow? Us beat up? Gonna bring some serious attention down on you guys. Won't be able to deal here for a long while. Maybe never again."

Bobby stepped closer, bat resting on his shoulder. "Well, you see, it's a shame. Probably will cause a little scuffle when Phelps is found at the bottom of the valley, all smashed up. He shouldn't have gone wandering around at night, huh? But when they find dope in his blood, they'll figure he was a junkie who got high and took off into the woods. You, however . . . "

He lifted the bat from his shoulder and pointed it at Micah. "You'll be a hero. Getting hurt falling down Blackfoot Valley, trying to save the kid." He paused, and then added, "If you don't want to get hurt worse, that is."

Micah stumbled back several steps—the pendant burning into his palm—and bumped into Phelps. "Baseball bat," he said. "Doc Jeffers'll be able to tell it was a baseball bat did the damage on us, not rocks."

This time Billy grinned, his yellow teeth gleaming in the night. It was a horrible thing to see, making Micah's knees buckle. "Yeah. Doc Jeffers would be able to tell. But we got a nice working relationship with him, see? He gets to buy product for some of his more under the table patients at a discounted price, so long as he ignores certain things."

"Here's the thing," Bobby said quietly. "Yeah, you've run into some shitty luck. Sometimes things go sideways in ways you don't expect."

"Exactly." Micah pointed at Billy, the pendant burning so hot he imagined there'd be a brand to mark its outline in his skin, later. "Things have gone sideways, all summer. You gotta see that."

"Problem is," Billy continued, "there are still consequences which must be paid. Regardless."

"So step away. Take your consequences like you got a pair," said Bobby, "and maybe we've still got a solid thing. You don't step away . . . "

Bobby Longtree took his bat off his shoulder and swished a practice swing through the night air, his meaning all too clear. "Take your consequences. Let Billy deal with the little shit who fucked this up for you."

At this, Phelps broke. He whirled and ran away, past the cabins and back into the woods, along the path toward Blackfoot Valley and its dangerous drop. Billy Longtree walked up the path, past Micah, and followed Tony.

Smiling, his gait relaxed and business-like as he twirled his bat.

Micah stood still, gaze darting from the receding Billy to Bobby, every muscle in his body pulled tight. Those bats would do serious damage. Phelps was done for. *He'd* make it through alive, but Micah knew, instinctively, what the "consequences" would be. A star quarterback for Indian Lake once crossed the Longtrees. Over the summer between his junior and senior year he "fell" hiking up Blue Face Mountain. Broke his leg in three places. It eventually healed, but his football career ended the day of his "accident." Micah knew exactly what his "consequence" would be.

But he was in great shape. The Longtrees were both strong and mean, but he was faster. He'd wait until Bobby came in for a swing, juke and dodge around him, then run hard as hell for the parking lot. He could get in his car and drive the hell out of here. Who cared if he wasn't paid for working this week? Who cared if he never worked here again? He'd rather escape intact. Phelps was fucked, but maybe Micah could . . .

His thoughts trailed off.

He'd already done this, hadn't he?

He didn't know how he knew this, but it rang in his head with absolute clarity. He'd already tried running. It hadn't worked. Bobby had caught him anyway.

The thought didn't make any sense. He didn't know where it came from, but there it was. Ringing in his head as he gripped the pendant tighter. He'd tried to run once and had gotten nothing but pain in return.

His knee ached with a phantom twinge.

He realized—feeling old, for some reason, much older than eighteen—there was no way to avoid his physical fate. But maybe something could be done about his spirit. Whatever the hell *that* meant.

Micah tensed, digging his feet in. Bobby's eyes lit up as

KEVIN LUCIA

he sensed Micah's intent. "Don't be a hero, Micah," Bobby said softly. "You're no hero. You're a special kind of stupid. That's what you are."

The Celtic infinity knot which he'd taken from Phelps . . .

found in the bag the shopkeeper gave him

. . . burned against his palm.

Micah wasn't sure when he'd done it, or even how, but at some point during Jimmy's monologue he'd slipped his hand into his right pocket. Now he clenched that weird pendent he'd found in the orange bag of Halloween candy the shopkeeper had given him.

Celtic infinity knot.

It felt warm against his skin; and it was growing warmer by the second.

Jimmy scowled and stepped close to Micah again. "You just did it, didn't you? Slipped back and forth. I saw you shimmer, just for a second. Not-here, and then here. How are you doing that? What did the shopkeeper do to you?"

A strange determination burned through Micah. For some reason, he no longer felt helpless or defeated. His spine stiff, his shoulders squared, Micah glared at Jimmy. "You can't just take me, can you? You need my *permission*. That's how this works. That's why you've had to chase me all over camp, why you didn't just *take* me and do whatever it is you're going to do. You need me to give up. To *let you*. There are like . . . rules to this."

Jimmy stood very still, hands clenched at his sides. Red glowed in his eye sockets, minutes crept by, until he rasped in a voice which didn't sound as if it came from a human throat. "But I can do whatever it takes to *make you* give up."

Jimmy leaned in close. His grave breath hissed in Micah's face. *"Whatever. It. Takes."*

With the speed of a snake, Jimmy drove a fist of hard bone into Micah's gut. Micah gasped as Mike Myers jerked him back by the neck, forcing him upright. His abdominal muscles screamed in pain.

Jimmy grabbed him by the shoulder, pulled him close, and whispered into Micah's ear, "You know the best thing about pain? It's like marinade. Soak a soul in pain and fear . . . "

Through slitted eyes, Micah saw Skull Face's nostrils twitch as he sniffed. "Boy-howdy. That's a *fine* meal."

Jimmy pistoned his arm back again and plunged his bony fist into Micah's guts—through cloth and flesh. Pain unlike anything he'd ever felt exploded in waves from his belly. Micah felt Jimmy's fingers digging into his intestines.

But he felt no blood.

When he looked down, Jimmy's fist had disappeared into his belly, up to the wrist. But he saw no torn flesh, no wound. It looked as if his belly was water, and Jimmy had plunged his fist into it.

"Is this real, Micah? Are my fingers playing with your insides, right now? Or is it an illusion? A glamour? If I grab a fistful of the squishy things in your belly and yank my fist out, would I have nothing . . . or a handful of your guts? Or . . . "

Micah gasped, unable to speak, mind blanked out not only by the pain but also the alien sensation of a hand closing around his . . .

"What if I grab hold of your spine, Micah? Rip it out and beat you with it?"

Electric pain blazed through him. Micah threw his head back and screamed.

In a grotesquely gentle gesture, Jimmy pulled Micah even closer, cradling his head against Jimmy's shoulder. "I can make it go away, Micah. Or make it last forever. Now that I've got a hold of you, whatever mojo the shopkeeper gave you to slip away won't work. I've got you, in this moment, and I can keep you in this moment, forever. So what's it going to be? I can make it all go away, if you want. It all depends on how badly you want it, how badly you need it."

Micah gagged on the blood slicking the back of his throat.

the right cosmic conditions
and the strength of will
Pain.

Blazing all through him, as Jimmy's cold fingers clutched his spine, impossibly. Pain, but now something else, as Micah squeezed the Celtic infinity knot so hard the edges cut into his flesh. As he felt the blood flow in his hand over the pendant, he felt something else.

Anger. *Rage.*

10.

AS JIMMY SQUEEZED his spine, Micah could only think of Amy, whom he loved—perhaps only after a dutiful fashion, but loved regardless. She'd been good to him. Had loved him even when he hadn't been easy to love. She'd kept him sane all these years. Warding off the darkness, preventing it from overwhelming him completely. Even facing the truth—in the midst of burning, white-hot pain—that he'd been ready to leave Amy for good, Micah found he wasn't ready to go. He wouldn't leave Amy. He would *not* be taken from her.

He squeezed the Celtic infinity knot, and felt a different kind of pain as the pendant's points cut deeper into his palm. A clear, bracing pain. He felt more blood flow over the pendant. It no longer felt warm. It *blazed* with a heat that burned all the way up his arm.

"What's it gonna be, Micah?" Jimmy's whisper in his ear was tender, almost a caress. "Are you ready to call it a night, or do I have to start playing mortician?"

Micah forced himself to look up, into Jimmy's eyes. "Go to hell," he rasped, and before Jimmy could respond, he closed his hand into a fist around the pendant, and, with every ounce of strength remaining in his body, swung his hand at Skull Face's head and slammed the pendant point-first into Jimmy's head wound, among the white things squirming there.

Jimmy spasmed. Light exploded from his eyes and his mouth, as it did from his lackeys and his queen. They jerked and shivered. An unearthly, howling shriek came from nowhere and everywhere at once. The King of Halloween, his Queen, and his court fractured into pieces of blazing glass. Light exploded everywhere, accompanied by a gigantic clap of sound, as . . .

II.

... MICAH TENSED, digging his feet in. Bobby's eyes lit up as he sensed Micah's intent. "Don't be a hero, Micah," Bobby said softly. "You're no hero. You're a special kind of stupid. That's what you are."

Micah said nothing, clenching and unclenching his hands. Bobby choked up on his baseball bat, but somehow Micah knew he'd be a fraction of a second too late to stop him. It had already happened. Deep down, Micah knew this. He'd let Bobby come over as he begged a second chance, and Bobby had administered the blows to his knee which had changed his life forever. He'd stood there like a lamb waiting for slaughter.

Not this time.

Micah's sudden pivot caught Bobby off guard as he turned and sprinted after Billy Longtree and Phelps, instead of waiting for his punishment.

He was faster and quicker than the Longtrees, Billy in particular. In several breathless minutes Micah closed in on the drug dealer as Billy was arcing his bat down toward the cowering Phelps, who'd tripped and fallen at the edge of Blackfoot Valley.

Micah had no clear idea what he was doing. Bobby was surely bringing up the rear, but Micah wasn't thinking. He was merely acting on the instinct that somehow, things must be done differently this time. He *must* do something else besides protect his own ass.

He lowered his shoulder and threw himself forward.

Before the bat could connect with Phelps' head, Micah plowed into Billy's back, shoulder-first. Billy gasped and his bat sailed off to the side. Micah's momentum flung them forward, pitching them into the air. Micah's foot, caught on a rock outcropping and arrested his fall, wrenching his left knee painfully ...

his left knee
not his right knee

   . . . but as he cried out in pain, a strange relief rushed through him, because tripping on the rock arrested his forward plunge. He twisted as he crashed to the slope, turning his face away from rocks, and his knee screamed as he did so.

Billy himself screamed—loud and shrill—as he plunged headfirst into the jagged depths below. His shrillness snapped off with a sickening thud and a *crack*.

Silence.

Save Phelps' whimpering as he lay on the ground on Blackfoot Valley's edge, somewhere out of sight. Micah rolled onto his side, trying in between hot blasts of pain rippling across his left kneecap to crawl back over the valley's edge. In jerking efforts, knee spasming, he finally threw himself onto level ground, where he collapsed.

Moaning, he clasped his ruined knee to his chest with both hands, realizing in a dim corner of his mind he'd dropped the pendant he'd been holding so tightly, the pendant he'd taken from Phelps—

from the orange bag of Halloween candy

But he didn't have time to worry about the pendent. He needed to get up. Needed to get Phelps moving and down to camp or away into the woods, because Bobby was coming with his bat. Soon as he'd seen what happened to Billy . . . what Micah had done to Billy . . .

With a titanic effort, Micah rolled over and crawled toward a nearby tree. When there, he rested his shoulder against it for a few seconds to gather his bearings. "C'mon . . . Phelps," he rasped. "Let's get going. He's coming. Bobby's coming, and he . . . " He gasped. Braced against the tree, levering his weight onto his good knee, he inched his way to a standing position. He grasped the cracked trunk with both hands; because of course he'd lost the pendant, the Celtic infinity knot . . .

His knee throbbed with pain.

His *left* knee, not his right.

He only had a minute to wonder about that, however, before he heard Bobby Longtree scream in rage, and felt the worst kind of pain imaginable explode against the base of his spine.

12.

MICAH LOST HIS hold on the tree. He crashed to the ground on his side. Bobby kicked him in the same place the bat had just struck. Micah wheezed, the pain squeezing his lungs so tightly he couldn't scream, or even whimper.

"You piece of shit! Where's my brother? *Where's Billy?*"

A faint whoosh of air. The bat swinging, a blast of pain exploding along his spine, and—

A dreadful, sharp *crack*, bringing with it a terrible sense of finality. All Micah could think of was Jimmy's hand wrapped around his spine, twisting mercilessly until it snapped like a twig in his bony hand.

Who's Jimmy?

He tried to move his legs in a feeble attempt to crawl away, but he couldn't. He felt maybe a faint twitch in his thighs, nothing more. All he could do was flop onto his back. Bobby loomed above, bat held high, poised to deliver one last blow.

Micah blinked, had time for one odd thought . . .

Amy

I'm sorry

. . . and he laid there, waiting for the end.

Longtree reared back, face twisting.

A different scream of rage split the night. One high and shrill, coming from someone much younger. It struck Micah like a thunderbolt.

The other bat, which Billy had dropped.

Tony Phelps, whom both Micah *and* Bobby Longtree had forgotten.

Startled, Bobby swiveled his head and looked directly into the path of the bat swung by a hysterical Tony Phelps. Phelps was a fraction of Bobby's size and not nearly as strong, but the swing caught Bobby unprepared and the bat smashed full-force into his forehead. He shivered once, and crumpled to the ground.

Phelps dropped the bat, hands dangling at his sides. He stared at Micah for several seconds, eyes unfocused, as if unsure of where he was or what he'd just done.

A fresh wave of pain hit Micah, and he cried out. This seemed to bring Tony back to his senses. His eyes focused and he paled. "Micah! Holy . . . are you okay?"

Micah tried to say something but, impossibly, more pain exploded all throughout his body, now coming from everywhere. That, and a strange bright light blossomed all around, filling the forest. A high-pitched ringing sound droned in his ears and drowned out Phelps' voice as the youth kneeling beside him disappeared into the bright white light . . .

13.

... WHICH FILLED HIS truck's cab, almost blinding him.

Micah squinted and glanced into his rearview mirror. A car sat behind him, its headlights on high. Micah shielded his eyes and looked again. The car looked low to the ground, but that's all he could tell. Its blazing headlights filled the cab.

A siren whooped. In concert, the blue and red lights on top of the car flickered to life.

"Great," Micah whispered. He couldn't imagine why one of Clifton Heights' finest had pulled behind him. He hadn't been speeding. He'd also only had one beer at The Inn, so he hadn't been driving erratically, either. Maybe a taillight was out? Whatever it was wouldn't amount to much more than an annoyance, but it was an annoyance he didn't feel like dealing with tonight.

The police cruiser's door thumped closed. Boots scraped on asphalt toward him. Micah sighed and rolled down the window with one hand, his other hand reaching for the glove compartment which held his registration and insurance cards.

The officer reached his window and shined his flashlight inside (courteously keeping the glare on the dashboard, away from Micah's eyes), but instead of asking for his license and registration, he said, "Micah? You okay?"

A strange sense of relief filled Micah as he turned and smiled at Sheriff Deputy Tony Phelps standing at his window. If you had to get pulled over by the police, and it wasn't Sheriff Baker, Tony Phelps was the next best card to draw.

"Hey, Tony. Yeah, I'm okay."

He realized, with an odd feeling of satisfaction, that he was telling the truth.

Tony nodded, smiling, looking amused but still a little concerned. "How long you been sitting here? I just pulled up, of course, but the light was green, and you weren't moving. Just wanted to see if everything was okay."

"Yeah, I . . . " Micah shook his head, his thoughts feeling muddled and distant, for some reason. "I was just thinking about some things. Got caught up, I guess." A thought occurred to him. "You don't seem too surprised it's me. Actually . . . you said my name right away. How did you know it was me?"

Tony shrugged, looking embarrassed and very young, reminding Micah of the sixteen-year-old he'd known a long time ago. He lowered the flashlight, faced Micah directly, and leaned against the truck. "Listen, don't be mad. Amy called. Said you were late coming home, and that she was worried. Mentioned you'd been at The Inn. So I stopped there, and Gus said he'd told you how the Valley was getting plowed tomorrow—how you freaked out and left. He felt bad, by the way. You know Gus. Big mouth, but big heart, too."

Micah nodded. Gus meant well, and he felt ashamed for his odd irritation at Gus retelling the story of how he'd saved Tony from Billy Longtree, and how Tony had in turn saved him from Bobby.

"Anyway. Took a guess and headed this way, out toward the Valley. Here you are." A pause, and then Tony asked carefully, "Were you headed there?"

Micah opened his mouth, but he paused. Unformed thoughts flickered on the edge of his mind, but he couldn't bring them into focus, no matter how hard he tried. Finally, he admitted, "Maybe. I'm not sure. Hearing they were tearing the place down after all these years . . . it shook me. I wasn't consciously heading there. Just driving around."

Tony offered a small smile. "Believe me, I know how you feel about that place. More than anyone. That last night? Wasn't your fault."

"It *was* my fault," Micah whispered, voice rough with emotion, nearly overcome with an abrupt swelling of guilt inside. "If it hadn't been for me, it wouldn't have happened."

Tony shrugged. His smile faded, face now somber and reflective. "I don't know about that. I was in a bad place back then, Micah. If you hadn't been dealing for the Longtrees, I probably would've found my way onto their radar anyway."

"But I put us in that situation," Micah insisted, though for some reason his self-loathing felt impotent and powerless. A shadowy memory of regret, nothing more. "Me. I made it happen. I brought you in."

"You could've stood there and let the Longtrees have their way with me. You could've run away. But you didn't. You saved my life, and in the process, got your spine broken. You can't walk anymore because of me."

Tony patted his deputy's badge. "I'm not a perfect guy. I've made lots of mistakes, even after cleaning up. I'm not sure how good a person I am. Honestly, I'm only an okay cop. I'm lucky Sheriff Baker is so laid-back. I'd get my chops busted a lot more under someone stricter."

He met Micah's gaze, his eyes bright and alive. "But I'm clean. I have purpose. I'm doing something, because of you. Because of what you sacrificed, which was . . . *everything*. I'm the one who should feel guilty. Not you."

Micah shook his head. "But you saved me, also. You could've run, too. If you had . . . "

A quick vision of Bobby Longtree standing above him, bat raised high, made him shiver. "It was too late for me. You throw in with folks like the Longtrees, you can guarantee losing in the long run. I was going to lose everything anyway, Tony. At least I lost trying to balance the scales, in what little way I could."

"You balanced the scales, Micah. In my book, at least." He paused. "Micah. You sure everything's okay? Everything okay at home, and with Sammy? I know the adoption process can be grueling."

Micah opened his mouth, planning on giving Tony a nice-sounding answer, but he said nothing at first, realizing he *was* okay, indeed. Not great, not super-fabulous, not leaping for joy. Life was still the same as it always had been, and tomorrow he'd go back to the same okay job doing the same okay things. But he *was* okay. The thirteen-year-old boy they were adopting had become part of their family over the past two years. The adoption had become more of a legal formality than anything else. "Adoption's going fine. Smoother than we thought, actually. It helps that Sammy's been such a good fit. Honestly, the legalities are like an afterthought. Soon as he started living with us, it felt right. Like it was meant to be."

Micah smiled. "And he's going to be a helluva basketball player someday, too. Kid's a natural."

Tony chuckled. "Well, he couldn't ask for a better Dad to teach him, that's for sure."

"I don't know about that. I'm not what I once was."

"Who is? Besides. Not only are you *still* the all-time leading scorer in Section 3, Class C history, you've also been the leading scorer in your adult league the last two years running. And I've seen those games, Micah. It's gotta be harder shooting from your wheelchair, but you still never miss, ever."

"I suppose." Micah took a deep breath, still distracted by the notion that something indefinable lingered just beyond his thoughts. "Y'know, I can't even tell you why Gus' story bothered me so much tonight, or why I bolted so quickly when he told me about the Valley. I was actually having a good time with him and Jimmy, watching the Knicks get roasted by the Spurs. Then he said something about the Valley getting torn down, and . . . "

Tony reached through the window, gripped his shoulder and squeezed. "Bad memories do that. They come up when you least expect them to. But tomorrow, Nuemann Construction is going to bulldoze the Valley into the ground.

It'll be less than a memory, my friend. You go home and get some rest." He thumped the truck's door, waved and turned back to his cruiser.

Micah nodded, smiling. He put his truck into gear but grabbed the brake lever, a sudden idea bubbling up, from where he didn't know. "Hey, Tony," he called out the window, "you ever find your necklace? The one I . . . well, the one I took from you? The Celtic infinity knot?"

Tony cocked his head, surprise written on his features. "Huh. I haven't thought about that in forever. Lost it that night. It probably fell into the valley. I never went hunting for it, that's for sure." He smiled, puzzled. "Why do you ask?"

Briefly, Micah thought of telling Tony about the weird pendant he'd found in the orange bag of Halloween candy the shopkeeper had given him. How it looked just like the one Micah had taken from Tony that night. The moment passed, however, and he shook his head. "No reason. Just a weird thought."

Tony chuckled. "Well, it's Halloween. The perfect night for weird thoughts, right?"

Micah was about to respond, but a low throbbing engine interrupted him, as well as the sound of a whining guitar riff. He looked up and saw, passing through the traffic light in the opposite direction, a gleaming midnight-black, restored 1977 Monte Carlo.

From the open window poured the thundering guitars and drums of Motley Crue's 'Shout at the Devil'. As the car rolled leisurely under one of the streetlamps and past them, Micah's heart sped up. He glimpsed a face done up in white makeup. Like a skull. The orange glow of a cigarette tip blazed against the dark inside the car.

Though it was probably his imagination, Micah thought he saw the driver give him a leisurely two-fingered salute as he drove by, after which the car sped up, turned right and drove away into the night.

Tony looked back at Micah and shrugged. "Like I said. It's Halloween. The night for weird thoughts, and even weirder sights." He pointed at Micah. "Get out of here. Amy and Sammy are waiting for you at home." He waved once more, then turned and walked to his cruiser.

Micah waved, disengaged the brake lever, flicked the turn signal on and executed a u-turn, away from Blackfoot Valley and toward home. As he put distance between himself and the ruins of the basketball camp, he relaxed. He would go home to his okay life, which was getting more okay by the day.

As he took the left turn which would send him home, he was struck by the notion that there was something in his left jacket pocket. However, when he stuck his hand in there, instead of touching something bigger, made of colder and more menacing metal, he found nothing but the strange necklace from the orange bag of Halloween candy. A clean feeling of relief surged so powerfully through him, Micah thought he might weep, though he didn't understand why.

There is a world in which we dwell;
And yet a world invisible!
And do not think that naught can be,
Save only what with eyes ye see;
I tell ye, that, this very hour,
Had but your sight a spirit's power,
Ye would be looking, eye to eye,
At a terrific company!
A thousand shapes are at your side,
A thousand by your bed abide,
A thousand, hellish demon sprites,
That bend ye to their foul delights!

Halloween, A Romaunt with Lays Meditative and Devotional,
by Arthur Cleveland Coxe

THE LAST WILL AND TESTAMENT OF THE NOT-SO-GOOD REVEREND FORD

I.

October 16th
Route 22 West

THE FIRST THING I noticed after turning off Route 28 North toward Clifton Heights, New York, was the amount of roadkill lying in the ditches. I grew up in the country and had seen my share of roadkill. Dead deer, dogs, cats, and gophers crawling with flies wasn't anything new. But after I passed the tenth dead animal—what looked like a gopher—I felt uneasy. It was only five miles from Route 28 North to Clifton Heights, and I was only halfway there. Ten dead animals seemed odd. Granted, I was under stress, but I couldn't shake the notion of animals driven to commit suicide by some unseen phenomena. A ridiculous thought.

Even so.

As I drove past stands of Adirondack pine, I remembered the time my father (the Good Reverend Ford) and I ran across a macabre discovery in the woods behind my childhood home. We'd been returning from a walk when we smelled a sweetish-sour odor coming from the woods.

My father made me wait while he investigated. I remember standing in the humid summer air, wondering what could possibly smell so bad, and instinctively knowing the answer. Something dead.

When my father returned ten minutes later, pale and shaken, I asked what he'd seen. He shook his head and said, "Let's go home." He refused to speak of it. When my father closed a discussion, it stayed closed.

Two days later, my best friend, Bob Owen, asked me while we were hanging out in the cemetery after church if I'd seen the skinned dead dogs my father found. When I said no, Bob gleefully informed me of the rumor my father had discovered ten dead dogs, skinned, arranged on the ground in a strange pattern. Everyone was talking about it (except in the Reverend's house, where only approved communications transpired). The local and state police were investigating.

"Who do they think did it?" My chest felt tight with apprehension. Years away from my closet-love for horror and the macabre (such trash was *verboten* in the Good Reverend's House), the thought of someone *willfully* killing and skinning animals other than game left me shaken.

"Probably Satanists," Bob said casually, as he sat on top of a tombstone washed blank with wind, rain, and age. "Y'know. Like those Mohammeds outside town."

"The Mohammeds" was a back-handed reference to the small Muslim community outside my childhood hometown. They home-schooled their children until high school and kept to themselves. At that time, I'd had little contact with them. Their community was largely self-sufficient. Because of this, for a long time I regarded them with an air of fearful mystery. They were *different*, of course. *Not Christian*. Even so, Bob's casual slight of them didn't make sense.

"But they're not Satanists. They're Muslim. They worship Allah and follow Islamic teachings from the Koran." This, of course, I'd learned in Mr. Jones' Social Studies class. Such things weren't discussed openly in my father's home.

Bob shrugged. "Yeah, but they're not *Christians* like us. They don't worship *our* God. Even your dad says so. And if they're not Christians," Bob screwed up his face with a grimace of mock disgust, "who knows what evil shit they do. Might as well be Satanists."

As I drove past a sign which read: CLIFTON HEIGHTS, 5 MI, I realized that moment was the first time I doubted myself, my father, and what he'd taught me to believe. However, I'd proceeded to shove those doubts down and swallow them. For the next thirty years. Until two months ago, when my daughter's death finally blew the walls down.

I shuddered as I passed another dead animal (a cat) lying sprawled and mangled in the ditch, though I didn't know why.

***

I nearly got into an accident shortly after entering Clifton Heights town limits, at a traffic light for the intersection of Haverton Road and Route 28. No cars waited in either direction while the light was red. When it turned green, however, just as I was pulling through, a midnight black Monte Carlo—a restored 1977, I thought—peeled down Haverton Road and roared across Route 28, cutting me off.

I slammed on the brakes, missing it by bare inches. Without thinking, I yelled out the window, "Watch it, asshole!"

Such language for a pastor.

To my surprise, the Monte Carlo screeched to a stop. Operating on instinct and anger, I upped the ante and stuck my hand out the window and flipped the Monte Carlo off.

The Monte Carlo sat there. Engine thrumming. A sudden, cold wave washed over me, making me feel like a fool. I quickly pulled my hand back inside the window, checked both ways, and continued down Route 28 North toward Clifton Heights. When I glanced into my rearview, the Monte Carlo was gone. That didn't make me feel better, for some reason.

2.

October 17th

CHECKING INTO THE MOTOR LODGE in Clifton Heights proved a simple affair. A credit card, registration form, and a security deposit later, and a pale-eyed bored young man handed me a brass key over the counter. It was attached to a blue plastic tile with a white #14 on it. Cabin 14, at the far end.

The cabin proved comfortably furnished. I slept well with no dreams. This would be the last night I could make that claim.

In the morning I decided to walk into town. Clifton Heights looked like the very picture of small-town Americana. All local stores and eateries, no chains, unless you counted the locally-owned Radio Shack. Quaint streets, and even the older buildings looked stately and venerable in their weariness. The people acted friendly and welcoming. Smiling, nodding hello, unlike the sullen reticence of York, PA, where I'd left behind my family and my congregation.

Even so.

As I stopped to sit on a black wrought-iron bench in front of Brown's Pharmacy, I sensed something beneath the surface of my surroundings. What exactly, I couldn't say. Just the suspicion of more existing in this small town than what I saw with my eyes.

To my dismay, while I watched people walking on the sidewalks and chatting in front of stores, I realized I was acting every inch the "watchful and wary" Christian on alert for the "snares of the devil," just as I'd been raised by the Good Reverend Ford. Had to be careful, because Satan "masqueraded as an angel of light." Looking for evil everywhere. Even in places it didn't exist.

Of course, my hometown, my congregation, my wife and son had turned out to be more than they seemed. As Great White used to say (always played very low on my Walkman and taped off the radio, because the Good Reverend Ford didn't allow such secular music in his household), "Once Bitten; Twice Shy." I most likely sensed duplicity in Clifton Heights because I'd been burned by the duplicity in those closest to me.

Still.

Something didn't feel right. Why the compulsion to turn down Route 28 toward this seemingly innocent town? Why stay here, of all places?

The night before, I'd caught William Malone's 1999 *House on Haunted Hill* on the cabin's flatscreen TV, on the Roku channel. The movie holds quite a bit of nostalgia for me. It was the first horror movie I ever saw. Away from home and free from the Good Reverend Ford's rules and constraints (even though I was attending seminary, and breaking seminary rules by attending a secular movie), several friends and I went to see it. Though it had gore, swearing, alcohol consumption and was rife with sexual innuendo, it most certainly was not the soul-shredding vehicle of depravity my father had always condemned horror movies to be. It wasn't exactly art, either, or even a particularly good movie. But in turns, it had proved suspenseful, exciting, scary, and humorous. It was a thoroughly enjoyable experience. I wanted more.In the movie, seemingly random people were invited to an old insane asylum for a party. As I sat and watched perfectly normal people enjoying life in a quiet small town, a voice whispered that, in similar fashion, I'd been invited to Clifton Heights. By what I didn't know, but something had beckoned me here, regardless.

As I sat there, a black car—an older one, its finish gleaming in the sun—drove slowly by. The black Monte Carlo which cut me off, and I'd yelled at. I felt sure of it.

3.

9:00 PM
Hyland's Pub

DONE WITH MY serviceable burger and picking at what remained of crisp steak fries, I let my gaze wander around the bar. It was a nice enough place, not much to distinguish it from hundreds of other establishments like it. Mahogany bar dotted with bar stools, running almost the length of the narrow building. Rows of liquor bottles against the wall behind the bar, and a mirror for all the drunks to gaze into. Booths against the opposite wall, and in what little space remained in the back, round tables with two or three chairs apiece.

I ate another fry and washed it down with a generous swig from my fourth bottle of Guinness Stout, thinking if only my congregation could see me now. Fulfilling the expected role of a fallen minister. Not even my second night in exile, and already degrading myself with the world's vices, downing beers in the devil's den. Of course, I'd been enjoying a beer or three on the weekends for over ten years, now. Just behind closed doors, of course. Safe from the prying eyes of the congregation. Beth had allowed this, though she'd never felt fully comfortable with it. My wife was raised by a Good Reverend, also.

Fuck this, I thought. *Might as well live up to the hype.* I tipped the Guinness back and finished it. Set it down and tapped the bar lightly. The bartender—a blank-looking man in his forties with a craggy, pitted face—appeared almost instantly. "Tullamore Dew," I said. "Three fingers. And another Guinness."

The bartender nodded. Within two minutes, another

bottle of Guinness and tumbler with three fingers of Tullamore Dew Irish Whiskey appeared at my hand. "Thanks," I said. "Start me a tab?" The bartender nodded and moved off to another customer.

I sipped the whiskey, savoring its smooth taste. Admittedly, I'm a new whiskey drinker. Only started experimenting with it about three years ago (though she'd been even more discomfited by this, Beth had also let it pass—because as it happened, her father the Good Reverend Williams had been partial to a glass or two of Jameson every Sunday afternoon following his sermon; behind closed doors, of course). This particular Irish whiskey had proved to be my favorite so far. Such a favorite, that if my old congregation knew how much I'd been drinking it, they would've fired my ass three years ago.

I let my gaze travel around the bar, which was surprisingly crowded given it was a weeknight. All sorts of folks milled about or sat at the bars and tables. Many of them blue-collar laborers. There was a lumbermill in town, I'd heard. Also a rock quarry nearby. Men dressed in overalls, jeans, blue chambray shirts, wearing Timberlands on their feet. Men with rough, unshaven faces and tired eyes, calloused hands clutching pint glasses or bottles of beer. Some of them were talking with men wearing gray shirts with their names stenciled on them. County workers, maybe.

I sipped from my whiskey and continued my appraisal of the bar's varied patrons. I've always been something of a people-watcher. Beth always liked to tease me for taking restaurant seats with a view of the front door so I could size people up as they entered.

It was true. Just in my nature. A reflex. I suppose all clergy people-watch to an extent. Church visitors, regular congregants, people coming to us for counseling. We develop a mental profile based on dress, body language, facial expressions, social interactions with others. Not for judgment's sake (at least, not for me), but more to establish a baseline on which we can build.

I noted younger patrons who looked like college students, most likely attending the community college nearby, Webb County Community College. They acted as a single unit. Sitting in their own booths and tables, not interacting with the laborers at all.

Down the bar from me sat two old men who looked like fixtures. One was balding while the other sported a thick head of white hair. Both their faces bristling with white scrub. Their eyes snapped bright and alive, however, as they debated over whether the hometown football team would make it to the state championships that year or not.

Some men wearing suits and ties sat at the bar. Suits designed to look much more expensive than they actually were. I saw them worn often enough in my congregation. I imagined these guys fancied themselves "movers and shakers", but more than likely they worked at the local bank, the small law office I saw on Main Street, or in the administration office of a retail store. They sat next to attractive women in their thirties or forties dressed like they were in their twenties, engaged in a casual flirtation which may or may not lead to something else.

The women drank mimosas or glasses of cheap wine, as if this was a high society country club. Having pastored a church for over fifteen years, I assumed most of these folks were married—just to other people. Their spouses were probably dutifully waiting for them to come home after "working late at the office".

After my walk earlier in the day, I relaxed in the cabin, flipping through the various free movie channels on Roku. I happened upon an older horror movie I'd never seen, *Fade to Black*, from 1980. In it, Dennis Christopher played a frustrated and rejected cinephile who, spurned by the world, went on a half-assed killing spree dressed as his favorite movie icons. Not merely wearing their masks, but *becoming* them.

A somewhat silly (if effective) exercise in horror-comedy, I'd thought about it all afternoon—and I couldn't help thinking about it now, examining the varied patrons of Hyland's Pub. It wasn't quite right to say everyone in life wore masks. More accurate to say everyone in life *became* the masks they wore, over time. They became what they needed themselves to be, or what others needed them to be, or what they perceived the world needed them to be. Some only became one person. Others, however, became so many different things for so many different people for so many different reasons they got lost and forgot who they'd originally been. Like Dennis Christopher's character, after becoming so many different faces, all sense of self sank beneath the artifice as the person became nothing *but* their varied roles.

I took a deep drink of my whiskey, thinking of the roles I'd played since childhood, into high school, through college and seminary, into marriage, parenthood, and my pastorate. Wondering how long ago I started drowning in my roles, and if the real me could finally claw its way back to the surface.

4.

October 18th
10:30 AM

ONE OF THE first things I did after settling into Cabin 14 was Google nearby used bookstores. I fell in love with them during seminary when, ironically, my love for the macabre and horror found its birth (a love carefully concealed from my seminary colleagues, of course). I realized that, when it came to reading material, I preferred horror written primarily in the 70s, 80s and 90s. Perhaps because of the prose, or perhaps because these horror tales were still largely moralistic, and therefore easier to square with my religious studies at the time. Regardless, when I finally moved into my own apartment and could start collecting horror novels (feeling a bit like Guy Montag hiding forbidden books behind an air vent) without fear of a Floor Dean discovering them on a random dorm check, I began visiting used bookstores in towns near my seminary, building what would eventually become a massive collection of classic horror and speculative fiction (something else I left behind in my flight). This was another "earthly vice" Beth grudgingly allowed me, but when everything first started happening with Lily, she demanded I throw out my book collection, saying my "sin" had caused our daughter's downfall. I flatly refused.

It was the first of many cracks in our marriage's foundation.

The only used bookstore in Clifton Heights—Arcane Delights—boasted a robust horror and speculative fiction collection. Not knowing if I'd ever see my own collection again, nor knowing how long I'd be on the road, I happily selected titles by my favorite writers: Ramsey Campbell, Charles L. Grant, T. M. Wright, Al Sarrantonio, and Ronald Kelly.

These books underarm, I moved on to browse the classics. My father the Good Reverend Ford prescribed me a heavy diet of the classics from an early age, deeming them the only "acceptable" form of reading besides the Bible (blithely ignoring the rampant sexuality and violence in Shakespeare's plays). Because of this, my first love before horror was the classics. I actually considered becoming a high school English teacher before my father's expectation of me to follow in his footsteps won out. Still, a whole section of my home library featured the classics.

As I browsed Arcane Delight's classics section, I wasn't sure what to look for. I certainly wasn't planning on rebuilding my collection in one fell swoop. I'd only booked Cabin 14 for a few weeks. I couldn't start collecting books in a cabin I was renting. I also didn't know where else I'd end up, or *if* I'd end up anywhere else. Even so, I searched the shelves for anything which jumped out.

At the beginning of the poetry section, a title caught my eye. *The Rime of the Ancient Mariner*, by Samuel Coolridge. I set my stack of horror novels on the floor, stooped and withdrew the thin, cloth-bound volume. Straightened and began flipping through the pages. I had a particular passage in mind, of course.

The Ancient Mariner was a favorite of mine. I discovered it in college, as I was secretly discovering the weird, strange worlds of horror. The poem fascinated me because even though it's largely considered a "classic work of literature" and therefore acceptable by the standards of the Good Reverend Ford and my seminary professors, it was, without a doubt, an eerie work of horror.

I found the passage I wanted and read it softly to myself:

Like one, that on a lonely road

Doth walk in fear and dread,
And having once turn'd round, walks on
And turns no more his head:
Because he knows, a frightful fiend
Doth close behind him tread.

After breakfast that morning, I caught an old favorite on a Roku channel dedicated to classic horror films. *Curse of the Demon.* In it, Dana Andrews plays an American psychologist grappling with the harrowing reality that the supernatural exists. The female lead, played by Peggy Cummings, read this passage from *Mariner* to him, warning him not to let his rational thought blind him to the supernatural threat closing in.

I closed the thin volume, picked up the other books, and added it to the pile. I tucked them under my arm and headed to the front counter.

Ironically, my situation is the reverse of Dana Andrews' in *Curse of the Demon.* I'm grappling with the reality that perhaps the supernatural doesn't exist at all. That nothing I've been taught my whole life is true. The 'frightful fiend' treading 'close behind' was unbelief. It had followed me since my youth, and now, it was closer than ever.

***

An energetic young woman with green hair rung me up at the register. She looked to be in her mid-twenties. Her pixie cut, wide green eyes and inviting smile reminded me of Lily. Several years ago, before our world fell apart.

She held up the Ramsey Campbell title—*The Overnight*—and grinned. "Haunted bookstore novel. I can relate."

I returned her smile. It was hard not to; it was so infectious. "Really? There's certainly a presence here. That's for sure."

I meant it. On the surface, Arcane Delights appeared to be nothing more than a trendy-shabby used bookstore.

However, underneath—like the town itself—something lingered. Whenever I'd rounded a bookshelf, I'd expected to see someone in the next aisle, waiting for me. I never did, but even so. Saying I'd felt a "presence" wasn't hyperbole. Unlike the rest of the town, however, it was comforting. Nothing to fear.

The young woman smiled wider. "Think it has presence now? You should be here after closing. That's when the store *really* lets itself be known." She paused and hit the TOTAL key. "That's twenty-two, fifty."

As I handed her thirty dollars (mindful that eventually I was probably going to need some sort of employment) I noticed the rainbow LGBT+ charm hanging from her necklace. Hoping I wasn't being too forward, I said, "I appreciate the necklace."

She smiled. "Thank you." She bagged my books and passed them over the counter to me. "Not everyone feels the same, unfortunately."

I nodded, and then surprising myself, said, "I lost someone close to me recently because our community . . . our *faith* community . . . refused to accept them. Someone I should've protected, and didn't."

I didn't want to, but I forced myself to meet her gaze. "I was afraid. Of losing my ministry. Of the fallout. Worse, I was afraid standing up for her was sinning. By the time I did try to stand up for her, it was too late."

To my surprise, the young woman's eyes brimmed with unshed tears. "It's never too late to stand up," she said, voice slightly rough. "I'm sure whoever you lost . . . I'm sure she understands."

Not sure at all, I nodded but remained silent, my words abruptly gone. I took my books off the counter, nodded to the young woman, and walked away, out the front door.

With that frightful fiend still treading behind.

5.

The Golden Kitty Gentleman's Club
11:00 PM

I SIPPED FROM a Heineken, content to nurse my beer for the time being. I didn't exactly get drunk last night at Hyland's, but those beers and the whiskey left me a little foggy, so considering this was only my second time ever in a strip club, I thought it a good idea to keep my wits about me.

I'd chosen a table in the back of the club, and I sat by myself. Dim, colored lights mounted in intervals around the club's ceiling pierced the murk. The stage was brightly lit, however, though of course I suspected the lights were angled to flatter the dancers.

I sipped my beer again, wondering why I'd even come here. I'd certainly no intention of visiting Clifton Heights' only strip club. I hadn't even known it existed until I'd heard two mill workers talking about it at Hyland's earlier, where I'd been eating dinner again, wings this time. Even then, I'd heard it as background noise, in passing, and initially dismissed it. But when I got back to Cabin 14, I couldn't settle in. Couldn't find any movies which looked interesting. Without even understanding what I was doing, I hopped into the car, Googled The Golden Kitty. Here I sat, an hour later. Still nursing my second beer.

I'd only ever visited one other strip club. Back in the city where I'd attended seminary, I worked part-time loading early-morning delivery trucks at a shipping company, and developed a nice group of decidedly *non*-Christian friends while there. Shamefully, I also felt a faint sense of guilt about their friendship (I was mingling with the World and

Its Vices!), and I dearly hoped they never noticed. They ended up becoming better friends than any I had at the seminary itself.

Anyway, after I'd been working there for six months, they somehow talked me into going to a strip club with them one Saturday night. In many ways it was an underwhelming experience, and weirdly conflicting because of that. Leading up to that night, I'd practically vibrated with anxiety. First off, it was an expulsion-level offense at seminary. For another, I felt besieged by the fear that exposure to all the free-floating lust and depravity of a strip club would surely turn me into a sex and porn addict.

Of course, neither happened. It was a big city, and the chances of someone from seminary catching me on my lone trip to a strip club were very low. Also, seeing naked women gyrating on poles and strutting across the stage didn't ensnare me in a life-long addiction to sex. I'd be lying if I claimed I wasn't aroused, or denied having a handful of erotic dreams (of the kind I hadn't had since I was thirteen) afterward. But I never went back on my own, didn't hoard pornography on my computer, or start sleeping around. Honestly, after my racy dreams faded, my experience didn't leave much of a mark on me at all.

Sitting in The Golden Kitty, I felt neither shame nor fear, nor guilt. Instead, I felt depressed. In my previous strip club experience, I'd (shamefully) viewed the dancers as avatars of lust and avarice, mere vessels of sexual desire run rampant, conduits of temptation which could taint my soul with but a glance. Now, however, all I saw in the strippers' mechanized bump and grind was an undercurrent of desperation and sadness.

When The Kitty's cheap speakers blasted tinny and generic techno-music as yet another dancer strutted onto stage wearing nothing but a thong, her generous and large-nippled breasts already swinging free, I didn't see a peddler of sin. Instead, I saw flatness in her gaze. Her stiff and obviously rehearsed movements. A wide, lascivious grin which looked faked, on a forced, paper-thin mask.

She called herself "Tawny Dreams". Maybe because she bore a passing resemblance to a young Tawny Kitaen, God Rest Her Soul.

Frankenhookers.

They were all Frankenhookers.

When my loading dock friends invited me over to watch a movie called *Frankenhooker*, I'd assumed they were trying to prank me into watching a porn movie. I'd debated declining their invitation, but in all honesty, my curiosity won the battle.

Of course, *Frankenhooker* wasn't pornography at all. It certainly featured lots of nudity, and the movie throbbed (no pun intended) with sexual overtones. But there hadn't been anything remotely erotic about a comedy in which a modern mad scientist tries to reanimate his dead girlfriend (who was killed in a tragic robotic lawnmower accident) by attaching her head to body parts culled from dead hookers in order to create the "perfect woman".

For some reason, as Tawny Dreams moved lethargically through her routine, I wasn't thinking about sin, sex, or temptation. Instead, I thought about the inherent—and possibly accidental—symbolism in a man butchering women (by accident) and using their ideal parts to make his girlfriend "perfect."

On the heels of that thought, I realized my wife, my church, and me—through my cowardly inaction—had done the same to my daughter, Lily. We'd mangled her into something unrecognizable, at the behest of a completely impossible "ideal."

My stomach soured. I left without finishing my beer, long before Tawny Dreams finished.

6.

October 19th
All Saint's Church
9:00 AM

I STOOD BEFORE the nave of All Saints Church on Henry Street, marveling at a unique blend of Adirondack rustic and Gothic interior. A reverence I wasn't used to hung in the air. You don't feel this sense of holy presence in most Evangelical churches today, my former church sadly included.

As I walked slowly up the nave toward the chancel, I let myself think freely—perhaps for the first time—how discontented I'd felt at the slow transformation of my church since I was appointed pastor. In the past few years, Sunday services had more in common with high-concept sales conferences than anything "holy." Every service needed just the right light placement, sound engineering, and most of all, well-rehearsed and choreographed worship. Musicians, choir, my assistant pastors and me, all delicately-balanced moving parts of an expensive and intricate performance.

Of course, I suspected larger Catholic churches with bigger congregations had undergone a similar transformation over the years. This particular church, however, seemed to have retained its simplicity. My old church hadn't felt this hushed in years.

A soft *click* issued from the chancel. I looked up to see the priest's side of the confessional vibrate slightly, as if the priest had just entered the booth, ready to hear confessions. I paused for a moment, unsure if I wanted to follow through with this. I wasn't Catholic. Wasn't sure I believed in anything, anymore. Not after what happened. I wasn't sure what purpose sitting for confession would serve.

The idea had lodged itself in my brain when I woke up this morning, however. I knew it would fester there unless I did something about it. Breathing deeply, I approached the confessional box, stepped inside the parishioner's side, closed the door and sat down.

A panel slid back with a soft *sssh-tunk*, revealing a grate. Beyond it, I saw the priest's silhouette.

"I'm Father Thomas," the priest said quietly. "How can I help you?"

I breathed in. "Well. I have to be honest. I'm not Catholic, though I used to pastor a church. Not sure if that makes a difference."

A good-natured chuckle. "God's house is for everyone, son. Regardless of denomination or creed." A pause, and then, "What troubles you?"

I took a moment to gather myself before, "I was in formal ministry for over fifteen years, Father. Studied in seminary. Grew up a pastor's kid. Religion has always been part of my life. In many ways, it *has* been a source of comfort over the years."

"But in other ways?"

I paused, wincing slightly at the priest's insight. "In other ways . . . organized religion. The church. Faith communities. Dogmas. It sometimes feels like there's no room to breathe. Be yourself. Be who you were *meant* to be. All my life, I've been acting. Wearing a mask. Putting on a show. Repressing an essential part of myself. Almost like religion and the church forced me to amputate a core part of my being, so I could fit in. Thing is, I did it willingly. Especially as a kid. Avoided the music, TV shows, books and movies my parents warned me about. No comic books, no cartoons. My father said I couldn't. Even as an adult when I had more freedom, I didn't use it. I hid my interests. Buried them. For fear of what the 'church' or my 'faith community' would say."

"But it was never quite enough."

"No. I always felt it there. Hiding. Who I really wanted to be. My true self. Its phantom limbs aching. Cut off, but still aching."

"Except it wasn't really gone."

I shook my head, even though the priest couldn't see me. "Not gone. Repressed. Buried. Something that's been stewing. And now, I'm afraid it's going to explode."

I licked my lips and continued. "This is going to sound strange, probably, coming from a former pastor . . . but do you watch many horror movies, Father?"

An affectionate chuckle. "No. But we have a young priest who's just started here, and he loves those sorts of movies. Lord knows why."

"During seminary I made friends with guys I worked with at a shipping company. They invited me over to watch horror movies. I went because it was against seminary rules to watch movies in the theater, or to watch horror movies on campus.

"Anyway, we watched this crazy movie called *Basket Case*. About conjoined twins. One is normal, the other twisted and deformed. Shunned because of their deformity, the brothers are actually *happy* in their unity. They're together, as they were meant to be. When they're surgically separated—without their consent—the deformed brother is left for dead."

The priest's silhouette nodded. "And you feel your true self is the deformed brother."

"Yes. Only I willingly accepted it. Hell, *I* did the amputating, all these years." I paused, collected myself, and continued. "In the movie, the rejected twin lives. Becomes fueled by hate. A hate which becomes murderous."

I swallowed. "All these years I've amputated essential parts of myself. My questions. My doubt. Dreams and goals which didn't line up with what my father said was 'God's Will'. Belief which contradicted 'sound doctrine'. All these

137

things I've willingly repressed . . . they never went away. They festered. Soured. And now . . . " I trailed off and looked into my hands, suddenly struggling for the words. "I'm afraid. I can't repress these parts of me any longer. Something happened . . . to set them free. My daughter died, and I . . . "

I swallowed and forced myself to continue. "I'm afraid. What will I be like if I let these parts of me come back? What will I become when I let them out?"

Silence. One which dragged on until it I looked up through the grate and whispered, "Father . . . ?"

I saw nothing.

No silhouette, no shadow. Even more, I felt an absence where before I'd felt a warm, open presence radiating through the grate. Now there was nothing but cold emptiness.

I waited several more minutes in a silence which felt less holy and increasingly oppressive by the minute. Finally, when I couldn't stand it any longer, I slowly—carefully, as if afraid of drawing attention to myself—stood, opened the confessional door, and stepped out.

I never once thought of opening the priest's side of the confessional, or knocking on it. I simply walked down the nave and out of All Saints, staring straight ahead, doing my best not to run, though I didn't know why I wanted to.

***

11:00 AM

Though I told myself I wasn't going to, later that afternoon, after eating lunch at the cabin this time, I looked up the rectory's number for All Saint's and called it. After three rings, a breezy-sounding woman answered, *"All Saints Church."*

I swallowed. "Hello. I was wondering if Father Thomas was in?"

A pause, and then the woman said, sounding confused,

OCTOBER NIGHTS

*"I'm sorry. Father Thomas passed away over ten years
ago. Fifteen, to be exact. Father Ward is our only priest.
Has been since then. Which is clearly listed in the directory,
I might add."*

Of course it had been. I'd looked it up before calling. I
simply needed to hear it for myself. "I'm sorry. My mistake."

"Who is this? I hope this isn't some sort of prank, this
being the anniversary of his—"

"So sorry. Goodbye."

I ended the call. Sat down on the futon, laid the phone
down on the coffee table with shaking hands, and sat that
way, very still, for a long time.

***

Boden Hill Trail
Raedeker Park
1:00 PM

I walked along Boden Hill Trail, one of three Adirondack
trails near the entrance of Raedeker Park, on the other side
of Clifton Heights. Hands in pockets, going slowly, looking
at the scenery—Adirondack pine, birch, low-lying brush—
without really seeing it, as my mind worked over this
morning's troubling experience. After refusing to think
about All Saints for several hours, I searched Google for
walking trails in the area. I found Boden Hill, and as I
walked, finally allowed myself to process what had
happened this morning at All Saints Church. Only two
conclusions made sense. I didn't like either.

The first; I'd imagined Father Thomas. In my stress and
grief, desperately needing another religious to talk with, I'd
conjured up the voice of a kindly old priest as an imaginary
sounding board. The second; Despite being dead for fifteen
years, I'd spoken to Father Thomas, and he'd spoken to me.

It was a good thing Boden Hill Trail offered easy
walking, because occupied as I was by my thoughts, it
would've been easy to trip over a root or rock.

Though it may seem strange, my crisis in faith—*Is there a God? Does It give a shit about us?*—didn't argue against believing in ghosts. At least, a certain *kind* of ghost. I could accept the reality that the energies of the universe acted in ways which couldn't be readily understood. The law of conservation of energy states energy can neither be created nor destroyed, only changed, or transferred.

For example: Ghosts. When a person dies, their energy has to go somewhere.

I kicked a small rock off the trail. It was a half-ass theory, to be sure. Even so, if a person's energy remains after their physical bodies die, what kind of energy might Father Thomas have left? I'd done a little research on the priest. What I found troubled me. He'd apparently died a violent death. At the hands of the current priest, no less, when Father Ward discovered Father Thomas attempting to sacrifice a child in some sort of demonic rite. In the confrontation, Father Ward sustained near-fatal wounds. Wounds administered by Father Thomas.

In *Lovely Molly*—a movie I watched shortly before Lilly died—the daughter of an abusive father moves back into her childhood home with her newlywed husband. A recently recovered heroin addict, she's instantly beset by haunting memories, nightmares, and strange occurrences. The movie plays it ambiguously enough to leave the viewer guessing. Was the female protagonist possessed by the spirit of her abusive father, or the spirit of whatever made her father abusive? Was she possessed by the negative energy left behind by the abuse, or merely "possessed" by the memories of her abuse?

Either way, as I continued my walk, I thought about the marks we all leave behind. Some of them are positive marks. Warm, pleasant, nostalgic. Some of them are powerfully life-changing, for better or for worse. Some of these marks, however, are stains. And stains do only one thing: they taint.

I wondered what stains I'd leave behind.

OCTOBER NIGHTS

***

1:45 PM

As I entered the clearing at the end of Boden Hill, which overlooked Owen Pond, my thoughts jarred to a stop at the sight of a pup tent. I stood very still, worried I'd stumbled upon someone's campsite. I was about to turn and quietly make my way back down Boden Hill when I saw it, poking out of the tent's unzippered front.

Something white.

Something *bone* white, and gleaming in the sun.

I stood there for several more seconds, heart beating faster, breath echoing in my ears. I had to be seeing things. That couldn't be what I thought it was. It couldn't.

I examined the tent best I could. It was a faded blue. Looked as if it had been there for months. Maybe even years, though that seemed impossible.

I breathed in once. Slipped my smartphone out of my pocket, and snapped the flashlight on. Telling myself I should leave, I took a tentative step closer to the tent, and to the white object sticking out of it. I felt ashamed at the slight weakness in my knees, but I forced myself to move closer.

I stopped in front of the tent. Close up, I could confirm that the white thing sticking out of the tent indeed was a foot stripped of all tissue, down to the bone.

I balanced on a precarious edge. Something inside whispered if I backed away and simply returned to my cabin, packed my things, and drove away from Clifton Heights, I'd narrowly escape crossing some kind of invisible threshold.

If I shined my phone's flashlight inside that tent, however. If I even glimpsed a portion of what I suspected hid behind its flaps, something would change. In All Saints, I'd briefly glimpsed something from a far, deep country. I believed that if I looked into that tent, I'd cross over *into* that far deep country, and I didn't know if I would return.

Of course, why else had I come here? Why else had I abandoned my family and my faith? To travel into that far deep country, in search of myself, understanding, and something . . . else. Returning was never a guarantee.

I knelt before the tent. Forced my hand to steady. Raised the phone, and shined its flashlight inside.

A skull glimmered in the light. Turned sideways, its unseeing eye sockets staring into that far deep country. Its hands were folded gently over its rib-cage, as if it had simply laid down and gone to sleep, never to wake again.

A tremor rippled through me. My thighs quivered, my knees buckled, and I slowly slid to the ground and sat there, staring into the tent.

7.

2:45 PM

I CALLED THE POLICE. They requested I remain on the scene until they arrived and I complied, finding a stump near the remains of a campfire and sitting on it. I angled myself so I couldn't see the tent's opening. A breeze had picked up and kept fluttering the tent's ragged flaps back, exposing its grisly occupant within.

When the Sheriff arrived, he questioned me with a surprising gentleness, listening to my account without interrupting. He nodded in all the right places, and made appropriate sounds of genuine concern.

When I finished my story, Sheriff Baker flipped open a small yellow notebook (a bit of an anachronism in a world of smartphones and tablets, which only endeared him to me more), and said, "Thanks for calling, Mr. Ford. Believe it or not, lots of folks around here wouldn't. People like to keep to themselves, I guess. Don't like getting tangled up in things. Makes missing persons cases difficult, sometimes. Drags out searches longer than necessary."

I found that strange, quite honestly. But then again, I'd already decided Clifton Heights was somewhat of a strange town. "Any idea who it might be?"

Sheriff Baker offered a regretful shrug. "No ID on the body. Have to send the remains to Webb County for dental records and forensics. Will take time, of course."

A question teetered on the edge of my tongue. I wasn't sure if I could make myself ask it. The sheriff's oddly regretful manner, however, pushed me over the edge. "I have to ask, Sheriff. I know I'm not from around here and it's none of my business. But it's awful strange, don't you think? Boden Hill Trail seems well-traveled. This look-out was listed on your town's website as a favorite tourist spot. Yet a corpse completely denuded to its skeleton? In an old tent which looks like it's been up for months? How could it have gone unnoticed?"

Sheriff Baker remained silent for a heartbeat. He didn't look angry at the question, not even annoyed, as you might imagine a small-town sheriff would be. He mostly looked sad, and—oddly enough? Lonely, too. As if he had to shoulder a lonely burden every single day that no one else could carry.

Believe me, I understood that kind of loneliness. All too well.

Finally he said, without averting his gaze, "The woods up here are strange, Mr. Ford. I know it probably doesn't make sense to you, but things around here tend to stay hidden, until they need to be found. That's the best way I can explain it. Hope you can understand."

I didn't know how to answer this, so I didn't. I simply nodded wordlessly. Sheriff Baker looked grateful as he returned my nod, then turned to supervise the careful— almost reverent—removal of the remains.

***

After reassuring Sheriff Baker I wasn't leaving town anytime soon (the Sheriff reassuring me he was only asking for procedure's sake), I allowed myself to be led back down Boden Hill Trail to my car, which I'd parked at the trailhead. A talkative young deputy named Potter escorted me. The friendly young man chatted incessantly about trivial things which didn't seem to matter. I mostly ignored him, politely nodding here and there. He didn't seem to mind, content to prattle on.

I sat in my car long after the police cars and ambulance (an odd overkill) had left. Staring out the front window at nothing, I couldn't banish the image of the skeleton lying in the tent in peaceful repose, hands folded over its rib cage.

Not even considering the impossible strangeness of it all, I couldn't stop thinking about the implications. Couldn't stop connecting the skeleton to my recent circumstances, because I'd always found a purity in skulls and skeletons in general. They were the ultimate truth inside everyone. It didn't matter how one clothed the outside, what lengths people went to preserve and protect the meat surrounding it. Eventually, time stripped everything away, leaving nothing but bones. Ideology, religion, political beliefs . . . none of that mattered. At the end of the day, only bones remained.

So many Christians view skulls and skeletons as horror props, grotesquely Gothic, occultist, distasteful, even demonic. Granted, skulls and skeletons have been co-opted for many occult rites and practices, by both frivolous dabblers and sincere practitioners. They certainly have been used to varying degrees of success as disturbing imagery in the horror genre.

However, I'd always believed them to be inherently divine. How could they not be, being of God's design? They were truer than anything else in the world. They were what lay inside all artifice. I'd always thought that terrible sense of intimacy is what really made people uncomfortable around skulls and skeletons. The sense of secret things made known. The unavoidable fact that, at the end of the day, we were all skeletons-in-waiting.

I gripped the steering wheel and made no move to start the car. Just twisted the faux-leather in my hands. I couldn't help but think about the skeleton and what it represented for me. As if things were slowly being stripped away from me. As time stripped the flesh from people's bones.

And it wasn't something which had started when I lost Lilly. It had been going on for a very long time. Probably even longer than I realized. Microscopic layer after layer of my faith, beliefs, doctrine, convictions, stripped away as the superficial meat they were. Lilly's death had only sped up the process. When everything was stripped away, what would I find? What would I be?

I shook my head and was about to start my car when I heard a low, rumbling throb. I looked up in time to see the glowing red taillights of a customized black car pull out of Raedeker Park and onto Samara Hill Road. I wasn't sure, but I thought it was the same Monte Carlo I'd almost hit at the intersection my first day here. The one I'd flipped off, calling the driver an "asshole." The one which I was sure drove by me in town the other day.

I shrugged off a creeping sense of unease, started the car and left.

***

On the way back to The Motor Lodge, it occurred to me quite forcefully how strange things were getting. Before my walk, during lunch, I'd caught the end of the 1959 *House on Haunted Hill* on AMC as I was channel-surfing. It stood out in stark relief, now. The scene at the end, with the skeleton (supposedly Vincent Price's murdered character) rising from a vat of acid. Clean, gleaming, perfect. I didn't know what to make of this. Seeing such a thing in a movie, then encountering something so bizarre and so similar in real life. It made me even more aware of the odd cinematic parallels I'd been drawing lately between horror films and my life—*uncomfortably* aware—so I forcibly thought of nothing for the rest of the day.

8.

October 20th
The Skylark Diner
12:30 PM

I PICKED AT my open-face hot turkey sandwich, but despite how good it smelled and looked, I couldn't work up the appetite to eat more than a few sporadic bites. Something was starting to happen. Something I didn't understand. Inside me, and in real life, too. I didn't know what to make of it, or if there was anything to make of it to begin with.

I'd made arrangements to come to the police station this morning and make an official statement about my discovery at the end of Boden Hill Trail yesterday. Nothing serious, just a recounting of the events. As it happened, Sheriff Baker had been honest about that. It was a low-key affair.

Horror movies, however, and their continued weird impingement on my life. *That* was another matter entirely. Yesterday's connection between 1959's *House on Haunted Hill* and my discovery on Boden Hill Trail had jarred me, badly. So badly I didn't watch any horror movies that night before bed. Almost as if I were anxious to prove nothing strange was happening.

But before leaving for the police station, I'd made no pretenses. I settled on the futon, turned on the flat screen, and started searching channels, intent on choosing the first horror movie which presented itself. Almost as if I was thinking, *What are you going to show me today?*

This morning's movie had been *Prom Night*, starring the inimitable Jamie Lee Curtis. I'd seen it many times before, and, as always, it was a pleasure to watch. Before I became a horror fan, I hadn't understood the mystique surrounding Jamie Lee Curtis. Why she had so many die-hard fans. Now I understood, of course. In her early horror movies, Curtis' on-screen presence overshadowed everyone else. It was easy to see how an entire generation fell in love with her.

As I watched the movie, I didn't experience any particular revelations. Jamie Lee Curtis ruled the screen as always, and despite having seen the film many times, its denouement still shook me. As the credits rolled, I shrugged with relief. No revelations. No weird clarity or insight. It was just a movie. I shut the television off, and went to the police station to give my statement.

From the moment I slid into my booth at The Skylark Diner, however, it all changed. I knew—almost immediately—why I'd chosen *Prom Night* that morning.

Sunday morning, of all mornings.

While I waited for a waitress, a family of five settled at a nearby table. Dressed in their Sunday best, I could tell. I'd seen the pews in my church filled with many folks looking like them over the years.

One of them stood out, of course. No matter how hard any pious, religious, righteous family wants to portray an image of Christian Familial Bliss, there is always one family member who stands out like a sore thumb. One who is always different.

Like my daughter, Lilly.

In this case, it was the son. He looked about thirteen or fourteen years old. Probably the middle child, as the other boy looked only about six or seven, and the daughter appeared to be nineteen or so. It made sense, of course. The middle child is often the "forgotten child," who languishes in the shadows of the oldest, or withers in the glare of the youngest. Most middle children know enough not to rock the boat and simply stick to their station.

Like I had.

Other middle children—like Lilly, and the boy sitting at the table near my booth—don't stand for it. They rebel (or try to) but often pay a heavy price for their rebellion, until they are someday able to forge their own way.

As Lilly would never be able to do.

The boy—lanky, tall, but with stooped shoulders and limp brown hair—wore all black. Black lipstick, eye-shadow, black clothes, shoes, even a nose-stud. From his ears dangled rainbow-colored triangles similar to the pendant worn by the cashier girl at Arcane Delights.

He sat still. Hands limp in his lap. He stared off over his father's shoulder at nothing. On a normal day he'd probably be scrolling through his smartphone, but the father most likely had a "no screen-time on Sunday" policy. Especially at after-church lunch. I'd established a similar policy, right before everything fell apart.

The father wore a black suit jacket, white button-down shirt, with a black tie. He'd combed his blond hair perfectly. Not a strand was out of place. His features and square jaw looked too chiseled to be real. I had a hard time believing my eyes. The man was the spitting image of my father, the Good Reverend Ford.

My breath quickened and my chest tightened. I was watching my childhood Sunday afternoons unfold. If the father depicted a nearly flawless rendition of The Good Reverend Ford, the mother proved an apt mirror for Mrs. Ford. Diminutive, doll-like, face made up with a small porcelain doll's smile forever frozen on her face. The Dutiful Biblical Wife, Commanded by the Lord to Support Her Husband in a Godly Manner.

The oldest daughter, sitting to the left of the middle son, wore a perfectly chaste (yet still tastefully stylish) dress. She wore a genteel smile which probably hid secret trysts with football players and clandestine joints in the girls' bathroom.

The younger brother, to the right of the middle child? A

toss-up. Either a perfect angel on the outside who liked to torture small animals (especially stray cats) out in the woods, or a little hellion whose exploits were always excused with the cliché platitude: "Boys will be boys."

Just like my childhood family.

Except the middle child, of course. In some ways, he was *too* obvious. Too much the outlaw, the "problem child." Obviously his rebellion had been informed by edgy yet very slickly-marketed music and "alternative" media, so instead of crafting his own identity, he'd just co-opted the one Hot Topic told him he should have.

I couldn't help but feel a pang of envy, however. In the most important way, this was not my childhood family, because I never rebelled. Instead, I chose to fit in, becoming a perfect clone of The Good Reverend Ford. Even if the Reverend Ford never noticed, or commented . . . until he condemned me, his son, for failing as a Man of God, a father, and a husband.

I laid my fork down, my stomach churning too much to even pretend to eat. The entire time, the father spoke engagingly with his perfect-looking older daughter, ignoring the middle Goth child while the doll-like mother shushed and admonished the squirming little boy, likewise ignoring the middle Goth child, just as I was ignored, all my life.

The waitress came and asked me if I wanted dessert. I declined. She left the check and said I could pay up front. As I stood, left a tip, and headed for the register, I wondered if things would've been different if I'd ignored Lilly like I'd been ignored, if I'd tried harder to mold her into what she "should've been." Instead, I'd interacted with my daughter. Validated her, shown interests in her interests. Listened to her instead of dismissing her questions. Allowed her to express herself. To be herself.

I paid my bill and left The Skylark, wondering if I'd set Lilly up for failure. Guaranteed her demise? Because I'd encouraged Lilly to be her own person, she was destroyed by her peers. "Pushed" to her death like Jamie Lee Curtis' little sister in *Prom Night*, publicly humiliated like Carrietta White in *Carrie*. Except, unlike Carrie White, she was never able to take the fiery revenge she so dearly deserved. The scary thing?

I wish she'd been able to. I wish Lilly had made her school and my church *burn*.

***

On my way back to The Motor Lodge, a restored black car roared past me in the other direction, engine growling. I told myself it was going too fast for me to get a good look at it . . . but that was a lie.

9.

FOR THE FIRST time in my life, I found I couldn't sleep at all. Even through the worst days following Lilly's death and the devolution of my life and ministry, I was always able to sleep, even if uneasily.

I wasn't able to fall asleep tonight, however. I tossed and turned until midnight, when I finally gave up. I went to the kitchen, grabbed a beer from the fridge, sat on the futon, turned on the TV and started watching horror movies, of course.

Something strange was happening to me in this small town, as the horror movies I was watching—or had watched, long ago—were starting to intersect with my life in strange, tangential ways. I was going to sit on that futon and watch them until I couldn't keep my eyes open, to see what they had to say.

The first movie I stumbled across was one of the most low-budget ones I'd ever seen, *Night Vision*, starring no one of consequence. However, it carried itself with a sort of charm other, higher-budget movies lacked. Also, it chilled me the most. It was about a stranger visiting the city to find himself, and to achieve writing stardom. Of course, I'm not in the city. I traded one small town for another, and the only writing I'd done was the diary I'd kept since coming here. However, I *was* a stranger in a strange place, just as Stacy Carson's character was in *Night Vision*.

Even more discomfiting was the movie's central conceit. It should be ridiculous. A Satanic VHS player beams horrific visions and horror movies into the young writers' brain, turning the stories he writes into reality. A silly concept that—despite the movie's independent charm—was hard to take seriously within the framework of the movie's narrative.

Even so, after the movie ended, I got another beer, sat down and drank about half the bottle in one go before I picked up the remote to watch another movie. Since I'd been in Clifton Heights, I'd watched more horror movies in several days than I'd seen in the past six months, and had reminisced on some of the first horror movies I ever watched.

For some reason, they had become more than movies. I didn't think anything supernatural was happening (not exactly, anyway), but I still remembered my first impression of Clifton Heights, after watching the 1999 version of *House on Haunted Hill*. As the characters in that movie had been invited to an insane asylum for a "party," I'd been invited to this picturesque Adirondack town. I was confronted with the impossible idea that whatever horror movie I watched in this town would reveal something to me. I didn't know what, or if these things would be important or merely pretentious navel gazing. I didn't know anything, really, except . . .

My daughter was dead. It was my fault because I hadn't protected her from the world, my church, my family, or myself. I'd never preach the Word of God again. My belief in God was up for grabs, too. I didn't know if I'd see my surviving family members ever again, or if I wanted to, or if they wanted to see me.

I had no idea where I was going. I didn't even know why I was here. When I left home, I'd packed my car, withdrawn only enough cash to last me a month, and headed North, until I stopped here.

My money was going to run out soon. I needed a job.

That was all I knew. I didn't think horror movies could help me answer the questions I had, but I also didn't know if answers existed at all.

With that thought, I finished my beer. Aimed the remote at the TV and cued the next movie. Maybe if I watched enough horror movies in a row, I'd see they were movies, nothing more.

I watched *Hellmaster*. A very strange movie starring a bored-looking John Saxon.

One Dark Night, starring Jennifer Tilly's sister Meg Tilly, and a bored-looking Adam West.

Mausoleum, a mostly incomprehensible movie with a woman sporting demon breasts.

I finally fell asleep on the futon, remote in-hand, halfway through *The Burning*, wondering what movies would've been made if Jason Alexander had kept his hair and never starred in *Seinfeld*, and instead had become the next Bruce Campbell.

IO.

October 22ⁿᵈ
The Skylark Diner
11:00 AM

"THIS IS A true story, son. Mark my words, it's a true story."

I folded my hands on the booth's table, meeting the old codger's watery blue gaze head-on. The old fellow had just told me the strangest, most unbelievable tale I'd ever heard. Something right out of *Humanoids from the Deep* (the 1980's version, not the 1996 remake), about something which lived in the depths of Clifton Lake. There was no way his story could be true in any shape or form.

Of course, that didn't matter. I'd started the day thinking about how tall tales and folklore lead to truth, and I'd come to The Skylark searching for the most unbelievable stories I could find. I'd found what I'd been looking for, so I didn't particularly care if the story was true or not.

The old man's companion—a slightly younger-looking man whose gray hair was pulled back into a ponytail—gave me an arch look. He nodded toward his friend. "This guy ain't told a true story his entire life. He *specializes* in bullshit. Trust me."

I looked back and forth between the two codgers, smiling and enjoying myself. Both of these men were a pleasing cliché. *The Old Farts Who Sit in the Same Booth in Their Favorite Diner and Bitch at Each Other Like Husband and Wife.* A cliché which existed because it was based on more than a gram of truth. Which maybe was true of the first story, told by Art.

Art waved a knobby and arthritic hand, snorting. "Oh,

you're one to talk, Georgie." Art leaned over the table, eyes comically wide. "He calls *my* story bullshit? One that almost *anyone* who's fished on Clifton Lake can back up? Ya oughta get a load of the yarns he tells."

Georgie—the one with the gray ponytail—scowled. "You hush up. You know I don't like talking about that."

"Pshaw. Don't get all shy in front of the youngin. Actin' like it's all taboo and forbidden." Art waggled his eyebrows at me and jabbed a crooked finger at Georgie. "Every damn year, Halloween night, after he gets a few under his belt, he'll tell whoever'll listen at Hyland's Pub the same damn thing. Don't be buyin' this act that it's some kinda taboo story."

Georgie's scowl deepened. "Tellin' it to townfolk is one thing. Tellin' it to an outsider?" He picked up his coffee, sipped, and shifted uncomfortably. "I dunno, Art. I dunno."

"Go on, you old coot. Fella is lookin' for weird stories for some book he's writin'. Tellin' him your Halloween yarn ain't gonna cause no harm. Ain't like this fella's gonna try an' chase your story down, right?"

At this he shot me an odd look. Grinning, face merry . . . but an odd light glinting in his eyes. A pleading light, almost. Of course, I'd already lied to them about writing a book on strange rural stories, so I did the sensible thing and compounded that lie with another.

"No, I'm not. Just need material for the book is all. If a publisher buys it, I'll make sure to credit you both in the acknowledgments."

Georgie looked at me doubtfully, scowled again, and then said in a reluctant voice, "All right then. About twenty years ago I was hiking up the old access road behind Shelby Road Cemetery when I came to a branch leadin' off in a different direction. Didn't remember no branch bein' there, so out of curiosity I hiked down it. At the end, I found an old graveyard out in the middle of the woods, and in the center of it, an old stone chapel . . . "

I'd gotten interested in stories—urban legends, cautionary tales—because of the movie I'd watched this morning. *The Final Terror*. A standard movie about forestry rangers stranded in the wilderness as a disguised maniac picked them off one by one.

What really grabbed my interest was the standard scene in horror movies of this kind. The moment when one of the future victims shares the legendary story about the killer who haunts the local woods they're in, and how victims' bodies have never been found. The story is shared around a campfire at night, or in the den of a cabin before a roaring fireplace, or in the car or van or bus traveling to the destination. Somewhere safe and quiet where nothing can go wrong, before the terror begins. However, like a dread Herald, the obligatory horrific backstory serves as a harbinger for what happens next.

Seeing as random aspects of horror movies had somehow become an integral part of my experience here in Clifton Heights, I was looking for the dread legend that would serve as a harbinger for . . .

Something?

So I came to The Skylark for lunch, hoping to find someone such as these two gentlemen. Soon as I saw Art and Georgie sitting in their booth (no doubt the same booth they sat in every day), I approached them, told them I was from out of town, and was here writing a book on legends and myths, and did Clifton Heights have any?

They proved happy to oblige.

***

Art's story, as I said, was truly unbelievable, the stuff of 'B' horror movies and the old EC horror comics. According to him, thirty years ago an old hill shaman named Clive Hartley cursed a man for trying to poach his traps. He was condemned to wander the swamps he'd been poaching forever. Art claimed to have seen this swamp beast when out fishing on Clifton Lake, as either a shadowed, mud-covered figure lurching ashore and disappearing into the woods, or as a human-shape swimming under his boat. Swore dozens of fishermen could back him up.

I smiled a lot during Art's tale, but he didn't mind. He was a natural-born storyteller, and thrived on my reaction.

Georgie, on the other hand, didn't relish his tale. In a halting, reluctant voice, he described hiking along this access road branch he'd never seen before, out to a forgotten graveyard in the middle of the woods where an old stone chapel stood. A haunted chapel, he claimed, because inside he was confronted with his worst fears. He said if he hadn't run immediately, he believed he would've been trapped inside forever.

The worst part according to Georgie? Every Halloween he returned to the old chapel in his dreams, only he believed he wasn't dreaming but was in fact going there in his sleep. He claimed (at this part he became distinctly uncomfortable, despite Art's eye-rolling), that whenever he woke from these dreams, the bottoms of his feet were always dirty, with twigs and pine needles stuck to them, from walking around the stone chapel barefoot.

Of course, both these stories served as classic horror movie myths. Art's more of the Roger Corman fare; Georgie's more like a folk horror movie A24 studios might release. As I thanked the two men and went on my way, I realized two things.

First, I hadn't thought about Lilly, my wife and surviving children, or my church during both stories.

Second, regardless of which I pursued, either story would serve me well as the cliché "horror movie legendary backstory." All I needed to decide? Did I want to be in a Roger Corman film? Or an art-house horror film about folk horror?

Time would shortly tell.

***

I decided about twenty minutes after leaving The Skylark. It proved to be an easy decision. As intriguing as I found the idea of a horrifying creature lurking in the swamps and in the depths of Clifton Lake, I couldn't ignore the implications of Georgie's story of a haunted stone chapel in the middle of a forest graveyard, which showed your worst fears.

My daughter had committed suicide. I'd walked away from the rest of my family, my calling, and the only life I'd ever known. I knew what my greatest fear was.

Would the stone chapel?

II.

Access Road Behind Shelby Road Cemetery
4 PM

I WOULD DRIVE out to Shelby Road Cemetery. Hike out to the old stone chapel and camp there for a few nights, until the stone chapel showed me my greatest fears. First, however?
I needed supplies.

Before that, I had to make arrangements with The Motor Lodge, let them know I was going to be camping somewhere for a few nights, make sure I was paid up through that time. The same bored attendant didn't react much when I told him my plans. He asked for payment in advance, so I wouldn't skip out. That was his only concern.

Next of course came camping supplies. I'd brought nothing of the kind with me. I visited the aptly named General Store and asked for the best supplies for a night or two camping out. The salesperson—an old fellow by the name of Novak—proved very helpful, albeit in a distracted way, much like the desk clerk at The Motor Lodge. With the exception of the friendly salesperson at Arcane Delights and Sheriff Baker, this had turned out to be typical behavior for Clifton Heights townsfolk.

I made it to Shelby Road Cemetery by four in the evening. After looking both ways and seeing no signs of traffic, I decided *hell with it*. I turned into the cemetery and followed its slightly overgrown road to the treeline and into the woods. The access road Georgie had talked about.

I parked just past the trees. Gathered my things into a backpack Novak was helpful enough to show me how to pack (I was on my own for the return trip). I locked the car, put the backpack on, and started down the access road as it wound its way through the woods.

What the hell was I doing?

Running away from my family and my responsibilities was the epitome of bad decision making, but at the very least understandable, given the circumstances. But spending money I really couldn't sacrifice on camping gear so I could hike into the woods looking for an abandoned graveyard with a haunted stone chapel that supposedly would show me my worst fears . . . when my worst fear had already been realized?

Insanity.

But even so, I set off at once.

I didn't see that black Monte Carlo on the way to Shelby Road Cemetery, but for some reason, that didn't make me feel any better.

***

After I reached the fork Georgie had talked about, the clearing and its abandoned cemetery and stone chapel was another twenty minutes down the trail. It turned out to be easy walking, the access road not nearly as overgrown as I expected. A good thing, because even though I'd kept up with hiking over the years, I hadn't done much of it with a full backpack.

I stopped at the entrance of the old graveyard and took in my surroundings before I entered. It was six in the evening, and dusk was falling. The clearing matched Georgie's description. About the size of half a football field, and oddly enough, no woods or brush. The grass wasn't mowed. It stood about ankle high. Almost frozen at that height. As if it had grown only so high, then stopped.

Tombstones dotted the clearing. About fifteen or twenty, scattered about in no discernible order. I decided to save a closer examination for tomorrow. From a distance, however, they looked *old*. Jutting from the ground at odd angles. The ones I passed were blank, names and dates scrubbed clear by time and the elements.

In the clearing's center stood the old stone chapel, just like Georgie said. I had no idea if it had actually been a chapel, of course. I was just using Georgie's description. No cross on the top, and the outside bore no markings of a creed. Even so, the place had a feeling to it. Like All Saints Church, but somehow more powerful. Older. Ancient, even. Standing before the stone chapel and feeling its presence was almost enough to erase my doubts about a divine Other.

It wasn't very big. Not much bigger than the cabin I was staying in back in town. Probably could hold only about ten or twenty people at once. Also, it didn't appear to have any modern conveniences. No electrical wires running to it. I'm sure there was no running water.

I toyed with the idea of exploring right then, but dark was falling even quicker. I thought it wise to get my tent pitched and camp set up, a fire going. As I slipped my pack off and started unpacking, for the briefest of moments I thought about bedding down in the chapel. I decided against it, however. I had no desire to sleep on a cold stone floor, and I didn't think it would have sufficient ventilation for a campfire.

Of course, the real reason came from instinct. The stone chapel wasn't a place to spend the night. Maybe I was just spooked by Georgie's stories of showing up here in his dreams, or seeing his "worst fears inside". Maybe not. Regardless, I felt a deep aversion to sleeping in the place. It wasn't a good idea. And not necessarily because of the dark. The idea of sinking into unconsciousness while inside the chapel made me uneasy.

I continued unpacking, and began setting up camp.

12.

I HADN'T TENT-CAMPED in years, but contemporary tents were much easier to assemble than the old ones. The tent I'd bought at The General Store (blue, I realized with a dim sense of dismay, for some reason) took five minutes to assemble. I had a fire going in half an hour. Heeding a gut feeling, I made camp alongside the stone chapel, away from its doorless entry. I couldn't say why. Something about facing that rectangle of darkness, or having it at my back, made me uneasy.

I'd packed enough food for two nights. Hot dogs and rolls, single-use packets of ketchup, a few travel bags of chips, and a few single packets of peanut-butter cookies. I'd brought bananas, oranges, and protein bars for breakfast. Also some sandwiches for lunches. Not much food, but I'd lost my appetite since Lilly died. I had several bottles of water, however.

As I readied camp, lit the fire and cooked hot dogs, I tried not to think about what the hell I was doing. On one hand, I'd always loved hiking and camping. Taking off for two days to camp while on my self-imposed exile made sense.

However, I wasn't camping at an approved Adirondack campground. I wasn't even primitive camping off an approved hiking trail. I'd spontaneously decided to camp near an abandoned stone chapel some old codger said was haunted. A place he still had nightmares about twenty years later, every October.

After I finished eating, I fished out my charged tablet (which I used to write sermon notes on, and would write sermon notes on no more) from my backpack, turned it on, and searched my downloaded movie collection. Figuring there wouldn't be any reception in the woods (there wasn't),

I'd downloaded several movies last night. Maybe watching one before bed would tire me out.

I should've known better. Not every horror movie I'd watched since arriving in Clifton Heights had offered hidden gems of revelation, but many of them had shown a weird synchronicity with the current course of my life. The odds seemed in favor of this continuing. But not because I believed any Guiding Hand was leading to those movies. For whatever reason, a part of my mind had been switched on, making me hyper-aware and receptive to just about anything.

I chose *Berserker* from my queue because it looked like nothing more than a standard low-budget 80s horror film. A group of twenty-somethings go camping at a remote cabin deep in the woods, in a county originally settled by Nords. There's a throwaway backstory about the berserker legend, and how spirits of Viking berserkers (bestial warriors) couldn't rest easy after death because of the atrocities they'd committed, so they forever haunted their bloodline, possessing innocent descendants with berserker rage and bloodlust when the conditions were just right. Of course, the backstory was conveniently vague as to what constituted the "right conditions."

The movie's plot proceeded on a fairly predictable course. It offered no surprises. I was suitably entertained, and also found myself admiring its heart. Though only a secondary character, I also liked the quiet and taciturn county sheriff. He reminded me, oddly enough, of Sheriff Baker (though I'd only met the man once) in his demeanor. He said little, watched much, and thought even more.

But after the movie ended and I'd shut down the tablet and hooked it up to its portable battery, that strange little voice—which had been piping up after every horror movie I watched—made itself known. This time, it said, very simply: *Blood wins.*

Even though it was part of a paper-thin exposition, the

movie's device of a berserker's destructive soul possessing one of its innocent descendants (through no fault of theirs) hit me hard. I'd become a pastor because it was expected. According to my father, The Good Reverend Ford, it was God's Will. I'd be *Using the Talents He'd Given Me for His Eternal Glory.*

Hallelujah, amen.

My oldest son (who now believed me a hypocrite, blasphemer, apostate, or, at the very least, a Deadbeat Dad and Deserting Husband), was heading off to seminary next year. Because at some point in his childhood he'd received the same message from me, The Not-So-Good Reverend Ford, that it was God's Will for his life, too.

Blood wins.

My father had certainly never run off from his family. He'd never abandoned his church. Even though his parenting had been harsh and distant, none of his children had committed suicide. Ironically, if I'd openly rejected Lilly like everyone else, I don't think she would've killed herself. I think it would've spurred her into self-defense. Anger was the flip-side of love. If I'd kicked her out of the house, that would've shown *some* emotion. Something.

But no.

I played Middle of the Road. I'd never exile Lilly, but I was too cowardly to support her. Sitting there, in my tent, I became convinced she'd killed herself *because* of my lack of reaction. In reality, I was an Anti-Berserker. Instead of destroying everything around me by ripping things apart, I allowed things to destroy themselves, because I did nothing.

Knowing sleep was hours away, I pulled my tablet back out, turned it on, and cued up another movie.

165

13.

I WOKE MY first morning in the abandoned graveyard with little fanfare. I'd had no dreams that night, and whatever "presence" I'd felt the night before under the cover of darkness faded with the sunlight. The clearing looked like nothing more than a clearing. The headstones, only old headstones. The abandoned chapel a building made of stone.

Even so, after I'd eaten a quick breakfast of a banana, a protein bar and an apple, I decided against poking around inside the old chapel. I didn't know why. Gone was the sense of foreboding I'd felt last night. It was daylight. I had nothing to fear.

I opted for poking around the clearing instead. At first there didn't seem to be anything unusual about it. However, the longer I walked around, the more I wondered. I'd no way of telling for sure, but I believed the clearing was a perfect circle. There was no way it could've grown like that naturally. It would've taken considerable effort to clear it that way, and why? How could it have remained that way all these years?

Also, after walking around and kneeling in several spots, I became convinced the grass was too short for a clearing abandoned so long ago. It didn't appear as if anyone had been mowing it. Just that the grass had reached a certain height and stopped growing. I started developing the crazy idea that forty years ago, the grass was the same height. Forty years from now, it wouldn't grow any higher.

The headstones also confounded me. Yesterday I

thought they were blank because the inscriptions had been scrubbed away by time. However, as I examined several of them, it didn't appear as if they'd ever had inscriptions at all. All of them appeared completely blank, belonging to no one. I didn't know what to make of that.

As a pastor, I knew it was customary for older churches to bury congregation members in small, adjacent graveyards. There'd been a graveyard behind my father's church, though there hadn't been one behind mine (being too modern and contemporary, of course).

Did these headstones belong to whomever had "attended" the stone chapel? If so, why were they blank? Were their identities secret? Why?

I thought again of poking around the chapel. Once more, I decided not to. This time, however, for good reason. I'd discovered the access road continued into the woods on the clearing's opposite side. This intrigued me. Georgie hadn't said anything in his story about the access road continuing into the woods. After filling a fanny pack with bottles of water, protein bars, and my small first aid kit, I set off down the other road.

After about twenty minutes the way grew narrower, becoming more of a path than a road. The trees grew much closer to the path. Seemed to crowd it, even. They also looked . . . less Adirondack, if that makes any sense. More twisted and gnarled. Looking like trees found in the South. As I picked my way forward, I continually stepped over roots which reached across the path, making walking a bit more difficult. The branches, too, extended into my way, scratching my arms and once—when I wasn't paying attention—my right cheek.

Reaching. A stupid idea, but one I couldn't diminish. The branches were reaching out to rake my face while roots stretched across the path to trip me. I didn't even realize how much harder the walking had gotten or how tired I was until my left foot didn't lift high enough to clear a large root.

My toe caught on it. I stumbled forward, hands flailing in vain to catch my fall as the ground rushed up to meet me.

My forehead struck the edge of a large rock half-buried in the ground. Bright sparks filled my vision as a painful pressure filled my head. Everything went dark.

For just a moment.

Then I rolled onto my back and blinked. The painful pressure still throbbed in my temples. I could feel the goose-egg swelling over my left eye. After lying on my back and catching my breath (staring at the branches above me, which reached across the path and formed an oddly seamless canopy above), I touched my left temple with a shaky hand. Winced at the sensitive swelling I found there, also relieved I felt no blood. Somehow, I'd managed not to break the skin, but I imagined I'd look quite the sight when I returned to town with a big swollen lump on my forehead.

I took my time and didn't rush. Just lay on my back and breathed in and out, the pain in my temples slowly fading. I stared at the intertwined branches above me. I got up when my vision started playing tricks on me, making it seem like the branches were twisting among themselves as I lay under them.

When I stood (feeling slightly dizzy but none the worse for wear), I frowned in confusion at the sight before me. Where the path had been only minutes before, those trees grew so close together the path disappeared. Among the trees, deep-green and slick looking vines twisted and twined among the branches and around tree trunks. They looked oddly normal and oddly out of place, at the same time. Sprouting broad, shiny leaves, and tendrils which anchored them to anything near. I certainly hadn't seen anything like it during my short stay in Clifton Heights. They were a darker green than the surrounding undergrowth, with a vaguely tropical look.

Apparently the second horror movie I'd watched last night, *The Crawlers*, was going to impinge on my life after all. It had been such an absurd and poorly-acted movie, I'd felt certain it wouldn't have any relevance. It had none of *Night Vision*'s charm, and while the sheriff in *Berserker* reminded me of the circumspect and quietly competent Sheriff Baker, the sheriff in *The Crawlers* reminded me of a low-rent Roscoe P. Coltrane from *The Dukes of Hazard*.

Even so.

Mutated tree roots, irradiated by the local power plant, which became sentient and attacked hapless townsfolk. And, here my way was blocked by strange-looking trees and very snaky vines which vibrated even as I looked at them. Preventing me from going any further. Forcing me back toward the clearing with the old stone chapel.

I stared at the trees, peering through the tangled vines and the crowded underbrush. I thought I saw the barest glimpse of the path continuing past them. I shook my head, turned around and went back the way I'd come, returning to the old stone chapel. I thought I heard *things* snaking their way through the brush behind me, but I knew it was the wind (had to be) so I didn't turn around.

14.

12:00 PM

WHEN 1 RETURNED to the clearing and my tent, my forehead was pounding from where I'd hit it. I grew very tired, and I lay down for a nap. As I slept, I dreamed for the first time since coming to Clifton Heights. I'd always had a vivid dream life, prone to surreal, bizarre vision quests during my slumber which rarely made sense upon awakening. But this was different. Everything felt clear. Tangible. Realistic. I knew it was a dream, despite how real it felt. Soon as I woke, gasping for breath, I remembered every bit of the dream down to its finest details.

It was Halloween night.

I was walking along a residential side street. Somehow, I knew it was in Clifton Heights. Kids in costumes toting bags swollen with candy dragged their parents along sidewalks, going from house to house. Costumed teenagers moved in packs with their friends. Every lawn boasted elaborate Halloween decorations. A ghoulish menagerie of ghosts hanging from trees by wire, zombies bursting from the ground, vampires hiding behind trees, and mummies rising from their sarcophagi. Jack-o'-lanterns blazed on every doorstep. Mystery hung in the air.

It was the perfect Halloween.

I realized with a start, as a ten-year-old pirate rushed by, followed by his beleaguered parents, that I'd dreamed this particular dream many times as a child. It was the only way I could celebrate Halloween, because The Good Reverend Ford didn't believe in "winking at the Devil's Night" by dressing up as a cowboy, an astronaut, an Indian, or as Frankenstein's monster. I always had to watch my school friends walk past my house on their candy routes without ever once being able to open the door, because The Good Reverend Ford didn't give out candy, either. He considered that "approval of the world's ways."

These dreams had faded as I became a teenager, of course. I never compared myself to teenage friends who still Trick or Treated, because after my sixth grade year, I asked my parents to transfer me to the local Christian high school. The assimilation of my father's worldview into mine was nearly complete.

I never allowed my children to celebrate Halloween either. Never spoke out against it like my father, but couldn't bring myself to condone it, because of course I had to "sacrifice" my "personal tastes" in order to set a "Godly example" for my family and congregation.

But I did allow my children to distribute candy. That was considered scandalous enough. Somehow, I think it only made things worse for Lilly. She never really grew out of her fascination with Halloween like her brothers did. She'd always stand in the doorway, a bowl of candy in her hand, gazing in longing at a world she couldn't partake in.

It was another useless half-measure.

In the dream, I was looking for someone. Someone I was supposed to protect. Someone I was responsible for. Someone I was supposed to guard. As I walked down the street (which seemed longer than it should be) the houses all looked the same and began to smear as my urgency increased. I'd lost track of her, though I couldn't put my finger on *who* . . .

I saw her.

Passing between The Mummy and Dracula. She glanced over her shoulder at me, face expressionless, before she melted back into the crowd.

Lilly.

I increased my pace, nudging through the abruptly crowded sidewalk, trying to reach her. I ducked, weaved, and pushed past people, but somehow never moved forward. My heart pounded, breath hitched, and my feet got clumsier with each step, but something inside drove me forward. I had to reach Lilly, had to . . .

About ten feet ahead, a little girl ducked past two Power Rangers, glancing back over her shoulder with the same flat expression. It was Lilly, but not the same one I'd seen moments before. That Lilly wore her customary teenage attire. Battered blue jeans, her black leather Goodwill jacket over her red and black flannel shirt, black t-shirt underneath that, hair dyed bright green, with a nose ring. *This* Lilly was about four years younger, with long black hair, dressed as a Gothic vampire—a Halloween costume I'm sure she would've chosen if we'd allowed. This version of Lilly also disappeared into the crowd after ducking past a group of girls, all dressed as different versions of Harley Quinn.

I kept going, but with each passing step, the sidewalk became more crowded. The crowds seemed to move as one being, pushing against me. Their faces looked strange. I didn't see Halloween masks anymore, nor could I differentiate features from one person to the next. As I kept pushing my way through the throng, everyone smeared into pale blurs.

The sidewalk abruptly turned a corner. I caught a glimpse of Lilly ducking around it to the right, dodging through bodies which seemed to part and then close ranks behind her. This Lilly was even younger. About eight or nine, and even worse—she wore a Cinderella costume I recognized.

She'd seen it at Walmart one Halloween and fallen in love with it. Begged us to buy it for her, even when we (Beth, actually, while I looked on stupidly) explained as gently as possible that "Good Christian Girls Don't Celebrate the World's Holidays." When Lilly begged for the costume and promised she didn't want it for Halloween or Trick or Treating, she just wanted to be a princess, Beth (again, as I looked on silently) lectured Lilly on "setting her heart on the Lord instead of on Earthly Things."

Her tiara flashed as she vanished into a press of bodies. A hysterical panic crested within me as tight bands wrapped around my chest, making it difficult to breathe. My vision narrowed and blackened around the edges.

A bellowing roar exploded from somewhere deep inside. I put my head down, dropped my shoulder, and charged through the grasping hands and flailing arms, barreling my way through . . .

Until I slid to a stop in the middle of the abandoned graveyard in the woods, facing the old stone chapel, its entrance yawning in a darkness blacker than the surrounding night.

At that moment, Georgie's rasping voice filled my head: *Place is cursed; if you go inside it'll show your worst fears, and you'll always go back there and won't ever be able to leave . . .*

A pale white hand reached out from the darkness and ran its fingertips leisurely down the stone, bending unnaturally at the wrist . . .

I gasped and woke up, feeling confused and disoriented, unsure of my surroundings. When I sat up, blinked and looked around, I immediately understood why. I was inside the stone chapel. Lying on its cold stone floor. I was naked, shivering as the stone's cold seeped into my buttocks and spread through me. My joints felt so stiff I thought I'd fall over if I tried to stand. I hugged my knees to my chest, wrapping my arms around myself tightly, trying to warm myself up . . . when I heard it.

A scratching from the chapel's far corner.

I squinted, shivering, teeth chattering as frosty breath plumed from me. I opened my mouth to shout "Who's there?" but said nothing as dull shock gripped me at the sight of the thing shambling out of the corner.

It was Georgie. But not the Georgie from The Skylark

KEVIN LUCIA

Diner. Like me, he was naked. But this Georgie was old—
not the hale and hearty sixty-something I'd met. This
Georgie looked eighty or ninety, and on the edge of death.
His fish-belly white skin hung from him in loose folds, his
head was completely bald and mottled with sores and liver
spots, and he'd lost most of his teeth. Worst of all were his
eyes, clouded with a milky-white film.

He reached a gnarled, trembling hand in my direction.
A flap of sickly gray and wattled skin hung from his arm as
he lurched. He opened cracked and bleeding lips, exposing
black, rotten gums. Something like a sighing moan came
out, nothing more.

Electric fear pulsed through me. Adrenaline loosened
my joints. I scrambled to my feet, convinced I couldn't let
him touch me because if he did, I'd never leave. Doomed to
return here like him, and I'd never find Lilly, ever . . .

My bare feet slid out from under me. I fell on my
stomach and chest and my forehead cracked the stone,
hard, in the same place I'd hit it when I fell on the trail. A
tremendous pressure filled my head. Weighed it down,
made it hard to think, hard to open my eyes . . .

Just give up, a voice whispered. *Just lay there and let
it happen. Let him touch you and doom you. It's what you
deserve, after all.*

For a moment, I relaxed. Prepared to give up and let go.
I heard the scraping footfalls dragging closer and steeled
myself for Georgie's cold, slick touch . . .

no

get up

get up, dammit!

I scrambled to my feet as if I'd been jolted with a live
wire of sparking electricity, jerking just out of reach of those
gnarled and clutching hands. I threw myself toward the
space where the doorway should be . . .

And landed with a spring-rattling *thump* on my bed in
Cabin 14.

I lay there, staring at the rough-hewn ceiling cross-beams, confused. After a few minutes, I sat up slowly and looked at myself.

I was fully clothed. Not only that, but wearing the clothes I'd packed for my return trip. I looked up and gazed around the bedroom, not understanding. Everything looked in order. In the corner, all my camping supplies were stacked neatly. The white-mesh bag I'd brought for laundry stuffed with maybe two-days' worth of dirty clothes.

What the hell?

My forehead throbbed. I reached up and touched the goose egg over my eye. I'd gotten it when I'd tripped and fallen on the other end of the access road, tripped on a root . . .

a root which grabbed me

. . . because I'd been careless and moving too fast. *God*, it hurt. Worse than anything in a real long time. In fact, it hurt so bad I'd laid down to take a nap, and then . . .

Nothing but a blank wall. Seeing my phone on the bedside table, I grabbed it, swipe-unlocked it, and looked at the date and time.

2:00 PM

October 22nd.

I'd lost a day and a half.

15.

October 24ᵗʰ
3:00 PM

IN *BRAIN DEAD*, Billy Pullman's character (a brilliant neurosurgeon) suffers a devastating brain injury which leaves him unable to differentiate between hallucinations and reality. As he fights for not only his sanity but also his life, he claws his way through various realities in a desperate attempt to understand what's happening to him.

It was one of the first horror movies I ever rented for myself, shortly after I got my own apartment. Like so many 80s horror movies, the garish cover didn't do it justice. I was expecting copious gore and botched lobotomies, something along the lines of H.P. Lovecraft's *Re-animator*. What I got instead was an astoundingly thoughtful rumination on mental trauma, insanity, our perceptions of reality, and our deep existential search for self.

The movie hit close to home. I'd also clawed my way through various perceptions of realities. My childhood perception of life, versus what the life of A Godly Servant should look like, as according to The Good Reverend Ford. The stiff, pompous, and sheltered reality of the seminary versus the raw, affable, sometimes vulgar but always compassionate reality of my loading dock friends. The confusing and contradictory realities of marriage, fatherhood, and the ministry. It all twisted, turned, and looped in on itself.

I'd felt like Bill Pullman's character for most of my life, and I felt like him as I walked in a daze from Cabin 14 to The Motor Lodge's main lobby, my mind sifting through the scattered images of the last two days. I remembered hiking out to the old stone chapel and its graveyard. Remembered my first night there, and my excursion down the other end of the access road until my way was blocked by strange-looking . . .

sentient

. . . trees and vines. I tripped on a root . . .

which grabbed me

. . . fell and hit my head. I couldn't remember anything concrete after that. Here I was, two days later, back at The Motor Lodge.

As I approached the front desk, I wasn't even sure how to broach the subject. How do you ask, "Excuse me, what day is it?" without looking like you've totally lost it?

Luckily, the clerk (the same bored man who'd checked me in) saved me the trouble by saying, "You were supposed to come back yesterday. Lucky no one wanted that cabin. Would've tossed all your stuff in storage and rented it to them."

He said this in a matter-of-fact monotone, completely impersonal, his expression never changing. I flashed him a fake smile I hoped looked genuine and said, "Sorry. Had so much fun, lost track of time. I can pay for another week. How much?"

He quoted the price in a bored voice. I opened my wallet (distantly realizing I was going to need more cash soon), withdrew money and handed it over the counter. He accepted it, rang me up, and handed back a receipt without even looking at me.

"Thanks," he mumbled, already turning his attention back to whatever he'd been doing on the desk's old PC. "Need anything else?"

I shook my head, though I needn't have bothered, because it wasn't like he was paying attention. "Nope. Everything's great."

His gaze didn't even flinch in my direction. "Just call. If you need anything."

I nodded and turned away. As I exited the main lobby and headed back to Cabin 14, I slowed and came to a halt, staring. My knees weakened and my hands started shaking slightly. Parked next to my rental was the black 1977 Monte Carlo I'd seen around town since I'd arrived. The one that had cut me off my first day here. The one I'd flipped.

Its engine throbbed a heavy metronome. Its black finish glittered and flowed. As I stood there, the driver's side window hummed down, revealing a smiling man wearing a battered Outback hat.

"Hey Wes," the man said, flashing bright white teeth in a big grin, "how's Clifton Heights treating you so far?"

16.

I ONCE CAUGHT my father watching a horror movie, though I didn't realize it was a horror movie then. I was eight years old. It was late on a Saturday night. I had to pee. As I opened my bedroom door, I heard the strangest sound—the blast of a loud horn. Like from a car or bus, but abnormally loud.

It came from the living room. From the television. The realization paralyzed me with shock. The Good Reverend Ford made us go to bed early so we'd be fresh for church Sunday morning. He forbade us from watching television Saturday night so we could "prepare our hearts to hear God's Word." It was also when he finalized his sermon for the next morning, "seeking the Lord's guidance."

That night he wasn't composing a message, studying his Bible, or praying. He was watching television.

How had this gone undiscovered until that moment? It was hard to believe I'd never gotten up to use the bathroom while Dad was "studying." Maybe when I was younger I'd been louder getting up, giving my father enough advance notice to turn the television off. Maybe that night he was just careless with the volume. Maybe it was an aberration. Maybe he normally never watched TV, but that night he'd gotten stuck with his sermon.

Regardless, there I stood. Frozen in the hallway at the bathroom door, listening to that horn and what sounded like a car revving its big engine. The rationalizations of this bizarre event came much later. Then, frozen in the hallway of my childhood ranch home, all I could think was: *Dad's watching TV! Why?*

Better yet, *What is he watching?*

You could creep just enough down the hall to get a view of the television in the living room while hiding from my father's chair. I took a few quiet steps, screwed up my courage, and peeked around the corner.

The movie was taking place out West, in a desert town, but it wasn't a Western. Folks wore clothes which only looked a little out of date. A crowd of women and children huddled inside the gates of an old cemetery, scared and crying. Around the cemetery, a large black car roared, its spinning tires sending up plumes of dust, its horn blaring an unnatural wail. Oddly enough, though the car could've driven through the open cemetery gates, it didn't. It pulled up to the entrance, revved its engine and blared its terrible horn. But it wouldn't enter. It circled the graveyard once more, engine roaring and horn sounding.

It can't go inside, my eight-year-old mind realized in a flash. *Something won't let it in.*

A cemetery is consecrated ground, whispered the voice of my Sunday School teacher.

I stood and watched for several more minutes, transfixed. That car—which I eventually learned was a heavily modified Lincoln Continental Mark III—was unlike anything I'd ever seen. Long, all black, powerful, its tinted windows glowing in the sun. It lurched forward on its front tires like a panther eager to kill. It wasn't hard to imagine the car was evil.

I heard my father shift in his chair and cough. Afraid he was getting up, I eased into the bathroom, closed the door quietly, peed, flushed, washed my hands and slipped back into the hallway, which had gone quiet. The television was off. I returned to bed undetected. The Good Reverend Ford never once intimated he'd known I was there.

I fell asleep surprisingly quickly, given the adrenaline pumping through me. I dreamed of that car all night. However, in the dream it didn't terrorize me or chase me down. Instead, I was driving it. Chasing down anyone who had hurt me, or those I didn't like. I was chasing my father in the black car, about to slam my foot on the gas and run him over. I woke up with a grin on my face. That was the most disturbing thing.

**

Of course the movie was *The Car*, starring James Brolin and Ronny Cox. I can understand why Dad had watched it. The story's morality is straightforward. The car is evil and it began the movie by killing people with "hidden sins" before it started killing anyone in its path. I was never disappointed I'd discovered him watching a horror movie when he was supposed to be composing sermon notes. Oddly enough, I felt more disappointed a weird movie had caught his interest, but he couldn't be honest and share that interest with others.

17.

3:00 PM

"HEY WES! How's Clifton Heights treating you so far?"

I stood and stared, unable to form a reply for several reasons. First, the Monte Carlo reminded me powerfully of the evil Lincoln Continental from *The Car*. Of similar shape, with oversized tires, and a predatory air. Its windows were likewise tinted black. The car's black finish glistened strangely in the sunlight, shifting like oil.

Another reason, of course, was the fact that I'd seen this Monte Carlo driving around Clifton Heights since I'd arrived in town. Embarrassingly enough, I'd given the driver the finger and called him an asshole when he'd cut me off at an intersection my very first day here. I wasn't exactly eager for a confrontation, especially given all the weirdness I'd experienced the past few days. The major reason I had a hard time finding words was more mundane, however.

The man's smile grew uncertain. He looked embarrassed, of all things. "You *are* Wes Ford, right? Hooboy. Here I am, driving up, just assuming who you are, singing out like a crazy man."

My wariness eased a bit, because he seemed genuine enough—but even so. I kept my guard up. "I'm Wes Ford. Who's asking? And . . . if you don't mind . . . how do you know my name?"

The man sighed regretfully, looking abashed, and my guard dropped more. It was hard, for some reason, not to warm up to him. "My Daddy always did say I was a bit presumptuous. Let's try this again." He coughed, took a slightly comical breath, and began again in a more subdued voice. "My name is Jimmy Graves. You were talking to a friend of mine at The Skylark Diner a few days ago. Georgie Hammoud? He said you're in town researching a book you're writing about haunted places. Did he mention me? He said he did. Said he told you about how I know *all* the haunted places around here. Of course, Georgie does lose track of what he says, so it's understandable if he didn't."

The only thing which kept me from wincing at my lie rearing its head again was trying to remember if Georgie had told me of such a friend. After a few minutes, I concluded he hadn't. "Sorry. I don't think he did. Or, if he did, I don't remember. It's been a busy couple of days since I spoke to him." I paused, then added, "You seem a bit on the young side to be such good friends with Georgie."

The man—Jimmy—chuckled. "I'm older than I look." He opened the Monte Carlo's door, disembarked, closed the door and leaned against it. He stood just over six feet. Wore that battered Outback hat, a white button-down shirt and jeans. He sported cowboy boots on his feet, which looked oddly out of place in the Adirondacks. He folded his arms across his chest and appraised me with a keen eye. Seemed like a perceptive fellow. "So you're writing about strange and haunted places," he said again. "How'd you get interested in that sort of thing?"

The words tumbled out of my mouth before I was even fully aware of what I was saying. "I'm a pastor. Well, former pastor. I've always been interested in the supernatural, I guess. Invested in the world beyond this one. I . . . " I snapped my mouth shut before I could vomit up the miserable backstory which had brought me here. I swallowed and opted for another lie. "I'm on sabbatical for a year. Seemed like a great chance to travel around. Do some research. See if this book idea has legs."

Of course, the only thing I was writing were my experiences since entering Clifton Heights, in the big leather-bound journal I'd brought with me. My last will and testament, if you will. I figured it could pass inspection as a "rough draft."

Jimmy grinned, his green eyes glinting in the sunlight. "Neat. Well, you're in the right place. Clifton Heights has strange and haunted places to spare. What brings you our way, if you don't mind my asking?"

I shrugged. "Just felt like stopping for a while when I got here. Something in the air, I guess. Seemed a good place to start my research."

Jimmy nodded. "You've got that right, friend. There is definitely something in the air around here. Anyway." He gestured toward town. "You want haunted places in Clifton Heights? I know them all. I'm sort of a freelance town historian. My family goes all the way back to its founding. It's in my blood, I suppose."

He peered closely at me, gaze suddenly probing. "I'd love to show you around. I know all the best sights, trust me." He raised his eyebrows and smiled. "Want to get a drink and some wings at Hyland's Pub tonight? Talk it over?"

A small part of me wanted to say yes—he had a magnetic personality—but the weariness and strangeness of the past few days caught up with me in a rush. I shook my head. "Honestly? I just got back from camping for two days . . . "

three

you lost a day and a half

" . . . and I'm beat. Think I'm going to lay low for the evening. Raincheck?"

Jimmy offered me another wide grin. "You went camping at the old stone chapel, didn't you? Georgie said you were planning to. That place is wild. I *bet* you need some rest."

He pulled a wallet out of his back pocket, opened it, and extracted a white card. "How long you plan on staying around?"

Of course I had no idea, but even so I said, "The end of the month, at least."

He held the card out to me, and I took it. "Halloween night. I'll give you a special Clifton Heights ghost tour."

I examined his card. It was plain white stock. On one side, in simple black print, it read: *Jimmy Graves.* I flipped the card over. On the other side, printed in black, more ornate script, it read: *A Night of Grave Delights!*

I held it up. "Nice hook."

He grinned wider, eyes alive. "Little play on the name, for the ghost tour. Kind of my tagline."

I smiled and tucked the card into my front pocket. Something was nipping at the back of my mind. I'd heard this motto somewhere else, but I couldn't place it. "A ghost tour would be great for the book."

"Excellent!" He opened the Monte Carlo's door and climbed in. Closed it, and before he rolled up the window, he smiled and said, "You won't regret it. And, because you're a friend of Georgie's, it's on the house. So long as you accept it."

His wording sounded odd, but I nodded. "Sure. Why not?"

He slapped the outside of the car door. "Fantastic. I've got such sights to show you, my friend."

The car throbbed to life. He raised the window and backed out of the space next to my car. For a moment I stood facing the midnight-black Monte Carlo, feeling distinctly like James Brolin facing down a demonic Lincoln Continental.

The Monte Carlo honked once, not sounding anything like a demon-possessed car. Just an average car. I waved, and the car turned and pulled out of the parking lot. It drove into town proper, quiet and meek as you please. As I returned to my cabin, several belated revelations hit in rapid succession.

One: I'd never told Georgie I was going to camp at the old stone chapel. How did Jimmy Graves know?

Two: His oddly-worded offer of a free ghost tour felt like

an invocation which, of course, featured heavily as supernatural catalysts in horror movies.

Three: Though it seemed ridiculous, his voice sounded very much like the voice which had told me to lie down in the stone chapel and give up.

Four: Why hadn't I asked him about seeing his car all around town? How did he not recognize the guy who flipped him off and called him an asshole? And if he did recognize me . . . why didn't he say anything?

Finally . . .

I've got such sights to show you.

He'd sounded almost exactly like Douglas Bradley as Pinhead in *Hellraiser*, and it felt like he'd known that. Had done it on purpose, to tease me.

The last part bothered me the most, for some reason.

***

Exhausted from my journey down the access road to the stone chapel and back, I decided on a nap before heading down to dinner, most likely to The Skylark again. I wondered if Art and Georgie would be there. Wondered if Georgie really was friends with Jimmy Graves.

I also figured it would be my last meal out. Tomorrow I needed to not only shop for provisions so I could start using the cabin's kitchen, but I also needed to look for some kind of employment. I'd run out of money soon enough, having left the bulk of my savings for Beth and the boys, which was the least I could do.

Which wasn't much.

Unfortunately, my nap didn't prove restful. I dreamed again of Halloween night. This time, Beth and I were answering the door for Trick or Treaters, but we weren't handing out candy. We were handing out Bible tracts—only the tract pages were sharp as razor blades. They slashed every Trick or Treater's hand.

Every Trick or Treater was Lilly.

Every time she accepted the razor-blade tract

submissively, squeezing it in her fist as it sliced deep into her flesh and drew blood. She stared at us through dead eyes devoid of light or life, face slack and wooden. Lily at age eight, costumed in the Cinderella dress Beth had denied her.

Age seventeen, in her black punk eyeliner and black leather jacket.

Age eleven, in the Gothic vampire outfit I knew she would've loved.

Alternate versions of Lilly paraded endlessly to our front door, dressed in Halloween costumes we never would've allowed for a holiday we forbade, accepting razor-blade tracts which slashed her hands to bloody ribbons, with nary a twitch of her eye.

Over and over.

I woke an interminable time later, bathed in cold sweat.

18.

6:00

BECAUSE MY NAP had offered little rest, I chose not to walk down into town after all. I had some leftover hot dogs and snacks, which served well enough as a makeshift meal. After yet another dream about Lilly, I didn't feel hungry anyway. I didn't watch any horror movies before going to bed, either. I didn't watch television at all. I was a bit tired of the weird confluence between horror movies and my life. Quite honestly, I wasn't in the mood for any more cinematic revelations. Somehow I knew I wouldn't be able to keep from watching them indefinitely, but for the moment I wanted—*needed*—a break. I also needed to acknowledge the reality of the situation.

I'd left my wife and surviving children without a provider. With no income. At the end of the day, fuck my congregation and pastoral duties. After their complicity in Lilly's death (and they *were* complicit, nothing could change my mind on that score), I didn't owe them a damn thing.

However, regardless of my feelings for Beth, I'd walked out on her and the boys. Granted, I'd left them the credit and bank cards. Even so, I needed to find a job soon—not only so I could keep paying my way, but also so I could send something home to Beth.

The problem was my email account didn't seem to be working. I tried numerous times that evening to access it, and kept getting an error message which said *This account does not exist*. It didn't work on my laptop, or on my phone.

Even stranger, when I jumped off the cliff and dialed first the parsonage number, then Beth's, a tinny robotic voice informed me both those numbers were disconnected.

I'd left only twelve days ago. Was it possible Beth had already changed her phone number, and the church had changed the parsonage number? Things like that happened faster these days, but even so. It didn't seem plausible. And I had no idea what was wrong with my email.

On a whim, I tried to log into our joint bank account from its website. I received another message saying my account "did not exist". That was even less likely. There'd be more red tape involved in closing a joint bank account, I felt sure. Especially when one of the account holders wasn't present. Especially after being gone for only twelve days.

I shut my laptop, sat back on the futon, and closed my eyes. A small headache had blossomed from the place where I'd hit my forehead a few days before (how many?), making it hard to think. Even if it meant risking another nightmare about Lilly, I needed sleep.

As I stood, however, I found myself gazing at the flat screen television on the wall. Wondering if maybe a movie would help settle my nerves. I actually caught myself sitting back down and reaching for the remote on the coffee table.

Somehow, I stopped myself. Closed my hand into a fist and stood. Gathered myself, and headed for the bedroom. I slept through the night, and I didn't dream at all.

19.

1 REMAINED IN or near my cabin for the next two days. I ordered pizza deliveries from Pizza Joe's (a place up the road I didn't remember passing on the way into town, and whose delivery guys all had the same blank stare as The Motor Lodge's desk clerk), took short walks up and down the road, wrote in my journal, and searched the local internet classifieds.

I didn't know what kind of job I'd find, but it didn't matter. I'd take a farmhand job. Something which would allow me to keep Cabin 14 for a little while longer and if possible, send money to Beth. How I'd do that, I wasn't sure. With the parsonage number and her number apparently changed, I'd no idea how to get a hold of her, or where she and the boys were living. Even so, it was the least I could do. Of course I'd become an expert at doing the *least* for my family over the years.

Especially Lilly.

Somehow I managed not to watch any horror movies during that time. I didn't even turn the TV on. When I wasn't looking for jobs or taking short strolls, I wrote in my journal, doing my best to recall everything that had happened since coming to Clifton Heights. The only experience which still remained fuzzy was my hike out to the old stone chapel. I did my best to write it all down, though it sounded fragmented and hallucinatory. For some reason I took comfort in this—that I couldn't remember everything that had happened out there.

20.

October 27th
11:00 AM

I'D MANAGED TO avoid watching horror movies the past two days, but that didn't seem to matter. Recollections of another movie I'd seen years ago confronted me not fifteen minutes after I left my cabin to walk into town.

The air felt pleasantly crisp, still lacking the damp cold of November. Maybe it was my imagination, but I'd always thought October had a certain smell. Hard to explain, really. A complex mingling of chimney smoke, hickory, dried leaves, apples (even if there weren't any orchards around), cider, an indeterminate kind of spice, and pumpkins. In spite of my father's refusal to celebrate Halloween, October had *always* smelled that way. I'd never spoken of it to anyone, however. Not even Beth.

Some Octobers smelled more "October" than others, of course. It varied from year to year, probably with my mood at the time. It was the same thing with towns. Clifton Heights smelled more of "October" than any town I'd ever visited. Maybe that was flight of fancy, but even so.

I was standing on the side of the road, enjoying the smell of October, when he called to me.

"Hello. Out for a morning stroll?"

I looked across the road and saw him, sitting in an Adirondack chair in front of a small yellow clapboard house. A man dressed in a red and black checkered flannel, jeans and boots, with long white hair pulled back into a ponytail and a bushy white beard. He wore darkly tinted glasses, even though it was overcast.

Curious, I looked both ways and ambled across the road

to him. Oddly, he got younger-looking as I approached. Up close, a man I'd initially taken to be in his seventies looked more in his late fifties, early sixties.

"Yes I am." I neared him and stopped. "Seems like a nice day for it."

The man offered me an amiable grin. "Indeed it is." He nodded at The Motor Lodge. "Visitor in town?"

"Yes. Staying for a few weeks, finances depending."

The man nodded and didn't press any further. That impressed me. He certainly wasn't like Art and Georgie, the kind of old coot who felt a right to know everyone's business. Especially newcomers. "Saw you had a visitor a few nights back. Fella in the black car. What was he pestering you about?"

I smiled. Maybe he was a nosy old coot after all. "I guess he runs ghost tours around town? Someone I met at The Skylark Diner—Georgie—told him I was interested in weird places. I'm thinking of writing a book on that sort of thing." The lie was coming easier now.

The man snorted. "Ghost tours, huh? That's what he's going with now?" He gave me a pointed look I could feel even through his tinted lenses. "He's a con man. Whatever he's offering, it's not worth the price you'll have to pay."

"Actually, he offered it free of charge. For the . . . book I'm writing."

Lies upon lies.

The man gave me a strange look. "Free is still too high a price when it's from him. Just mind yourself. Fella's a con man, through and through."

I folded my arms, becoming more interested by the moment. Also realizing that part of me believed the old man was right. I *had* sensed something slippery about Jimmy Graves. "If he's such a con man, why doesn't Sheriff Baker run him in? I've met the sheriff. He seems like a good man. Forthright guy."

The man shrugged. "The sunuvabitch deals with

intangibles. He's not peddling stolen merchandise or anything illegal. Not taking people's money, running moonshine, or anything like that. His promises never turn out like they're supposed to. But it's not *illegal*, per se. Wrong, yes. Not anything Sheriff Baker can legally charge him with, however. Especially because people *choose* to accept the things he offers."

My interest quickly changed into confusion. "I'm not quite sure I follow."

The man sighed and shifted in his chair. "Don't pay me no mind. I'm an old duffer sticking his nose into other people's business. Mind yourself around him, is all."

I smiled. "'Old duffer.' You don't look so old."

The man grinned. "I'm older than I look. Him too."

"Huh. That's exactly what he said."

"Yeah. We're the same age. He'll deny it, though."

Interesting and as a weird as the conversation had gotten, it was time to get going. I needed to get lunch and look for a job. "Well, I'll be on my way. Nice talking with you. I'm sure I'll see you again."

The man smiled and opened the book sitting in his lap. "That would be a pleasure, son."

I turned and made it a few steps before he called out. "Son?"

I glanced over my shoulder.

Giving me an oddly sad smile, he said, "Whatever you're looking for . . . that fellow can't give it to you. Remember that."

There seemed no adequate response, so I merely nodded and continued down the hill.

***

When I reached the bottom of the hill and was about to turn onto Main Street, that movie memory hit me.

The Sentinel.

I looked back up the hill. I could make out the man sitting in his chair in front of his little yellow clapboard house. From my vantage, it appeared as if he was looking down over Clifton Heights. As if he was watching over the whole town.

In *The Sentinel* a blind priest watches over the gateway to hell, holding the depraved forces of evil at bay. I couldn't keep the similarities out of my mind. The Sentinel, sitting in the top floor of a brownstone overlooking the street. The man, sitting in his chair, looking out over Clifton Heights. The blind priest, holding back the forces of darkness, and the man warning me against Jimmy Graves. Jimmy Graves, who drove a shining black Monte Carlo which closely resembled the demonic black Lincoln Continental from *The Car*.

I stared at the man sitting in his chair. "This is real life," I whispered, "not a horror movie."

Even so, a chill rippled down my back. I turned and walked down Main Street, unable to make myself believe it.

21.

8:00 PM
Raedeker Park Zoo

MY FIRST DAY on the job search turned up empty. All the places I found in online classified ads had been filled months ago. To be fair, they weren't jobs I'd be very interested in. The Mobilmart on Haverton Road. Cashier at The Great American Grocery. Can and bottle sorter at a recycling center called The Can Man. Waiter at Henry's Drive-In Diner.

I ate lunch at The Skylark, hoping to encounter Art or Georgie or both. I saw neither of them. I thought about asking the waitress about them, but decided against it, for some reason. After lunch I walked around town some more, hoping to stumble upon job openings.

Eventually I gave up and headed back to The Motor Lodge. Once there, I used some cash from my dwindling supply to order a pizza from Pizza Joe's, which was once again delivered by the same vacant-eyed teenager who'd delivered all the other pizzas. I was tempted to ask him if he was Pizza Joe's only delivery boy, but decided not to. Something in his vague manner and distant gaze discouraged me.

After dinner, tired of walking, I drove to Raedeker Park to stroll through the zoo. It was an odd place. Some of the exhibits were exceptionally well-done. The animals in good health and obviously well-cared for. Other exhibits were empty and ramshackle, and looked like they hadn't housed animals in years. Still others looked as if they'd been under construction for just as long.

I'd left the zoo and was returning to the parking lot at

the top of the hill when it happened. Walking past a small playground before the parking lot, I saw several children clustered together near the swings from the corner of my eye. I didn't pay them any mind until I heard . . .

"Leave me alone!"

"Why? Gonna fucking cry, *lesbo*?"

A sharp cry, and then a *thud*. Laughter, cackling and shrill, like a bunch of hyenas.

I stopped and regarded the group closely. They looked like they were probably in fifth or sixth grade. They loomed over a kid on the ground, who they'd presumably pushed off the swing. I hesitated, wondering if I should do anything or just keep walking. It wasn't any of my business. Not my kids, and I was a stranger in Clifton Heights, with no authority over them whatsoever.

Gonna fucking cry
lesbo?

The slur propelled me forward. Before I knew it, I stood behind them. The crackling anger in my voice surprised me. "What's going on?"

The four kids turned detached gazes toward me. Two girls and two boys. A blond, a redhead, one with brown hair, one with black. Expressions flat and wooden, mouths straight lines.

I had never been a stern disciplinarian, much to Beth's dismay (and the dismay of my father, The Good Reverend Ford, of course). According to her (and my congregation) I was too easy-going, too permissive, too lax. A congregation member once called me too *kind* and too *compassionate*. I had a good heart but was *misguided*.

In any case, I felt distinctly uncomfortable returning those stares, not only because I'd stepped out of my comfort zone but also because I was acutely aware these kids didn't seem the slightest bit concerned about my involvement in their affairs.

"It was an accident," the blond girl with ponytails said in a flat voice. "We were just playing."

"Yeah," agreed the redhead with freckles, his voice sounding like it came from a deep well. "An accident. Didn't mean it."

I glanced at the girl lying on the ground at their feet. She looked to be the same age. Dressed in the same kind of clothes as them, no discernible differences between them . . . except for the look of anger and fear pinching her eyes, and . . .

My breath caught in my throat when I met her gaze and recognized the unique shade of brown-green in her hazel eyes. The upturn of her pert nose, the slight gap between her front teeth.

Lilly.

It was her. Despite all the common sense in the world arguing against it. I knew it was her. My daughter as a nine-year-old. My daughter who'd been pushed off the swings and called *lesbo*. My daughter who cowered at the feet of merciless bullies.

My throat tightened with anger. I swallowed and managed, "Is that true? Was it an accident?"

The girl—*Lilly*—stared back. I knew this moment, of course. Everyone in authority over children did. When the target of bullying is put on the spot by an authority figure and has the chance to speak out against their oppressors, or keep quiet, knowing that speaking out will only make things worse, and that keeping quiet will only earn a brief reprieve.

"C'mon, Mister," the girl with straight black hair said in an emotionless tone, "we were just playing around. We didn't mean anything by it."

I looked at the girl lying on the ground (Lilly). "Is this true?"

She said nothing. Just kept staring at me. She wasn't going to let me off the hook by giving me any kind of answer, especially by saying, "Yes, they're right, nothing happened." She was going to leave it in my hands, and I knew why.

Too many times—because I was so *compassionate*, so

forgiving, so *merciful*—I'd let bullies weasel out. I hadn't pressed them. I'd accepted the plea of "we were just fooling around," telling myself I was letting it go because I didn't want to make it worse for the victim. I told myself that, and I believed it.

Even when it involved Lilly. When I thought kids were whispering about her in church, when parents gave her lingering glances of disapproval, I told myself that, as Pastor, I couldn't use my authority to make things easier on my daughter, because that would be seen as favoritism. It wouldn't set a "good example". Would only make it harder for her in the long run by singling her out. I told myself that, and I believed it.

Right up until the day Lilly killed herself.

The girl who bore such an uncanny resemblance to my dead daughter . . .

it is Lilly

. . . stared at me and said nothing.

"All right," I said, jaw clenching in barely restrained anger, "get the *hell* out of here."

I met each of their gazes. "I know what you guys are doing. I *know* you pushed her off that swing. I heard what you called her. Get out of here and go home. Wherever that is."

"You're not from around here," the brown-haired boy said coldly. "You don't belong here, so you can't tell us what to do."

The kid was absolutely right, and a few years ago, such a bold challenge might have derailed me. Not now, though. Something had changed. In those cold, murderous eyes— yes, *murderous*—I saw the eyes of everyone who had killed Lilly. The church's pious, rigidly conservative and upwardly mobile teens (who, despite their shiny Baptist veneer, drank, smoke, and fucked with the worst of them behind closed doors), the little biddies who'd looked down their nose at my daughter because of her green hair, black clothes, leather jacket, ripped jeans and nose-rings, the sarcastic and misogynistic men who shook their heads and behind my back mumbled *"Men who can't keep their household in order can't be expected to lead a church."*

Even the eyes of Beth. My wife, who'd shunned Lilly more and more as the years passed and Lilly tried to find her own identity. Picking every little fight she could with Lilly. Her older brother who avoided her also, and her little brother who always asked, "Why are you so weird? Why do you like girls? Billy says yer goin' to hell cause you do," with nary a word from me. I saw all of them in the eyes of these little bastards, and I hated them for it.

I stepped closer, feeling a mean delight when they stepped back. "I don't give a damn what you think. Get the hell out of here. I'm not leaving until you do. You're right, kid," I addressed the one who'd challenged me, "I'm not from around here and don't have any authority. I don't care. I know what happened here, and I'm not going to let it go on. I'll take her . . . "

Lilly

" . . . down to the zoo entrance and tell them what I saw. I'll have them call her parents, and then I'll tell them what I saw."

The boy with the brown hair smirked, as if I was inconsequential. "They won't believe you."

Something cruel pulsed through me. I smirked back. "I don't care. I'll make it up. Tell them what I *think* happened. Either way, I'm not going anywhere. I'm staying here until you little fuckers leave."

The boy's smirk vanished. He didn't look scared, though. More like bored. "It doesn't matter, you know," he said in that strange, flat monotone of his, "you can't save her. It's too late. You always try, but it's always too late, and it's always your fault she's dead."

My mouth fell open. An ice-cold fist clenched my guts. Before I could say anything, they scurried off in separate directions out of the playground, looking like nothing more than adolescents scattering so they wouldn't get into trouble. I stepped after them but of course I couldn't follow, my mind a riot of confused thoughts and conflicting emotions as those words echoed in my head . . .

can't save her
too late
your fault

After several minutes, I looked back to the little girl who so strongly resembled Lilly. She'd vanished.

***

In 1981's *Bloody Birthday*, three kids born during a solar eclipse grow into pure evil beings. Leading up to their thirteenth birthdays, they embark on a spurious, depraved murder spree. No reason is ever offered for their murderous impulses or their evil, save that they were "born under an eclipse." They are simply evil, and they love to kill. No explanation necessary.

In some ways, that was a comforting thought. Evil wasn't a choice. It was biological. Something in the genes. Something was wrong with evil people. They were bent, twisted, for no other reason than they were. They couldn't help hurting and killing, and it wasn't their fault they loved it. They were made that way. Born under the wrong star, their evil was a cosmic hiccup. Another aspect of an uncertain universe.

I knew different.

Those who played a hand in Lilly's death, chose to. They chose to shun her. To spread rumors about her. Bully her. They chose to bombard her email and social media with messages and YouTube videos about homosexuals going to hell. They chose to vandalize her locker (at the "Christian school" Beth had insisted we send our kids to). They chose to slip those tracts onto her desk at school when the teachers "weren't looking." And their parents chose to either turn a blind eye, or outright condone it.

What did I choose?

I chose to do nothing.

I did nothing about the entire *rack* of tracts in our Outreach Center. I chose not to confront the deacons and Sunday school teachers about the pranks their kids pulled on Lilly in school and in church. I chose not to confront my eldest about him ignoring Lilly after she came out, preferring to "give him space". I chose not to reprimand my youngest for telling Lilly she was going to hell, because he was "just being a kid, after all".

Did I ever stop my wife from bullying her own child?

I did nothing.

I didn't show Lilly any visible support, either. I had my "ministry" to think about. Didn't want to "wink at sin." Had to show a "united front" with Beth. No discord could be allowed. Absolutely not.

I did nothing.

I *chose* to do nothing.

Which made me more of a monster than all the evil children in every horror movie in existence.

22.

October 28ᵗʰ
10:00 AM

I WANTED TO wake early the next day and hit the streets before nine for day two of my job search, but I'd slept badly the night before, caught in the grip of another nightmare about Lilly. I didn't wake up until nine-thirty. After a meager breakfast of cereal and toast, I managed to get myself together by quarter of ten. I considered driving, but until I could find some kind of job, I needed to save money for my spare diet and my cabin.

As I left the parking lot and walked into town, I waved at the man sitting in his chair. He waved back and smiled, but didn't call out. I expected him to return his attention to the book open in his lap, but he didn't. He kept looking at me, face inscrutable behind those shades. Reminding me, uncomfortably, of my association of him with the blind priest in *The Sentinel*, and of his warning about Jimmy Graves. I nodded again, looked away and continued down the hill.

***

I heard the loud music before I saw the car. Didn't recognize the tune and the vocals were indistinct, but the music sounded like it was from the 80s or 90s. Definitely the "devil's music" the Good Reverend Ford railed against in my youth. Such music did not lead to thinking upon things Holy and Good, and it certainly didn't "direct our eyes unto the Lord."

Even back then I sensed the shallowness of those claims. Especially since I spent my entire high school career (at a Christian high school, no less) furtively listening to

OCTOBER NIGHTS

Mötley Crue, Guns'n Roses, Def Leopard, Dokken, Pearl Jam, Nirvana and others on my friends' Walkmans while on the bus rides to and from school. Listened to the same rock music all the deacons' sons were covertly listening to themselves, taped in secret off the radio.

Never once did I feel the urge to murder, maim, hurt others, blaspheme the Lord. Rock music didn't stoke my lust any worse than average sixteen-year-old hormones did. I certainly wasn't running around raping girls, participating in orgies, or knocking up cheerleaders.

As I turned the corner onto Main Street and neared the town square and its small park, an insidious voice (oddly sounding like Jimmy Graves) whispered as I drew nearer to the music: *Of course, the Good Reverend Ford would say Satan's influence is subtler than that. Because you listened to it in high school, you listened to it on the sly all through college, listened to it in the car when you were alone, even listened to it when driving with Lilly, and you let her listen to it on her own. Now she's dead because you weren't Godly enough to keep her under control. Guess that devil's music ruined you after all.*

The music came closer. When I looked up, I saw a 1979 white Pontiac Trans AM driving down Main Street toward me, music blasting. It hugged the curb. I quickly saw why. A rangy young man wearing a cut-off denim jacket leaned out of the driver's side window, wolf-whistling and shouting, "Hey baby! Hroooo! Stop runnin away and be nice, Momma!" at the young woman scurrying along the sidewalk away from him.

The man leaning out the window drove with one hand. With the other, he stuck two fingers in his mouth and blew a piercing whistle. The girl flinched, scowling.

An icy fist clenched my heart. The angry scowl. Pierced lip and eyebrows. Dark eye shadow, green hair and wide, luminous eyes . . .

Lilly.

It was Lilly, walking toward me on the sidewalk, away from the stalking rock'n roll asshole following her in his vintage 1979 Pontiac Trans Am. It didn't matter how impossible it was. Just like I'd seen a nine-year-old Lilly getting bullied by kids at Raedeker Park last night, I was watching her get harassed by an asshole in a souped-up compensation for his manhood. Even worse, the sidewalks were oddly empty. Storefronts closed. There weren't any other cars about. Not a police cruiser in sight.

The same anger from last night pulsed through me. Without quite understanding myself, I broke into a trot toward the girl . . .

Lilly

. . . and the car slowly following her. "Hey! Excuse me! Miss . . . are you all right? This guy bothering you?" The car jerked to a stop, engine rumbling. The driver fell silent and stared at me. The girl stumbled to a halt and stared at me, eyes wide and trembling, without any of the relief I'd hoped to see. Instead, I saw stark terror.

She shook her head. I wasn't sure, but as I drew near, I thought she whispered, *"No."*

I met her gaze. It *was* Lilly. Teenage Lilly, several months before she killed herself. It had to be her. I didn't see any recognition in her features, however. Only mad fear.

The driver of the Trans Am finally spoke, all sneering bravado and malevolence. "What's your problem, asshole?"

I stepped past the girl (Lilly), gripping her shoulder tightly. It shook, and felt cold even through her black hoodie. I placed myself between her and the white Trans Am. "What's my problem? What the hell is *your* problem?"

The rock music thundering from the Trans Am's speakers cut off. An oppressive silence fell over the street, sending cold prickles along my shoulders. I regarded the young man as he exited his car. He looked like he was in his twenties, and every inch the stereotypical headbanger of the late 80s. Acid wash jeans ripped at the knees and thighs.

Under his sleeveless denim jacket, a Judas Priest t-shirt screamed in all its 80s glory. Inverted crosses dangled from each earlobe.

He stepped forward, boots scuffing the sidewalk, thumbs hooked in a belt with a grinning silver skull buckle. "My problem is *you*, fucknuts," he said in a menacing tone. "Was just having some fun is all." He flashed a cruel smile over my shoulder. "Ain't that right, sweetie? Just havin' some fun."

I glanced over my shoulder at the girl. Head lowered, staring at the sidewalk, hands stuck in her hoodie pockets. She wasn't going to look up, I knew, or say anything. Just like she didn't last night.

It's not the same girl.

It is.

She wouldn't defend herself. It would be left to me, because I'd failed her so badly in real life.

I turned and met the headbanger's gaze. "I'm sure she *wasn't* having fun. Get your ass in your car and head on your way. Before I call Sheriff Baker."

The headbanger threw his hands up in mock surrender. "Oh no! The Sheriff! What'll I do?" His smile faded, replaced by a cold, dead expression. He stepped closer, within five feet. "Sheriff Baker can't do shit. No one can. Besides," he folded his arms across his chest, face relaxing into an insouciant expression. "You're not from around here. Can't tell me what to do, 'cause you don't belong here."

My guts twisted as I recalled the kid's words last night. *You don't belong here. Can't tell us what to do.*

I had never been a violent man. Never got into fights as a kid. Of course, I'd been raised to "turn the other cheek" and if that cheek was struck, to "offer the other cheek also." Raised to believe it took more courage *not* to fight back.

But that was bullshit.

All bullshit.

A low-level rage flushed through me. Clenching my fists,

I closed the distance between myself and the headbanger until only two feet remained between us. A delicious sensation of uncontrollable mania pounded behind my eyes. What the hell was I doing? Was I really going to take a swing? Risking brass knuckles, a switchblade, who knew what else?

Something shifted in the headbanger's expression. His eyes narrowed. Nostrils flared. Lips pulled back to reveal teeth which looked pointed, canine-like, and (though it had to be my imagination), his entire face shifted. Cheeks became higher and more pronounced. Nose crooked and bent. Skin cracked and weathered. Eyes flaming a deep, hellish green. Hair oily and dead, hanging from a flaky, raw scalp.

"It doesn't matter," it said in a guttural voice. "You can't save her. It's too late. It's always too late . . . motherfucker!"

It threw back its head and bellowed in laughter. I stumbled back, blinked, and he was just an asshole headbanger again, laughing hysterically at a middle-aged man trying to get his ass kicked. He returned to the Trans Am, opened the driver's side door, and got back inside. Closed the door, shook his head and said, "You don't belong here, asshole. This ain't your town, so fuck off."

He started the Trans Am up. Its engine growled to life. This time I recognized the song blaring from its speakers, and it seemed frighteningly appropriate.

Mötley Crue's "Shout at the Devil."

The headbanger put the Trans Am in gear, executed a sharp U-turn and peeled away, tires screeching and engine roaring. It shot off down Main Street, in the direction of what I thought was Shelby Road Cemetery. Again, I was shocked at how empty the streets were. How the Trans Am's roaring exit drew no attention from the stores at all.

I wasn't surprised, however, to turn and find the teenage version of Lilly gone.

***

Black Roses is an absurd horror movie playing on the Satanic Panic of the 80s, turned up to eleven. A rock band made up of demons, which uses demonic rock music to seduce teens into becoming demonic "black roses" (hence the movie's title) to help spread their evil across the world.

I'd never bought into the Satanic Panic's hysterical fears. Even as an easily influenced Pastor's kid. I didn't think rock and roll was the devil's music then. I didn't believe that as an adult or as a pastor, though of course I had to disapprove of it, "for the good of the congregation."

But as I stood on the sidewalk and gazed down Main Street where that Trans Am had disappeared, I still felt the menace which had flowed off the headbanger. Thought of the split-second his face changed into something horrible—something demonic—and the hellish fire burning in his eyes.

You don't belong here.

Rattled, my thoughts dark and confusing, I turned to walk back to The Motor Lodge and Cabin 14, in no mood to search for a job, wondering if it really mattered.

23.

I SPENT THE rest of the 28th in the cabin, watching one horror movie after another. My experience with the 80s headbanger and yet another version of Lilly had shaken me up enough that I didn't care if I ran out of funds and The Motor Lodge tossed me out. I'd seen something in the headbanger's face. Something decayed and evil, and it had been harassing Lilly. Just like the kids harassing the nine-year-old Lilly the night before. Either that, or I was going crazy.

I didn't bother keeping track of the movies I watched, because I knew that didn't matter, either. If they impinged on my life or revealed something, they would. If they didn't it wouldn't matter.

For lunch I decided hell with it and called Pizza Joe's. The line was busy, so I contented myself with whatever I could rummage from the meager supplies I had left. Some hot dogs, a bag of chips, and an apple. I sat on the futon, ate, and watched horror movie after horror movie, trying not to think of the strangeness which had taken over my life or the nightmare I'd suffered the night before—another one about Lilly.

There was a Halloween party in our basement Rec Room, which was decorated with black and orange streamers and balloons, and cardboard monster cutouts taped to the walls. Dozens of kids were present, but I couldn't see their masks, or what they'd dressed as. They melted together into a tangled mass of flesh. A dizzying collage of leering faces, claws, fur, bulging eyes, gaping mouths and pulsing green skin.

Beth clapped her hands. The fleshy mass lurched toward a tub filled with water and floating apples. Before us stood a middle-grade Lilly, dressed as a classic witch. Pointy black hat, flowing and tattered black dress, face painted green and plastic crooked witch's nose held on by a rubber band.

Beth clapped a hand on Lilly's right shoulder. I mindlessly followed suit, clamping her left shoulder. I could feel Lilly quaking in fear. I tried to make myself look at her, but I couldn't, lest I see the accusation burning in her eyes.

Beth forced Lilly to her knees. I pushed down, also. She raised her other hand, and screeched, "Behold! The *witch*!"

The mass of costumed flesh groaned, "Behold the witch!"

"Behold the blasphemer, the profaner!"

The crowd echoed her in moaning symphony.

"Behold, she who gives herself over to unnatural urges, and spits in the Face of God!"

I opened my mouth to say something, *anything* to interrupt Beth, but I couldn't. I squeezed Lilly's shoulder. All I felt was cold, hard bone.

"Behold the witch! If she drowns, she's purged of her sin, her soul cleansed forevermore! If she survives, she's damned to hell!"

The crowd of misshapen faces and malformed bodies pulsed, shouting with glee. I opened my mouth, but it didn't matter. Beth shoved Lilly head-first into the tub of water. I helplessly did likewise. We held her under while she thrashed, but didn't drown, and the crowd roared even louder . . .

When I woke from that dream, I cried like a baby for the first time since coming to Clifton Heights.

24.

5:00 PM

ĄROUND FIVE I was getting hungry for more than hot dogs and chips. I looked at my rapidly dwindling cash supply and decided I could at least afford another pizza. I called Pizza Joe's and they were busy again, so I decided to drive there. According to Google, it was only fifteen minutes up the hill.

First, I went to the Mobilmart on Haverton Road and bought myself several cases of Sam Adams from a bored-looking cashier with the name *Jessica* pinned on her polo shirt. I was low on money, and would soon be out. Not enough to pay for another week at The Motor Lodge; not enough to buy more than two or three meals. At that precise moment, however, I didn't care. I had beer. I wanted pizza. I was going to sit and eat pizza, drink beer, and watch horror movies until I passed out.

I set Google Maps to Pizza Joe's. Drove back up the hill, past The Motor Lodge. On my right, the man was sitting in his chair. He waved. I ignored him and drove on.

The trip took me twice as long as Google Maps originally estimated. Every few minutes my phone's robotic and slightly feminine voice said *"Recalculating,"* adding five minutes onto my trip time. What Google had initially projected as a fifteen-minute drive became twice that. I didn't hear *"Destination is on the left"* until thirty minutes later. Very high up the hill, back into the woods, where a pizza joint seemed unlikely. Regardless, I stopped, checked both ways, cut a sharp U-turn, parked on the other side of the road, and looked out the window . . .

At nothing.

No Pizza Joe's. No building of any kind. Nothing but a vast expanse of heaved and cracked asphalt shot through with weeds. Back in the overgrowth, I saw something which resembled a foundation of sorts, but I couldn't see for sure.

I sat and stared for several minutes, head spinning. I looked down at my phone and saw Google Maps had reset itself. I typed "Pizza Joes" and clicked *Search*.

Google Maps thought about it for a moment, then said: *no results.* I opened the Google App and searched, "pizza near me." The only result was *Chin's Pizza & Wings* on Main Street.

I set the phone down. Pulled onto the road without bothering to check for traffic behind me. Drove down the hill, and rolled to a stop just before The Motor Lodge, across from the man sitting in his chair. Heedless of other cars (thankfully there weren't any) I rolled down the window and blurted, "What happened to Pizza Joe's? Up the road from here?"

The man frowned slightly. "Pizza Joe's? That's long gone. Burned down in the late 70s or early 80s. Arson. Insurance fraud or criminal skirmish between gangs. No one really knows for sure."

I stared at the man, mouth slightly agape, and not caring. After a few minutes I swallowed, gathered my shredded wits about me, and managed, "But . . . I've been getting pizza deliveries from there for days."

At this, the man's expression turned somber. Sad, almost. "Yes," he said, his voice tinged with regret, "I'm sure you have."

I opened my mouth to ask why, how that was possible, what did he mean . . . but I couldn't speak. There weren't any words. I closed my mouth, shook my head, and turned away to park my car before my cabin.

As I did, I felt sure I heard him whisper, "God be with you, son."

***

I still had my beer, of course. I sat on the futon and drank bottle after bottle, watching horror movies without seeing them, forgetting their plots soon as they ended. At some point, I microwaved the last of the hot dogs, and ate them. I didn't taste them, but they stilled my grumbling stomach. Somewhere in the middle of *Doom Asylum* I passed out on the futon.

Thank God I didn't dream.

25.

October 29th
10:00 AM

I STARTED MY day waking on the futon with a pounding headache. A glance through slitted eyelids at the coffee table showed the damage. More empty beer bottles than I wanted to count. Considering I wasn't a seasoned drinker, I'd gone way over my limit and was paying a heavy price.

Luckily I wasn't nauseated. Yet. After shuffling into the bathroom, downing Advil and sipping water, I made my way to bed, crawling under the covers. My headache subsided, and I slipped into a deep, restful sleep. I didn't dream that time, either.

When I woke two hours later, around eleven, my headache was mostly gone. Not only was I desperately thirsty, I felt famished, too. Unfortunately, most of my supplies had been depleted. Remembering The Motor Lodge put out a continental breakfast every morning, and also had vending machines in the lobby, I headed there after I showered and dressed.

An employment opportunity finally presented itself when I entered the lobby and headed to the tray of bagels, apples, and oranges next to the coffee urns and vending machines. It came in the form of a different man—one I hadn't seen before, with long brown hair and thin, hatchet-face—swearing into his phone. His features were sharp and pointed, eyes flashing, and he talked with more authority than a mere desk clerk.

"Are you kidding? That's *bullshit*. Way too high."

As I selected a cinnamon-raisin bagel (which felt like it was a day away from being stale) and worked on slicing it and buttering it, my ears pricked up. I'd acquired many handyman skills during my college and seminary years. Roofing was one of them. As I poured myself a coffee and dumped a liberal amount of cream into it, I openly listened in on the clerk's increasingly agitated phone conversation.

The man's scowl deepened. "Oh, hell no. No way I'm falling for that shit. I finance this through you, you'll roast us with interest."

I bit into the bagel—finding it fresher than I'd expected—chewed, sipped from my coffee, and approached the front desk. I swallowed, cleared my throat, and said, "Excuse me?"

"Hold on." The clerk looked at me and said curtly, "What the hell do you want?"

"I'm Wes Ford. Staying in Cabin 14? I've got lots of experience shingling roofs. What's the trouble?"

The clerk narrowed his eyes, but his scowl faded slightly. "Shingles on Cabins 1, 2 and 3 just failed building inspection. Asshole inspector says all the other cabin roofs should be re-shingled, too."

I'd worked on similar situations before and knew the lay of this land well. "Let me guess," I said as I nodded at the phone, "that guy's charging an arm and a leg."

The guy snorted. "About it."

"Are you the owner here?"

"I'm the manager. Owner's hands off. I make the money decisions around here."

I'd figured as much. "How much is that roofing guy charging?" The desk clerk told me and I nodded. "Listen. I'd have to price the supplies—it's been over fifteen years since I did any shingling—but I bet I can cut that estimate by half."

The man's scowl disappeared completely, his eyes widening. He held up a finger and said, "Wait a sec." Put the phone back to his ear and said, "Forget it. I'm going a different way."

He hung up and waved me toward the desk. I sipped my coffee and stepped forward. He said, "Quote me a price."

I thought a bit. Adjusted for assumed inflation and increase in materials cost. The clerk nodded. "You're right. That's half of what everyone else is quoting." He waved me closer. "Here's the deal. I *need* Cabins 1-3 re-shingled, and could use the rest of them re-shingled, also. Can you start this afternoon?"

I nodded. What else was I doing?

"Fantastic. Go down to The General Store. We got an account with them. I'll call ahead, say you can charge the supplies to us. Get what you need, start working. If I like the results, I'll hire you to do the rest. Sound fair?"

I nodded. "Absolutely." Turned and left, rinsing the rest of my bagel down with my coffee. I'd found employment in a very unexpected place, right when I needed it. Granted, I hadn't done roofing in a while. I was sure to be rusty, but I figured my skills would return quickly enough.

I felt better than I had in days. Almost good enough to forget I'd been ordering pizza from a pizza joint which didn't exist anymore. Almost good enough to forget many other strange things.

I held those thoughts at bay, however, as I returned to my cabin before going to The General Store. I'd found work. I needed to get to it, while I had the chance. It would do me good. Keep troubling thoughts at bay. For a while, anyway.

But not forever.

I knew that sure enough.

26.

Hyland's Pub
9:00 PM

A DAY OF physical toil delivered exactly the results I'd been hoping for. Purpose. A clearer head. A semblance of peace. As I'd figured, things felt clumsy at first. I was flexing skills I hadn't drawn on in years. In due time, however, muscle memory served me well. I fell into a numbing routine which quieted my mind. I'd finished shingling Cabin 1 and was starting Cabin 2 by six when the manager came out and told me I could call it a day. Even better, he paid me in cash for the day's work, on the spot. I decided to head down to Hyland's for dinner and a few drinks to celebrate.

Predictably, a few drinks turned into many drinks, and I got way more than I expected.

***

I sat at the end of the bar, minding my business, feeling good if a bit fuzzy from all the beers I'd put down. I wasn't exactly shit-faced, but I certainly wasn't sober anymore, either. After dinner I ordered myself a pitcher of Saranac and worked on polishing off the whole thing until my mind felt relatively free. Too many strange things had happened, but at that moment, buzzing happily, I felt relatively unburdened. I'd taken a yellow cab to Hyland's, so I planned on drinking a few more beers and maybe a shot of whiskey for good measure.

I hadn't watched horror movies at all (another benefit of working: I kept *busy*) and nothing strange had happened. Thankfully, I also hadn't seen any more versions of Lilly. I felt sure if I got just a bit drunker (not as badly as last night), I'd sleep soundly, with no more dreams.

My future was still terribly unclear. I didn't know where it led, or how long it would last. I felt completely cut-off from my old life. I'd long since stopped trying to access my email and bank account, and though my smartphone still worked, I'd noticed a few days before that all my Contacts were now gone. Erased, as if they'd never existed.

I'd bought myself some time with the roofing job, but eventually that would end. What next? Maybe I could stay on at The Motor Lodge as a handyman. The desk clerk certainly didn't seem the type to dirty his hands. What I didn't know about maintenance far outweighed what I did know, but I was a fast study.

One thing I *was* sure of?

My journey was coming to an end. Halloween was in two days. So far I'd seen nine-year-old Lilly and teenager Lilly. Which would I see next? Was I *really* seeing her . . . or going crazy?

"Heavy thoughts, sweetheart. You don't lighten up, you'll sink into the bar."

I looked up and couldn't help staring. A woman with long blond hair stood next to me, wearing a clinging black dress. Her bright green eyes seemed to drink me in, the corners of her mouth turned up in good-natured mirth. She nodded at the stool next to me. "Seat taken?"

I smiled, face flushing with heat, feeling like a tongue-tied teenager overrun with hormones, feeling guilty also. But still I gestured grandly at the stool, hoping I didn't look too eager. "Be my guest."

She slid onto the stool, her movements supple, like liquid silk. She folded her hands demurely on the bar and gave me an inquiring look. "You're new here. Aren't you?"

It was a statement, not a question.

"I am. Got into town around the 14th. Staying at The Motor Lodge."

She lifted an eyebrow. "What brings you into town?"

I opened my mouth, the lie of writing a book about

myths and legends waiting on my tongue. Something glimmered in her eyes, however, which killed the lie right there. "I'm . . . kind of on a personal sabbatical, I guess. Trying to sort some things out."

She smiled wider. "Trying to find yourself?"

I snorted. "I suppose. Though that's a bit cliché for my tastes."

She laughed, and I laughed with her. It was an infectious sound. She sobered quickly, however, and peered at me closely. "Who left? You, or her?"

I stared at her, my mouth hanging open for several seconds before I could manage, "My . . . my daughter died."

She pursed her very red lips, looking intently thoughtful. I braced myself for the inevitable—and justified—barbs about leaving my wife in her time of need.

Instead, she gently laid her hand over mine and said softly, "What was her name?"

For a moment I couldn't think. A pleasant, soothing warmth spread from her hand into mine, which sent a wave of tingling warmth up my arm and throughout my body. I felt even drunker than I had moments before. It became very hard to concentrate, and also?

I felt powerfully aroused, for the first time in over a year.

Dimly, I remembered she'd asked me a question about someone's name. Who? It was . . . it was . . .

A crystal-clear image formed in my mind of a little girl in a bright blue skirt, wearing a red THING 1 t-shirt from *The Cat in the Hat*. A name formed on my tongue. I slurred, feeling even drunker. "Lilllly. Her name's Lilly. My . . . daughter."

Instantly my mental image in my head of Lilly wearing her Dr. Seuss t-shirt dissolved into nothingness. It was as if the memory had never existed. As if that little girl had never existed. In that moment, I couldn't remember what Lilly looked like as a child.

I glanced numbly at the woman. Her wide green eyes

swirled, deep pools of emerald. Just looking into them made me feel good. Made me feel free. As if everything which had burdened me over the past few months—the past few decades—was slowly being stripped away, layer by layer.

Her full red lips parted as a languorous sigh slipped between them. I experienced a powerful urge to kiss those lips. To breathe in her breath, and let her breathe mine. I found my gaze drifting downward to her ample cleavage and settling on the generous globes of flesh her dress barely contained.

Her fingers entwined with mine, sending even more intense waves of pleasure up my arm and into my chest. "Lilly. Such a pretty name. What was she like? Especially in her teen years. I adore teenagers, I must admit. So full of life, and . . . energy."

I guiltily pulled my gaze away from her chest and stared into the mirror behind the bar. I hated my reflection. The dark circles under my eyes. The dazed, unfocused pupils. The thin face and weak jaw. The reflection of a man lost and adrift, bereft of meaning and purpose.

Oddly enough, I had a hard time seeing her reflection. The glass looked smeared where it should be. I only saw an indistinct shape which vaguely resembled a woman. I was apparently far drunker than I'd thought.

"So, Lilly, the teenager. What was she like?"

She squeezed my hand. I turned back and met her dizzying gaze, thinking about Lilly's gradual transformation from a compliant, dutiful, and circumspect middle-school girl to a melancholic, neo-punk, teenage malcontent. I thought about her average wardrobe going into the seventh grade. Jeans, t-shirts, and generic backpacks bought at Wal-Mart, her black hair pulled back into a sensible ponytail.

Slowly, as the woman gripped my fingers tighter, her index finger massaging the back of my hand in slow, sensuous circles, my image of middle-school Lilly grew fuzzy, indistinct, and then dissolved.

. . . and then I thought about Lilly's almost overnight transformation into a punk-rock teenager who wore all black. Black jeans, black t-shirts with white Anarchy symbols on them, and a black jean jacket she'd decorated with pride rainbows, occult symbols, and Clorox-washed slogans like PUNK'S NOT DEAD and EAT THE RICH.

Beth had stridently disapproved. Criticized, hounded, pestered, bullied. My oldest son told Lilly he was "disappointed she was copying the World". My youngest started asking Lilly, *"Why are you dressing so weird? Is it because you're going to hell?"* My parents and in-laws expressed their barely-concealed disapproval with cold shoulders and thinly-veiled barbs about how "girls don't know how to dress like proper ladies in these days" and the congregation at large looked at Lilly askance.

And me?

I'd loved little-girl Lilly and middle-school Lilly (both of whom I couldn't seem to remember, no matter how hard I tried), but I'd secretly adored punk-rock Lilly for her courage in risking to be her own person, to experiment and investigate herself.

But could I support her openly? Defend her transformation to her mother? Protect her from the congregation's stares and whispers? Shield her from her older brother's condemnation and the jeers of her peers?

No.

I didn't condemn her, but I couldn't bring myself to support her openly. I did nothing, which I'd become an expert at.

The woman's fingernails dug into my skin, sending pinpricks of delicious pain into my hand. Erotic pain. I shivered and realized vaguely I had a powerful erection which strained against my jeans, so hard it hurt, yet felt wonderful at the same time.

The woman squeezed my hand and sighed again as my image of Lilly the punk rock teenager dissolved and disappeared. I could no longer remember what she looked like.

Though I still felt good, and now aroused, a small part of me realized something was wrong, too. As good as I felt, something bad was happening to me, but I wasn't sure what. I had a hard time holding onto the thought, as waves of pleasurable warmth coursed from the woman's hand into my body.

I looked at her, opened my mouth and tried to speak, but I couldn't. I felt lost in her gaze, which swirled in bright green, bottomless eddies. Those lips (which I not only wanted to kiss but also wanted to feel all over my body) glistened. She moved her hand up to my forearm. I wanted her to move it to other, more private parts, and yet, that small part of me loathed her touch, though I didn't know why.

The woman sidled closer. Dropped her hand onto my left thigh, and began to massage it slowly. With no shame, my mind conjured fantasies of this woman and I coupling in an animal-like frenzy, in every position I could imagine. My skin buzzed with desire. The pressure swelling in my crotch demanded release, feeling wonderful in its pain and pleasure.

"What about . . . your wife. Tell me your favorite memory of her."

It was when Lilly was born. When the nurse handed her to me (all six pounds, seven ounces of her) and I handed her to Beth. Who'd looked at our daughter with love and hope, for the first and maybe last time . . .

The woman's hand slid up my thigh and grabbed my rigid member through my jeans. She squeezed it, gently. A surge of electric pleasure throbbed through my groin. I didn't climax, but it was a near thing, as my memory of Beth holding baby Lilly dissolved and flitted away like so much ash.

She leaned closer and put her lips to my ear. Her warm

breath caressed my skin, almost sending me over the edge as she whispered, "Let's go somewhere more . . . private."

Practically numb with paralyzing arousal, I nodded speechlessly. When she stood, I did also. As she took my hand and walked away, I followed her like so much sheep.

***

Lilly saved me.

My mind swirled in a whirlpool of lurid images and desire as I stumbled toward the door, after the woman. The vague idea plagued me that I'd given up something precious, that I was going to sacrifice all I had left, but I couldn't make myself understand what I'd given up, or if it even mattered. No coherent thought could withstand the torrent of lust bombarding my mind and heart. Beth hadn't looked at me with desire in years. Having done her "Godly duty" and borne me children, sex meant nothing more to her than an occasional obligation.

But the way this woman looked at and touched me made my body vibrate. As I followed her to the pub's exit—winding through patrons sitting at tables and the waitresses serving them—I would've gladly given her everything I had left until nothing remained, had not the door to Hyland's opened a few steps before we reached it . . .

And *Lilly* walked in. Hand-in-hand with another woman. But this was a Lilly I'd never seen before. A Lilly I'd never get to see. Gone was the shy-anxious smile I'd seen since childhood. Gone also was the teenage angst and punk affectation. This Lilly wore clothes any modern young woman would wear to a bar. Jeans, a white stretch-shirt under a black button-down shirt, open and untucked, sleeves rolled up to the elbows. Black hair in a loose bun, a discreet diamond nose-stud her only item of jewelry.

She was smiling. Showing white teeth, lighting up her expression, reflecting the joy in her eyes. A joy I never saw in her while she lived. The source of her joy was obvious. The woman she held hands with: Black, with deep and rich chocolate skin, hair buzzed close to her scalp and dyed blond, eyes bright and happy, smile matching Lilly's in every ounce of her joy.

They walked past, oblivious to my presence. I turned and stared after them as they melted into the crowd, telling myself it wasn't Lilly. It *couldn't* be. Even so, I craned my neck, trying in vain to pick her out of the people hugging the bar.

The woman squeezed my hand, sending a new wave of desire pulsing through me. I turned and followed her as she tugged me through the front door and out into the parking lot. "My car is over here. Let's . . . "

An aching pressure built in my head, swelling against my skull, dousing my arousal. I yanked my hand from hers and staggered away, pressing both sides of my head, which felt twice its size. Images—dozens of them, *hundreds* of them—flooded my mind as all my memories of Lilly came rushing back.

Something twisted deep inside my head, and *snapped*. The pain vanished.

I straightened and stared at the woman, heart pounding, stomach clenching, ears ringing. "What . . . what did you do to me? What *are* you?"

Whatever allure the woman had held was gone. My body no longer thrummed with lust when I looked at her. Physically, she didn't appear any different—but instead of desire, I felt disgust. Her eyes no longer swirled with an entrancing green, either. Maybe it was because I was drunk, or maybe it was dark outside, but her eyes were twin pools of the deepest black I'd ever seen. Almost liquid, pulsing in her sockets.

She approached me slowly, with the casual menace of a confident predator. "You can't save her," she said in a deep, gravelly voice. "You can never save her. No matter how hard you try. It's too late. It will always be too late."

Something compelled me away from her. An urge which

demanded me to get out of there. I was still drunk, though, so I stumbled and lurched when I tried to sidestep her advance. She closed the distance in a flash, hand striking like a snake, latching onto my throat with a vise-like grip, cutting off my air. To my horrified astonishment, she lifted me several feet off the ground. Fingernails digging into my skin. She brought my face close to hers, her mouth opening impossibly wide, showing more teeth than a human should possess.

She stopped. Nostrils flaring like an animal picking up an awful scent. Whatever she smelled displeased her. Disgust rippled across her features as she hissed, *"You're not ready."*

With a heave, she dashed me to the ground like a ragdoll. My head crashed into the asphalt parking lot. Darkness rushed in, but as I lay there, head throbbing, I saw her turn smartly on one heel and walk toward a car. Its red taillights burned against the night as its grumbling engine roared to life. The passenger side door opened on its own. She got in, slamming the door shut behind her. The car— midnight black, its finish glinting under the orange parking lamps—backed out of its parking spot, and sped out onto the road. I dimly registered it as looking like Jimmy Graves' Monte Carlo before I passed out, and knew no more.

27.

October 30ᵗʰ
9:00 AM

I WOKE THE next morning with an even worse hangover than the last. The light filtering through the bedroom's blinds made my forehead throb. When I moved, my stomach rippled, and gorge was rushing up my throat as I scrambled from the bed and stumbled to the bathroom. I barely made it to the toilet in time. I seemed to vomit forever, my head pounding with each heave.

After what felt like hours, I crawled back into bed. Somehow making it under the covers, cursing myself for letting the new job and source of cash go to my head last night at Hyland's. Eventually I'd have to get up, gather myself, and spend the afternoon finishing Cabin 2's roofing. A prospect I didn't look forward to.

Lying there, my thoughts took an odd turn. For some reason, I thought about one of the movies I'd watched during my most recent binge. *Def by Temptation*, briefly staring Samuel L. Jackson, also starring James Bond III (seriously), who also wrote, directed, and produced. In it, an evil succubus is determined to destroy a pastor-in-training (played by James Bond III, son of dead preacher Samuel L. Jackson) by any means necessary.

As I drifted off, for some reason I was thinking about what a succubus would be like if it ate not blood or energy, but memories. Especially painful ones. Sleep blurred those thoughts, however, before that train of thought could go further.

28.

1:00 PM

SOMEHOW I EVENTUALLY dragged myself out of bed, showered, dressed, ate some toast and drank a lot of water. By noon I was able to start working on Cabin 2's roof. I wasn't exactly excited about it. Regardless, I set myself to the task, and estimated I'd finish by six or so.

By three, however, my head was pounding again, and my stomach was finally rumbling for something more substantial than toast. The manager (whose name was Terry) hadn't been tracking my progress at all, so I had enough time for a quick break to hydrate and make a sandwich.

Instead of sitting and eating in the cabin, however, I wandered outside, initially intending on sitting at one of the picnic tables in front of the main building. Across the road, the man was again sitting in his chair before his little yellow clapboard house, keeping watch over who knew what. He saw me and raised a hand in greeting. I bit from my sandwich and crossed the road toward him.

As I drew near, it occurred to me I'd never asked his name. I thought that odd. Even odder, I had no inclination to ask him his name any time soon.

"You've been busy the past few days," he said by way of greeting. "I see Old Man Kretzmer found someone to give him a deal on cabin roofing."

I raised an eyebrow. "Old Man Kretzmer?"

"Archie Kretzmer. He owns The Lodge. Owns the Mobilmart on Haverton Road, and The Golden Kitty, also. Not so's you'd ever know it, though. He's somewhat of an 'absentee owner'. Lets his managers run things. Not much for making appearances." The man grunted. "Hell, I don't even remember the last time I actually *saw* Kretzmer. He's quite the recluse these days."

The man gave me a piercing look. "The Lodge manager paying you okay? Not low-balling you or anything?"

I shrugged, because of course I'd "low-balled" myself by bidding half under the other contractors. Certainly couldn't complain about not getting paid enough. "It's enough. I've been looking for a job the past few days and coming up empty. I was honestly getting a little desperate, so this worked out okay."

The man closed the book in his lap and said, "I didn't ask so as not to be intrusive. It really isn't my business what you're doing in Clifton Heights. But I'm going to make a deductive leap and guess that whatever or whomever you've left behind, you're not going back. Hence the lack of funds."

I finished my sandwich, chewed and swallowed, and put my hands into my pockets. When I'd first arrived in Clifton Heights, I'd felt reluctant to talk about my past. Maybe I'd still harbored notions of returning home, someday. Of finding a new way. As my time in Clifton Heights had grown increasingly stranger, however, I'd grown ever more aware I most likely wouldn't return from the path I'd chosen. I had no idea what lay at the end of it, but I felt freer now, discussing what had led me here.

"You're right. I won't be going back. I can't. I no longer believe in what I was doing and why I was doing it. It just . . . took and took and took, and never gave back. And those I've left behind . . . " I looked away, guts twisting with guilt and remorse. "I don't think they want me back. Don't want anything to do with me. I've tried to contact them a few times, and . . . " I faced the man. "It's like, to them, I don't exist anymore. Whatever that means."

The man raised his eyebrows and gave me an odd look. "Have you considered actually *leaving* Clifton Heights? Going home? This town can feel . . . strangely cut off from the outside world, at times. The normally reliable ways of communicating often become unreliable with little or no warning. Especially for newcomers who haven't acclimated, yet."

I grunted. "Things normally reliable become unreliable, huh? Like if I call a phone number and order pizza from a place called Pizza Joe's half a dozen times, and after getting delivery from them every time, but when I try to drive there, Google Maps directs me to a thirty-year-old pile of rubble?"

Though it was probably my imagination, I felt the weight of the man's gaze from behind his sunglasses. "Did the pizza boxes *say* Pizza Joe's on them?"

"No. They're generic pizza boxes lots of places use."

"Did the delivery guy wear a uniform or hat with Pizza Joe's on it?"

That I hadn't thought of. "No," I admitted, "every time the guy—the *same* guy, I might add—wore a red polo shirt and a red ball cap. No name on them."

The man shrugged. "There you go. Must've ordered from somewhere else by accident. Maybe the phone numbers got crossed up. Happens often enough out here. Could be why you can't get hold of anyone at home."

I looked at him skeptically. "That sort of thing happens 'often enough out here'?"

He shrugged. "You get used to it, after a while." He paused, his face assuming an expression I couldn't decipher. "Has *he* come around recently?"

My confusion must've shown on my face. He shifted, sat forward, and said, "The one I warned you about. Our local . . . conman."

"Ah. Jimmy Graves, you mean?"

The man winced and sat back. He sighed heavily. "You need to take care, son. There's some names which shouldn't ever be spoken aloud, lightly."

I was about to ask him why when a distant rumble from up the hill distracted me. I looked, already knowing what I'd see.

A shiny black 1977 Monte Carlo. Slowly coming around the curve, down the hill toward us. It drove at a leisurely pace, and for some reason, I was reminded of the strange woman I'd met at Hyland's last night—the one who, according to my hazy memories, had hit on me, then acted badly when I declined.

The car rolled to a stop before us. The tinted window slid down with a hum, revealing the smiling face of Jimmy Graves.

"Speak of the devil," the man said softly.

"Wes! Glad I caught you. Was thinking of you the other day. Still up for a ghost-tour on Halloween night?"

I didn't look at the man sitting in his chair, but I could almost feel his displeasure as I nodded, "Sure. Sounds like a great time."

Jimmy slapped the steering wheel. "Fantastic! You won't be disappointed, Wes. I promise."

"Afternoon, Jimmy," the man said from his chair. His voice sounded different, somehow. Older. Colder, with stern authority.

Jimmy looked past me, as if he hadn't seen the man when he'd pulled up (somehow, I knew this was an act). His smile grew. "Well, well. I see you've made a new friend, old timer! Good for you!"

Something twisted in Jimmy's features, turning his smile into a sneer. "You don't have many of those left. Do you?"

I felt the man's anger simmering behind me, like a cresting wave.

Jimmy's unpleasant expression faded, replaced by his amiable grin. He looked at me and said, "He's a card, that one is. Tells great stories, but don't believe them all! He *loves* pulling people's legs. Tells some real crackers. Especially the one about us being the same age."

The man finally responded. "You're just vainer than I am. Obsessed with keeping up appearances is all."

Jimmy tossed his head back and laughed uproariously. Wiping tears from his eyes, he said through chuckles, "See what I mean? This guy's *hilarious*."

"Yeah," came the disgruntled reply, "I'm a laugh a minute."

"Anyway," Jimmy said, calming down, "I'll pick you up tomorrow night. Eight sound good? I'll give you a proper tour of this strange old town."

He stuck his hand out the driver's side window. "Deal?"

It seemed an odd formality. Shaking over a ghost tour. In a split second, gears turned in my head as I thought of how the man sitting in his chair hadn't ever spoken Jimmy's name, not once. I thought of another movie I'd watched on my recent binge. *Madman*. A simplistic but oddly entertaining movie about an evil and undying serial killer summoned by anyone who speaks his name aloud.

Just like I'd spoken Jimmy's.

I took his hand. It had a pleasant, dry grip. "Wouldn't miss it."

He shook, released my hand, and offered another dazzling, white-toothed grin. "Excellent! I'll see you tomorrow night."

The tinted window hummed up, hiding him from view. The Monte Carlo—it's black finish swimming like oil— pulled away from the road's shoulder and rumbled down the hill, into town.

I expected the man to say something, but instead heard nothing. Surprised, I glanced behind me and felt even more surprise when I saw his empty chair. He had gone. Probably back inside his little yellow clapboard house.

I stood there for a moment, staring at the yellow house, thinking. At the end of *Madman*, the surviving female camp counselor willingly enters the madman's lair to confront him. I couldn't help relating my upcoming ghost tour with Jimmy Graves to entering the madman's lair, and I wondered what fate I'd meet.

29.

8:00 PM

I'D FINISHED CABIN 2's roof and was just starting Cabin 3's when I called it quits around seven. I worked at a leisurely pace after talking with Jimmy Graves and the man in his chair, so it took me a little longer than the previous day. While I worked, my hands operated on remote as my mind turned over thoughts about phantom pizza joints, malfunctioning GPS, old stone chapels, and reflections of my dead daughter.

7 PM came quickly. As before, Terry paid me in cash for the day's work. I showered, changed, and decided to walk into town for something to eat. The Skylark Diner was closest, and best of all, *wasn't* a bar. I had no intentions of replicating last night's experience.

I enjoyed an excellent hamburger and steak fries which somehow tasted better than any burger or fries I'd ever eaten. As I'd expected, I didn't see Art or Georgie in their booth. Hadn't seen them since the day Georgie told me about the old stone chapel. Even more, I was starting to believe they were both figments of my imagination. The thought bothered me more than it should.

After I ate I walked the streets, enjoying the various Halloween decorations of the homes and shops. Over the past few days, like a great slumbering beast finally waking, Clifton Heights' Halloween Spirit was coming alive. Jack-o'-lanterns flickered on more and more porches. Front lawns were transformed in diverse tableaus of the macabre. Zombies rising from graves, mummies lurching from coffins, ghosts hanging from trees, and contemporary monsters like Jason Vorhees, Freddy Krueger and Michael

Myers lurked about. Some houses went all-out, featuring huge animatronic skeletons, witches, and evil clowns on their front yards. Others offered simpler fare. Black and orange streamers, cardboard black cats, amiable ghosts, and friendly Jack-o'-lanterns in windows.

As I traveled Clifton Heights' sidewalks, listening to my shoes scuffing concrete and crunching brittle autumn leaves, I felt both pleasure and sadness as I took in the sights. Lilly would've loved all this. She always begged us to drive around town during the Halloween season so she could see the neighbors' decorations.

Of course, Beth wouldn't hear of it. No matter how many times I broached the matter behind closed doors. My oldest son reprimanded Lilly, saying it was dangerous to enjoy something so "worldly." My youngest told Lilly it would be boring. I, of course, said nothing.

I could've taken her myself. Picked her up from school early. Or we could've sneaked out on a weekend. But if anyone saw us, it wouldn't have looked good to the congregation. Their pastor driving his daughter around to look at all the "pagan" Halloween decorations. So of course I never did.

As I randomly turned onto Clinton Avenue, I heard a gentle murmur which sounded like a crowd talking as they waited anxiously for something to begin. Down the avenue I saw a line of people on the sidewalk in front of a stately old Victorian house. It was the most lavishly decorated of all the Halloween exhibits I'd seen so far. Fake spiderwebs draped the siding. Different kinds of animatronics hung out of every front window. Witches, vampires, zombies, evil clowns and evil little girls. I craned my head to look around the crowd and saw the front lawn made over into a meticulous rendition of a graveyard . . .

not dissimilar to the graveyard around the stone chapel
    . . . replete with zombies bursting from the ground.

Draped across the front porch a banner read in garish horror font: *Feldpausch Horror House!*

I smiled sadly, thinking how much Lilly would've loved going into a scare house such as this. She'd never broached the subject (probably didn't dare to) but somehow I knew houses like these and scare parks would've been right up her alley.

I stumbled to a halt and stared, my hands shaking in my pockets, my mouth hanging open slightly as an invisible hand squeezed my heart. At the doorway a woman wearing white face paint and vampire fangs, dressed in a tattered Victorian dress splattered with fake blood, admitted groups into the scare house. She looked as if she could've stepped straight from an Anne Rice novel. Though I couldn't hear her words clearly, she spoke with a grandiose tone and gestured emotively, so I assumed she was playing her role to the hilt as she admitted customers. It wasn't her I was staring at, however.

It was Lilly.

Again.

Another Lilly I'd never seen and would never see. Not the grown-up and self-assured Lilly I'd seen at Hyland's last night (though that memory was still fuzzy, something about a woman trying to take me home?), but also not the moody, depressed and withdrawn Lilly I'd known (and failed) before her suicide. This Lilly looked like she was maybe nineteen. She'd moved out of her punk/all-black phase, into what looked like a more original phase. Hair dyed a bright pink, wearing an obscure anime t-shirt cut at the midriff (which would've driven Beth to apoplexy), and cargo pants.

While sixteen year old Lilly had worn sullenness like a second skin, and adult Lilly looked well-adjusted and even happy, this Lilly giggled, laughed and bounced on her toes in excitement, seemingly unable to keep still as she chatted with her friends as they waited their turn to enter Feldpausch House. Expression animated, eyes wide and gleaming, white teeth flashing as she talked excitedly. She fairly vibrated with energy.

The Victorian vampire mistress gestured grandly to the front door. Lilly and her friends squealed and, clutching each other, clambered into the darkness beyond.

I joined the line and waited my turn.

**

I wasn't sure what the point of this was. Lilly and her friends were at least twenty people before me. By the time I entered Feldpausch House, she and her group would be through and well on their way. Even so, I felt compelled to follow her, even if at a distance. Which, of course, replicated my parenting of her. Always at a distance. A *safe* distance.

Twenty minutes later, a young man dressed in remarkably authentic period dress and makeup which had transformed him into the Hunchback of Notre Dame, accepted my $20 admission fee and secured a paper wristband on me. Ten minutes later I stood on the porch with four guys receiving the Victorian vampire mistress's over-the-top introduction. I listened with only half an ear, staring into the doorway's darkness, where Lilly had disappeared thirty minutes before.

The Victorian vampire said something ridiculously overwrought, then gestured us toward the doorway. I strode forward, ignoring those behind me.

I stepped into darkness.

The others followed, muttering to each other. Their banter sounded good-natured but predictably edgy. I felt nothing. And it made me sad. I should've been enjoying this. Heart pounding, adrenaline flowing, breath short and rapid. Instead, it just felt like one more thing I was compelled to do, whether I wanted to or not.

The door slammed shut behind us, plunging the hallway into absolute darkness. My fellow travelers shouted and swore, laughing shakily and complaining with mirth. I stood and said nothing.

A low, wailing moan drifted down the hall toward us. Clearly from hidden speakers, but the others reacted with the expected shouts. As the wail faded, dim green lights flared to life on the walls, filling the corridor with their haze. Impatient and not willing to wait for those behind me, I plunged ahead, consumed by the irrational notion that somewhere in here, Lilly was trapped, and only I could save her.

You can't save her
it's too late
always too late

My quick strides left the others behind. I felt sure they'd be grateful, because my absence would allow them to enjoy themselves without having a stranger in their midst. For my part, I wasn't about to let others slow me down.

The corridor stretched on forever, longer than seemed possible. Garish, horrific portraits hung on the walls. Scenes of torture and bloodshed straight from Gustav Dore's portrayal of hell, but I ignored them all. I also ignored the fake spiders and bats attached to the walls and ceiling. As I approached a closed door to my right, I clenched my fists in anticipation . . .

The door slammed open and a werewolf leaped out, snarling, saliva drooling from its maw. In daylight it probably looked fake, its fur stiff and artificial and its maw and fangs rubbery and manufactured, but in the hall's garish green glow it looked real, and the body it was dragging behind it . . .

Its head lolled over. In the surreal green lighting, I saw eight-year-old Lilly's dead, staring face. Her throat was torn open, exposing pink flesh and white gristle. My previous indifference dissolved, replaced by real, heart-squeezing fear.

"Can't . . . can't save her. Ever."

I wasn't sure if the werewolf said that, really. It spoke mostly in guttural snarls and yips. However, as I glanced from the dead and mauled eight-year-old Lilly to the werewolf, I saw the truth in its blazing yellow eyes. Eyes which looked too real. I couldn't save her. Ever.

The werewolf roared at me again. I couldn't help flinching. In glee, the werewolf pointed its snout to the ceiling and howled. Then it yanked eight-year-old dead Lilly and dragged her back through the doorway.

The door slammed shut.

I heard it, through the door. Thick and wet ripping sounds. Chewing. Slurping. Feeding.

My stomach twisted. I lurched forward, but no matter how fast I stumbled to the hallway's end, the sound of feeding followed.

**

I saw countless versions of Lilly die. Somewhere in the back of my mind I understood my trip through Feldpausch Horror House couldn't have taken that long. It couldn't possibly have so many rooms, it couldn't possibly be so big. I stumbled on, however, never once trying to turn back. I viewed each atrocity with a detached numbness, as if somehow the connection between me and my soul had been severed by an unseen hand.

And I was utterly alone. The others in my group never caught up with me, nor did I run into any other groups. I also knew that—if anyone else was in this house besides me—they weren't seeing what I saw. I'm sure they were treated to all the cliché elements of a scare house. Monsters, ghouls, and demons played by half-hearted local actors, and decorations which would look ridiculous in the daylight. My visions of torment were for me, alone.

Eight-year-old Lilly, devoured by a werewolf behind a closed door.

In a lavish boudoir the adult Lilly I saw at Hyland's lay prone on a voluminous bed of white, wearing a white gown, staring sightless at the ceiling while a woman who looked strikingly like the one who'd hit on me at Hyland's last night ravaged her neck, feeding hungrily on her flesh and blood. The woman paid no attention to me as she ate and drank. Bright arterial blood squirted from Lilly's neck in crimson fountains.

In a blood-splattered operating theater, a mad doctor (which looked dishearteningly like Beth) injected a long, gleaming, wickedly pointed needle into sixteen-year-old Lilly's neck, with a great flourish and a violent thrust. Blood and glowing green fluid spurted from the injection point. Lilly thrashed in a bone-wrenching seizure, arms flopping and legs jerking, head whipping back and forth. Face contorted in pain unimaginable, dead eyes wide and empty.

I saw baby Lilly. She was naked, screaming, with a vaguely satanic symbol painted on her belly in blood. Red-robed cultists held her aloft in a dimly lit grotto (I didn't question how a grotto could be so authentically replicated in a house; the question was moot, by then). They placed my crying baby on an altar, and I turned my head as the cultists' chanting rose to a crescendo. I knew if I saw the knife plunge into my little girl, I would truly, indeed go mad.

Baby Lilly screamed once, then fell silent.

As I stumbled blindly past, I knew I couldn't deny that two of the cultists looked like Beth and I.

One room opened into a starlit field (which made no sense, I knew) where a pack of zombies chased down a screaming eighteen-year-old Lilly with neon green hair. She never had a chance. In no more than four or five strides, the fast and ravenous zombies pounced on Lilly and dragged her to the ground. Decaying ligaments and rotten organs pulsed through their tattered skin. Shattered and broken teeth dug into her flesh and tore out muscle in great bloody chunks. She disappeared beneath their withered and gray limbs, her screams quickly replaced by the sounds of their frenzied feeding. Zombies which, despite their decayed and ruined features, looked hauntingly like members of my old congregation.

It went on.

Much longer than was possible.

Uncountable versions of my dead daughter, killed in horrific, grotesque ways; killed in subtle, mundane ways. Hung, stabbed, dismembered, drowned, gored to death, sacrificed, electrocuted, poisoned, killed over and over . . .

Until the last.

I stumbled through one last doorway, my sanity held together by bare threads. I swayed on my feet, looking dully upon the final—and the worst—display of Lilly's death.

She hung from a cross. Naked. Somehow, I knew she represented the embodiment of every Lilly there'd ever been, and never was. She'd been cut and slashed all over, ribs and thighs crossed with long red welts.

Beth faced her, holding a whip. It wasn't just any whip, either. It was a scourge whip, embedded with nails. The same whip Roman soldiers used on Christ before His crucifixion.

Silently, with a wooden expression, Beth cranked her arm back and snapped the scourge at Lilly. It struck Lilly, carving bright red trenches across her abdomen and upper thigh. Trenches which instantly welled with blood.

Beth reared the whip back again and delivered another cracking blow, this time peeling back strips of flesh at Lilly's hip and ribs, exposing quivering muscle and ribbons of gristle. Another strike dug deep into Lilly's left shoulder.

With each blow, Lilly's body shook. Otherwise, she didn't move. Never flinched, or tried to avoid a blow. She made no sounds, and she stared into the middle distance because, of course, she was already dead.

Beth struck her face with the scourge, laying the cheek open to the bone, exposing a quivering white sack which was most likely her nasal cavity. It slipped free and sagged down Lilly's face in a wash of blood and water. Beth continued to destroy Lilly's face, each slash of the scourge gouging out eyes, raking her forehead, until nothing but shredded meat remained where my daughter's face had been.

Next to her, a vision of me stood. Silent, motionless, doing nothing. Face slack and eyes just as dead as Lilly, hands hanging uselessly.

I sank to my knees and squeezed my eyes shut, but it didn't matter. The image of my wife flaying our daughter had been burned into my brain. I didn't sob or cry out, I didn't scream or rage. I simply fell away inside myself, all senses fading, until all I heard was the *hiss-crack* of the scourge snapping into the air.

***

"Hey, buddy. You okay?"

A hand gently squeezed my shoulder. I blinked, awareness leaking back into me, and looked up at the person standing over me. I didn't know his name, but I recognized him. He'd been one of the strangers admitted into Feldpausch House with me.

I was sitting on the curb of Clinton Avenue, just past Feldpaush House. Full night had fallen, and Johann Sebastian Bach's "Toccata and Fugue in D Minor"—that creepy organ riff everyone knows—blared from Feldpausch House's outside speakers. A line twice as long trailed down the sidewalk away from the entrance.

"You okay, pal? That last room was a doozy."

I looked back at the man and nodded, whispering, "Yeah. I'm fine. Just a little shook up is all."

The man smiled. "I don't blame you. These things usually don't rattle me . . . but that was *intense.*"

I thought about asking his thoughts on the last exhibit, but decided against it, already knowing he hadn't seen what I had. "Yeah," I said. "It sure was."

He nodded down the sidewalk, where his friends—the others in our group—stood talking animatedly about their experience. "I'm heading out with my friends. Sure you're okay?"

I wasn't, of course, but I ran an amazingly steady hand through my hair and said, "Yeah. I'm good. Gonna rest here a bit, then call a cab."

He patted my shoulder again. "All right then. Have a good night." He walked away and then, as an afterthought, tossed over his shoulder, "Happy Halloween!"

I raised a hand. "You too."

He nodded again and walked away.

I put my head in my hands and kneaded my forehead with my fingertips. The various images of Lilly's multiple deaths layered over one another, one bleeding into the next. Killed by every kind of monster possible. Zombies. Vampires. Witches. Occultists. Mad scientists. Werewolves. Ghosts. And the worst monsters of all: her parents.

I rubbed my face, raised my head, and looked down night-shrouded Clinton Avenue. Jack-o'-lanterns offered glowing smiles to the darkness from dozens of porches. Behind me, Bach's eerie organ tune kept blaring. The line of people waiting their turn buzzed in anticipation.

Despite my breakdown at the end, I realized what I'd seen in Feldpausch House was almost too over-the-top to be taken seriously, taken as a whole. Every monster conceivable had killed Lilly, and though I'd felt fear every time, it had been muted and distant. The only time the fear felt visceral and cutting was when Beth and I killed Lilly. Beth directly, and me indirectly, by my inaction.

It reminded me (unsurprisingly) of a ridiculous movie I watched years ago when Beth spent one weekend at her sister's. This was before kids, before a ministry, back when folks were still renting and watching VHS tapes. Back then I could visit the local video store and rent what I wanted, with no worries about what the "community" or the "congregation" thought. Regardless, guilt still nipped at my heels the whole time, like I was slipping off to a strip club or X-rated Adult Video store in the dead of night.

I came across *Spookies* right away. A buxom blond in a

white dress menaced by a dizzying array of monsters. The movie was labeled as a "night of unrelenting terror". I took the box off the shelf and to the front desk, telling myself I was renting it for the "unrelenting terror" and not the buxom blond.

What I saw in Feldpausch House (with the exception of the truly horrifying last scene) reminded me of *Spookies* because, just like in the movie, there was too much to process. In *Spookies* the initial monster effects were moderately impressive (especially for such a low-budget movie), but by the end of such a long-winded and confusing menagerie of monsters, I no longer cared.

Also, I was starting to feel as if my life was being run by the same confused mage who spent the entirety of *Spookies* muttering a nonsensical over-arching narrative which seemed to have little to do with the action playing out on the screen. None of the varied and ill-fitting parts of the story seemed to work together in any kind of conceivable way.

As I slowly, achingly stood, I wanted to tell myself that's what my life had become. A nonsensical hodge-podge of story elements which didn't fit together or make sense. But as I started walking back to The Motor Lodge (I didn't call a cab; I didn't want to deal with people at that moment), I knew that wasn't true. Since returning from my walk to the stone chapel, I'd seen different versions of Lilly menaced by threatening figures who told me I couldn't save her. I'd also encountered an entrancing woman at Hyland's (whom I barely remembered, but now thought of as a succubus), who'd tried to get me to forget Lilly in a real way.

Tomorrow night, a stranger who drove a strange black car was taking me on a "ghost tour" of Clifton Heights, a tour another stranger—a man who sat in his chair all day long watching over Clifton Heights—warned me against.

My life wasn't a hodge-podge of disparate parts with no meaning, much as I wished it was. It had a terrifying meaning; one I didn't want to face.

KEVIN LUCIA

30.

October 31ˢᵗ

WHEN I FINALLY made it to The Motor Lodge, I went into my cabin and straight to bed. I didn't drink myself into oblivion and I didn't watch any more horror movies. I felt beyond that. I walked numbly into the bedroom, stripped naked (oddly, the first time I'd never felt guilty for sleeping nude), slipped in bed beneath the covers, and fell asleep immediately.

I didn't dream.

Halloween morning, I woke without fanfare at ten. I ate another breakfast of cereal and toast. Afterward, I got into my car, and realized I wasn't going back to finish my work on Cabin 3's roof. Maybe today would be nothing more than another day. It might pass. I might wake up tomorrow with nothing changed. Maybe all my experiences since coming to Clifton Heights were products of a mind broken by guilt and remorse, a soul weighed down by exhaustion. Jimmy Graves was nothing more than a small-town grifter. The old man sitting in his chair an eccentric coot. Maybe it all meant nothing.

But maybe it meant everything. Either way, as I pulled out of The Motor Lodge's parking lot, I decided today wasn't a day to spend fixing roofs. Halloween had always been celebrated as a time of transition. When thresholds between worlds were crossed. I was going to cross a threshold of my own before its end, and I believed no matter what the outcome, I'd be changed by it, forever.

***

I drove around in a daze that morning. I wandered from place to place, my mind running on autopilot. I visited The

Skylark Diner and mechanically ate lunch, no longer concerned about conserving my funds. Art and Georgie weren't there. I'd expected they wouldn't be, of course. By then I felt more and more sure they'd somehow never existed in the first place. Even so, I was disappointed not to see them.

I visited Arcane Delights, but the friendly girl with the Pride earrings wasn't working. A man my age was. The store's owner, probably. I browsed the horror section, but left without buying anything, feeling strangely certain I wouldn't be needing books anytime soon.

I saw signs for KAMINSKY'S HALLOWEEN CORN MAZE. On a whim, I followed them to a sprawling farm on the town's outskirts. Cars and trucks filled a gravel parking lot. A large wooden sign directed visitors not only to the corn maze, but also to a pumpkin patch.

I spent an hour wandering the corn maze. The air felt pleasantly crisp, with a light breeze which sifted the corn stalks as I walked through them, bringing up memories of not only the farm back home, but also *Children of the Corn*. I didn't feel as if something malignant walked behind these rows, however. More like something watchful. Something waiting. In a way, it felt vaguely comforting.

The corn maze was aptly decorated at random intervals with mannequins dressed as various monsters. The usual vampires, ghosts, zombies, and also more contemporary villains such as Leatherface, Jason Vorhees, and Michael Myers lurked among the cornstalks. In daylight they looked merely amusing. At night, I imagine more chilling.

I didn't see Lilly.

I hadn't expected to. For some reason I felt if I was going to see her again, it wouldn't be until tonight, on Jimmy Graves' ghost tour.

Other folks wandered through the corn maze. Oddly enough, they paid no attention to me. They talked with each other and enjoyed themselves, but no matter how many passed me by, not a single person acknowledged my presence. After a time, I had to repress an odd urge to start bumping shoulders with them, just to see if they'd notice me. I felt relieved when I exited the maze without doing so. What if I'd bumped into someone . . . and they hadn't noticed?

What then?

31.

BEFORE GETTING INTO my car, I browsed the pumpkin patch, following a half-formed thought about buying a pumpkin to carve into a jack-o'-lantern. Obviously, considering the Good Reverend Ford's thoughts on Halloween, I'd never had the pleasure. The only time I'd asked if we could as a kid, I received a lengthy explanation about the legend surrounding jack-o'-lanterns—that the light inside represented the fires of the devil. Being "faithful to God" meant "hating the things of the world." Beth, of course, never allowed our kids to carve jack-o'-lanterns either.

When I was single, before I met Beth, I never carved one for myself. So strong did my father's admonitions against it echo in my mind.

As I browsed a field of pumpkins in all shapes and sizes, I decided to buy one. I would carve my first—and most likely *only*—jack-o'-lantern. I found a suitable one quickly enough. Almost perfectly spherical, about the size of my head.

On my way to pay, I passed a slightly grizzled, older man and a younger helper busily loading pumpkins into the back of a restored red 1945 Ford pickup. The older man wore denim overalls, a denim jacket, and a wide-brimmed straw hat. His gravelly voice rasped in an oddly familiar way. I thought I'd heard it before (or one just like it), but as I paid for my pumpkin, I couldn't quite place it. As I walked to my car, the red truck—its back full of pumpkins—drove past. The younger man must've told a joke, because the older man was laughing through his rolled-down window. His laugh cackled, and I knew who it reminded me of. Yet another horror movie hearkening back to my days watching horror movies with my loading dock friends.

Hack-O-Lantern. One of those terrible horror movies which was great fun to watch. As a young seminary student, I'd expected the movie's portrayal of the occult and Satanism to unnerve me, given the horror stories I'd been fed my whole childhood—but instead I found myself laughing at the oafish redneck cult leader grandfather and his redneck Satan worshipers. The man in the red truck at Kaminsky's resembled the Satanic grandfather perfectly. Right down to the cackling, raspy laugh.

It seemed ridiculous—in the face of everything I'd experienced so far—to think Clifton Heights played home to a Satanic Halloween Cult run by an over-the-top Satanic grandfather whose only wish in life was to recruit his grandson into his redneck Satanic Halloween cult. Based on what I *had* experienced, however, the idea didn't seem so implausible at all.

32.

Halloween Night
8:00

AS SEEMED BEFITTING, I watched the original *Halloween* (not that I have anything against Rob Zombie's remake) on the cabin's flatscreen as I hollowed out the pumpkin, scooping its stringy innards and seeds into a Tupperware bowl I found in a kitchen cupboard. Having never carved a pumpkin before, I was unprepared for the feel of its slimy, stringy inner matter sliding along my fingers.

As I cut out eyes, nose, and worked on the mouth, in the background, Dr. Loomis expounded on the nature of pure evil and its unrelenting destructiveness. I thought about how odd it was. Being raised to believe horror movies were so evil, when so many of them depicted stark divisions between good and evil, or spent most of their stories debating the nature of good and evil.

By the time *Halloween* ended and Laurie Strode—the original final girl—survived, I'd finished my first and most likely only jack-o'-lantern. I'd opted for a traditional look. Because I'd kept it simple, the first-time results weren't bad. If only life and parenting were as simple as carving pumpkins.

Satisfied with my finished product, I glanced at my phone and saw it was quarter to eight. Nearly time for Jimmy Graves to pick me up for my Halloween ghost tour of Clifton Heights. I picked up my jack-o'-lantern and went out to wait for him.

33.

**Halloween Night
8:00 PM**

AFTER POSITIONING MY jack-o'-lantern on Cabin 14's front porch, the tealight I'd purchased inside, I stepped back to admire my handiwork. It looked quite nice. Though electronic light wasn't quite as warm as candlelight, my jack-o'-lantern grinned brightly against the growing dark. I wished I could grin so brightly against my own darkness.

An engine rumbled up behind me, as if appearing from thin air. Tires crunched to a stop on gravel.

It was time.

I turned and appraised the Monte Carlo. It looked even blacker at night. Its glossy finish swam under the parking lot's halogen lights. Its engine thrummed, resonating deep in my guts, almost as if we were vibrating on the same harmonic.

Jimmy Graves didn't get out. He didn't honk the horn, rev the engine, or roll the window down. The Monte Carlo merely sat there. Staring me down, its engine throbbing.

I decided not to waste time. I rounded the car and reached for the passenger door handle. It felt ice-cold. So cold my fingers ached. Even so, I grabbed hold and pulled. The door swung open. I didn't look inside. For some reason, at that exact moment, I didn't want to.

No sound. No radio. Jimmy didn't speak. I put my hand on the roof of the car, but before I got in, I looked behind me, across the road. I could barely see the man sitting in his chair in front of his little yellow house. I had no doubt he could see me just fine. He offered a simple wave, nothing more. As if he understood nothing could stop me from taking Jimmy's tour. I waved back, got into the car, and pulled the door shut behind me.

34.

AS IF AN unseen hand flipped a cosmic switch, the Monte Carlo's radio blared to life soon as I shut the door, playing a tune which took me a few minutes to place. It clicked, finally. Heavily ironic, to say the least.

"Shout at the Devil" by Motley Crue.

Jimmy Graves sat in the driver seat, dressed exactly the same as every time I'd seen him. Smiling his wide, white-toothed smile. "Wes, my man. You ready for a night you'll never forget?"

I returned his smile, though my stomach twisted with the sudden certainty the man who sat in his chair was right. This was a mistake. Maybe my last.

"Absolutely."

Jimmy grinned wider and slapped the steering wheel. "Excellent! This is going to blow your mind, I promise."

He shifted the car into gear. We backed out of The Motor Lodge's parking lot, onto the road. I got a brief glimpse of my jack-o'-lantern grinning a flickering red-orange into the night. I was overcome by a wash of nostalgia for something I'd never experienced. I wondered what it felt like to return home from a night of trick or treating to the welcoming warm glow of your jack-o'-lantern's grin. I wondered if I would finally get to experience that welcome home tonight . . . if I returned.

***

At the bottom of the hill, we turned onto Main Street and then down a residential side street. Kids and teenagers dressed in every kind of costume imaginable populated the sidewalks. Younger ones hand-in-hand with their parents. Slightly older ones jogging just ahead of their parents, and teenagers traveling in their own packs. Almost every doorstep or porch had at least one jack-o'-

lantern glowing in the night, and lawns were decorated to the nines.

The Monte Carlo rumbled along, riding much smoother than I somehow thought such a big car would. "Shout at the Devil" had faded into another song, a vague tune by AC/DC which sounded familiar but I didn't recognize.

An especially boisterous group of adolescents scrambled by on the sidewalk outside, screaming in happiness. Jimmy chuckled and shook his head. "Ain't anything quite like trick or treating on Halloween night."

I shrugged and tried to ignore the buried disappointments rearing their heads. "I wouldn't know. We weren't allowed to when I was growing up. I never let my kids do it, either."

"Really?" Jimmy glanced at me, looking sorry. "That's too bad. Still," he looked ahead, expression turning thoughtful, "maybe that was for the best. Today's Halloween is tame, but its roots are ancient."

He glanced at me, eyes wide and gleaming. "There's a power to Halloween. A power which still survives today. It's out there, even now. Swirling around everyone, however innocent or ignorant they may be." He shrugged and looked back to the street. "Maybe protecting kids from Halloween is a good thing. Especially at such a young age."

He fell silent for several minutes. The only sound was the vague AC/DC tune playing on the radio, until I asked, "So where are we going?"

This brought Jimmy back to life. He glanced at me, smiling widely, eyes electric. "You love horror movies, right?"

I nodded, not bothering to ask *how* he knew I loved horror movies. It just seemed like something he'd know. "Sure."

"Ever see *Boys in the Trees*? Australian flick. Indie, but well done."

I shook my head. "No. Heard of it, but haven't gotten around to watching it yet."

KEVIN LUCIA

"Oh, it's a beautiful film. Wonderfully shot. Very atmospheric, and poetic. Not a 'horror' film, exactly . . . but definitely a Halloween film."

He gave me a strange look. "It's all about stories, Wes. How stories can be more real than real life. It's about the power of stories. What they can teach us. Each place we'll visit tonight has its own story. I'll share them with you. Hopefully they'll help you find your truth." He looked at me. "Because that's why you're here, isn't it? To find your truth."

I opened my mouth to answer, but before I could speak, I heard the man's voice whisper in my head: *he won't give you what you're looking for.*

I shrugged. "Maybe. Or, maybe I just want to see some spooky sights."

He grinned, serious demeanor vanishing into excitement. "That, I can promise you!"

***

Fifteen minutes and several turns later we left Clifton Heights' residential area and turned onto an asphalt road which looked like it hadn't been used in twenty years. It was heaved and cracked in places, going over to weed. Jimmy drove slowly, almost at a crawl. Five minutes in, we passed a leaning metal sign pock-marked with rust and bullet holes. It read: *Adirondack Scenic Railway.*

We broke from the trees into what used to be a fairly large gravel parking lot. Weeds, shrubs, and small trees had taken root across the lot. Jimmy pulled up to a long wooden building and parked. A sign on the building—once a brilliant maroon with gold letters and trim, now faded to the color of rust—bore the same legend as the rusted metal sign.

Jimmy grinned at me, showing too many teeth, his eyes wide. "Ready?"

I was already unbuckling my seat-belt and getting out. "After you."

***

Our destination wasn't the building—an old train station from when the Adirondack Scenic Railroad stopped at Clifton Heights, according to Jimmy—but an old boxcar at the far edge of the parking lot. Jimmy led the way with a flashlight, sketching out the train station's history as we walked past it and approached the old boxcar.

"Townsfolk don't like to talk about why this branch of the Adirondack Scenic Railroad shut down," he said conversationally. "Like lots of things in this town, there were plausible stories easy to swallow. 'No one rides trains anymore.' Or, 'kids today just don't appreciate history.' The *real* reason, of course, is that when they cleared this land to begin construction for the depot the summer of 1897, construction workers uncovered several Indian burial mounds. Not an entire graveyard, mind you, but even so." He shot me an amused look. "I know. How cliché can you get, right?"

"Where are the tracks?"

He gestured back to the building as we stopped at the old boxcar. "Behind the station, in the woods. That's where the boarding dock is. There wasn't any way to bring tracks into town, so that's why they built the depot out here. Anyhow, it never attracted much of a crowd. People just didn't like coming here. The rumors about passengers who vanished shortly after disembarking, strange-looking and quiet engineers depot staff didn't recognize, and consistent stories of a midnight train—when the Adirondack Scenic Railroad only ran between the hours of 9AM and 7PM—didn't help. The foot traffic died off so badly, it was decommissioned in 1994 when planned renovations never happened." He shrugged. "Did the depot shut down because of lack of interest, or because it was built on Indian burial mounds? Draw your own conclusions. Either way, people around town still insist they hear the midnight train passing through at the strike of twelve." He aimed the flashlight at the old boxcar. "In any case, *this* is what we're here to see."

He fell silent. I examined the boxcar under his flashlight's beam. Its wheels and undercarriage long gone, it sat crooked on the ground. Rust had consumed the car long ago, leaving no identifying marks. Strange-looking vines (reminding me uncomfortably of those vines I saw out past the old stone chapel), crawled over the car, inside and out. The boxcar was riddled with holes eaten away by rust, and the vines had woven their way through them. It was hard for me not to imagine the vines themselves eating holes in the metal.

Jimmy shone his flashlight through the boxcar's open door, illuminating piles of sodden clothes and mounds of other indistinguishable debris. In the gloom, I also saw what looked like an old wooden crate. Jammed into the crate, swollen objects which once may have been books.

Jimmy shifted the flashlight slightly. Next to the crate, I glimpsed the hollowed-out, rusted remains of what might've been a small, propane stove. Not unlike the one I'd seen my father use on our camp-outs.

"Someone lived in here," I murmured.

"Yes. Doesn't look like much now, but compared to what he'd grown up in, it felt like a king's castle to Edmund Glover. When he couldn't take any more of his father's beatings and his mother's excuses, he stuffed a ratty old bag bought at a thrift store in his hometown of Booneville and ran away, while his old man was sleeping off his latest drunk and his mother was slaving her fingers to the bone washing stained sheets at The Booneville Motel. He helped himself to whatever cash he could find—just recompense, he believed, for sixteen years of bruises, cuts, and cracked cheekbones—and left on a bright, sunny, Tuesday afternoon. After several days of wandering and sleeping in the woods, he eventually hitched a ride to Clifton Heights, and found a new home here."

He fell silent again.

I stared into the boxcar's shadowed depths. For some

reason I didn't want to look at Jimmy Graves, for fear I might find his face subtly changed into something alien and horrible. I cleared my throat and said, "What happened to him?"

"Do you truly wish to know?"

Part of me didn't. Part of me, however, knew I couldn't finish this night without knowing. "Yes."

"Well then."

***

The old boxcar next to Clifton Heights' abandoned train depot served Edmund Glover well for three glorious months. July, August, and September. The rust had yet to work its decay, so after sleeping outside for five nights (it rained on him two nights in a row), Edmund found the boxcar heavenly shelter. He dried his clothes in short order. The boxcar proved easy to make clean enough for his purposes.

He packed a few sandwiches and carried a jug of water with him, but the sandwiches went quickly, and despite the thick blackberry bush fortuitously growing next to the boxcar, food became an issue. After spending his first night in the boxcar on a metal floor and enduring a rumbling stomach, Edmund dressed in cleaner clothes, made himself as presentable as possible, and walked into Clifton Heights in search of food.

With the two hundred dollars he'd stolen from his mother and father, he bought enough food for two or three weeks from The Great American Grocery, wisely purchasing mostly nonperishable goods. Crackers, beef jerky, nuts and raisins, canned fruit and ravioli, bread, and even peanut butter. When he bought hot dogs or pre-made hamburgers, he only got enough to cook all at once. He also purchased a small assortment of plastic silverware, a metal plate for cooking over the fire, matches to make said fire, skewers for hot dogs and a spatula for hamburgers, and a can opener.

After two weeks, he bought a small propane camping

stove and a sleeping bag from The General Store, tired of sleeping on the boxcar's metal floor and trying to cook ravioli or soup in a can over a campfire. Because he worked hard to keep his clothes clean and he self-groomed as much as he could (there's a creek nearby to wash in), Edmund attracted little attention from the locals, even when buying his moderate amounts of camping gear.

Of course, it was summer. Clifton Heights was more wooded than Booneville, so kids his age camping out over the summer was probably common. He realizes now was the best time to buy such things, because in the winter, he would surely attract more attention.

Edmund shouldn't have worried about that, of course. He wouldn't make it past September.

Edmund found a surprising amount of reading material given away at the local library and used bookstore. Yellowed and worn paperbacks, musty cloth-bound hardcovers. He treated them like manna from heaven, because reading was his favorite thing to do. It was one of the many reasons why his father, Pete, always called him a *sissy pussy fag,* because he'd rather read and sometimes write than learn how to tune up a car or go hunting.

He always enjoyed fishing, however. It was one of the few things he and the old man had in common. One of the only things his father taught him. A pole, hooks, and a filleting knife are one of his earliest procurements from The General Store. The cashier raised his eyebrow at the filleting knife, but Edmund lied and said it was for his father. Though his filleting skills proved clumsy at first, he eventually got the hang of it. Every Saturday and Sunday afternoon he treated himself to a fresh-caught lunch of either small-mouth bass or panfish.

His first several weeks in the boxcar, Edmund worried someone from Booneville would come for him. The police, social workers, his parents. No one ever did. And why should they? To social workers in Booneville, white-trash runaways like him were a dime a dozen. Saying the CPS services in Booneville was overworked was like saying the desert was hot and the ocean was wet. Most of the cops were part-timers or weekend warriors whose love for the law extended to their love of wearing a uniform and a gun on their hip, no further.

And his parents?

His mother was probably relieved, because she'd no longer have to repress the daily nagging guilt at not lifting a finger to protect him. The only reason his father would come after him is the money, and Edmund believed his father no doubt saw the two hundred dollars a just price for getting his *sissy pussy fag* son out of his life for good.

This, however, isn't a story by Horatio Alger about a plucky young homeless boy who, through his undying perseverance, hard work, and unflagging optimism, pulls himself up by his own bootstraps and makes his way in the world. It may've begun that way, but it most assuredly won't end that way, because the universe wasn't a hopeful place where all a person needs is determination and a positive attitude to survive. It was a cold, merciless place which ate innocence alive and then shit it out without another thought.

Edmund's idyllic vagabond existence came to an end simply because he made a crucial mistake, one he can hardly be blamed for. We all want to fit in. Belong to something bigger than us. It's an essential part of human nature. Unfortunately, Edmund forgot another essential part of human nature. A darker, more ravening part.

The strong devoured the weak. Always.

Knowing his funds wouldn't last forever, Edmund looked for work with local farmers. Somewhere he can collect money under the table, no questions asked. He found such a place at the Drake farm, on the other side of town. Over the years Mr. Drake hired more than one young man such as Edmund to help bale and stack hay. Edmund was unused to such manual labor but after a week of trial and error, he learned well. Mr. Drake was gruff but patient. His fellow workers seemed like okay guys.

But they weren't.

Far from it. They smelled the difference in Edmund, though Edmund wasn't aware. He hadn't enough world experience to know how some detect people who are different like a wolf smells its prey from miles away.

His *father* knew he was gay. He'd raised him, after all. But Edmund had hidden this deep down inside. He believed that when his work friends invited him out for a few beers at The Stumble Inn, they were warming up to him. Accepting him as "one of the boys."

Of course Edmund had been drinking since age fourteen. It was how he'd survived the last two years. He'd never drank whiskey, however, and he was only sixteen. So after several shots of Wild Turkey, when they asked him where he was from, he drunkenly said nowhere, that he lived in an old boxcar up by the abandoned train depot.

One can only imagine how this information pleased his co-workers. To know he belonged nowhere, and to no one. After several more drinks and something one of the men dropped into his drink when he wasn't looking, Edmund descended into a deep, dark, walking blackness.

I suppose you know what happened next.

When Edmund woke the next morning, he was a twisted jumble of blazing pain. He woke face-down in the boxcar. Head feeling twice its normal size. Eyes swollen shut from being punched there repeatedly. His ribs throbbed. When he breathed, sharp stinging pain zapped through his lungs with each inhalation. Several of his teeth felt loose. When he spat, he expelled gobs of bloody mucus.

His pants were around his ankles. Everything *back there* felt raw, and also . . . greasy. Dirty. Next to him was a broken-off broom handle, smeared with dark clots of blood. When he shit, there was blood in his stool. He knew, then—without a doubt—what happened.

As the morning sun filtered into the boxcar, he saw it spray-painted on the wall: *Eat shit and die, fag. Next time, it won't be wood up your ass.*

For a brief moment, he thought of making his way to the police. Asking for help. But he chose not to. This was before Sheriff Baker, you see. A man of the law who actually gave a damn. Back then, the police in Clifton Heights were no different from those in Booneville. Edmund somehow knew it wouldn't be worth the effort.

As he tried to move around the boxcar, trying to manage something to eat, he also realized he'd never make it into work. Several of his ribs were most likely cracked. He probably had a concussion. And, as he lay against the boxcar's wall, he realized what they did to him with the broken-off broomstick damaged something inside. He hadn't stopped bleeding after taking a shit. Had bled through his pants, and realized he was bleeding elsewhere, too. Somewhere deep inside of him.

Edmund was still a stranger in Clifton Heights, so he knew nothing about the whispered stories of the depot's "midnight train." That night, after lying all day in an ever-widening puddle of his own blood, as he felt his life slowly slipping away, he didn't know what to think when he heard the piercing wail of a train whistle and the *roaring-clacking-hiss* of a train coming to a stop outside. And he cringed away—as best he could—from the strange-looking conductor (dressed in a style long out of date) who stepped soundlessly into the boxcar and approached him.

But when the conductor—who had no face, just a blank expanse of glowing white flesh—took his hand, Edmund stood, and his pain and despair fell away. A numbing peace descended over him. He left with the conductor and boarded the midnight train. Some say he still rides it today, as the train returns every year on Halloween night, searching for lost souls to join him.

The three men from Drake's farm who'd taken Edmund out for beers were found dead in one of the men's cars, sitting on McHenry Road, on the tracks, the only place in Clifton Heights where the old tracks crossed a road. While the car showed not a scratch, all three men were mangled beyond recognition. Limbs and heads torn off, their bodies ripped to pieces. Some say it looked as if they'd each been hit by a train and dragged for miles.

***

"Locals say if you come here at midnight on Halloween, you can hear the midnight train's whistle blow. As Edmund returns, looking for anyone as broken and lonely as he."

I blinked, disoriented, as images of a brutalized sixteen-year-old boy broke apart and faded. A cold shiver passed through me as I struggled to understand what had just happened. Why I felt so odd . . .

I leaned back and felt cold metal. I realized I was sitting on the floor of the boxcar, huddled against the wall, hugging my knees to my chest. Phantom pains ached all over. My face and especially eyes which, for a moment, felt swollen shut. I took a breath and my ribs burned sharply for a split second. I scrambled to my feet in panic, my feet banging echoes against the boxcar's floor, and pain . . . *down there*, the worst pain I'd ever felt . . . flared to life, then vanished.

I gaped at Jimmy Graves, standing in the boxcar's doorway. He wasn't smiling. His expression was blank and wooden. Eyes wide, deep, and dark. In a flat voice he asked, "Did you like that story?"

I tried to speak but couldn't as I felt my throat clench. I swallowed, then managed, "What . . . what the *hell* was that?"

Jimmy did smile then, only it was small, and mean-spirited. "It was a story. Like I said. Sometimes stories are truer than real life. If the storyteller is any good, the stories they tell take on an existence of their own. A real, tangible . . . sometimes *painful* existence."

His smile spread into a grin, nothing like the jovial expression I'd gotten used to, exposing many white teeth. "And I am an *excellent* storyteller. One of the best. Anyone will tell you."

I swallowed again. Closed my eyes and massaged my chest as I tried to slow my breathing. "Did that story actually happen? Was there an Edmund?"

"See for yourself."

I opened my eyes and looked where Jimmy pointed his flashlight, on the boxcar's wall behind me. A round circle of white light illuminated a partially faded spray-painted message. Most of it was lost to time, but the first part read:
Eat shit and die fag

I gathered myself and looked back at Jimmy. "Anyone could have painted that."

Jimmy shrugged. "Sure. But do *you* believe that?"

I didn't answer.

He nodded back toward his car. "Ready for the next stop? That one's even better."

I stood there for a moment, debating my options. Thinking about the man who sat in his chair, and his warning about trusting Jimmy Graves. For the first time, I consciously admitted to myself how dangerous Graves might be. His "story" had put me into Edmund's life, whether he'd existed or not. I'd felt everything he'd felt. Everything he'd experienced in the story—every violent and vile thing—*I'd* experienced.

And of course, even though nothing like that had ever happened to Lilly, she'd certainly been threatened with such things. By her "fellow Christians." It was part of what drove her to suicide. If I continued with Jimmy . . . what other "sights" would he show me? To what end?

he can't give you what you're looking for.

Something hard and stiff-necked rose inside. I nodded. He grinned wider, turned and walked back to his car. I followed. I had little other choice.

35.

THOUGH I'D SPENT the last few weeks in Clifton Heights, I'd stuck to Main Street, Raedeker Park and a few residential streets. I hadn't ventured into its countryside, so after Jimmy drove away from the abandoned depot and continued along nighttime backroads, I had no idea where we were headed.

The Monte Carlo's engine thrummed. The radio continued to blast generic 80s hard rock, but gone was Jimmy's chatty, upbeat banter. He drove in grim silence. Eyes firmly ahead. Hands gripping the steering wheel so tight his knuckles turned white. I realized then that even if I'd tried to escape back at the depot, I wouldn't have been able to. I'd shaken Jimmy Graves' hand, and come along willingly. My fate, whatever it might be, was sealed.

Eventually we turned right onto a narrow, rutted, one-lane dirt road. It cut through the woods. Trees crowded the road with overarching boughs forming a ceiling above us. After about ten minutes, the one-lane road widened into a small gravel clearing.

Jimmy parked the car. Said nothing and got out. I did likewise and followed him to the clearing's edge, where he stopped and shined his flashlight at what proved to be the rocky base of a large hill. Not a mountain, exactly. But not a knoll, either. His flashlight illuminated a gaping hole of darkness barred by a rotten wooden gate. On the gate hung a sign which read: DANGER.

He pointed his left hand in a vague direction behind us. "Back that way about three or four miles is the old French farm. Nothing but moldering debris now. Twenty years ago, it was the biggest farm in Clifton Heights. So big it employed most of the Clifton Heights teenage boys over the summers to get its work done. That wasn't enough help, however. So the French's did what many farming families did back then. They became experts at working the foster care system. They'd take on five to ten foster kids at once, so long as they were old enough and fit enough to work the farm year-round. The French's made sure they attended school at Clifton Heights High—*most* of the time—so it was a win-win for the Webb County Foster Care system. A daily regimen of hard work, discipline, order, and they attended school. *Mostly.* They were absent when the farm got busy, but the school didn't mind. Nor did the foster care system. Of course, there were rumors. Scandalous stories." Jimmy offered me a wry grin a little closer to the one I'd become used to. "Some of the foster kids complained of sub-par treatment. Of being locked in basement quarters more like prison barracks than anything else. Ungodly long work days, poor feeding, and cruel punishments. Also, girls complained of Mr. French and his teenage boys taking an undue liking to them. Also claiming the French's encouraged the male foster teenagers to have their way with the girls, too. Regardless of age. No one believed them, of course. Everyone saw them as juvies. Cast-offs. Attention-seeking riff-raff."

My stomach clenched, because of course I remembered—shortly after she'd entered her punk phase—when Lilly came to me with accusations of the Christian school Dean making advances when he called her into his office to "discuss her immoral behavior." Beth refused to let me pursue the matter, berating me into believing Lilly was acting out.

"That's why Josie did what she did. Why she had to put a stop to the abuse. Make sure the boys on that farm never touched her again. She lured them to her favorite hiding place," he gestured his flashlight at the black hole barred by the wooden gate reading DANGER, "this old silver mine, and made them pay."

***

Josie Travers had no memory of her birth family, having been removed from their care as a toddler. This was a blessing, because quite frankly, her birth parents weren't worth knowing, and their tawdry behavior not worth mentioning. Suffice to say, had she remained with them two outcomes would've awaited her: death by parental negligence in a variety of tragic ways, or death by her own hand when she became old enough.

For the most part, Josie's foster care life was benign, if numb and transitory. Every few years she was shuffled from family to family, fortunate to never experience abuse or mistreatment, but her stays never lasted long. The seemingly endless parade of foster parents treated her distantly, less like a child, more like a border.

Until she comes to live on the French Farm in Clifton Heights. Life was unpleasant there, even hard and occasionally terrifying, from the first day. Unpleasant, in that Mr. and Mrs. French didn't even treat her like a border. Here, she was an indentured servant who should feel fortunate to be offered room and board in exchange for her labor. The days were long and hard. Though she was never hit or beaten for her mistakes, she believed that day wasn't in long coming.

The nights terrified her, because even though she was only eleven, she knew why the two French boys—older, bigger, stronger, with the leering eyes and grinning teeth of hyenas—snuck into their basement barracks at night. She understood what those muffled grunting sounds and squeaking cot springs meant. Why some of the girls cried out in pain and fear as the boys grunted and the cots squeaked. She knew that for the moment she was too young to attract their attention, but her time would come soon. Also, she'd heard whispers that—even though the elder French had yet to pay her mind—he wasn't particular about age at all.

Unlike poor Edmund, however, Josie was cut of a

different cloth. Who knew why some people were made the way they were? Why some were ill-suited to survive in this world, and why others had the will and fortitude to fight back preemptively? Was it God's Will? Had He chosen some to be survivors, and doomed others to suffering and misery? Almost better to believe it was random, than think a Big Distant Someone determined our fate.

Regardless, Josie understood the looming danger. She realized it was only a matter of time before she received a nighttime visit from either the French boys or from their father. She had to act soon. She refused to suffer those muffled grunts blowing stinking hot breath into her face, or hear the cot squeaking beneath her.

Josie was aptly armed to defend herself. How?

She believed in magic. In the supernatural. She believed that on All Hallow's Eve, the walls grew thin between worlds, allowing beings from other dimensions to pass into ours. Contrary to popular belief, not all these beings wished us harm. That was Josie's big secret. The reason why she'd never really been alone, no matter how distant and mechanical each foster home felt. Since she'd been able to walk, Josie had seen ghosts. Played with them, and talked with them.

She once tried to talk about them to others, but when her fellow foster siblings picked on her and called her crazy and her foster parents began looking at her oddly, she stopped and kept it to herself. It was better that way, because for some reason, while her ghosts loved her and would never hurt her, she'd always sensed they didn't feel that way about other humans.

In every foster home she'd lived at, she found a special place to talk with her ghosts. In one house, the dusty attic no one was allowed in. In another house, an old playroom in the back of the house the other kids didn't like. In yet another, the cool and dry basement, which scared her fellow foster siblings with its spiders, and its darkness.

OCTOBER NIGHTS

When there wasn't farm work, the French foster children were allowed surprisingly free rein. On such a free day, Josie wandered through the forest behind the farm until she came to an old silver mine, long-since abandoned. The tracks were pulled up and the mine only extended about fifteen feet before ending in the rubble wall of the cave-in which closed it fifty years prior.

The opening of the mine was stable enough, however. For two years Josie regularly snuck off there to commune with her ghosts. They told her ghostly and weird tales of strange and far-off worlds. She regaled them with the events of her day. Together, they made up their own strange tales of wonder and terror. As her fears of the French boys and their father grew larger, she shared them also. The ghosts grew angrier, promising to exact revenge should Josie wish it.

At first, Josie recoiled from the thought. By nature she was kind and generous, and wished no harm on anyone. But as the nights passed, filled with muffled and frenzied grunts, pained cries and squeaking cots, as more of the older girls shuffled through their days with glazed, empty eyes, something hardened in Josie. She determined never to look at the world through such a glazed stare, so she and her ghosts began scheming. When would they bring their plan to fruition?

Halloween night.

During the weeks leading up to Halloween, Josie began paying attention to the French boys. *Flirting* is what the older girls called it. Complimenting them on their appearance. Saying nice things to them. Even giving them long looks, like the women gave men long looks on television.

The ghosts told her this was the best way to lure the boys to the mine. Though she didn't believe them, really (she was only eleven and not that pretty at all), to her mildly horrified shock she realized it was working. She was now drawing their notice. Lingering stares from wide, hungry eyes. Big smiles whenever she entered the room. Long pats on the shoulder for doing well on her chores. Candy bars slipped to her when the other children weren't looking.

Even a doll bought from the thrift store in town. She was really too old for a doll, but she acted as if it was the greatest gift she'd ever received. She crushed herself to each French boy in turn with clinging hugs, and it sickened her to feel the heat of their desire wafting off them.

They were primed. Due to visit her at night and foist their "attentions" on her, soon. So she took the plan to the next level, as she'd discussed with the ghosts. She told the French boys of the silver mine she'd discovered. The boys recognized it immediately. She told them how she loved to go in there because it was "so dark and scary" and she "loved to be scared". Feeling sick to her stomach and only barely holding down her nausea, she told them how cool it would be for all three of them to go there Halloween night.

It was easy. So easy it made her want to vomit. Three days later, as night fell, she led the French boys into the woods behind their farm. They were sipping from a bottle of whiskey they'd swiped from their old man. Making leering comments of barely disguised innuendo about how she shouldn't worry, if the mine was too "scary," they could make her "feel better." She pretended she didn't know what that meant. To her disgust, this only excited them more.

It was a quick walk through the woods. By the time they reached the mine, darkness had fully fallen, and they'd gotten out their flashlights. As they broke from the woods, there loomed the entrance to the old silver mine, its dark opening somehow blacker than the night.

She suggested they lead the way, knowing they'd make her go first. The oldest French boy snickered and said something along the lines of, "Oh naw, naw, you ain't wrigglin' away on us. You go first, we'll come *behind*."

His younger brother found this hilarious and snorted

guffawing laughter. Josie tasted bile in the back of her throat, but she smiled innocently, again pretending she had no idea why he was laughing.

She led them into the mine. The boys fell silent, cowed by the darkness, most likely sensing the ghosts, even though they couldn't speak to them like she could. They walked for a very long time in an increasingly oppressive silence. They walked longer than the mine actually was, but this didn't surprise Josie. The ghosts arranged this. It was all part of the plan.

Eventually the boys' impatience won out over their uneasiness. The younger one said, "Fuck this. Let's get it on an' get the fuck outta here." To Lilly, he sneered as he stepped forward, hand out-stretched, "C'mere, you. Ain't gonna be blue-ballin us, that's fer damn . . . "

His foot caught on something and he grunted. His older brother behind him complained, "What the fuck's your problem?"

"Somethin's got my foot. I can't fuckin move."

Another grunt. "Shit. Me too. What the hell . . . "

"Hey, now somethin's got my other foot. What the *fuck*, man . . . "

The whiskey bottle smashed against the ground. Its glassy crash echoed in the darkness.

"HOLY FUCKING SHIT!"

Josie turned. Though she was good and generous by nature and normally wouldn't wish harm on anyone, what she saw brought great joy to her heart. The French boys, pointing their flashlights downward and screaming at the rock encasing their feet and slowly oozing its way up their calves. It had somehow become soft and liquid, pulsing and surging over their thighs like a viscous, rubbery matter. They jerked, howled, and clawed at the pulsing liquid rock slowly devouring them—to no avail.

Josie stayed and watched until the end. Until the liquid rock poured over their heads and down their throats and solidified, choking their screams off into silence. She smiled sweetly at them and walked out of the mine, leaving them for her ghosts to finish off.

***

"No one ever found the French boys, of course. They were presumed run off, tired of toiling under their abusive father. Whatever Josie's ghosts did to them, nothing remained. As you can see, there aren't any teenager-shaped stalagmites around."

Like in the boxcar, I blinked, shrugging off a moment of disorientation. Also, I couldn't move my feet. It felt as if something was holding them together. Trapping them in place. I cried out and kicked them free, looking down. In the glare of Jimmy's flashlight, I saw nothing but a pile of rocks cluttered around my feet. Clustered, really. As if encircling them.

I breathed deep and looked at Jimmy. Unlike at the boxcar, he was smiling widely, looking as if he was enjoying himself immensely. "And what's your charming 'Halloween hook' for this lovely spot?"

Jimmy chuckled. "Well, the story goes that Josie grew up to write horror—quite successfully—under a pen name. I won't tell you which; you won't believe me. However, as she grew, she had less and less need of her ghosts. Especially as she began creating her own. Her ghosts, supposedly, remained here. In this very cave. And they're lonely. Have been since she left. They desperately want friends. So desperately, they're willing to do *anything* to curry favor. Worse things than they did to the French boys, even."

At that exact moment, so theatrical it angered me, a low, howling moan wound its way up from the mine's shadowed depths. Surprised at the unreasoning fear which tightened around my spine, I kicked the rocks aside and strode past Jimmy and out of the cave, muttering, "Let's get on with this."

"Oh, we will," he said, voice ringing with false jocularity, "because the next sight is the best of them *all*."

36.

SOMETHING ABOUT THE outline of the building lit up by the Monte Carlo's headlights struck a chord in me as Jimmy Graves pulled up to our next stop, but I couldn't place a finger on why. Just that it seemed familiar, somehow. In an awful way.

I got out and followed Jimmy Graves. As he aimed his flashlight at the place, tight bands of fear wrapped around my chest. It felt like my heart stuttered. My throat tightened. It was very hard to breathe.

A huge red barn. Not just any barn, either. Our neighbor's barn. Where Lilly spent so many summers tending to our neighbor's horses. A childhood chore which had grown into one of the few things she loved. She passed so many contented hours feeding, brushing, and caring for those horses. Near the end, they were her true family, the barn her true home.

It was also the barn she killed herself in.

I stumbled to a halt. "No," I rasped. "I can't see this. I can't."

Jimmy Graves said nothing. He walked forward, flashlight beam bouncing before him. I lurched after him helplessly.

***

It was different this time. Jimmy offered no narrative or monologue. Of course, he didn't need to. I already knew this story. In the barn, I stood next to a silent Jimmy Graves and helplessly watched it unfold.

Lilly was talking to one of our neighbor's (the Greene's) horses. Champ, I thought. And talking wasn't quite the right description. Sobbing into the horse's russet mane fit better. She slowly worked a brush down his neck. I was too far away to hear what she said. I felt grateful for that small mercy.

She sniffed, mumbled something else into Champ's mane, then moved on to the other horses, lovingly brushing them and speaking to them softly. I of course knew what had preceded this moment. A knock-down-drag-out fight with Beth, because Lilly had come home with her head shaven. Not buzzed, but shaved down to her skin.

Beth lost her mind. Started screaming at her, pointing her finger in Lilly's face, accusing her of making a "statement" about her "sinful perversion" and calling her a disgrace and an embarrassment. She blamed Lilly for the criticism I'd been experiencing among the congregation (criticism I'd rightfully earned all on my own), and came two steps short of calling her a tool of Satan to destroy my ministry.

Lilly said nothing.

Which was odd, because since she'd gone "punk", she'd toed up to Beth and gave as good as she got. Vehemently dismantling all of Beth's invectives and turning them against her. Lilly would never know how proud I was of her for standing her ground that last year.

But this last time, she didn't fight back. I don't know why. Maybe she felt tired. Maybe she knew it didn't matter. Beth would never have given in. So Lilly stood there and took it. Tears streaming down her face as she quietly sobbed. This only incensed Beth further. Before I could say or do anything, Beth did the unthinkable. She cranked her arm back and struck Lilly in the face, open-handed.

The blow cracked like a gunshot. The kitchen—where the argument had taken place—fell silent. Beth stared, unbelieving what she'd done. I stood there, motionless, the impossibility of what had just happened paralyzing me. Lilly cupped her cheek and stared at Beth, eyes wide and filled with tears.

She looked at me, once. Opened her mouth, but closed it. Turned and fled the kitchen, the house, and across the road to the Greene's barn.

We hadn't followed right away. I'd convinced Beth to give her space, because I assumed she was visiting the horses for comfort. She wasn't, however.

She was saying *goodbye*.

I stood next to Jimmy Graves, watching helplessly. The Greene's were away that weekend. They'd hired Lilly to watch over their horses. Which meant there was no one around to stop what happened next.

Lilly found about ten feet of rope in the tack room, where the saddles, bridles, and other riding gear were kept. Made the noose. Tied one end to the bottom rung of the ladder leading up to the barn's hayloft; tugging the knot tight. One thing Lilly had learned well in her time with the horses was how to tie a knot that wouldn't slip.

She looped the noose and the rest of the rope around her shoulder. Climbed up the hayloft, which had to be about fifteen feet. Once there, she tossed the noose over the nearest ceiling beam. She caught it. Without hesitation, she secured the noose around her neck. Cinched the knot— probably the most secure she'd ever made—tight.

She bowed her head and closed her eyes. Was she praying? Asking for forgiveness from a God who had— according to her mother, her church congregation, and her childhood faith—ultimately condemned her? Or was she simply taking one last moment to shore up her courage? I would never know.

She opened her eyes.

Breathed deep.

And she leaped off the hayloft, into open space. Her momentum did the job quickly. The snap of her neck cracked sharp and clear across the barn. She hung from the noose, arms limp at her sides, head bent at an unnatural angle, her body swaying gently, back and forth.

Eerily, the horses didn't react. They merely chuffed. Pawed their stables, and looked at Lilly. Swaying above them.

I wanted to close my eyes, but couldn't. I wanted to run screaming from that barn, but my muscles quivered in paralysis, my joints locked. The worst was yet to come, and I could do nothing but watch it happen.

I heard voices approaching outside the barn. One of them was angry and sharp. Beth, tired of giving Lilly space, ready to renew her attack. The other was pleading, conciliatory, and, of course, weak. Me—pleading in vain with Beth for leniency.

Beth stalked into the barn. Striding angrily, arms swinging at her sides, blue eyes flashing. She made it about four steps before her daughter's gently swaying figure caught her eye. She stumbled to a halt. Eyes wide and unbelieving. Mouth open and working silently.

"Oh my God."

I blinked, and was no longer standing next to Jimmy Graves. I was following Beth into the barn. Staring at my dead daughter hanging from a ceiling beam. A part of me cried out, deep inside at the unfairness, the injustice. I wouldn't reenact this moment, I *wouldn't*!

I couldn't stop myself, however. I followed the script, like a robot follows its programming.

"Oh my God," I whispered again.

Beth sank to her knees. Stared silently at Lilly's rigid body, swaying side-to-side from the ceiling beam above. She bent over. Buried her face into her hands.

And she *screamed*. A long, wailing screech ripping its way out from the deepest part of her guts, tearing her apart inside. It rose and fell and rose and fell, each scream more ragged, as if she were rupturing the very blood vessels of her throat. She screamed until her voice died away completely, and still she screamed hoarse, rasping gasps.

I stepped forward, but the air shimmered and a wave of disorientation passed through me. My vision blurred. When it cleared, Beth was standing, not kneeling. Dressed in an old sweatshirt and tattered jeans. Lilly no longer hung from the ceiling beam. The paramedics had come and gone along with the police. The funeral—which we'd stumbled through blindly and silently, like strangers instead of husband and wife—also in the past.

This was it.

The last day I saw Beth. She'd gone missing, and I'd come over here, suspecting to find her at the scene of Lilly's death. Here she was, staring up at the ceiling beam where our darling little girl had ended her life.

I opened my mouth, my throat tight with all the things I wanted to say, *needed* to say, but couldn't. "Beth," I whispered hoarsely, "Beth, I . . . "

Beth whirled on me. Instead of the grief or despair you'd expect to see on her face, I saw instead anger and rage. She jabbed a shaking finger at the ceiling beam which had once borne our dead, swaying daughter. "This is *your* fault," she said through gritted teeth. "Your fault. And now she's damned to hell!"

I raised my hands, mind-numbing grief and horror warring with anger of my own. "*My fault?* You've done nothing but hound her for the last two years! Every day, over every little thing!"

She advanced upon me. I backpedaled instinctively. A coward, up until the end. "Let her *find* herself, you kept saying. Give her room to breathe. Discover her own identity. She trafficked in filth and perversity, flaunting her sin in the face of God, and you did *nothing*. Said she was just trying to figure herself out. Trying to *express* herself." She jabbed her finger at the ceiling beam again, her voice rising to a hysterical screech. "Well, she *expressed herself*! Are you proud? ARE YOU PROUD?"

What happened next defied all logic and reason. Her face twisting into a snarl, Beth howled in an unreasoning rage and plunged at me, swinging her hands wildly. She caught me upside the head and face with several hard, open-handed slaps which rocked my head on my neck. Blinding pain flashed through my temples—and something else, finally.

My own rage.

At watching Beth do nothing but wear down our beautiful little girl since toddler-hood. At every single cutting word and sarcastic sneer she offered me and Lilly over the past four years. At the disparity between the smiling, gentle façade she offered the rest of the congregation as the "pastor's wife" and the cold, frigid shrew she'd become at home. At the *audacity* of her blaming our daughter's suicide on me, when she was the one who'd been knotting that rope from the moment Lilly started becoming her own person.

Rage filled every part of me. Blanked out all thought and reason. I grabbed Beth by the forearms, fingers clenching into her flesh so hard she cried out. With an inarticulate cry born of every single bad feeling I'd kept bottled up my entire life, I shoved her away from me.

She stumbled back. Her left foot caught on her right, throwing her off balance. Arms flailing uselessly, she plummeted to her side and down, straight for the lip of a wheelbarrow. The side of her head clanged against it, but the *snap* of her neck cracked the air much louder. The loudest sound I'd ever heard, in fact.

Her body thumped to the barn floor in a heap. Head lolling just as unnaturally as Lilly's, above us. I stared at Beth's prone body. I was filled with an overwhelming numbness.

In an instant, many things became clear. Why I wasn't able to contact Beth at the parsonage or on the phone. Why there'd been no record of our bank accounts. Why I'd been so convinced there was nothing for me to return to.

I felt an icy cold hand grip my shoulder. It wasn't a comforting gesture, or a compassionate one. More like a prison guard restraining a flight-risk convict. I turned and looked into the stony, uncaring face of Jimmy Graves.

he won't give you what you're looking for

"One more stop," he said in a dead, empty voice. "No need for the car, this time."

He snapped his fingers.

***

I blinked. We were no longer in the barn where Lilly killed herself. We were now in a clearing in the woods at night. I looked around, finding the spot vaguely familiar. When I saw the tent in the middle of the clearing—a tent I now recognized as the one I'd bought at The General Store—I realized where I was.

The clearing at the end of Boden Hill Trail, overlooking Owen Pond. Where I'd found a tent I now realized was an older version of the one I'd bought. In which I'd seen the skeleton of an unidentified man.

"Not really unidentified," Jimmy spoke casually, lifting the thought from my brain. "You just never ran into Sheriff Baker again. And there's a good reason why. Baker may be a fucking goody two-shoes who mucks up the works now and again, but even *he* knows there's some things he can't mess with. He identified the body all right. He just knew there wasn't anything he could do about it."

I looked at Jimmy. He was all smiles again—but this time, I could see the expression for what it was. The hungry glee of a wolf right before it feeds. "What do you mean?"

He tipped his head, stuck his hands into his pockets, and wandered toward the tent, its open flap ruffling in the breeze. "I've got one more Clifton Heights legend for you. Every few years, a couple weeks before Halloween, some poor sap who's new in town makes a gruesome discovery after hiking up Boden Hill Trail. A skeleton in an old tent which looks like it was pitched years ago. Impossible, of course. That a body could've lain here undisturbed or undiscovered all that time. Flesh rotting away to the bone. The tent still standing."

Jimmy Graves smiled and shrugged. "Of course, this *is*

Clifton Heights. A nice little town on the outside, where the rules of the normal world don't always apply. Especially during the month of October. Sheriff Baker dutifully responds to the 911 call about a body found at the end of Boden Hill Trail and he dutifully interviews the caller, knowing ultimately what's going on but also knowing there isn't a damn thing he can do about it. He also always identifies the body, of course, and the cause of death, after forensics comes back a few weeks later. The day *after* Halloween, of course."

Jimmy's grin spread, finally revealing what I'd suspected had been there all along. Rows and rows of sharp, inhuman teeth. "You know what the forensics report says? The man died of a self-inflicted gunshot to the head. And it always turns out to be the man who found the body in the first place. A man who has since disappeared from his cabin at The Motor Lodge."

I didn't doubt the truth of his words, realizing they were truer than anything else he'd told me. I felt nothing in response to them. No anger, no remorse, regret, or sadness. Just a yawning emptiness, and one simple question. "Why? Is this punishment? Am I atoning? Making things right? Is it a test? Am I not supposed to go on your ghost tour or go to the stone chapel in the woods? Is there some secret key to unlocking all this, and I have to keep trying until I get it right?"

I did feel something as he tipped his head back and laughed so hard his shoulders shook. Cold surprise, and also, finally: fear. A deep, yawning, existential dread.

As Jimmy's laughter tapered off, he wiped the mirthful tears from his eyes. Sauntering toward me, he shook his head and said, "None of the above. No punishment. No atonement. There's nothing you can do to escape. No key to turn the lock and set you free. It doesn't matter how you do it differently each time, because there's no meaning to this, at all. No reason. You know why this is happening? Why it happens *every* Halloween?"

He stepped close, face to face with me. "Because I find it *fun*," he hissed. "That's all."

He smirked. "Happy Halloween, Wes. See you next year."

He snapped his fingers.

***

The first thing I noticed after turning off Route 28 North toward Clifton Heights, New York, was the copious amount of roadkill lying in the ditches. I grew up in the country and had seen my share of roadkill. Dead deer, dogs, cats, and gophers crawling with flies wasn't anything new. However, after I passed the tenth dead animal, I began feeling uneasy . . .

And ye are, every day, the hand,
The tool of an infernal band,
That with you dwell, are one with you,
And govern ye in all ye do,
Save, when ye live in prayer, or hear
A silent whisper in your ear,
From one, your friend in heav'n and earth,
The guardian angel of your birth.

Halloween, A Romaunt with Lays Meditative and Devotional,
by Arthur Cleveland Coxe

ONE LAST PITCH

I.

May, 2013
The Commons Trailer Park
1:30 PM

"I'M GETTING *SO* trashed tonight. You've *no* idea."

Jessica Hagarty didn't respond as she studied her Anatomy textbook, trying to tune out her friend's chatter while she crammed in some last-minute studying. She had a lab examination Monday. Even though going out with the girls to celebrate Raye dumping her boyfriend had seemed like a good idea earlier, she was already regretting it, aware of how much she still needed to study. She had to review the last three chapters (taking her own notes, because that always helped her learn better than the classroom lectures), and read at least two more before the examination.

"I mean it," Raye said, perched on the arm of the sofa next to Jessica, applying red lipstick, compact mirror in hand. "I'm drinking until I can't remember that bastard's name. *And*, if I see a cute guy tonight . . . "

"You're going to ignore him and spend the night with your girlfriends. *That's* what you're going to do." Jessica highlighted a paragraph in her textbook. Glanced up at Raye and added, "At least, that's what you've been telling me all week."

Raye dropped both her lipstick and the compact mirror into her lap. "I know. I know. But if I see a cute boy who wants to dance, can't I play a *little*?"

Jessica snorted. "How'd you meet Cliff?"

A grumble-sigh. "UGH. I know, but c'mon." Raye threw an arm around her shoulder. "I wanna have *fun* tonight."

"Get off me, willya? You're practically in my lap."

"*Jessicaaaa*," Raye crooned, "pweese let me have fun tonight. Pwetty pweese?"

Jessica couldn't repress a snort of laughter as she shrugged Raye off. "*Fine*. Have fun." She arched her eyebrow, wagging a mock-stern finger at Raye. "Not too much fun. You wanted me to be DD *and* a rebound buffer. I take this charge very seriously. Have fun. But you're coming home with us tonight, because *if* I let you go home with some sweet young thing, I'll never hear the end of it when you eventually break up with said sweet young thing a year from now because *he* cheated on you, too."

Raye offered a lopsided grin. "How come you're so good to me? Always looking out for me even when I'm acting like a little shit."

Jessica smiled tightly, thinking many things she'd rather not. About how she'd always looked after others. Especially Mom. How she'd cooked dinner most nights. Washed dishes, cleaned their trailer, mowed their tiny lawn. Vacuumed, dusted, and done the laundry. How she'd shouldered the bills by working two jobs when her mom left the trailer to her when she met Barry (a lineman at the lumbermill) and moved into his trailer on the other side of town.

She thought about these things in several seconds, then forced a wider, more carefree smile. "We've all got a part to play. Guess mine's mother hen."

The other girls—Miriam and Samantha—squealed in glee as they moved down the trailer's cramped hall from the bathroom toward the den. Raye squeezed Jessica. "You're too good to us, sweetie. Definitely."

As she joined the other two, all of them already high and chattering away, Jessica grunted and returned her attention to her studies, muttering to herself, "Yeah. I'm a damn saint."

2.

Clifton Heights High Baseball Field
3:30 PM

SCOTT KENNSINGER STOOD on the mound. Arms loose, right shoulder tingling, mind resting in that quiet place it always went to before the windup and pitch. Nothing else in the world existed but the ball tucked snugly into the palm of his hand, and the catcher, who was flashing his favorite sign.

Fast ball.

Time to bring the heat.

It was the bottom of the ninth. Bases loaded, with two outs. They were ahead 1-0, but Clifton Heights' best batter, senior Chris Testani, was stepping up to plate. He looked more like a nose-tackle than a baseball player. A monster with a barrel chest and tree-trunk legs, he had a reputation for blasting out homeruns in situations like these.

Scott wasn't worried. His shoulder hummed with coiled strength, ready to throw his third out to end the game. He'd been on fire today. Every pitch had been on the money. He was in the zone. A private little world in which he heard every tap, whisper, and scrape. Where he saw every lead off before it happened, and knew exactly where and when to throw the ball.

They were going to win.

He was going to win. He had to, because this was his life.

The mound.

The ball.

His arm. The speed.

The pitch.

This was everything. Up here on the mound he didn't worry if Mom had gotten home safely last night without drinking herself to death, or if she'd thrown up in her sleep and drowned in her own puke. He didn't have to wake her and get her sober so she could spend the day numbly bagging groceries at The Sure-Save, all before he got ready for school.

He didn't have to wonder who she'd brought home Friday or Saturday night, or wonder if she'd slept with one of his classmates' wayward fathers . . . again. He didn't think about his own father and wonder why he'd left, where he was, or who he was. Up here, on the mound, he could just be.

His fingers tightened on the ball. He looked down. Closed his eyes as he always did before every pitch, to center himself. His focus narrowed to a razor-sharp point. Something rose inside him, eager for release. He was ready.

In an instant, however . . . everything changed.

"Fuckin retard! *Move!*"

Cleats scrambled in the dust and a wooden bat clattered to the ground. Something struck the chain-link backstop, making it buzz like a storm of angry metallic bees. Then that something thumped to the ground.

A shrill, agonizing cry pierced Scott's ears. Driving a cold spike into his brain. He winced and looked up, but the sun's light burned his eyes. He had to shield them with his pitcher's mitt. Someone cried out—*inside* his head—and his ears started ringing.

Then, the shouts came.

"Hey, kid . . . what the hell's wrong with you?"

"Move your ass! We're trying to play a game, here!"

Murmurs seeped from the crowd. Something much worse ebbed and swelled underneath. A constant hum which gathered a strange sort of substance, pressing against Scott's thoughts. Chuckles. Snorts. Laughter. Whispered under-breath, but still there, regardless.

Scott clenched the baseball tightly in his right hand. The Clifton Heights bat boy sat on the ground against the backstop, a bat rolling lazily at his feet. Testani loomed over him, brutish face twisted in scorn, fist upraised.

The boy must've gotten in Testani's way as he was retrieving the previous player's bat. Testani had shoved him or perhaps just bumped into him. The boy had stumbled, hit the chain-link backstop, and bounced off it to the ground. Now—despite the umpire striding forward with an upraised hand—Testani looked like he wanted nothing more than to put the boy's lights out.

Testani and the bat boy's uniforms were the same, but they were not teammates, and never would be. Not in this world, anyway. Scott understood, far too well. Growing up in a trailer park, raised by a mother who drank herself into oblivion every weekend, and had slept with more than one of his classmates' fathers, Scott knew the only difference between him and that bat boy was his fastball, nothing more. His success on the diamond was the only thing which saved him from the same kind of humiliation the bat boy was experiencing right now.

Coaches from both teams were in motion, trying to intervene, but Scott didn't look at them. He couldn't. He could only look at the boy, sitting in the dust, as Testani cursed and took a menacing step toward him.

Scott gripped the baseball tighter, fingernails digging into leather. Sweat trickled down his forehead, into his eyes, stinging them. He felt feverish and faint. His suddenly damp uniform clung to him. His heart pounded. It was hard to breathe, as if he'd just finished running a marathon.

Time stopped.

Everyone froze.

Testani standing over the boy. The two opposing coaches rushing from their dugouts to prevent a minor disaster. The umpire reaching out to restrain Testani.

The boy staring at Scott. Wooden face hanging slack and

emotionless. His mouth formed a straight line. Blue eyes glowed in his passive face, the irises swirling in a way Scott had never seen. They didn't just look at him. They looked *into* him. Into the quiet place in his mind, where he always went before every pitch.

Please.

Help me.

Make them stop.

Scott blinked once. His heart pounded in his head, ears ringing even worse. It was all he could hear. Sunlight glinted off aluminum bats and hard plastic helmets. Fans standing and complaining. Scott saw very little of this, entranced by blue eyes that looked so alive, he felt lost in their depths. The ringing in his ears rose into a droning hum.

Please.

Will you help me?

Scott nodded and whispered, "Yes."

His fingers twitched around the baseball, while his shoulder flexed. With a grace born of throwing old balls through tire swings for hours, Scott spun into a tight, smooth wind-up and threw the ball with everything he had.

His release was true.

He brought the heat.

The ball left his fingers with a snap of leather against flesh, hurtling toward the batter. Just as the umpire was about to grab Testani's shoulder, the ball plowed into Testani's face with a bone-splitting crack. A fine, red mist sprayed the air, spattering the umpire's face with little red dots.

Testani howled and crumpled to the ground, knees drawn to his chest. He rocked in the fetal position, clutching his face, screaming in high-pitched, whiny gasps. The umpire froze, hand still reaching to where Testani's shoulder had been, staring unbelievably at Scott, mouth working silently.

Shouts rang out from the crowd.

"Holy shit, Scott!" Coach Hamilton pounded the infield toward him, the other coach following, looking furious. "What the hell's wrong with you?"

Scott straightened and looked at the angry, confused faces rushing at him. The coaches, players, and the umpire, finally loosed from his shocked paralysis, and screaming, thumbing him out of the game. He mouthed the words *I'm sorry* but the truth was, he wasn't sorry at all. Didn't feel anything. He just stared past them at the baseball, smeared in crimson, as it rolled around home plate in the bloody dust and mud.

The ringing in his ears swelled into a crescendo until something twisted and snapped in his head. He coughed. Blood spurted from both nostrils, down and over his lips. His bladder released and soaked his groin with warmth. The sharp scent of ammonia stung his nostrils.

Shakes took him.

He bent over and puked into the dust. His throat stinging, he rose into a half-crouch and staggered away from everyone, his feet dragging as he stumbled and weaved in no particular direction. His cleats got tangled up with each other and he fell forward, striking the ground shoulder-first.

Scott flopped over onto his back, chewed his tongue, and twitched under the wide blue sky. Darkness fell inside his head, leaving nothing but the memory of deep blues and a voice that whispered . . .

Thank you.

OCTOBER NIGHTS

3.

Lake George
The Adirondack Brewery
5:00 PM

THEIR WAITRESS PLACED a circular slab of pine on the table before them. Cut into it were slots for shot glasses. Jessica still nursed her Pepsi.

"Thank *you*," Raye gushed, face glowing. Nodding, the waitress moved on, leaving Raye and the other girls to enjoy their shots while Jessica tried to read a photocopied article she'd brought with her.

"Okay girls. Here's to the single life, and all the pretty boys we can manage!" Miriam and Samantha cheered and picked up their shot glasses along with Raye. "Salut!" They tipped back the shots, then banged the glasses back down.

The juke box blasted something by Black Eyed Peas. Raye squealed and threw her hands up. Samantha followed suit. They stumbled out of the booth toward the Brewery's small dance floor.

Miriam glanced at Raye and Samantha, looked back at Jessica, and deadpanned: "Shitfaced much?"

They both snorted, then dissolved into laughter. Jessica loved Raye to death. She was full of life, and lived it to the fullest. However, she also ran the edge, often too fast. It was still early, but she and Samantha were already drunk. Maybe she'd get lucky and Raye would crash early, so they could go home and she could get a decent night's sleep after all.

Miriam nudged Jessica with her shoulder, nodding at the article. "Are you *actually* trying to study? That's hardcore."

"You know me. I love to party." Jessica sipped her Pepsi, swallowed and added, "Actually, this isn't a nursing article. It's about autism. I've gotten interested in the subject."

"Autism. Isn't that what Dustin Hoffman's character had in that movie with Tom Cruise? Like Down's Syndrome, or something?"

"No. Well, yes about the Dustin Hoffman thing, but it's not like Down's Syndrome. Down's is chromosomal. Something genetic that shows up on a test. You can tell if a child is going to be born with Down's. Autism . . . " She shrugged again. "No one really knows what causes autism. There's no way of 'testing' for it. No way of knowing if someone will have it or not. No one knows why some folks have a little autism or why some can't ever live normal lives."

Miriam stared with wide-eyed wonder. "Wow. You're really into this nursing thing, aren't you?"

Jessica tipped her head, considering. "Yep. But this," she gestured at the article, "doesn't necessarily have anything to do with nursing. This one kid I sometimes get called to watch—you know, the Department of Social Services has me as an on-call aide these days—his name's Evan, and sometimes I hang with him at his house until his mom or dad gets home from work. Working with him has gotten me interested in autism. Maybe something to look into when I graduate."

"That's really awesome. Y'know? I wish . . . " Miriam paused and looked away.

Jessica sipped her Pepsi, swallowed, and asked, "Wish what?"

Miriam shrugged, looking at Raye and Samantha prancing around the dance floor. "We have fun. We always do." Miriam offered Jessica a wistful smile. "But you have fun without getting trashed. You're working all these jobs and doing so well in school . . . "

This time it was Jessica's turn to nudge Miriam. "Hey.

You're working through school too. Waitressing at The Skylark ain't a walk in the park."

Miriam snorted. "I guess. It's just . . . you've got something the rest of us don't. I don't know what it is. It's something special, though. Something the rest of us can never have."

A chill ran through Jessica at the words *something special*. She didn't know why, but Miriam's odd comment unsettled something deep inside. She was about to ask Miriam what she'd meant, but before she could utter a word, Raye and Samantha had returned to their table, two college guys they'd met on the dance floor in tow. Miriam instantly perked up, the melancholic expression on her face disappearing as if it'd never been. Jessica smiled and nodded in all the right places, unable to shake the foreboding which had settled onto her like a cold blanket.

4.

Commons Trailer Park
2:00 AM

"JESSSSICA. HEEEEY. Watchoodoin? Jesssicaa!"

Jessica shifted Raye's head against her shoulder and dug around in her purse for the trailer's keys. Of course the purse hung on her left side, trapped between her body and Raye's staggering dead weight. Should've gotten the keys out soon as she'd parked, but she'd been too focused on making sure everyone made it out of the car without falling or puking.

"Hey. C'mon, Jess." Miriam leaned against Samantha, who was leaning against Miriam. "I gotta pee. Bad."

Jessica snorted. "You *always* have to pee. Got the bladder of a two-year-old."

"Nuh-uh. Too many shooters. And shots. And those blue things. The ones with the plastic umbrellas in 'em."

"Blue things," Samantha crooned. "Bluuuuuuuue things."

Jessica nudged Raye's weight to the left and sighed. "Raye, hon. Can you lean against the trailer for a minute? Can't get my keys."

"Surekaywhatev." Raye swayed off Jessica's shoulder and slumped against the trailer.

Free of Raye's weight, Jessica plunged her hand into her cluttered purse, rummaging through lipstick, tissue packages, packs of gum, a lighter and a box of menthols, spare tampons, and God knew what else, until her hand closed around the metallic jingle of her keys. "Yes! Finally."

Seconds later they were inside. Lights on, door shut behind them, Raye stumbled to Jessica's threadbare couch, where she flopped down face-first. Miriam and Samantha leaned against each other and sang nonsense songs as they staggered down the cramped hall to the trailer's tiny bathroom. Jessica made a beeline for her bedroom to get changed and into bed.

In her room, she kicked off her flats, unzipped her jeans and wriggled out of them, and kicked them into the corner. She shucked her panties off with one hand, tossing them into the clothes hamper. Her blouse followed, then her bra, and then she was rummaging through her dresser for a big t-shirt to sleep in, mentally reviewing the subjects she had to study tomorrow.

That's when she heard it.

Samantha's panicked cry.

"Raye. Raye! Oh, *shit*! Jessica!"

Alarm pricked her spine at the cry. She snagged a random T-Shirt, tugged it over her head ran out of her room, trying not to trip over scattered clothes and textbooks. Samantha sat on the couch, hovering over Raye, now on her back, presumably turned over by Samantha, who was patting Raye's cheeks lightly, calling insistently over and over, "Raye, honey . . . wake up. *Raye*."

Jessica rounded the couch, glancing at Miriam, who was twisting her hands uselessly, whimpering. Fear and worry throbbed in Jessica's chest. "What's happening?"

Miriam shook her head, sobbing, eye-liner streaking down her cheeks. "I . . . I dunno! Samantha yelled something to her and Raye didn't answer so she came out here, was gonna j-jump on her, and . . . "

"Samantha?" Jessica knelt beside the couch.

Face twisted with worry, Samantha looked helplessly at Jessica. "Jesus I think she drank too much! She's hardly breathing!"

"Move."

Samantha obeyed Jessica's clipped tone without question. They switched spots, Jessica sitting softly on the couch, leaning over Raye's still form, Samantha on the floor next to them. Miriam whimpered and sniffed in the background.

Jessica took Raye's hand and spoke loudly. "Raye? It's Jessica. Raye?" Pinched her wrist, looking for a pulse, finding a weak one which felt thready and erratic. Raye's hands were damp and cool, her skin pale. Jessica reached up and lifted one of Raye's eyelids with a finger.

Barely a flicker, the pupil dilated, badly.

"Shit. How much did she drink? Anyone know?"

Samantha hugged herself and shrugged. Now that she was no longer trying to wake Raye, she displayed signs of panic herself. "I don't know! Lots of beers and Tequila, but . . . "

Her eyes lit up. "Jello shots. When you had to pee right before we left. Those frat guys from Potsdam were doing Jello shots in the back. She sneaked back there and downed a whole handful. I tried to slow her down but she said 'Fuck off' so I said 'Fuck you, too' and left and . . . "

Her hand flew to her mouth. "I can't believe I forgot! I was just so tired! It's my fault! I left her! I never should've left her . . . "

Jessica shook her head. "*Not* your fault. Raye's a big girl and makes her own choices, but we gotta make her puke and get that shit outta her. That and call 911 and . . . "

Samantha stared for a heartbeat, mouth wide open. Trembling, but otherwise frozen.

"Dammit, Samantha!" Jessica turned on her, snarling. "She's gonna fucking die!"

Samantha lurched, as if slapped. She stood and stumbled toward the phone in the kitchen. Miriam whimpered. Jessica turned her focus on Raye. Grabbed a shoulder with one hand, cupped the back of her head with the other, about to tip her onto her side, stick a finger down her throat . . .

Desperation gripped her, and something else. Something ice cold and burning, and hard as steel.

Anger.

Rage.

She and Raye were good friends. Not terribly close, not even that intimate. But Raye was young, alive, full of energy. So she'd gotten careless and had too much to drink? So what? Some asshole frat boy had probably over-mixed those Jello shots, looking to get someone like Raye blind-drunk for an easy score. It wasn't fair.

She didn't deserve to die.

Not for this.

Jessica wasn't going to let her.

She squeezed Raye's shoulder. Breathed deep, and rasped, "Dammit, Raye. Stay with me, you hear? *Don't* die, dammit. *Don't die.*"

Jessica's gut twisted. Her head throbbed. The room wavered, her vision blurred, and for a moment she couldn't breathe. Her hands warmed where she gripped Raye, and though she knew it was crazy, it felt like her fingers were dissolving and melting *into* Raye, deep into her, reaching down and . . .

Everything faded away.

The room. Samantha, yammering on the phone from the kitchen. Miriam, whimpering behind her. All of it gone, except this couch, her, and Raye.

Something flowed into her, from Raye. Filled her up and made her queasy. Raye shuddered and sighed. Her pulse surged and throbbed in her neck under Jessica's thumb. Everything snapped back.

Miriam still whimpering. Samantha fumbling her address on the phone to 911. Raye, breathing.

She blinked. Rubbed her eyes and mumbled, "Geethus. Whatfuckintimeisit?"

Miriam gasped.

The phone—dropped from Samantha's nerveless fingers, no doubt—slammed against the wall, swinging from its cord. It bounced once, twice, three times.

Jessica opened her mouth to speak, but something surged up from her guts. Bile, flooding her throat. Suddenly the room was spinning. Her skin and teeth felt numb. She tried to push off the couch to run for the bathroom and the toilet, but her legs buckled and threw her face-first to the floor.

On her hands and knees, her forehead scratched against the trailer's thin carpeting. Shrill voices clamored, asking what was wrong, *what happened, Jessica are you all right . . . ?*

The floor tilted. Her stomach spasmed and rippled. Cold sweat burst from her pores. Her breath and heartbeat pounded in her ears, head, brain. Sour saliva mixed with bile filling her mouth. She gulped once, tried to swallow, keep it down . . .

She arched her back and vomited liters of booze she hadn't consumed, until nothing remained. The sour, rotten smell of her puke twisted her stomach and ripped several hacking dry heaves from her, burning her throat and cramping her stomach.

One last heave. A burp, and a cough. Then, at least having the presence of mind to push away from her vomit and flop onto her back, Jessica passed out.

OCTOBER NIGHTS

FOUR YEARS LATER

5.

Thursday
October 29th
8:30 AM

STANDING IN THE middle of his small apartment over Chin's Pizza & Wings on Main Street, Scott Kennsinger stared at his ringing cellphone. It wasn't Mom, because he hadn't given her this number when he'd moved out two years ago. She was usually too busy messing around with Steve from the lumbermill to bother calling, anyway. It certainly wasn't Buddy, one of his few real friends from high school. Buddy had suffered a bad accident at the landfill a few months ago. Last Scott knew, Buddy was in ICU over at Clifton Heights Memorial, in no shape to call anyone. That only left work, and it wasn't them, either. There was no number. 'Private Caller' flashed on the screen.

The phone kept ringing. A second or two passed. Biting the inside of his cheek, he answered it. "H-hello?"

Static buzzed, then: *"Is this Scott Kennsinger?"*

The voice sounded pleasant and warm. Scott still felt uneasy, however, because he couldn't imagine who'd be calling. "S-speaking." He bit the word as short and curt as he could—but as usual, he sounded illiterate, not tough.

"Scott! Great! I wasn't sure if this was the right number or not. The Blue Sox's GM was fuzzy on the last four digits you listed on your scouting questionnaire last Spring. This was my fifth try. Almost gave up." The line crackled with

good humor. *"Sure hope your curveball is better than your handwriting."*

Scott swallowed, understanding now. Every year on the first day of Spring try-outs for the local Double AA team, the Utica Blue Sox, players filled out scouting questionnaires, keeping alive their dreams of someday getting called up to the majors. Scott never really thought much about that, however. The Sox usually cut him by the second day, every year, and this past Spring hadn't been any different. In fact, he didn't even remember bothering to fill the damn thing out.

"Scott? You still there?"

Scott shook his head, as if waking from a bad dream. "Yeah. Sorry. I'm tired. Worked a lot of overtime this week."

"A working man, I get it. But listen: what if I told you maybe you don't have to work overtime, anymore?"

Scott frowned. "Who is this?"

"Scott, my name is Jimmy. I'm a recruiter for a sports development and management group. We handle baseball, football, basketball players . . . hell, even some golfers. We have clients playing at all levels, from Triple A to Single A, even in the pros. We pride ourselves on taking care of our athletes."

Scott's confusion only increased. This sounded like every minor league player's dream. The only problem? He hadn't done anything since he quit high school. Had been cut from the Sox the last four years. Why was this guy calling *him*? Why now? Six months after Spring tryouts?

"Listen, thanks for the call, but I'm gonna be late for work if—"

"Just a few more minutes. You won't regret it, trust me. Here's the deal, Scott. Professional sports teams thrive every year on the strength of diamonds in the rough. Unsigned talent other teams and organizations pass over. It's my job to find those diamonds. You, my friend, are one of them."

Scott's jaw worked, but he couldn't make the words come. Back in high school, he'd hated talking to scouts and coaches. They'd talked too fast, firing cliched promises at him with machine-gun intensity, never giving him time to think. Got so bad, he'd stopped picking up the phone at home. He refused to leave class (even though he hated school) to meet with visiting scouts. Eventually he'd begged Coach Hamilton to send them away. Now, like then, his mind swirled at this guy's rapid-fire speech.

"Listen, I don't get it. Every spring the Blue Sox cut me by the second day. Why are you calling m-me? Especially so long after tryouts?"

"Diamond in the rough, remember? Look, the Blue Sox GM has been dying for you to put it together so he can keep you, but he's starting to think you gotta leave town to do that. Get away from your past. Sometimes that's what ya gotta do, Scott. Drop your baggage where you are, move on, and start over." A pause, and then, *"What happened to Chris Testani wasn't your fault. It was a bad throw, Scott. That's all."*

Scott closed his eyes. Swallowed thickly, his stomach churning. He'd heard that so many times, from so many people. It didn't matter because none of them understood.

They couldn't, because they didn't know the truth.

Apparently misinterpreting his silence for offense, the recruiter said, *"Sorry, Scott. Hate to bring up bad memories. But here's the thing. That shit—excuse my French—happens all the time. Chris Testani was a fine player. Maybe, if things were different, he would've played college or Single A ball. But he's not you. You're special. Trust me on this, kid."*

Scott swallowed. His heart was starting to pound, and a tell-tale buzz rose in his ears. His head was starting to ache too, which wasn't a good sign. He had to get off the phone. "Sorry. I'm late for work. Thanks for saying all those nice things, but I'm not interested."

"Please, Scott." The voice deepened, and for some reason, its resonance unnerved him. *"This is the chance of a lifetime. Don't throw it away. It won't come back again, and if you pass on it, you'll kick yourself every day for the rest of your life."*

"Trust me. I already do."

"This is a chance to reclaim your dreams, Scott. Think about it. Your dreams. You can have them again . . . if you want it bad enough." A pause, in which something heavy lingered in the air. *"Don't you want your dreams back, Scott?"*

Scott bit his tongue. An acrid despair swirled in his belly. "Sure. Who doesn't?"

"So c'mon. I'm in your area. Let me come around Saturday, run you through a workout. What do you say?"

"Saturday's Halloween."

"I know! Perfect day to change your life, Scott. A time of transformation, to be sure."

Scott glanced at the wall clock. He was going to be late. His boss Deyquan hated that, worse than anything. Whoever this guy was, he'd made a mistake. What he offered, Scott couldn't take. He didn't deserve it.

But still.

What the hell?

"Sure. Whatever. Gotta be during the day, though. I w-work Saturday night. E-everyone else wanted off."

"Fabulous. I'll put things into motion."

"Sure. Gotta go."

"All right then. I'll give you a call! This'll be the best Halloween of your life, Scott!"

Scott hung up without answering and stuffed his cell into his pocket. He glanced at the clock again and swore. Cutting it close. He headed for the door, but stopped when his gaze fell on it.

His eyes narrowed. There it sat, lurking in piles of old socks and rags he used to change his Kawasaki's motor oil, waiting where he'd tossed it after coming home from work yesterday.

Damn.

Couldn't he leave that thing home? Just this once?

He knew the answer, of course. Pursing his lips, he grabbed the old, battered baseball. It was mottled dark brown in places. His fingers molded to its curves. It fit neatly into his palm, like it had been made special for him. He carried the damn thing everywhere. He didn't know why. Maybe to remind him, every day, of what he'd thrown away.

Literally.

Damn.

How sadistic was that?

Every day he tried to leave his apartment without it. But every day, no matter how long he stood there and fought the urge, he always gave in.

Today was no different.

He grabbed the baseball, stuffed it into his jeans pocket and headed out the door, resolving to forget about the mystery recruiter's promises (somehow he'd forgotten to get the guy's full name) and focus only on what he could control. Everything else could go to hell, for all he cared.

6.

**The Commons Trailer Park
8:30 AM**

SOMEONE WAS YELLING. Jessica Hagarty rolled over and blinked twice. She'd worked overnight and hadn't gotten home until 6 AM. Her lower back ached from standing on concrete the whole night. Lucky for her, she was working another nightshift tonight.

Someone kept yelling. She groaned, rubbed her face, and tried to push away the sleep-fog which clouded her mind.

"Jessica!"

Someone definitely yelling her name and pounding on the trailer's screen door. Rent wasn't due, so it couldn't be that. Plus, that voice sounded young and desperate.

"Jessica? Are you home? Please! It's Cody! Mom's sick! Took some pills or something!"

Not rent, but a scared kid.

Cody.

. . . I think she took some pills or something . . .

Shit!

Jessica came awake, scrambled out of bed, and grabbed last night's jeans off the floor. Shrugging into them, hopping on one foot, she called out, "I'm up! Cody, did you call 911?"

Cody's voice hovered between a wail and a whine. "No! Can't! Landline and cell are dead. Mom couldn't pay the bills last month and . . . "

"Hold on!"

She pulled a T-shirt over her head. Grabbed a flannel hanging from her dresser, aware in the back of her head she wore no bra, it was cold out, and even though Cody was a nice and right-now very scared boy, he was also a *teenage* boy. And he sort of had a crush on her.

He doesn't just have a crush on you, does he? He worships you a little. Of course, he's also afraid of you, too.

Like everyone else.

She shrugged the flannel on. Rushed to the door, hastily buttoning it high enough to cover any potential cleavage. Soon as she opened her trailer's door and saw Cody's wide, shimmering eyes, she felt bad about those thoughts. She could be naked and slicked in baby oil and he probably wouldn't have noticed. He stood on her small porch, hugging himself and trembling, whether from the late October chill or fear, she couldn't tell.

Words tumbled over each other, nearly incoherent in their jumbling. "Mom . . . she . . . she's layin' on the bed, not breathin' so good . . . won't wake or talk or nothin' . . . "

She pushed all the way through the door and out onto the porch. Grasped Cody's elbow and tugged him down the porch steps and toward him and his mom's trailer, trying to speak in a calming tone. "Hey. Slow down and look at me. What happened?"

Cody breathed deep and wiped his nose with the back of his hand as he stumbled along after her, a distinctly childish gesture which made it near impossible to think he'd sneak peeks down her shirt. How old was he, really? Thirteen? Too young to deal with the shit his mom pulled.

Not fucking fair.

Then again, what was?

"I . . . uh . . . " he looked away as they quickly walked, visibly drawing himself together. The heartbreaker? He'd already calmed down a little, because he was used to this. It happened all the time. The initial shock. Then panic and desperation. The explanations. Etcetera, ad infinitum. "I woke up early to make breakfast for us. She skipped dinner last night. Didn't feel good. Went straight to bed. Stomach bug or somethin'."

KEVIN LUCIA

Stomach bug my ass.

Cody sniffed. His voice had deadened now, because he'd done this too many times before. "Finished making breakfast, called her but she didn't come. Didn't think nothin'. She does that, sometimes. Lays around in the mornin' before gettin' up."

"How long before . . . "

Cody swallowed. Looked at her, then away. "Don't know. Ten minutes. Maybe twenty? I finished eating, called her again. She didn't answer. I washed my plates. She still hadn't . . . I went to her room, knocked. Didn't hear anythin' and I . . . "

Cody's breath hitched. He broke apart again. A guilty shadow passed over his face. She almost guessed what happened next. "Relax. What'd you do next?"

"I went in. Not supposed to without permission. Mom likes her privacy an' all."

I bet. Easier to shoot junk that way.

Jessica shook the recrimination off. She wasn't being fair to Cody's mom, Shelly. Things had been hard for her. But that didn't give her the right to keep doing this to Cody.

So why keep helping her? She obviously wanted out of this life. Why not just let her go and be done with it? Or even better . . .

You could do it yourself. Put death in, just like you take it out. Never tried it before, but you can do it. Would be a mercy. To her, and Cody.

She shuddered and pushed the horrible thought (which had been coming more and more often lately) away.

"It's okay." She squeezed his elbow as she tugged him along. "No one's gonna hate you. Promise."

He swallowed. "Okay. She was lyin' on the bed. On her back. Starin' up at the ceilin'. Eyes all shiny. Droolin'. Bottle of pills in her hand. Didn't see which ones, but it looked empty . . . "

Shit.

" . . . and she was wearin' only her bathrobe. That silk one? An' it was open an' all . . . " Cody's face nearly crumpled, tears welling in his eyes. "I didn't mean to look, *honest . . .* "

Pity swelled inside. "Course you didn't." She stopped, turned him by the shoulders, and pushed him gently towards the Commons entrance. "Get to Phil Hacker's trailer, out front." A jerky nod. "You wake his ass up. Tell him your mom's sick and needs an ambulance. Tell him *Jessica Hagarty* said so."

because he's a little afraid of you, too

"Got it?"

Another quick nod.

"Quick. Beat feet, kiddo. I'll see to your Mom."

He gave her a sad glance. Eyes shining with admiration and gratitude and *yes*, a little fear. Then he took off running toward Phil Hacker's trailer.

Jessica turned and sped up as she headed toward Shelly and Cody's trailer. It was only a few rows over. Took her five minutes to get there. The door hung open—the way Cody had probably left it—yawning a darkness which made her uneasy. Something about the way it shifted in that black rectangle. Like it was liquid, and waiting.

For her.

She skidded to a rustling stop in the drive's loose gravel. Stared at the looming darkness. Her flesh puckered, because there *was* something waiting there. Jessica shivered and tried to push away a cold, cloying sensation which clung to her skin like an invisible film. She thought about the other times she'd butted heads against the darkness.

During Jimmy Thompson's pneumonia last winter. Mauve Walker's diabetic shock three months ago. Matilda Givens before cancer finally got her last Spring. Juney Bugg's OD. All the other times she'd brought Shelly back from the edge.

She gritted her teeth against the chill in her bones and forced herself towards the trailer and up the porch's front steps. She breathed deep, then plunged through the dark doorway.

She stopped and looked around. Dark and thick in here. Just an old trailer like hers. A little messier, though. Shelly had never been one for housekeeping, and though Cody did what he could, he was just a kid. Housework wasn't his thing. It shouldn't have to be, really.

Bedroom. To her left, down the hall.

As she moved that way, a sour odor hit her. Decay. Age. Mildew. How could anyone live this way? Her own trailer was cluttered, mostly with clothes, magazines and her old nursing textbooks. She kept up with the trash and washed the dishes at least.

Poor Cody.

Last room, at the end of the trailer. Door open as Cody had left it. Beyond, an even deeper darkness swirled. She felt it there. The darkness she'd seen in the doorway. The same cold presence she'd felt so often the last four years. An ice-cold blackness which didn't want her here.

Go away, bitch.

She's mine.

Jessica clenched her teeth, stepped into the pitch-black bedroom to try and beat back the cold blackness once more.

7.

Bassler Road
10 AM

SCOTT LOOKED UP into the sun and blinked. For a moment, he thought he was back on the mound before the wind-up, sweating on a hot Saturday afternoon in May. The crowd whispered in his ears, his glove's leather creaked against his hand . . .

No.

Not there.

Here.

He blinked again. His hand curled around something smooth with ridged laces, his fingernails digging into old leather, and the crowd's whispers melted into the wind rustling through leaves. In a rush, the sun became too bright. Scott glanced down and rubbed his throbbing eyes with his free hand, gripping leather as awareness trickled back into him.

He scuffed his feet. Heavy, steel-toed Timberlands thumped metal. The bed of a truck. A county truck. Not pitching. Working. Standing in the back of a Webb County pick-up truck, painted bright yellow, just like the vest and hardhat he wore every day. Bright yellow, just like his old baseball uniform.

He squeezed the hard leather thing in his pocket and sighed bitterly. Always that damned ball.

Something jolted him—the truck jerking to a stop—and he swayed. Other boots scuffed and banged on metal around him as men scrambled from the pick-up's bed onto an old, cracked strip of asphalt he'd come to know well. Bassler Road, just outside Clifton Heights.

Scott rubbed the bridge of his nose between his index finger and thumb, fighting down a yawn. He hadn't been sleeping well. Too many bad dreams. Also, he'd run out of his meds a couple weeks ago. Hadn't had the cash to refill his prescription since. He always slept better on his meds. Off them, he felt too jumpy to sleep, which made him tired all the time, too. Always jumpy and tired. Not a good combination.

"Kennsinger! Move your ass! County ain't payin' ya to daydream."

Scott blinked and shook off his fatigue, though it was reluctant to let go. He looked up at his foreman, Deyquan, whose black face glistened with sweat. The skin around his eyes and nose was pulled tight from a lifetime spent both in the harsh summer rays and blistering winter winds.

"Yes sir." Scott rubbed his eyes once more. Let go of the ball in his pocket, adjusted his hardhat and jumped down to the road beside Deyquan, whose wide-shouldered form dwarfed his, even though Scott wasn't small himself. "Sorry. Not sleepin' so good lately."

They followed the rest of the road crew towards several fallen young saplings and a broken birch tilting dangerously along the road. Scott remembered now. Bad thunderstorm last night. Tore up trees all over the county, littering the backroads with branches and other debris. Power lines down everywhere. The crews sent to clean those were lucky. At least the lines were already down where workers could see them. It was worse when a leaning tree could fall and snap a line unexpectedly.

"Yeah, you been twitchy lately." Boots scraped asphalt as they neared the trees. "Don't get me wrong, you been workin' fine. Better'n some of these idiots, that's for sure. You just been real dreamy the past few weeks."

Scott glanced at Deyquan, surprised to see concern in the foreman's eyes. "Sorry. Just been real tired."

They stopped at the road's shoulder. "Look," Deyquan

said, gripping his elbow. "You say you been sleepin' bad but haven't missed a day of work in weeks. We finish here, take the rest of the day off."

Scott shook his head and grinned tiredly. That was Deyquan, sure enough. All bluster, no real bite. "That's okay. I need the cash. I'll be fine."

Deyquan slapped his shoulder. "Whatever. Offer still stands."

"Thanks. Hey," he said as he thought about his odd Halloween meeting with a stranger on the phone who claimed to be a recruiter, "maybe Friday I could take the day off? I got this thing Saturday . . . " He stopped.

Scott's thoughts lagged, as if caught on a mental fishhook. He stared at the swaying birch, the power lines and the trees beyond. He swallowed. The salty taste of copper flooded his mouth.

The sky was so blue. It reminded him of the bluest pair of eyes he'd ever seen. Eyes which had burned past his skin and looked deep into his soul.

"Scott? You all right?"

Scott kept staring. It felt as if sparks were firing in his head. All in a row, like a string of Black Cats going off. He felt his jaw working. Heard it clicking. His tongue twitched but he said nothing, though something was there, a name . . .

"Scott?"

Vaguely, from a great distance, he felt Deyquan grab his shoulder and shake him. "Hey. Where you at, man?"

He felt it coming together in his head finally. He saw it. Swirling columns of blazing particles forming a terrible picture. His heart skipped, stomach clenching as his flesh puckered.

"Shit! Scott!"

Deyquan grabbed both his shoulders and shook him harder. "Damn! It's another seizure! Scott, you off your meds? Someone call fuckin' 911 now . . . "

A name formed and took on substance. Tumblers in his

mind rolled and clicked. The name flashed in big, burning letters before he actually whispered it, unheeding of Mack's shaking and yelling.

Redman.

"Redman," he murmured, "Sasha Redman."

He felt Deyquan's rough, calloused hands clasp his cheeks. "What? What is it, Scott? What about Sasha?"

He snapped back, blinked and saw Deyquan's face inches from his, twisted in concern and fear.

The new guy on the crew. The funny one with all the jokes. Redman. Sasha Redman.

Shit.

He's gonna die, RIGHT NOW, unless . . .

Move!

Scott tore away from Deyquan and sprinted down the gravel shoulder, where Sasha Redman and Derek Barton worked on a fallen sapling. Deyquan's cries faded beneath the pounding of his boots on gravel and the thudding of his heart.

Sasha is gonna die!

Three steps later he heard the leaning birch give way with an air-splitting crack. Shouts rose behind him, exploding into a frenzied crescendo. Then, the sound they all feared and hoped never to hear above them. The snap-hiss of electricity, free and deadly in the air.

He felt it against his back. An electric snake, swinging down, wanting to catch Sasha square in the chest. He ran harder. The air hummed as the wires raced him to Sasha. His feet and heart pounded in time. He tried to scream at Sasha to move, run, something, but all he could manage was to click his tongue like a skipping record.

Sasha turned, eyes widening. He froze over the tree he and Barton were working to tug into the road. Derek stiffened for a moment, then yelled and pawed at Sasha's shoulder, trying to get him to move, but Sasha remained.

Hands glued to the thick tree branch he'd been tugging. Scott was so close now, he could see Sasha's lower lip twitch, just once.

The air warmed and snapped behind him.

He wasn't going to make it, unless—

Scott dove. His shoulder slammed into Sasha's chest. His momentum tossed them several feet forward as his arms wrapped around Sasha and tried to pull him down and away from the snapped power line.

Was there too much slack?

How close were they to the next power pole?

Would the line clear the ground and swing above them? Or drag through gravel and dirt, right into them?

Scott and Sasha hit the ground in a flurry of arms, legs and flying dust. The truth hit Scott's brain with actual, physical pain. Too much slack. It'd hit the ground, drag and roll, hissing right into their feet and fry them both. Grabbing two fistfuls of Sasha's shirt, he rolled them away towards the county truck, away from the lines.

Blinding pain hit his mind and stabbed his eyes. He cried out, gurgling nonsense as his jaws clenched and his teeth ground together.

Oh shit.

God, no.

Shouts pealed. Boots pounded towards them. Scott and Sasha lay on the ground. Sasha stared over his shoulder at the power line coiling and sparking mere feet away. Scott's eyes bulged as he clutched Sasha's shirt, the shakes starting to set in . . .

"Holy shit! That was unfuckinbelievable! Scott, how the hell did you know that—"

"Goddamn, that was close! Scott, I ain't seen you move that fast since you stole home base in the state playoffs, back in—"

"Holy Mother Teresa, Sasha! You'd better pick up Scott's tab at The Stumble Inn for the next year."

Deyquan's worried voice broke through the babble. "Back off! Scott, man . . . you okay?"

Scott's jaw clicked and his mouth opened, but he couldn't speak because the thing was *here*, that dreaded thing he hated . . .

Seizure.

His head jerked back and he spasmed. Somehow he knew his fingers were still locked onto Sasha's shirt and that he was jerking the other man around, but he couldn't stop. Couldn't force his fingers to unclench. From far away, he heard someone yell "911!" as strong hands grabbed his shoulders and tried to hold him still. Through it all, brilliant blue eyes blazed in the darkness that descended upon him.

8.

The Commons Trailer Park
1 PM

JESSICA RECLINED IN an Adirondack chair on her trailer's cramped front porch, wearing the same outfit she'd thrown on this morning. Her bare feet rested on the railing as she nursed her third beer. Her last, because much as she wanted to, she couldn't drink herself silly. She had to work late-afternoon into the evening tonight, and was due at 2:30 PM.

A small charcoal grill sizzled next to her. Tendrils of smoke carried the scent of cooking hamburger, which set her stomach rumbling. She hadn't eaten much today. Just a vending machine lunch of chips and soda as she'd waited with Cody at Clifton Heights Hospital for word on how Shelly had fared after her most recent "accidental overdose of sleeping pills".

Jessica scowled. Sipped her drink, and vowed that if Shelly Livingston wanted to die so badly, next time she'd listen to the nasty little voice which had been bothering her lately and let Shelly die. Save everyone the trouble.

She instantly felt horrible. Along with a chill, thinking the strange, dark voice she'd been hearing lately was starting to sound so reasonable. She set her beer on the deck and leaned forward, elbows on knees. Closed her eyes and rubbed her temples with her fingertips. She saw Shelly Livingston sprawled on her unmade bed. Open bathrobe revealing everything as she stared blindly at the ceiling.

The image flickered to the darkness looming in the corners of Shelly's bedroom. She remembered touching Shelly's frigid, ice-cold skin . . .

She blinked.

Rubbed her eyes with the heels of her palms.

The image faded. She sat back, sighed, and grabbed her beer. She took a generous swig, wondering if maybe she should call off at work. They could manage without her for once.

She *had* to work tonight, of course. Couldn't afford not to. She'd made good ground the last two years. Paying tuition bills and saving up. Hadn't heard from a creditor in almost seven months. If she kept it up, she'd have some of her smaller bills paid off, then maybe she could increase her payments on those school loans. Start paying more than just the interest . . .

Get real.

Nothing's going to change. You should give up, now.

Her tremulous enthusiasm lost steam as that damn *voice* came back. For a moment, some black part of her heart listened to it. Sympathized with Shelly's numerous suicide attempts. Maybe that's what she should do. Go for one last big ride. Take the easy way out.

Her stomach curdled, not only because she found the concept disgusting, but also because it struck too close to home. Made her wonder just what it would take to push her over the edge, like Shelly.

She grunted. "Fuck that noise."

Angry at herself for even thinking it, she picked up the spatula resting on the chair's arm, and flipped the hamburgers.

When the EMTs arrived (after Jessica puked up the pills Shelly had taken), they'd worked quickly and efficiently. After checking Shelly's vitals, they eased her onto a stretcher and loaded her into Clifton Heights' only ambulance. The EMTs didn't bother asking any questions. They'd already answered too many emergency calls to the Commons involving Jessica. They'd gotten used to it, by now. Jessica's version of the story was the only one they'd hear.

After the ambulance left, Jessica spent money she shouldn't have on a cab and took Cody to the hospital. As they had too many times before, they waited in semi-silence in the GI Trauma waiting room, speaking in monotones about random trivialities. School, the weather, how the Utica Mets were doing, until yet another stern-faced but aloof doctor emerged with the prognosis that while Mrs. Livingston was out of danger, she'd need to spend the night for observation.

They'd visited Shelly briefly. As always, she'd begged Cody's forgiveness. Sobbing, promising to turn over a new leaf. He'd tearfully forgiven her. Jessica assured Shelly she'd keep an eye on Cody and the trailer until she went to work.

So it went.

Same old story.

As Jessica lifted her beer and drained it, she heard from her front steps: "Jessica? Uh . . . Ms. Hagarty? Think your burgers are burning."

Jessica blinked and returned to the present. Looked up and saw a concerned-looking Cody standing on her porch's front step, elbow leaning on the railing. She glanced the grill and saw flames curling up and around her charring burgers.

"Ah, damn."

She sat forward, grabbed a plate and the spatula from the chair's arm and gently pried the burgers off the grill and onto the plate. On quick inspection, only the edges looked crisped. Cody had warned her just in time.

She balanced the plate on her thigh, plucked a bag of rolls from next to her feet, and smiled at Cody. "Thanks. Day-dreaming, I guess. Probably would've burned them to a cinder, if not for you."

Cody shrugged, face and eyes blank with fatigue. "No big."

"Also. What've I been telling you about calling me *Ms. Hagarty*?" She gave him a pointed look. "Makes me feel old. Damn, kid. I'm not even twenty-five yet." She offered him a big smile. "<u>But</u>, you were trying to get my attention and save my dinner, so I'll cut you some slack. This time."

This brought a faint, flickering smile. "Gee. Thanks."

With the spatula she flipped a burger onto the bun. Her heart ached for Cody. He'd just turned thirteen. How many times had he weathered his mom's suicide attempts since the last boyfriend left her four years ago?

Too many. She saw it in his shadowed eyes, reluctant smile, and hollowed cheeks. Kids his age weren't built for this kind of shit. Weren't meant to bear such heavy burdens. It took a toll.

She knew better than anyone.

She grabbed ketchup, squirted some on the burger, topped it with the other bun, and asked, "How's your Mom?"

He shrugged again as she bit into the burger and chewed. He looked away, voice barely above a whisper. "Just got off the phone. She's okay. Tired. Cryin' and apologizin'. Promisin' she'll get better an' things'll get better an' she'll try harder an' all that." He made a fist, eyes flinty. "That's a lie. Everyone knows it. Month or so, she'll get lonely an' start drinkin' again. Or start drinkin' and feelin' lonely, an' she'll just do it again. Like always."

Jessica chewed and swallowed, coughed lightly. "She's had a hard time, kiddo," she managed. "She's not well."

Even in her ears, the words rang hollow.

He shook his head and sighed. "I get so scared an' messed up when she does this. An' sometimes . . . " he looked down and kicked the front porch's first step. "She's tried so many times, now. Gotta wonder if she even wants to be around, anymore. So sometimes I wish . . . "

She sat up quickly, shifted the plate to her lap, sensing his next words and wanting to spare him. "Hey, listen . . . "

He continued unabated. " . . . Sounds horrible, but sometimes I wish she'd do it when you're workin' so you can't help her. So it'd be too late. So she could just have her way an' be done with it."

There it was. What the little black voice had been whispering to her. All this time, she thought she'd been doing good. Saving Shelly, giving her second, third, even fourth chances others never got.

What if she *hadn't* been doing good? What if she'd been delaying the inevitable, making it hurt worse for everyone involved. She wondered about all the others, now. Had she wronged them, somehow, in the same way?

"Listen kiddo, I . . . "

Cody shook his head, face hard and unyielding. "It doesn't matter. One of these days she's gonna get what she wants, and there won't be anything any of us can do about it."

He turned and left Jessica's porch, walking away on stiff legs. Jessica dropped the burger on her plate. She was no longer hungry.

9.

The Golden Kitty
Route 28 North
11 PM

CHRIS TESTANI LEANED back in one of The Golden Kitty's recliners. An alcoholic numbness throbbed in his head, threatening to push him over the edge into unconsciousness. He fought against it, however. This private dance had cost him fifty bucks he couldn't spare. Especially since he'd gotten fired from the lumbermill a month ago, showing up to work drunk. No way was he blacking out and missing it.

He grunted and forced himself to sit up, the thought of his dwindling finances pulsing anger throughout him. Testani latched onto it, drawing energy from the fire sparking inside. It was Kennsinger's fault he was almost broke. *All* of this was Kennsinger's fault. He'd ruined everything the day he'd ruined Testani's face and his chances at pro baseball.

"Hey there, sleepy."

The stripper squatted near the edge of the room's small stage. Her husky voice made him burn inside, waking him up some more. "Thought you'd nodded off."

Testani eyed the limber dancer hungrily. She smiled, stood, and began her routine. Swaying her hips as she sauntered back to the pole in the middle of the stage. The pleasant heat in his groin blossomed and spread through him as he devoured her with his eyes. She was wiry and muscled, strong and firm. As she glanced back over her shoulder at him, he knew she was faking her steamy gaze—but he didn't care. It made him feel good, as she leered at him . . .

Her expression shifted slightly. The lustful mask slipping just enough to allow a moment of disgust bleed through. It happened in an instant. There and gone, but it didn't matter.

She'd seen his face.

Seen the gifts bestowed by Scott Kennsinger's fastball. A badly-healed cheek bone and eye-socket. Misshapen, warped . . . disgusting.

Inhuman.

His desire faltered.

That oily hate rose up again, threatening to overwhelm him. He stared at the stripper, pretending she *hadn't* seen his ruined face, telling himself she *wasn't* disgusted by him, that her clearly feigned expression of need and hunger was real. He tried to concentrate on the way she ran her hands down her breasts to her sides, to her hips, desperate to push away the hate boiling inside.

It didn't work.

Because of Scott Kennsinger.

Everything had been aces before that day four years ago, when Scott ruined his life. He'd ruled the halls of Clifton Heights High with an iron fist. A god on the football field, wrestling mat, and especially on the baseball diamond. He had college scholarship offers for all three sports. All the girls in school wanted him. All the guys wanted to *be* him.

To top it off, he'd been a good student. He didn't study, exactly, but reading and good grades came easily to him, like everything else always had. Even though his old man hadn't cared about anything he'd done (nothing Testani did impressed *that* fucker), the world had been his to conquer.

Until that day.

He shuddered, trying to push those thoughts away. He refocused on the stripper as she swayed to the hypnotic beat of canned dance music, her back pressed against the pole. Multi-colored spotlights on the ceiling glinted off her sweat-slicked, smooth flesh. Body glitter sparkled on her forearms, thighs and breasts. She smiled at him and winked, pretending she *wasn't* disgusted at the ruin of his face.

But it wasn't working.

Perhaps sensing his flagging desire, the stripper grabbed the pole, hooked her right leg on it and spun around once. The pole rattled. She leaped off it and pounced onto all fours. She crawled to the edge of the stage like a prowling lioness on the hunt, eyes faking her need.

At the stage's edge, she slowly stood. Placing her hands on her hips, she offered him a playful smirk. "You look tense. You seriously need to relax."

Testani nodded and forced himself into the routine, pretending he didn't see how her gaze flinched away from the crushed side of his face. "Yeah, baby," he rasped, "let's do this."

It felt scripted and pathetic, but he didn't care. Anything to shove down the self-loathing he felt. Anything to quench the hate boiling inside. The stripper smiled wider, but he knew why. She sensed easy money.

He met her gaze, enraptured by how the lights accentuated her soft facial curves. Desperate need pulsed inside. Before he could stop himself, he leaned forward out of his seat, grabbed the edge of the stage and snarled, "That's right. Fucking *whore*. Give it to Daddy."

The stripper's money-hungry look vanished. She jerked away, eyes suddenly bright and wary, no longer lustful. "Easy, Tiger. We don't play rough like that, here. Ain't that kind of place."

There it was, glittering openly in her eyes.

Contempt.

Disgust.

Fear.

Which only made him angrier. He leaped from his chair to lean against the stage's edge. "What's wrong? Don't like how I look? Huh? Think I'm fucking *ugly*?" He yanked back his hoodie and pointed at the warped side of his face. "Take a look! Take a close fucking look!"

The stripper backed away. He leaned over further and swiped at her leg, but he missed and his fingers grasped only air. "I paid my fifty bucks! Get back here and do your fucking job!" Scrambling, he got one knee over the edge and onto the stage as he reached again—

Stars exploded across his vision as pain flashed down the side of his head, stabbing into his neck and shoulder. She'd kicked him in the same place Kennsinger had ruined his face. He looked up and saw her crank back a muscled leg to do it again. "Asshole!"

His head rocked.

Pain flashed down his spine.

Liquid warmth pulsed where the toe of her high-heeled shoe had torn his skin, down along his crooked and lumped cheekbone. Stunned but insane with anger, he reached and clawed, trying again to crawl onstage . . .

. . . and everything became shouts and grabbing. Huge hands yanked him away from the stage. Someone screamed. Curses filled his ears as it all spun around. The floor, chairs, tables, lights.

Alcohol swirled in his gut. He couldn't hold it down any longer. He puked on himself and the floor.

More curses, and the hands dropped him. A sour stench assaulted his nose. He'd been thrown into his own vomit. With a wrenching intestinal heave, he puked again.

Someone muttered, "That shit stinks."

"Get him outta my club. Now."

Hands grabbed his collar and dragged him a few more feet. They lifted him, then launched him airborne. The cool night bit his skin as he flew. He slammed down onto asphalt, forehead cracking pavement.

"Don't come back, asshole! Or we'll fuck you up, *then* call the cops!"

A door slammed.

The night fell silent and still. Chris Testani curled into

a fetal ball. Snot bubbled from his nose and mixed with blood, sweat, tears and vomit. He cried up at the uncaring stars.

IO.

SCOTT KENNSINGER WOKE slowly and opened his eyes. He stood on a pitcher's mound. *The* pitcher's mound. Footsteps behind him ascended the wooden steps from the dugout and onto the field. They stopped. Someone waited for him there.

He turned.

Familiar sky-blue eyes stared at him. Unruly, blazing white locks spilled from under a hat with an unbroken brim. Not a player—but Scott knew that, didn't he? A bat boy, then. No . . . *the* bat boy. The one who changed his life forever.

Scott started to speak, when a throaty rumble interrupted him. He glanced up. Just past the bridge, he saw black tinted windows and headlights staring him down.

A black car.

A Monte Carlo, he thinks. Maybe a 1974? A '77? Its finish shimmered like a slick sheet of black beetles. As he stared at the car, something cold washed over him, making him feel dead inside. His head throbbed. Looking at the car made him dizzy. The air around it rippled. Shadows oozed from beneath it.

He couldn't look at it for very long. His stomach rolled as the car's surface shifted, slick as oil. He looked away to the boy and tried again to speak, but he couldn't. The Monte Carlo's engine throbbed against his mind. He clapped his hands over his ears but still the pain swelled, making it hard to think. The boy stared, silent and still.

A great rush filled Scott's head.

The Monte Carlo revved.

A high-pitched keening pulsed against his brain, and his stomach muscles clenched in primal fear. Scott cried out and crumpled to his knees as the pain in his head exploded.

Blood burst from his nose and poured down over his mouth. He gagged; insides squirming but even as he heaved, nothing came up but small dribbles of blood mixed with mucus.

The Monte Carlo revved again.

Tires squealed on asphalt. Scott managed to look up, and saw the car speed over the bridge, down the road toward them. A great pressure inside his head exploded and he plunged into the cold dark, as he . . .

II.

Saturday
October 31st
Halloween Night
6:00 PM

... OPENED HIS EYES. Rolled over and glanced at the old digital clock sitting on his even older black and white television. His shift at the gas station started in an hour. Still sleepy, head still aching slightly from his seizure and from a strange dream he couldn't really remember, he threw back the blankets, swung his feet to the floor and sat up on his futon. He rubbed his face and kneaded his forehead with his fingertips. Dropped his hands into his lap, headache only marginally eased. "This sucks," he whispered.

He sighed and ran a hand through his hair. He shouldn't complain. He didn't feel all that bad, actually. Just wrung out, with a slight headache. He probably could've even worked the road-crew yesterday, if Deyquan wasn't such a stickler about following doctor's orders. Old Man Kretzmer, who owned the gas station where he worked the night-shifts, didn't suffer from such quirks of morality.

He cracked his neck and rubbed the tight spot where it met his shoulder. He'd been stupid. Spending so much money this past month tuning up his motorcycle instead of spending it on his seizure meds. Of course, if his Kawasaki died and he couldn't make it to either job, he wouldn't be able to afford his meds, period.

Of course, there were worse things than the seizures. The premonitions, like the one he'd suffered Thursday right before his seizure, of the power line breaking and killing Sasha Redman. If those started coming back, like they had after that day on the baseball diamond four years ago . . .

He squeezed his eyes shut. No. It had been a fluke. A freak thing. That's all.

It wouldn't happen again.

With great effort he pushed those thoughts away. He didn't have time for them. According to doctor's orders Scott shouldn't work on the road crew until next Wednesday. Which meant he needed to work tonight and tomorrow night and pick up extra hours at the gas station next week, if possible. He eased off the futon and shuffled to his apartment's tiny bathroom for a shower.

Fifteen minutes later, Scott yawned while he tucked his purple and white work polo into his faded black jeans. He glanced into the mirror on the wall over his clothes dresser, making a lame effort to look presentable. With his fingers, he raked away unruly, coarse blond hair. Deep circles hung under his eyes. He'd slept worse than usual the past few days. Too many strange nightmares about that day on the pitcher's mound, the boy with 'Evan' stitched on the breast of his uniform, and a strange black car . . .

Scott ran another futile hand through his hair. He felt overtired and overstressed because he'd been sleeping poorly, and he didn't want to think about it anymore. But he'd taken his last dose of Tegretol weeks ago. He could have another seizure at any time. Worse, another vision which brought on a seizure . . .

It had been a fluke.

It wouldn't happen again.

It *couldn't*.

His cell rang. He looked down to where it lay on his dresser and stared at it for several seconds. An eerie sensation of synchronicity struck him. Two days ago, he'd received that odd call from the sports recruiter, right before leaving for work.

Right before he had a vision, and a seizure for the first time in four years.

Coincidence.

Has to be.

Scott peered at the phone's screen. 'Unknown Number' flashed. He should probably let it go. If it wasn't the sports recruiter, it was probably a sales call of some kind. And did he really want to talk to the recruiter, anyway?

Don't you want your dreams back, Scott?

Surprising himself, Scott reached out, grabbed his phone and answered the call. "Hello?"

"Scott! Hey kid, look—I'm really sorry. My schedule went crazy the last two days, and I totally dropped the ball. You remember me, right? Jimmy?"

Scott paused. A strange feeling curdled in his belly. An odd premonition. A certainty that, while life right now seemed cruelly difficult, it was better than what this "recruiter" could offer. He was gripped by the urge to hang up his phone and never answer another call from 'Unknown Number' ever again.

Even so.

Don't you want your dreams back, Scott?

He coughed and said, "Yeah. I remember you. It's okay. I've been . . . busy the past few days, too."

"Scott, my offer still stands. This may sound weird, considering it's Halloween night . . . but give me the go-ahead to set up a work-out. I'm confident you'll give me a class-act performance. Then you can have the life you've always dreamed of. Quit the damn gas station and the road crew."

That feeling in his belly worsened. At the same time, however, an opposite and almost equally powerful feeling rose up inside. Hatred. He hated his life. Hated working at the gas station. Hated what happened to him four years ago. Hated the seizures, and everything else. And even though he didn't hate working on the road crew or Deyquan, he didn't like it much, either (though he liked Deyquan just fine). Despite feeling strangely afraid of this guy's call, he almost felt more afraid of the dull future stretching out before him.

Fuck it.

"Sure. Why not? Set something up. I'll give it a shot."

"Fantastic! Scott, you won't be disappointed, I promise! And I know I won't be disappointed. I believe in you, pal. I really do."

With that, the strange unease curdling his stomach vanished. This guy was a huckster, plain and simple. More than likely he'd never call back. Even if he did set up some sort of workout for him, Scott would probably throw as badly as he always did. The best this guy could offer was a bench spot on a piss-ant farm team even smaller than the Utica Blue Sox. Nothing worth getting worked up about.

"Okay. Thanks for calling. Gotta get to work."

"Totally understand. Like I said—you won't regret this. And this is a special night, right? You know what they say about Halloween! 'Tonight's the night! The night of grave delights!'"

"Sure. Whatever." Scott hung up and stuck his phone into his pocket. He finished getting ready for work. And of course, he remembered that damn baseball, which he still felt compelled to stuff into his pocket on the way out the door.

For the most part, he shoved aside the recruiter's ridiculous promises, with the exception of two uneasy thoughts. One: it seemed odd a sports recruiter would call him so late at night, on *Halloween*, no less . . . though maybe not so odd. A guy who freelanced probably didn't keep regular hours. Even so. Something about it didn't sit right.

Two? Though he wasn't positive, Scott was sure he'd never listed his job at the gas station, or on the road crew, on the Sox's recruiting questionnaire. How had the guy known about it?

12.

The Stumble Inn
6:30 PM

CHRIS TESTANI SAT at The Stumble Inn's long, pitted bar. In the spirit of the season, someone had strung up orange and black crepe streamers around the ceiling. Cardboard cutouts of jack-o'-lanterns, witches, ghosts, Frankenstein's monster and Dracula hung from the mirror behind the bar. Instead of the regular glass dishes for the peanuts and pretzels, someone had filled cutesy dishes of jack-o'-lanterns and various monsters, and spaced them out along the bar. The Stumble Inn was even offering themed, brightly-colored orange and green mixed drinks for the occasion. A large plastic jack-o'-lantern sat next to the cash register against the back wall, glowing with electric light.

Head hanging, his old high school ball cap pulled to his nose, Testani saw none of this. He stared dully at his last pint of beer instead. He'd gotten drunk by five, after walking in with his last seventy bucks. He'd spent most of it on shots of cheap whiskey, chasing them with pints of equally cheap beer.

The gash on his forehead burned from where the stripper had kicked him two nights ago. The wound proved largely superficial. He'd patched it up with gauze and tape. In some ways, it actually made him feel less horrid. It hid his deformed and warped eye socket and cheekbone, gifts of Scott Kennsinger.

He mechanically raised his pint. Sipped and swallowed. It tasted stale, but it was all he could afford. Too bad it would be his last beer, ever.

When he'd dragged himself from bed this morning in

the apartment he'd be evicted from next Saturday, (he was two months late on rent), he'd numbly showered, fixed his wounds, dressed and left with his last two hundred dollars. He had a buddy who owned a ramshackle store on the outskirts of Booneville. A gun shop humbly named "Bob's Guns."

There, for one hundred and fifty dollars, he'd purchased an old .38 Special and a box of shells. After, he'd driven here and now he sat, bent over his warm beer, the .38 jammed under his belt, pressing against his belly and hid by his untucked flannel.

He took another drink and belched. The gas stung his nostrils. Somehow, he held down the bile.

In a dim corner of his mind, Testani knew he couldn't blame his current circumstances completely on Kennsinger. It wasn't Kennsinger's fault, directly, that he'd shown up to the lumbermill a month ago, too drunk to run the line.

He also couldn't blame Kennsinger for the way he fought with everyone at the mill. Even guys he considered friends. Over his four-year career there, he'd almost gotten into a dozen fist-fights over petty disagreements. In many ways, he probably should've been fired years ago for that alone.

He never saved his paychecks. Spent them at The Stumble Inn and The Golden Kitty. He'd been late on his rent several times. This was just the final straw. He never serviced his beat-up and dying 1985 Isuzu pickup truck, which he'd been driving since high school. None of these things could be blamed on Scott Kennsinger. This, Testani knew, if only in a dim way.

Scott certainly didn't pour booze down his throat for him, either—but he more than happily blamed his drinking on Scott, anyway. Which also didn't make sense, because he'd been drinking since he was sixteen.However, his burgeoning athletic career and scholarship potential had restrained him, at least a little. He hadn't wanted to go too crazy at a beer-banger and blow his chance at getting out of this shitty town.

Then *that* day came. Kennsinger going nuts and rocketing a fastball straight into his face. Shattering his right cheekbone and eye socket. No way his mother (who'd taken off two years ago) could afford the expensive reconstruction surgery to make his face look normal again, so his face healed all wrong. Warped. Misshapen. No way he could play college sports with that kind of damage. Even though the eye itself hadn't been harmed, he'd never have quite the same vision again.

After the surgery it had taken almost a year for the pain to recede. A year before he could even think about finding work. During that year, he sat in his mother's run-down house (a reflection of the woman herself) and drank.

He'd eventually gotten the job at the mill. Moved into a crappy apartment over Chin's Pizza and Wings, on Main Street. He'd thought the break would give him new purpose. Instead, he just sat in his apartment and drank every day after work. When he wasn't drinking at The Stumble Inn, or The Golden Kitty.

He had become his father.

In his irrational, booze-addled mind, Testani believed he *could* lay that at Kennsinger's feet. If it hadn't been for that fastball, at the very least, Chris Testani might be playing on a farm team somewhere instead of drinking himself to death in his hometown.

He lifted the pint and drained it, swallowing with a grimace. Set it down and waved a vague hand at the bartender for a refill. He still had twenty bucks left. He'd drink the rest of that away, and afterward, hopefully he'd have the courage to do what needed to be done. The courage he didn't quite have, yet.

13.

7:00 PM

SCOTT WAS CRUISING down Route 28 South through Clifton Heights and towards work when he saw it. Idling at the intersection ahead, where Havertown Road crossed the interstate. A big black car, sitting at the stoplight. Its engine throbbing, low and throaty. Tinted windows shimmered. Chrome trim and exhaust glinted against the night, almost unnatural in its luminescence.

Plenty of guys in the area loved their restored muscle cars. It was practically a required proof of manhood. He'd seen three of them this past month.

This one looked different, however. Familiar, also.

Like he'd seen it in a dream.

Or a nightmare.

He didn't usually heed the traffic lights at this intersection. He just eyed Havertown both ways and sped through. Tonight, however, he braked and skidded to a gravel-crunching stop. Oddly enthralled, he stared at the black car which, up close, he saw was a Monte Carlo. What year, he wasn't sure. Regardless, it had been restored and customized. Its black metallic finish rippled like the surface of a deep pool. Its tinted windows inspired unpleasant ideas about what sat behind the wheel.

a black car

a Monte Carlo

its finish shimmers like a slick sheet of beetles

He fidgeted, shrugging off a sudden, odd premonition. It was probably only a trick of the night, or maybe just the car's slightly over-sized tires, but the Monte Carlo seemed to crouch forward. As if straining against an invisible leash. Waiting for some unfortunate prey to cross its path.

Silently, the passenger window slid halfway down.

Icy fingers trailed along his spine.

Soupy darkness swirled inside the car. Though he saw nothing, he felt something watching from inside. Unbidden, the sports recruiter's final words on the phone came back to him:

Tonight's the night!

The night of grave delights!

Seconds passed. Scott raised his foot, fingers tensing against the motorbike's throttle, but he couldn't push off. It was like something he'd once seen on Animal Planet. He was a gazelle hoping its stillness would hide it from a predator's tooth and claw. The Monte Carlo was . . .

More seconds passed.

The light changed and the car's window hissed upward and closed. Heavy metal clanked somewhere in its guts as it shifted gears. Thrumming lazily, it rolled through the intersection and pulled away. It seemed forever before its red taillights disappeared around the bend at the bottom of the hill.

Scott released a burning breath.

With it, his unease faded. Obviously it had been some asshole—probably drunk—having fun at his expense. Whatever. He didn't have time to worry about it tonight.

His scalp prickling at the thought, he glanced at his wristwatch. Sure enough, he was late. Cursing, he gunned his Kawasaki and shot through the intersection towards work, the Monte Carlo and its oddness fading from his thoughts.

Almost.

14.

SCOTT'S KAWASAKI BURPED into the parking lot of the 24-hour Mobilmart on Haverton. Squeezing the brakes and releasing the throttle, he killed the engine and skidded to a bumpy stop before a bike stand. He pocketed the key, toed the kickstand down, dismounted and unwrapped the security chain he kept looped around the motorbike's handlebars. He had no idea who'd want to steal such a gas-guzzling piece of shit, but with his sketchy finances he couldn't take any chances. If someone snatched his bike, he'd be forced to take a Yellow Cab to work, walking when he couldn't afford that.

After securing his motorcycle with his old high school padlock (also fucking ironic), he stood and saw Jessica Hagarty crying through the gas station's front window. The image startled him. Signs for garage sales and local concert playbills framed a face which looked lost and sad.

She blinked.

The moment passed. Jessica scowled and turned away. She bent over the cash register and resumed counting out her drawer, which meant he *was* late, by ten minutes or more.

Damn.

He jogged toward the entrance. The electric doors hissed open and ushered him inside. Jessica ignored him, but that was to be expected. She'd ignored him since he started working here. She was probably sorry she'd looked at him for even a minute. Figuring two could play that game, he spun on one heel and stalked to the office without a backward glance.

"You're late. I was supposed to punch out ten minutes ago."

He ducked into the office. "Whatever," he mumbled

under his breath. Between the weird persistence of that recruiter who was probably a scammer and his odd encounter with the Monte Carlo, he didn't have the patience for her attitude.

"I heard that, Kennsinger. Don't be an asshole. Not tonight, please. I don't have the patience for it."

There was a pause, filled with clinking change and ruffling bills. "Just get your drawer and ring in."

He went to the manager's desk, punched in and grabbed his plastic-wrapped cash drawer from the shelf. He turned to leave . . . and froze. Jessica was facing him. She eyed him with a frown.

He tried to form a snappy remark, but it sputtered and died. Was just as well. He didn't do snappy. He probably would've sounded stupid, anyway.

"E-excuse me. Gotta cash in, right?"

She stared at him silently. He wished he could say something smart and clever. Something that would set her back on her heels. This would be the perfect time.

Not tonight, please.

I don't have the patience for it.

He opened his mouth. Closed it, and swallowed. His throat felt thick and dry. For some reason, he couldn't summon up the urge to pass a cutting remark.

Finally, she spoke. "Get out there." Edging past him, she stuffed the drawer onto the second shelf, turned and crossed her arms. "Something to say?"

He glared at her over his shoulder but as usual had no comeback. Futile anger burned in his guts. He gripped the cash drawer so tightly his knuckles ached.

"Get to work," she said quietly. She turned, sat down at the desk, and started filling out her end-of-shift paperwork.

He stared at her for a heartbeat, but she'd returned to ignoring him again. Whatever else he was, he wasn't a lurker. He left the office and headed to the register.

15.

The Stumble Inn
8:30 PM

CHRIS TESTANI RAISED his pint to his lips and slugged back the last of his beer. Swallowed regretfully (even though it tasted like warm piss), because he'd finally run out of money. This was it. The last bit of booze he'd ever swill.

He set the pint back on the bar gently, almost reverently. As if it were a holy relic. In a way, maybe it was. This wasn't The Last Supper and that glass wasn't the Cup of Christ. More like the Pint of Chris, and this certainly was his Last Call.

Testani's hand drifted to the cool metal of the .38 tucked under his belt, hidden under his T-shirt. As he touched it, he thought about getting help. Drying out. Maybe he should turn himself into the cops or something. Old Sheriff Beckmore was a soft touch. Always had been. He'd gone to school with Chris' old man—played football with him back in the day—and Chris had distant memories of Beckmore trying to get his father help at one time, also. Before the old man became a lost cause. Maybe Beckmore could do the same for him.

The thought was compelling in its brief clarity. Chris stumbling into the police station. Turning the .38 over to whoever was working the night desk tonight. Asking them to put him in the drunk tank so he could sober up. For just a moment, Chris saw this with such vividness, his heart sped up.

Dim reality reared its head. Overshadowing this hopeful dream. Maybe Beckmore *could* help. Get him into AA with Father Thomas at All Saints. Maybe he *could* dry out for a week or so. But where would he go? No way Mr. Chin would let him skip rent again, no matter how hard Beckmore leaned on him. He had no friends to crash with. No place to stay.

There was the YMCA in Utica . . . but how would he get there? It was over an hour away. How would he attend AA? Maybe Father Thomas' reach extended that far, but in a strange environment, surrounded by people he didn't know or trust, how long would any kind of sobriety last?

He also thought about everyone in Clifton Heights. Former fans and classmates who'd watched his quick descent into a workman-like alcoholism. Folks who'd done nothing and said nothing through years of abuse at his father's hands, and also stood by and watched him destroy his life, silently shaking their heads in pity. No one had offered help all these years. Who'd help, now?

The harsh reality of his existence washed away his dim dream of recovery. He had no one. No friends left from school, and he'd quickly destroyed the brief friendships he'd made at the mill. Any kind of recovery was doomed to a short life, only forestalling the inevitable.

"All right then," Testani muttered, shifting on his barstool, "let's get this fucking show on the road."

He gripped the bar's edge with both hands, bracing himself. Was about to stand when the bartender's voice—suddenly in close proximity—asked, "What'll it be?"

Testani's thoughts snagged, confused, because he thought the bartender was addressing him. Looking up, however, he saw the stout bartender (a gruff but amiable guy named Gus) addressing a man standing next to Chris. A guy wearing—of all things—an outback hat and black trench-coat. He thought for a moment maybe it was some sort of half-assed Halloween costume.

Staring at the guy, however, Chris didn't think so. The hat threw odd shadows on the man's face, hiding everything except for the guy's nose and mouth. It made Chris uneasy, for some reason, though he didn't know why.

"I'll have a Devil's Delight," the man said in a smooth, pleasant voice. Something about it put Chris instantly at ease. Made him feel good. Warm. Peaceful, even. "Seems an appropriate drink, considering the night, yes? Oh, and heavy on the vodka and brandy, if you please."

Gus nodded and fixed the man's drink, mixing fruit juices, vodka and brandy. Chris sat and stared at the stranger as a soothing warmth spread through him. He felt like he'd taken a strong hit off a joint, but the feeling pulsing through him was stronger than a high. Purer, somehow, offering great clarity. He felt more focused than he had in weeks.

The stranger accepted the drink from Gus. Nodded once, lifted the glass in salute to the gruff bartender. Tossed it back in one smooth motion, downing it all at once, without the slightest reaction. He set the glass down, tapped the bar, and said in that same pleasant voice, "Start me a tab?"

Gus nodded and began mixing another. In minutes, he handed the stranger a second drink. The man saluted with the glass again, saying, "Thanks. I'm good for a bit." Gus nodded and moved down the bar to serve other patrons.

The man turned smoothly and offered a wide smile. "Hello, Chris. How's Halloween treating you?"

16.

"HELLO, CHRIS. How's Halloween treating you?"

Chris couldn't speak. He opened his mouth, but nothing came out. The man smiled, shrugged, saluted him with his glass, said, "Cheers," and took a healthy drink.

Feeling lightheaded and *good* (for the first time in a very long time), Chris nonetheless suffered pinpricks of shame as he clumsily lifted his pint glass in a half-assed salute of his own. "Same to you. 'Cept I'm kinda . . . out."

The man frowned. He looked sad, as if Chris had just informed him of a great personal tragedy. "Out of booze on Halloween? That won't stand, at all."

He whistled down the bar. "Excuse me?" Held up his glass, and nodded at Chris. "The same for my friend? Put him on my tab, also."

Gus handed two beers to waiting customers, and started fixing new drinks. Minutes later, two glasses of the pinkish-red concoction appeared before them. The man exchanged his empty glass for one of the full ones, and with an amazingly steady hand (considering how much he'd already had), Chris picked up the other glass.

He saluted the stranger. "Thanks."

The man smiled, exposing perfectly square, white teeth. "Cheers." He tossed back the full glass like it was water.

Chris took a generous sip of his own. He shuddered slightly at the perfect blend of vodka, brandy, and fruit juices. He'd never been a mixed-drink guy. He preferred beer and straight whiskey. This drink, however, proved shockingly refreshing. Even though his belly glowed with its warmth, his head felt clearer than ever. Emboldened by this, he emptied the glass.

His senses buzzing even sharper, Testani set the glass down and nodded at the stranger. "Thanks. That really hit the spot."

The man smiled and nodded at the glass (oddly, Chris still couldn't make out the man's eyes, his hat casting shadows there). "Have another. Might make you forget about the .38 tucked under your belt, and what you're planning on doing with it."

Chris blinked, speechless, at first not comprehending the man's words. He swallowed down a tight throat and finally managed, "How . . . how did you . . . ?"

The man nodded at the bar. "Have another, Chris. Will clear your head."

Chris glanced at the bar, where two more glasses of Devil's Delight sat. The man snagged his glass. Like before, he emptied it in one swallow.

Instead of reaching for his, Chris's hand strayed to his belly, fingers searching for the .38. Instead of cool metal, however, he touched his own skin.

"Looking for this?"

He glanced up and saw the .38 gleaming in the man's hand. The stranger held it by the barrel, up where anyone could see, if they looked in their direction. A sudden flush of panic overwhelmed his confusion at how the man had taken it without him knowing. "Jesus! What the hell are you doin'? People are gonna . . . "

The man smiled and waved Chris's protests away. "No worries. People tend to only see what they want. And I, my good friend, am *very* good at making people see only what *I* want. Rest assured, all anyone sees right now is two guys sharing a drink."

The man set the .38 down on the bar and gestured at Chris. "Go on. Bottom's up. Like I said. It'll clear your mind. Get you thinking straight."

Feeling disoriented, Chris glanced down at the glass he'd apparently picked up without noticing. He licked his lips and hesitated, a small part of him thinking something was very wrong.

But he was so thirsty.

He raised the glass, saluted the man, tipped his head back and threw the whole thing down. The cool liquid fire scorched his mouth and throat. Though it made him cough slightly, a warm sense of wellbeing instantly suffused him. His belly glowed hotter with satisfaction.

"Attaboy. Now listen." The man grabbed Chris' shoulder with a firm, comforting grip. Chris gazed into the shadow under the man's hat, looking for his eyes and finding nothing but swirling darkness. But not a terrible, menacing darkness. A warm kind of darkness. The kind he'd like to sleep in. "I know about everything, Chris. What happened to you. What Scott Kennsinger *took* from you."

As if conjured by the man's words, Chris' cheekbone and his eye-socket flared with throbbing hot pain. "How do you know about that?"

"I've been watching both of you for a while, Chris. I'm a talent scout, of sorts. You and Scott have always had something special. More than others. I've been watching you both because I wanted to know if you can take your talents to another level."

Though it hurt his ruined cheekbone (as it always did), Chris grinned. "You mean . . . pro ball?"

The man tipped his head. "More like Triple A, with a chance to advance. You and Scott had a spark others didn't." He held up a finger. "Very *different* kinds of sparks, mind you. Scott's was a gift from another. Something given to him. You got yours from your Daddy. He *made* your spark."

Chris's thoughts turned dark and oily at the mention of his father and the old man's drunken rages. The things he did to Chris's older sister when deep in his cups. The impact of his open-handed slaps to Chris's mother, and his fists crashing into Chris's temples. Then, that one time . . . that one awful time, after his sister ran away, and Mom locked herself in the basement . . . the things his old man had done to *him*, until his hunger was sated.

As if sensing Chris's thoughts, the man squeezed his

shoulder and spoke in a gentle voice. "I know how hard it was for you, Chris. The pain, the *degradation* you endured. I wouldn't wish that kind of treatment on my worst enemy."

Despite his warm feelings, Chris thought this was a lie.

The man squeezed his shoulder again. "But you survived. Became hard. *Strong*. And that sunnuvabitch got what he deserved, didn't he? No one knows, Chris, but I do. I was fucking *proud*, son. Of how you sneaked out to The Drunken Otter that one night when he was drinking with the boys, and cut the brake line to his Monte Carlo. That was some deft work. Proof of how special you were."

Chris felt no shame or guilt at the mention of his darkest secret. Instead, a glowing pride filled him. A sense of satisfaction at a job well-done.

"He'll never hurt anyone ever again, Chris. Because of you. You had the strength of will to *end* him. No way Scott Kennsinger would ever have the guts for something like that." Almost as an afterthought, he added, "Drink up, son. You've got a full night ahead."

Chris looked down and felt no surprise when he saw his glass refilled. He eagerly tossed its contents down as the man continued, his tone turning somber. "Scott Kennsinger did you wrong, Chris. He tried to take everything from you."

Chris licked his lips, which were starting to feel numb. "Damn straight," he mumbled, looking down into a glass that was mysteriously full once more.

"And he *did* take something from you, I'm afraid. Something vital. He ruined you, my boy, on a deeper level than just your face. Sent you on this dark road."

"Fuck yes," Chris mumbled as he raised the glass to his lips, sipping slower this time, even though he still felt good and clear, clearer than he'd felt in years.

"You can take it all back, y'know. Tonight. If you want."

This grabbed his attention. Chris frowned and looked up into the shadows where the man's eyes should be. "Whaddya mean?"

The man grabbed both of his shoulders and squeezed. "He *didn't* take everything, Chris. You've still got it. The strength. The hardness. It's just buried deep inside. I can help bring it out."

Chris took another healthy sip, and looked deep into the darkness beneath the man's hat. For the first time, he saw something which might be eyes. Softly glowing orbs of red-orange . . . which didn't make sense. They didn't look like eyes at all. More like seething coals in a fire.

"How?"

The man's throaty chuckle sounded good-natured and amiable on the surface. Beneath it, however? Something crackled like dry leaves scuttling across cold concrete. "It's Halloween night, Chris. A night of limitless potential. The air itself is different tonight. You remember, yes? That one night Daddy somehow stayed sober and took you Trick or Treating? You remember your costume?"

Chris nodded slightly. He did remember. A-Rod. Alex Rodriguez. He'd dressed in his "official" A-Rod New York Yankees uniform, complete with cleats and a Louisville Slugger. He'd even slicked his hair back and dyed his face brownish with cheap Halloween face paint bought at Brown's Pharmacy.

For some reason, Dad was sober that night, and took him Trick or Treating. Didn't call A-Rod a "lazy-ass spic" once. Everyone greeted him by calling out, "Hey, A-Rod! Swing for the fences!" It felt like the greatest night of his life.

"Yeah," he whispered. "I remember."

"Of course you do. Because it's Halloween. A night we can be anyone we want, and do anything."

Chris looked deep into the man's glowing ember eyes. "Tonight's the night," the man whispered, "the night of grave delights. Those delights are yours, Chris. They're waiting. All you have to do is take them back from Scott Kennsinger. All you have to do is give me permission to help you. Will you do that?"

KEVIN LUCIA

The question hung in the air.

Waiting, expectant, pregnant with possibility.

Chris looked down into his once again mysteriously full glass. He'd lost everything. Dignity. Pride. Purpose. Meaning. He'd tried to get over it, but he couldn't. His future spread out before him like a rotting corpse, and he'd come here to end it, once and for all.

"Fuck it," he whispered.

He tossed back the drink. Thumped the glass down on the bar and looked deep into the man's burning ember eyes. "Hell yes."

The man smiled. "Well then. Let's go outside, shall we?"

17.

IN WHAT FELT like a blink of an eye, Chris and the man with burning ember eyes were standing outside in The Stumble Inn's parking lot. The man held out Chris's gun. He accepted it with an eagerness which felt right and true. "I think we've found another use for this, now," the man said as Chris took the gun back. "Also, I have something else for you. A Halloween gift, you might say."

Chris opened his mouth to speak, but fell silent as an approaching rumble interrupted him. He peered into the darkness on Route 28 and saw . . .

He gasped.

Twin beams of light splashed over him as a car pulled into the Inn's parking lot and drove up to him. He blinked, confused, and raised a shaking hand to shield his eyes. His heart sped up as the car rolled to a stop and parked before him.

A black 1977 Monte Carlo.

Its headlights flicked off, leaving spots in his vision for a few seconds. As they faded, he could see the car clearer. Long and sleek, the Monte Carlo stretched out, its black finish swimming like liquid metal under the Inn's parking lamps. Front fenders and hood sloped forward, leering at him in casual disregard. Chrome trim gleamed. The car sat slightly high in the rear on oversized tires.

The idling engine pulsed, resonating in Chris, from the bottom of his feet all the way to his head. Judging by the engine's heavy, rhythmic throb, Chris guessed it had a Chevy 502 under the hood. Maybe even a 572. Just like his father's. The one his old man had driven straight into a tree the night Chris had cut his brake lines.

"Go on," the man whispered. "Take a closer look."

Chris stepped closer, peering through narrowed eyes.

KEVIN LUCIA

The tinted front windows gave back his wavering, ghostly reflection, back-lit by orange parking lamps. The car cast off emanations of strength and power as the Monte Carlo filled his vision. He saw nothing but flowing black metal. Its big block engine throbbed in tune with his heartbeat.

The car was hungry. He felt it, skin prickling with its desire.

"It's yours," the man said, "along with this."

Chris faced the man, who was extending something with his right hand.

A Louisville Slugger.

"One more thing. There's this girl. She's been mucking up the works for a few years now. Getting in the way of some deals I've been trying to close. She's got spark, too. Got it from the same place as Kennsinger, actually. But I can't use that kind of spark. It's actually been getting in the way. I need you to snuff her spark out, if you come across her. Can you do that for me, Chris?"

Chris licked his lips and nodded. "Fuck yeah."

The man smiled. "Swing for the fences, A-Rod."

Chris accepted the bat, the wood feeling deliciously cool and smooth against his skin. With a click, the driver side door of the Monte Carlo opened.

18.

The Mobilmart
9:30 PM

SCOTT HAD BEEN thinking about the possibility of looking for a job in Utica. Maybe in a factory or warehouse, when Jessica approached the counter and abruptly said, "Why the hell are you working here? You could do better, you know."

The question caught him off guard. He looked up at the cigarette rack hanging over the counter and pretended to count the Marlboro Menthols, Virginia Slims and Pall Mall Light 100s. Anything not to face her, because what could he say?

help me
make them stop

Jessica wouldn't be ignored. "Look, Kennsinger. I've had a bad day and I'm being a bitch. I'm sorry."

Scott coughed as he continued counting cigarette boxes. "Thanks."

"So. Why are you here? You're not like the other losers who've worked for Old Man Kretzmer."

"I . . . " He glanced at her, then quickly back up to the cigarette boxes, confused, pleased and terrified at Jessica's sudden, unexpected interest. "I just . . . "

Jessica remained patiently silent.

He finally pretended to stop counting the cigarette boxes. Folded his arms and tried to look anywhere else but at Jessica, fighting back a rising tide of aggravation, maybe even fear. "I don't like talking about it." He swallowed. Looked away, and continued. "I . . . had a seizure my senior year in high school. And . . . "

I hurt someone
bad

" . . . someone got hurt. I quit school after. Just didn't want to be there anymore."

Scott took a deep breath and forced himself to meet Jessica's gaze. "I work a day job, too. For the county. I like it, but the health insurance isn't enough to cover my seizure meds." He shrugged. "So I work here, too." He didn't mention his seizure from the other day, how work wouldn't let him come back until his doctor cleared him. He figured she didn't need the whole song and dance.

Even so, Jessica's face softened. She crossed her arms, expression oddly sympathetic. As if she could relate. "Seizures, huh? Like epilepsy?"

"I guess. Except . . . "

Memories of a sun-swept Saturday afternoon blossomed in his head. The feel of the ball in his one hand. The glove on his other. The sun beating down on his shoulders . . .

help me
make them stop

Though he hated it, he found himself digging into his pocket and clutching the hated memory of that day. The baseball he couldn't seem to get rid of. Somehow, clenching it gave him the strength to push on. "The doctors don't think it's epilepsy. They don't know what causes it."

He paused, curious himself, now. He probably shouldn't ask. Most likely she'd just get pissed. Even so. "What about *you*?"

She frowned. "What about me?"

Her reaction wasn't nearly as defensive as he'd feared it'd be, but it was still enough to throw him off-balance. "I mean, you don't seem the type to work here, either. You're better than this place, too."

Jessica's laugh sounded surprisingly relaxed. "Wow. Are you flirting with me?"

He opened his mouth as his face warmed with embarrassment, but she continued before he could protest.

"What can I say? Shit happens. You plan on your life going one way, it turns out different, and you make do. Couple years ago, I wanted to be a nurse. Went to college for it, even."

"What happened?"

She shrugged and smiled, but the hard lines on her face told a different story. "Shit happened. That's all. Now, here I am. Three years later, trying to pay off college bills for a degree I never quite earned." Jessica waved, acting as if it wasn't important, but Scott could see by the shadow passing over her face it was. "You do what you can to get by. That's all any of us can do."

He opened his mouth—to say something lame, probably—when the *ping* of the doors interrupted him. Two men walked in; one heading toward him, his wallet out, presumably to pay for gas. The other heading back to the beer coolers.

Scott shot a quick glance past the man standing before him, hoping to catch Jessica's eye. She'd already vanished into the back office, so he regretfully accepted the twenty the man handed to him and rang his gas purchase up.

19.

SOMETHING WONDERFUL WAS happening to Chris Testani. He hadn't left The Inn's parking lot yet. He'd sat in the Monte Carlo for what seemed like hours, grooving to Rob Zombie, Korn and—amazingly enough—every other band he loved. But it wasn't just bands he liked. It was their specific *songs*. The ones he listened to before every athletic contest to pump himself up. Especially baseball. The radio seemed to be playing the same mix he'd listen to on bus rides to away games, and while he sat in the bullpen waiting his turn at bat. It was like someone had programmed every single one of those baseball songs into the car's radio.

He shifted in the comfort of the driver's seat and sighed. He clutched the .38 in his right hand. The Louisville Slugger lay across his lap. He hummed and tapped his foot along with the music's beat. Underneath, the car's engine pulsed, sending vibrations through him. He felt so good he could barely stand it. He felt *happy*. He hadn't been too happy lately, had he?

No.

He'd been all used up. Broken. Worn down and defeated. Life had sucked, and . . .

He frowned.

Why had things sucked?

He couldn't remember.

That bothered him, slightly. It also bothered him that he didn't know why he felt so happy. He couldn't remember the "fine print," as Daddy used to say.

Of course, thinking about Daddy wasn't good, at all. That just made him feel dirty inside. All that grappling, panting and grunting in the cold, sweaty dark with Daddy . . .

The car's engine throbbed in his ears and washed away memories of Daddy, making him feel even better. Best not to think about Daddy. That just got him upset, which wouldn't do. He had too much to accomplish. Too much to do with this wonderful, shiny black car.

The car's engine kept throbbing.

Yes.

He'd better get going. He had important things to do. Best be on his way.

The car asked a question. Exactly how a car could ask him a question, Chris wasn't sure. But like it was best not to think about Daddy, it was also best not to think about how a car could ask him a question, so he concentrated on the question itself. He nodded and licked his lips. Smiled. "Yeah. I'd like that. A lot."

The car asked another question. Chris thought about this for a moment, but the answer was simple. "Everything. I'm all yours."

This made the car happy. Chris could tell by the way its engine purred.

The Monte Carlo shifted into gear and rumbled as it backed out of its parking space, somehow all by itself. Chris didn't care, though, or ask how or why. He just smiled because his new car made him happy. One hand tightened around the .38 and the other around his Louisville Slugger as he thought how very *happy* he was, indeed. And why shouldn't he be happy?

It was Halloween night!

The night of grave delights!

And it was time he got his.

20.

BUSINESS PICKED UP for the next twenty minutes as a variety of customers stopped by. Teenagers getting soda and snacks, wearing fright masks and colored wigs. A few tired-looking construction workers. College guys picking up twelve packs, probably for a Halloween frat party at Webb Community College. A few clusters of haughty college girls, buying hard sodas and wine coolers, probably for their own Halloween festivities.

Scott was ringing up the last customer in the store after a steady stream—a rough-looking bearded man wearing a Carhart jacket and a CAT hat—when he felt something pull his thoughts away. He glanced out the window. What he saw tightened his stomach muscles. At one of the gas pumps sat the black Monte Carlo he'd seen earlier. Its passenger side window was down. Inky darkness swirled inside. Though it was impossible, he thought he heard voices coming from the car. Through the gas station window, into his head. Wailing screams and cries, waxing and waning. Terrible voices whispering of terrible things from some far, distant place . . .

As he looked, entranced, he heard the gas station's glass doors *ping* and slide open. The man in the CAT hat cursed. Scott turned in time to see a baseball bat swinging through air. It hit the side of the man's head with a loud *crack*, spinning his CAT hat off his head in the midst of a fine spray of blood.

The man hit the floor hard enough to shake the counter. Jessica ran out of the office, shouting, sliding to a halt and falling silent, her eyes wide with fear. A dark figure swung the baseball bat down over and over, each swing ending with a dull, wet thwacking, as if someone was pummeling a sack of meat. Droplets of blood splattered onto the counter before him, and Scott felt his unwilling gaze drawn toward their wet redness.

A loud *click*.

He'd heard something like it before, but only in the movies.

A hammer pulled back on a gun.

"Hello, fucker."

Scott forced himself to look up. His gaze traded the droplets of blood shimmering on the counter for a yawning black muzzle, behind which hovered a hauntingly familiar, twisted and ruined face and mad, glittering eyes. Eyes which Scott had last seen four years ago.

Icy dread crept down his spine.

Chris Testani.

The guy whose life he'd ruined.

Testani's twisted face smirked, revealing jagged teeth which looked sharper than they should. Flesh was twisted up in scarred knots around his ruined cheek bone and eye socket. "Tonight's the night," Testani rasped, teeth clicking. "The night of grave delights! And I'm about to get my delights, Scott. Finally."

21.

IN THE DAYS when Scott ruled the pitcher's mound, the world lived and breathed in his head. Colors burned brighter in the sky. Smells stung his nose, sharp and pungent. Cleats scraped against dust-grimed bases and clicked against stones while uniforms whisper-rustled against dried-sweat skin.

Standing tall on the mound, ball snug in his glove, he flowed out into the world, and it flowed into him. When he was pitching, he knew his purpose. It felt good. Felt right.

He'd never been to church but he wondered if maybe that's why people went. They felt right there. He'd lost that. Thanks to a boy who'd stared into the bottom of his soul and asked for help, Scott had lost his sense of rightness. Since then, the world had retreated to a tin echo of a symphony he'd once known by heart. He no longer had purpose. He no longer belonged, forever disconnected from the bigger thing which had made things feel *right*.

Standing behind the counter of the Mobilmart #9 in Clifton Heights, Scott Kennsinger abruptly plugged back in. The world flared to life once more. His eyes absorbed details with the same precision he'd once used to break down batters at the plate.

The black mouth of a gun loomed in his face.

Quick death lurked within.

The man in the Carhart jacket gurgled from the floor.

Testani's other white-knuckled hand gripped a Louisville Slugger, its end clotted with thick red blood. Scott imagined if he looked closer, he'd find chunks of scalp and matted hair clinging to it.

His gaze flicked sideways.

Jessica had flattened herself against the wall. Eyes wide, nostrils flaring.

He looked back to Testani's face. He'd never seen him up close before the accident, so he'd no point of reference. Even so, there was no way the man could've looked worse than he did at this moment. His face was drawn and gaunt. Thin lips pulled back from teeth in a hungry grimace, exposing shiny pink gums. Old, unwashed clothes hung limply off a thin frame. Even worse, Scott beheld, up close, what he'd done to Testani. The twisted scar tissue knotted up on the cheekbone and wrapped around a dented, deformed eye-socket, making the right side of his face look like something out of a black and white horror film.

Gun never wavering, Testani growled, "Like what you see? You did this to me, Kennsinger." He punctuated each point by jabbing the gun's muzzle at him. "You. Did. *This.* To *me!*"

Scott swallowed. "I'm sorry. I didn't want—"

"DON'T!" Testani slammed the Louisville Slugger on the counter, left it there, and jabbed a finger at him. "Don't bullshit me! You took everything away from me. *Everything!* And you made me into . . . into *this!*"

He jabbed the gun at Scott again. "I'm gonna take it back, you hear me? I'm gonna do him proud, so he'll take me up to the big leagues with him. Like he said, Scott—tonight's the night!"

Scott's mouth dropped open, his memory clicking furiously, calling up a voice which had spoken to him over the phone earlier that day . . .

tonight's the night
the night of grave delights!

Scott clenched his hands into fists. The urge to stick his hand into his pocket and grasp the hated baseball felt nearly uncontrollable. He breathed once, then swallowed. Desperate breath hissed through his teeth. "Oh, shit."

"Yes. Yes! Shit, yes! It's all shit, because you turned it into shit! Everything in my life is shit because of *you!*"

Testani's face shone with sweat, eyes bright and

gleaming. "But he's given me another chance, Scott. To take things back, to make things right. And when I do that, he's gonna take me to the top. To sit at his right hand in a place where black stars spin in black skies. He's the Yellow King, and He's taken off His mask and shown me His true face! All I have to do," he reached out and tapped Scott's chest with the gun's muzzle, "is make you pay."

Scott stared into Testani's brimming green eyes. The connection was instant, like staring into Jessica's eyes through the window glass—only this was horrible and nightmarish. He looked deep into Testani. His breath caught at the dark things he saw twisting there.

"Make. You. Pay." Testani's voice rasped like old sandpaper. "And then after that, I'm gonna find that little shit who made you throw that ball, make *him* pay, too, and then . . . "

Something *clinked*.

Rubber squeaked against tile.

Scott would never know why Jessica did it. Maybe she'd snapped, choosing fight over flight in some sort of manic response. It didn't matter. Before Scott quite understood what was happening, Jessica was swinging the old fire extinguisher from the wall next to her at Chris Testani's head.

Somehow, Testani sensed it coming. His eyes widened and he screamed, pivoting on his right foot, allowing the old extinguisher to swing harmlessly by him.

22.

CHRIS HADN'T EXPECTED anyone else to be here. Didn't matter, though. He'd handled it fine. Beating in that redneck's skull with the Slugger, which had felt fucking fantastic.

He hadn't expected the girl to be there, either. At first she hadn't mattered, because she'd just screamed and thrown herself against the wall. She was nothing, just like Daddy had always told Chris he was nothing. Like all the girls in high school thought he was nothing after Kennsinger ruined his face. He could handle her, easy.

Then the bitch tried to swing a fucking *fire extinguisher* at him. Just after he set the Slugger down (which hadn't been smart; he knew that now). She'd been fast, too. Almost got him.

Good thing Chris was faster.

He pivoted on his right foot, opening with his left. The fire extinguisher swooshed harmlessly by. It clanged on the floor, the impact jarring it out of the bitch's hands. Keeping the gun pointed at Scott, Chris flung out a vicious backhand and smashed the bitch in the face. Delicious pain pulsed across his knuckles as they cracked against bone. His arm shuddered all the way to his shoulder.

The blow threw her back into a rack of DVDs. She slammed into it and bounced off the glass doors, knocking the rack over and spilling DVD cases onto the floor. Recovering quickly, she scrambled onto her hands and knees, and pressed back against the glass. Bleeding from her nose but glaring at him, fit to kill.

"Shouldn't have done that, bitch," he said through clenched teeth. "Now I gotta make you pay, too . . . "

He stopped.

Looked into her eyes, and saw glistening anger—but also something else. A glow. A glitter.

A *spark.*

Breath whistled and hissed through his teeth. "You. He *told* me about you. Told me to take care of you, too."

Fire flickered in her eyes. She screwed up her face and spit a thick gob of mucus at his feet.

Testani swung the gun to point it at her. "Let's take care of you first," he rasped.

The bitch's eyes widened. Testani's dark and twisted soul crowed at the sight.

23.

SCOTT BLINKED. Each moment had flowed into the next, almost too quickly for him to see. Chris Testani attacking the man at the cash register, then pointing a gun into his face. Jessica trying to run. Testani punching Jessica so hard he'd probably broken her nose. Now this: Testani swinging to point the gun at Jessica, finger tightening on the trigger.

She's dead.

I'm next.

Without thinking he leaped forward, scrambled onto the counter and pushed off, diving at Chris. All sound faded, save the squeak of his sneakers on the counter-top, his breath roaring in his ears, and his heart pounding.

Testani spun, snarling. The .38 popped but the shot went wide. Distantly, Scott heard the window behind him smash as he slammed into Testani and knocked him away from Jessica, to the floor.

They hit cement tile and rolled, arms and legs thrashing. Oddly, there was little sound. No cursing or yelling, only grunts and gasps, smothered by a surreal silence. He managed to pin Testani's gun hand to the floor. With his free hand he snatched a fistful of Testani's shirt and jacket. Scott's fingers brushed his skin as they struggled on the cool tile. A rush of images slammed into him, pushing him down beneath waves of misery, pain, and desperation. A blazing hot sensation burned his hand and raced down his arm.

He closed his eyes.

His head throbbed.

The taste of copper filled his mouth and he wanted to scream . . .

no Daddy, not again . . . don't touch me anymore I'll be a good boy I won't tell Mommy or Teacher anymore I promise I'll be a good boy, a real good boy just please don't touch me there again

. . . but he could only gasp as he twisted the fabric harder. Blood pulsed from his nostrils with his heartbeat. His brain burned. He couldn't let *go*. Testani trembled in his grip as . . .

he thrashed under Daddy's cold, alien touch, enraged yet sad at what was being done to him

. . . Scott jerked. Phantom lines of fire blazed on his back, cut by . . .

the belt, please Daddy not the belt I'll do anything whatever you want just no belt no belt

. . . and in Scott's head, he heard Testani rasp: *Hate you. Hate you all. Gonna kill you. Kill you ALL.*

Something in his head twisted. A terrible pressure squeezing his brains. With a cry he jerked out of Testani's head and back to the real world, rolling on a gas station floor, struggling with a lunatic for the gun now wedged between them. Words tumbled from his lips, out of his control. "Not your fault! You were a kid! Couldn't stop him!"

Testani pulled at the gun while jerking his head side to side in short, erratic sweeps. "No! You don't get to see that! Not allowed! NO!" He arched his back and howled. "Shut the fuck up! He promised me! *He promised!*"

Their shoes squeaked on the floor as they kicked, thrashed, and rolled. The words Scott spoke next chilled him, because he didn't understand where they came from or what they meant. "He lies. He always lies."

"No!"

"You don't deserve this! Don't have to—"

Testani twisted the gun in Scott's hands. Scott grunted and pushed the gun away. They yanked it back and forth; muscles straining and joints throbbing.

Testani screamed.

The .38 roared.

Scott blinked and gasped and . . .

24.

... WOKE SLOWLY, the pain in his head receding to a dull throb. He breathed; tasting cool and crisp air which stung his throat with a sweet-sour tang, like aged cider. He took another breath, savoring its essence. It filled him with a sense of peace and belonging. Gave him more strength than he'd felt in years.

An elusive darkness flitted along the edges of his thoughts, however. He swallowed a faint, coppery taste in the back of his throat.

He slipped his hand into his pocket.

As always, there it was.

The baseball. He clutched it, sickened because he just couldn't escape it, but comforted by its presence, regardless.

"Okay," he murmured, "let's do this." He took one last breath of delicious air, and opened his eyes.

He stood on a pitcher's mound, examining the details. The chain-link fence marking the outfield's farthest edges. Beyond that, a bank reaching up to Gato Road, which ran over Black Creek Bridge. Across the street, Bassler Memorial Library, and screeching somewhere off in the distance, the wooden buzz of the lumbermill which always seemed to be running, even during ball games.

He knew this place.

His career ended here, after all. In Clifton Heights.

There was something behind him.

Waiting.

Scott turned and saw him standing at home base. Someone with familiar blue eyes, staring at him. He wore the same spotless baggy uniform over his thin frame. The brim of his cap was still flat. The number 15 blazed on the front of his jersey, with the name *'Evan'* stitched on the breast.

Scott opened his mouth, but before he could speak he heard laughter. What sounded like a boy and a young woman. He turned and saw, sitting on a park bench, two people tossing pieces of bread to waiting squirrels. One of them was the bat boy. Evan, dressed in regular clothes. A t-shirt, shorts and sneakers.

The other was Jessica. A slightly younger, happier, smiling Jessica. Sitting with the bat boy, laughing with him at the squirrels begging for more breadcrumbs.

From home plate, Scott heard Evan whisper: "He lies."

He looked away from the younger Jessica and the other Evan and turned to home plate. The bat boy said, "He always lies, Scott. Always. That's what he does. Don't listen. Don't accept what he offers."

Scott wanted to ask what the hell that meant. What was this? A dream? A hallucination? Is he dead? But a throaty rumble interrupted him.

Scott spun and saw it on Black Creek Bridge.

Tinted windows staring him down.

The midnight black Monte Carlo. Even in the sunshine, its black finish shimmered strangely, crawling like a slick sheet of black-shelled beetles. The wind blew warm against Scott's skin and the sun glowed overhead, but a cold worm of dread burrowed into his guts as he looked at that car. A cold river flowed from it, washing over him, making him feel empty and dead inside.

Pain flashed through Scott's head. Looking at the car made him dizzy. Its finish seemed to slide and ooze, and it throbbed with each pulse of its engine. He couldn't look at it very long. His stomach roiled with slick nausea at the way its surface shifted like black oil.

Turning away, back to the boy, he tried to speak—but a sinuous throb slammed into his mind. The painful beat mingled with the Monte Carlo's engine. He clapped his hands over his ears but still the pain swelled, overwhelming all thought. Behind him, the Monte Carlo revved, a high-pitched keening against his brain. He cried out, crumpling to his knees, holding his head, screaming.

Screaming, and not just him. The younger Jessica and the other bat boy sitting on the bench with her. Screaming, also.

The world spun. The air shimmered, grew fuzzy, splotchy, pulling apart at the seams like a video losing its cohesion. Blood burst from his nostrils, pouring over his lips, into his mouth. He gagged, his insides twisting, but nothing came up.

The Monte Carlo revved again.

Its tires spun and squealed.

Gears thunked and gravel spat as Scott heard the car speed off the bridge, towards them. The pressure inside his head exploded with a great flash of pain. He plunged into an empty, cold darkness, lit only by burning blue eyes as he . . .

25.

... BLINKED AND WOKE UP.

Scott Kennsinger stared at the gas station's white ceiling tiles and thought, *On the floor. I'm on the floor. Why ...?*

Scott closed his eyes.

In the darkness, images spun. Testani. The gun. A black Monte Carlo that wasn't really a car. The bat boy in his uniform, from that day on the mound. A younger Jessica sitting on a park bench with the bat boy.

Scott.

Wake up.

C'mon, snap out of it.

Scott opened his eyes again to see Jessica kneeling next to him. She was scowling, though something like worry and fear glimmered in her eyes as she said, "Idiot. What the hell? Could've been killed."

He opened his mouth, but she shook her head. "Can you sit up? I think you had one of those seizures you were talking about."

He nodded slightly. Breathed in, and eased himself into a sitting position. Nausea curdled in his belly. He licked his lips and tasted sour bile. He glanced at Jessica, looked away and mumbled, "Think I'm gonna be sick ..."

He leaned away from her, bent his head and closed his eyes. He again breathed deeply. His stomach twitched and quivered. He burped, several times. Seconds passed.

He didn't throw up, but it was a near thing. He swallowed once more and looked behind them. A grisly sight met his gaze. His stomach trembled and he thought he might puke, after all.

Chris lay supine, arms and legs splayed, head turned away. A dark red stain soaked his shirt, spreading from his belly outward. Blood puddled on the floor underneath him.

He glanced to the front counter. At its base lay the big man in the Carhart jacket. His forehead—where Chris must have hit him with the baseball bat—looked caved in. The shattered red mess oozed blood and other white matter.

His stomach clenched. He looked back at Jessica. Her gaze met his, unflinching. Blood had congealed on her nostrils and smeared along her upper lip, and the bridge of her nose looked humped and swollen.

"Your nose. It's probably broken."

She shrugged and glanced away. "Probably."

He swallowed. Bits and pieces of colors and pictures swirled around in his head, but they refused to come together. "When?"

She looked back at him, saying nothing.

"When did you know the bat boy?"

She frowned. "Who?"

Scott thought for a moment, calling up the image of the bat boy in his mind, thinking about the name stitched on his breast.

"Evan."

Her eyes widened. "How do you know about that?"

An unusual calm settled over him. As he spoke, his words flowed, free and easy. He never stuttered once. It actually scared him a little, because he wasn't sure if he was the one talking.

"You worked with him. As an aide. When you were studying nursing. You would take him to parks. Movies. On walks. To Clifton Beach. The library. But something . . . happened. And you stopped. Because . . . "

Jessica sucked in a deep breath and gnawed on her lower lip for a few seconds before responding. "Something happened to me. And it . . . changed me."

Scott continued, still feeling as if someone else was speaking through him. "*He* changed you. The boy. Evan. Just like he changed me. I don't know how, but he did. He made me . . . made me throw a baseball at . . . "

"Wait." Jessica's brow furrowed. "Evan was the bat boy for the high school team for a short time, until something happened. An asshole on his own team pushed him down when he got in the way, and then someone . . . "

Realization dawned in her eyes. "It was *you*. You threw that wild pitch. Because that asshole knocked Evan down." She glanced at Chris's body. "Holy shit. That's what he was talking about! You ruining his life. *That's* the guy you hit with the baseball!"

She looked back at him, eyes wide. "What the hell is going on?"

He shook his head, because he didn't know. So many puzzle pieces were still missing, and even though he thought part of a picture was forming . . .

Something rustled.

He turned. Jessica followed his gaze to Chris' body. Silence swelled and filled the gas station. Dimly, he noted a vague coppery scent in the air. Then a whiff of something else, like shit and spoiled meat . . .

Testani's right leg jerked.

Jessica grabbed his arm.

Testani's left leg kicked, and she dug her fingernails into Scott's bicep. A ripple of motion trembled along Testani's torso. His exposed skin bulged and stretched, as if thousands of small beetles scuttled underneath, yearning for freedom.

"What the *fuck*?" Jessica rasped.

Testani jerked once more, then lurched upright. He sat very still. Eyes closed, face slack, mouth hanging open. Something black and thick trickled from his nostrils.

Somehow, Scott scrambled to his feet. Jessica clung to him in uncharacteristic fear as they edged towards the front doors, step by dragging step. As they inched past Testani he began to sway, swirling at the waist in small circles, as if weaving to a dance only he could hear. His flesh pulled tight across his face. Something pressed through from the other side.

They'd almost gotten to the door when they heard the liquid, gurgling laugh.

Testani's head whipped around. His eyes snapped open, showing only a liquid, swirling black.

Outside, the Monte Carlo roared to life. Scott glanced from Chris to the car. Its black finish glinted and rippled under the station's halogen parking lights. It revved over and over, rocking on tires which looked engorged.

"Scott."

The voice slithered into his brain, making him sick and dizzy again. Greasy sweat leaked from his pores. He shivered, because that wasn't Testani's voice, at all.

"Scott!"

He turned, following Jessica's horrified gaze. Somehow, he managed to croak, "No. Not fucking possible."

"C'mon, Scott," the thing crooned in an all-too-recognizable voice. Black oil spilled from its mouth, thick and viscous, coating his chin and neck. *"It's Halloween night. Anything is possible!"*

Oh fuck. It's him.

The guy on the phone.

The sports recruiter.

Jimmy.

The thing chuckled wetly. Shiny black bubbles popped from clotted nostrils. Its skin undulated like rubber sheeting stretched too thin over a thousand pinching mandibles as it tried to stand, its limbs trembling.

Outside, the Monte Carlo thundered.

It finally got to its feet and took a trembling step toward them. *"Tonight's the night, Scott! Of GRAVE FUCKING DELIGHTS!"*

It lurched forward.

Scott exploded for the front doors, dragging Jessica behind him. She abandoned her tough-girl exterior and followed. The shambling thing screamed. Scott's heart slammed high into his throat as he heard it scrabble behind them on wet tile.

The front doors hissed open. He and Jessica shot through them. Moving on instinct, he pulled her towards his parked Kawasaki.

The Monte Carlo's headlights snapped on, bathing the parking lot in a shifting, unnatural light. Casting their shadows long and capering, in a parody of their flight. The car's strange engine revved again.

They were only a few feet away from the Kawasaki. If they could get there in time, he and Jessica could—

The Chris-thing and the Monte Carlo screamed together, freezing Scott's guts into hard, jagged ice.

26.

CHRIS DIDN'T FEEL so good, anymore.

Pain blazed deep in his abdomen. It felt like someone had dug his insides out with a huge ice cream scoop. In his middle, a troubling cold spot had blossomed and was now spreading its empty numbness through him. He wondered what would happen when that emptiness filled him. Deep inside, the boy who had been Chris trembled at the thought of surrendering to the biting cold.

Also, something was pushing out of him. He didn't know what. It felt like his skin had gotten too tight, or that he was swelling up, because his insides desperately wanted to rip through his flesh. This made it hard to run. His joints, suddenly bulging and swollen, locked up as he scrambled towards the gas station doors. He kept slipping on blood-slicked tile.

The Dark screamed. Chris screamed too, and the Monte Carlo outside roared with him. This made him feel better, despite the creeping cold in his guts and the things inside pressing against his skin. If he got to the car, everything would be fine.

Which was good, because everything was wrong. Not like He'd promised at all. Fucking Scott had hurt the Dark somehow. Hurt It bad with something bright and glowing, and this hurt Chris too . . .

it's not your fault Daddy touched you like that

. . . and now the Dark burned with an icy hate. This scared Chris, because the Dark had seemed so calm and assured, soft as silk. Now It raged out of control inside him, pulling him in a thousand directions at once. The Dark hated Scott's silvery glow, hated Scott, hated that girl . . .

Chris's boots squelched in the trail of blood he left behind. He slipped and crashed to his knee. Something popped outside. Sounding like distant fireworks or a burping lawnmower or . . .

Someone kick-starting a motorcycle.

The Dark crept behind his eyes, shoved him aside and hurled Chris to his feet. It propelled him out the door, shambling on creaking joints which popped and tore.

The burping caught, coughed, and stuttered into a tiny, burbling clatter. Chris and the Dark screamed as he slammed against the Monte Carlo's passenger side door, jerked it open and scrambled inside.

27.

SCOTT HEAVED UP and down once more on the Kawasaki's kick-start. The little engine coughed and died.

"Shit! Come on!" He tried again.

And again.

"Go!" Jessica shouted into his back, arms wrapped tightly around his waist. *"Go!"*

He kicked again. The motorcycle sputtered, jerked, and wheezed.

Nothing.

"Fuck me!"

"Scott, get us the *fuck* out of here!"

The Monte Carlo roared behind them.

"Go!"

Scott slammed down the kick-start once more, twisting the throttle so hard he thought he might rip it off. The Kawasaki trembled, coughed, spit and hiccupped—then fired up.

The car thundered. Its tires squealed against pavement. Its pounding engine rushing up from behind.

Jessica screamed.

Scott gunned it. The Kawasaki shot forward, wobbled at first with the extra weight it carried, but Scott leaned forward, corrected for this, and they sped out of the gas station's parking lot, onto the dark and empty road. The Kawasaki's headlight briefly pierced the darkness ahead. Then the Monte Carlo's headlights swung around and swallowed the yellow dot in a sea of white as it roared in pursuit.

28.

BACK BEHIND THE Monte Carlo's wheel, chasing down Kennsinger and that girl . . .

get them get them get them get them GET THEM!

. . . Chris felt fine. His insides felt much better. The cold had faded. The mangled meat and muscles in his gut had squirmed back together. With each pulse of the car's engine, the Dark washed over him. Making him feel strong.

The Dark chuckled as it flowed through the car. Chris still wasn't sure how this all worked. The swirls of Dark in his head and all around felt so strange, but he thought he understood a little, now. The Dark came from some Other Place. Somewhere Outside. All the Dark wanted to do was eat and destroy. The Dark hated this world and everyone here. Hated the Creator and everything He stood for. Wanted nothing more than to tear everything to pieces.

Chris hated lots of things, too. He hated Daddy most of all. Hated the way he'd beaten him and Mommy, the way he'd touched him. Most of all? Chris hated himself with a vibrant fury which felt everlasting. Something the Dark feasted upon with glee.

However, somewhere deep inside, Chris had splintered. A very small and terrified part of him didn't hate at all. It just screamed in pain. The small part knew the Dark would use him up until there was nothing left. Then it would jump to someone else, leaving what was left of Chris to be eaten by cold and dead hungry things which hate the living. The scared part of Chris tried to tell the rest of him this, but the rest of him wouldn't listen. That part only wanted to destroy everyone who had hurt him. The Dark whispered into his ear all the things he could have, if only he did what the Dark asked.

Part of Chris cried.

The other part grinned.

The Dark whispered and pumped through Chris as if It was pulsing from the car's dark engine. The scared part of Chris retreated as the other part screamed, pumped a fist and stomped on the gas. With a howl the Monte Carlo bore down on the tiny burping motorcycle. In seconds the Dark would have what It wanted, and then . . .

A roar filled Chris's head. Something bright, clear and pure.

The Dark shivered and screamed.

The smaller part raised its head and stared.

The other part howled in rage.

Blazing light poured into the Monte Carlo. Chris tried to look, but everything shook. Metal cymbals crashed and banged. Glass shattered into high pitched notes as something slammed into the Monte Carlo and everything flew apart.

29.

THE MONTE CARLO was gaining. He felt it. A dark, throbbing presence bearing down on them. It wouldn't stop. It would run them down, and leave nothing in its wake.

He looked over his shoulder. Past Jessica's terror-stricken face, eyes squeezed shut in fear. For a moment, he saw the bat boy. Evan. Standing on home plate, his blue eyes shining. The image dissolved, replaced by the blazing twin suns of the Monte Carlo's headlights.

"No," Scott whispered. And then, deep inside, from the very core of his being, his heart screamed *NO!*

A wave pulsed out from him, sending a wall of emotion and energy slamming into the Monte Carlo.

30.

IN THE MIDDLE of the intersection of Haverton Road and Route 28 North, the raging black Monte Carlo slammed into nothing. Metal, plastic, and glass exploded into a glittering, expanding halo. Parts rained everywhere. The Monte Carlo's rear launched into the air. For a moment, it looked like it might flip forward. The moment passed. The rear slammed down to earth. Its tires exploded on impact.

A shock-wave clipped the back tire of Scott's fleeing Kawasaki, kicking it out from underneath him and Jessica, tumbling them onto the cold, hard asphalt. Their arms and legs tangled as the Kawasaki slid on its side for several screeching feet, showering sparks, before coming to a rest.

The Monte Carlo's engine sputtered and died. Its radiator hissed and spat into the suddenly quiet night.

31.

SCOTT KENNSINGER GROANED. Leaned up on his elbows, raised his aching head, and peered at the wrecked Monte Carlo. Its front was caved in and its windshield was spider-webbed with cracks around a gaping hole in the middle. The car looked like it had run head-on into a giant's outstretched hand. The hole in the windshield showed nothing but darkness, yet even so . . . *something* squirmed in that darkness.

Chris.

Or, what he'd become.

An ululating cry froze Scott's heart. What remained of the Monte Carlo's front windshield exploded outward. Glass flew everywhere and showered the road with tinkling shards. A dark hulking shape clawed its way through the Monte Carlo's empty window, onto the hood. Scott couldn't see it very well—it shifted in a darkness which pulsed and flowed from the Monte Carlo's liquid, sinuous black finish. But what Scott *could* see . . .

A bloated, swollen form. Hairless, shiny and shifting black. Shaped in the rough approximation of a man. Sharp, needle-point teeth lining a gaping maw. Serpentine appendages which lashed the air, and two burning-red coals glittering where eyes should be, bright and angry. It roared, slick-black flesh rippling as it flexed on all fours, ready to pounce.

Next to him on the cold asphalt, Jessica groaned.

32.

JESSICA HELD HER head and groaned. She'd been knocked off a motorcycle. Or something? While running away from a midnight black Monte Carlo driven by an evil-monster-zombie-thing that wanted to kill them.

Of course.

That made *perfect* sense.

She pressed her forehead against the cold, wet asphalt, which actually felt soothing. Her nose throbbed. She could barely breathe through it. Every part of her ached. Cold as the road felt, she wanted to curl up and sleep for hours.

But she couldn't.

Because that *thing* was still out there. Whatever the hell it was . . .

A connection snapped alive along her blurry synapses. Between the Dark Thing in the Monte Carlo, and the cold dark she fought off whenever she healed people. Most recently, Shelly Livingston.

He told me about you

Told me to take care of you, too

Oh.

Shit.

Slowly, she raised her head and hissed between her teeth as pain coursed in electric arcs down her neck. She shifted, tried to get up, but her bruised muscles screamed in protest. She settled for rolling onto her right elbow and leaning back against Scott. She shivered at how comforting he felt.

She rubbed her face and looked up.

And felt the world fall beneath her.

33.

CHRIS TESTANI RAGED. Everything had been going so well. He'd chosen Chris to do His Good Work. Had given Testani to the Dark, because the Dark fed on hate, and Chris hated everything and everyone but most of all hated himself. In return the Dark had offered him strength so he could destroy the world that hated him, starting with the one person he hated most in this world (because he'd already killed Daddy), the one who'd ruined his life.

Scott Kennsinger.

no that's a lie you've always hated yourself because of the things Daddy did to you, those awful nasty slimy naughty sticky things in the dark

Scott FUCKING Kennsinger!

The thing which used to be Chris turned into something else. Its shifting body writhed and changed. The Dark surged outward in a blast of darkness, colder than anything he'd ever felt as he and the Dark screamed as one.

The Monte Carlo shifted, slowly melting and flowing into him. Its great black engine throbbed with life, but it wasn't just an engine now. It was something more.

A heart.

A black, pulsing, beating heart. Fueled by rage, fear and a cold, penetrating Dark from beyond all things.

Chris screamed as they shifted and became something new. Something powerful. Something much bigger and badder than Daddy had ever been. Too bad Daddy wasn't here to see the powerful and hungry thing his worthless, good-for-nothing son had become.

Deep inside, however, Chris knew part of Daddy was in the Dark, now. With the Dark inside him, Daddy was inside him, too.

Just like old times.

And Daddy was very proud.

34.

THE THING THAT used to be Chris screamed as it mutated and grew. Scott shuddered. Jessica leaned against him, burying her face into his shoulder, for the first time openly showing her fear.

He swallowed cold air. It bit his raw throat and hurt his lungs. Nothing made sense. From the moment Chris had stepped into the Mobilmart and clubbed that man to death, to *this* moment, sense had flown out the window. He stared, open-mouthed, speechless, as the thing which used to be Chris and the car melted into each other, staggered upright—maybe seven or eight feet tall—and slouched towards them.

Scott glanced around, mind on the verge of completely collapsing. Just as he was about to wrap his arms tight around Jessica, close his eyes and wait for the end, he saw where they'd come to rest after crashing.

A long gravel drive leading to an abandoned farm.

Scott scrambled to his feet and pulled Jessica up. "There!" he screamed, pointing towards the gravel drive. They stumbled forward, Scott's heart pounding, ears ringing, breath whistling through clenched teeth, muscles aching everywhere. He didn't know if they'd make it but at least they wouldn't die cowering in the middle of the road.

A lashing sound sliced the air.

Pressure cinched tight around his throat, cutting off his breath. Something cold and slick snared him around the neck. He clawed at the leathery appendage, but his fingers found no purchase on the taut muscles which flexed around his throat.

The ground sped away.

His feet kicked as the Thing yanked him high into the air. Black spots peppered his vision. He opened his mouth but nothing came out. Distantly, he heard Jessica screaming below. The Thing lifted him higher, squealing in delight. He clawed at the fleshy appendage coiled around his neck, his vision blurring . . .

no

no

No!

Like before, Scott screamed the word, deep in his head. A gut-wrenching wave of vibration pulsed outward from him. It slammed into the thing. He held onto the mental scream as long as he possibly could.

Noooooooooooooo!

Bright light exploded, as the Thing's agonized scream blasted the skies.

35.

SCREAMING, THE THING dropped Scott. Somehow he managed to land, roll awkwardly, and come upright unharmed. He scrambled to his feet and stared, mesmerized by horrified fascination.

The *Thing* had transformed into a sprawling, unimaginable horror. All shifting shadow, liquid darkness, refusing to assume any one shape but looking like so many things at once.

a gigantic spider with thousands of bulging eyes

a man-squid which lurched along on slime-coated tentacles

a gigantic man-o-war

a scorpion with too many legs and claws and stingers

a great mass of tentacles beating the air

It shook and screamed as he stood and stared, legs weak and rubbery. The Thing towered above him, its form morphing into various shapes, flickering and melting back and forth between them. Scott thought about trying to summon another one of those strange mental screams, but he couldn't. He felt sick, disoriented by the ever-shifting forms.

"Scott!"

Someone grabbed his hand. Jessica. She grabbed his hand and pulled him toward the dilapidated farmhouse at the end of the drive.

It lumbered after them.

36.

THEY'D BARELY MADE it into the old farmhouse's living room when the front door slammed open and something thundered down the front hall, howling.

They turned. Jessica screamed, but Scott could only stare at the dark form (smaller, now) vaulting into the room. In the dim light, it looked more like Chris again, its eyes a liquid black.

Tentacles spread behind It. Black, writhing, stretching out into a sickening parody of angel wings.

The Thing lunged.

Tentacles snapped towards him.

Scott leaped away, flailing for Jessica's hand, but he missed and hit the floor. The air cracked above him as it ignored him and darted past. Someone's scream choked off into a gurgle.

Jessica.

Scott slammed into the far wall shoulder-first, spun and flattened himself against sheet-rock and peeling wallpaper. His lungs hitched at the sight before him.

The Thing had swelled again, filling the room. Off to the side, lifted to the ceiling by tentacles around her neck, dangled Jessica.

It laughed. Low, deep, and gurgling.

With slow, measured strides It approached him, holding Jessica high in the air as she clawed and screamed silently. It spread its human arms wide in a mocking gesture, as if to embrace him, hissing in pleasure.

It spoke in a voice of swarming, buzzing locusts. *"Who first? You, or this one?"* It leered at him. *"I should do you first. Take back what belongs to me. But this one."*

It brought Jessica near to its liquid, ever-shifting face.

She reacted with a burst of primal fear, kicking and jerking, hysteria twisting her face.

"He wants this one, especially. She's been getting in the way of His Good Work. No longer."

Adrenaline thrummed in Scott's veins. His arms and legs jittered. He had to do something, now. While the thing's attention was focused on Jessica. His legs and thighs tensed as he clenched his fists, but at that exact moment, Jessica met his gaze. Communication passed between them. Scott didn't hear anything specific. Just a vague sense to *wait.*

Scott nodded.

Jessica's face relaxed as she stopped clawing at the tentacle circling her neck. She closed her eyes, reached her hand out, and—*gently*—pressed it flat against the thing's flesh.

Blue light sizzled and hissed around her fingers, culminating in a bright flash of crackling energy which snapped louder than a thunderclap. The Chris-Thing holding her jerked away, its slimy black hide dissolving, face writhing as It lurched away and screamed.

Now.

Scott pushed off the wall with everything he had and dove forward, no clear plan in mind, only one thought thrumming in his head: *Get Jessica.*

It screamed. Hurt, confused and angry.

Scott's feet pounded the wooden floor. Arms and legs pumping, breath thundering in his ears. He felt good. Fast. Alive, because even pitchers had to run bases, sometimes. It was the bottom of the ninth. Bases loaded. They were down by one, with two outs on the board, and even though he'd never been the fastest guy on the team . . .

Scott Kennsinger stole home.

Slimy tentacles lashed at his face.

He ducked and dove, hands outstretched.

His palms thudding against Its chest. To his amazed

horror, his hands sunk up to his wrists in what felt like slick putty. He grabbed *something* underneath which twisted and coiled.

It screamed.

He gasped.

And went inside its heart.

37.

SCOTT MOUNTED THE old house's leaning front porch. Jessica was already there, waiting. She looked at him, eyes wide and filled with quiet terror. "What happened?"

He shook his head. "I'm not sure, but I think . . . "

Silence.

They looked at the front door, then back to each other. "Sounds crazy," he whispered, "but I . . . *think* we're supposed to go in."

Doubt shadowed Jessica's face and haunted her eyes, but she didn't look afraid. "Are you sure?"

"Yeah. Think so."

"Who opens it, then?"

Scott swallowed. "Me. I think." He looked at Jessica, feeling doubt too, but also a strange resolve. "It's what I do, I guess. Open doors."

Jessica grunted and waved at the door, sounding a little more like her old self. "Be my guest."

Scott reached for the tarnished doorknob, but stopped and glanced at Jessica. "What do you think is in there?"

She spoke immediately, though she also looked puzzled at her answer. "Truth."

A morbid levity filled him. "That certainly clears things up. Thanks."

Jessica scowled, though for the first time ever, Scott saw affection in the expression. "Just open the door, dumbass."

Scott shrugged. "Whatever."

He squared his shoulders and faced the door. Breathed once, then grabbed the doorknob, twisted and pushed. The door swung silently open to a bright, blinding rectangle of light.

Her bravado returned, Jessica didn't hesitate. She plunged into the light. It devoured her whole.

Scott swallowed, staring at the burning rectangle. Light spilled from it onto the floor where it pooled at his feet. It curled along the doorframe, crawled along the walls and porch, a luminescent mist of white fiery tongues. He released a breath he didn't realize he'd been holding.

Behind him blared a discordant jumble of sounds. Howls, wails, moans, screams, clicks and hissing. Scott reached out and placed a hand flat against the white mist filling the door. Instantly, the horrible sounds faded away.

Scott fell quiet inside, for the first time in four years. Before those voices could muster a new assault on his heart and mind and soul, he stepped through.

38.

THE BLINDING RECTANGLE of light changed into a long, dim hallway. The transition was seamless. They felt it more than anything else, moving from the comfort and peace of the porch into a hallway with a dank chill which seeped into their joints.

Scott swallowed. "Where are we?"

"I'm guessing somewhere that thing doesn't want us to be," Jessica whispered as they moved slowly down a hall which seemed to lengthen with every step. "I heard whispers on the porch, before you showed up. Couldn't understand them, but the words . . . they sounded . . . "

She paused. "Wrong. Dead. *Angry.* And we're going somewhere those voices don't want us to go. Where that is, exactly . . . "

"Chris," Scott whispered, struck by an unusual clarity. "It's the only thing which makes sense. We're going somewhere inside Chris. Somewhere It doesn't want us to be."

They continued down the moldering hallway. Took several turns as the hall bended and twisted in ways which defied geometrical logic. They took another sharp right, and then they stopped before another door. As they stood there a bone-chilling despair leaked into them. Something swelled behind the door. Bending the wood, as if it wanted to break free.

The door pulsed. Then it contracted, settling back into its frame.

Scott glanced at Jessica. She nodded. He took a deep breath, swallowed, and grabbed the dull brass doorknob. The cold metal stung his hand and he hissed between his teeth.

But he held on.

Biting his tongue, he pushed past the dread roiling in his guts, steeling himself against the knob's frigid cold, and turned the knob. He pushed the door open.

A wall of invisible ice knocked the breath from him.

He staggered for a moment, but the cold fades, leaving behind only a dull chill crawling on his flesh.

He entered the room. Took in sports-hero wallpaper with hulking linemen, diving halfbacks, soaring power forwards and wind-milling pitchers. Rock posters hung askew on the walls. Dokken, Iron Maiden, Judas Priest.

On top of a tall, dark mahogany clothes bureau sat rows of meticulously arranged model cars. Trans Ams, Corvettes, NASCAR and DIRT stock cars. Next to the bureau was a small, rickety wooden desk, littered with plastic parts, rubber wheels, a few half-painted engine blocks, rolled up tubes of Testors airplane glue and small, empty jars of Testors enamel . . .

. . . and the model of a gleaming, midnight-black Monte Carlo. Its finish sliding, shifting, shining liquid, as if freshly coated with paint that would never dry.

A bookshelf stood against the far wall, jammed full of various kinds of books, everything from old, worm-eaten detective pulp novels to The Hardy Boys, Tom Swift, Danny Dunn, The Sugar Creek Gang, a smattering of Choose Your Own Adventure novels and the entire set of The Chronicles of Narnia. A box on the floor held magazines and comics jammed in no particular order, their titles hidden. Somehow Scott knew them all. Sports Illustrated, Boy's Life, Ranger Rick, Highlights, assorted Marvel and DC comics, Whitman Comics.

To the far left was a bed with sports blankets and comforters matching the wallpaper. There, huddled on the bed's edge, pressed into the room's corner . . .

Scott first saw feet sheathed in Keds. Tapping a nervous rhythm on the bed. Up from them stretched gangly legs in scuffed and worn jeans, attached to a wide torso cloaked in a black hoodie. Long arms, covered in sleeves, hugged knees to a thin chest.

Behind that, hidden in the hoodie: a pinched, drawn face.

A child, a boy, and a teen carrying burdens too heavy for someone so young. A child, a boy, a teen, occupying the same body, rocking back and forth on the bed, whimpering softly.

Scott slowly approached the bed. Reached out a tentative hand and whispered, *"Chris."*

The child-boy-teen cried out and jerked his head up. Something dark, feral, and ugly twisted his face as he shrank farther back into the corner. "Don't touch me!"

Scott felt an emotion much bigger than his experience. He wondered if this is what it meant to feel your heart breaking. Something bitter and sour rose in the back of his throat. "Who did this to you?"

The child-boy-teen's wide black eyes trembled as he whimpered, "It hurts. Please make it stop. Please."

"Let me," Jessica murmured. She moved beside him. Slowly, she took Chris's hand. Unclasped it from the child-boy-teen's knee and pulled it away. Even as her fingers touched Chris's skin, the child-boy-teen's tremors eased as he gazed anxiously—maybe even hopefully—at her.

Jessica turned Chris's hand over. He jerked and whimpered, almost pulled his hand and arm away. He looked at Jessica, face cracking, on the verge of collapse. "No. P-please. D-don't. It's b-bad. Too bad. Too . . . "

"Shh. It's okay."

Something in her tone calmed Chris. The child-boy-teen sucked in a deep, watery breath, bit his lip and nodded. Jessica offered a faint smile, looked down and pulled the sweatshirt's sleeve to Chris's elbow . . .

Scott couldn't make sense of it, at first.

Lines and angles and curves, cut deeply into the skin.

Jagged edges swollen, purple, puckering, crusted with

dried brown blood, seeping dark, almost black fluids which trailed all over Chris's forearms . . .

He stared, lips pressing together, jaw tight.

As the lines, angles, curves, and swollen jagged edges coalesced into meaning. *Letters*, carved into scarred, tough and leathery flesh healed from countless other cuts and slashes. Letters most likely inscribed by the stinging metal tips of Exacto knives, the knife of choice among teenage model car enthusiasts.

Scott peered closer.

Four letters swam in his vision, unwilling to spell a word, at first. Finally, dreadfully, he pieced them together.

E

V

I

L

'EVIL'

Breath escaped through Scott's clenched teeth, like he'd been punched in the kidneys. Jessica cradled Chris's arm, grazing rough, twisted scar tissue with her fingertips. Afterward, she gently laid Chris's left arm down and reached for his other arm, which the child-boy-teen let her have without resistance.

Jessica rolled this sleeve up.

Because the shock had lessened somewhat, these puckered and blood-crusted lines coalesced into words and letters much quicker.

D

I

R

T

Y

'DIRTY'

Scott closed his eyes as immense pressure built in his head. Pressing against eyeballs, eardrums, face and teeth. How could anyone do this to themselves?

How did someone not *know*?

The truth, of course, was one Scott knew all too well. Because someone hadn't wanted to.

Scott looked at the child-boy-teen and swallowed. Opened his mouth but couldn't speak. He stuttered and finally found words which felt pale and lifeless compared to the emotions swirling inside.

"Chris . . . I'm so sorry. I wish . . . I wish I could . . . "

The pale child-boy-teen shook his head, eyes hooded and dark. "Doesn't matter. I'm evil. That's why Daddy did those things to me. I'm evil."

Chris pulled his arms away from Jessica.

Hugged his knees to his chest and withdrew into a rocking ball, huddling into the corner once more. "My fault," he whispered, face bleak and wooden, eyes flat pools of dead black, "my fault he did those things, because I'm bad and dirty and evil."

Scott felt an unfamiliar anger bloom inside. "No. It's not your fault. It's *not*."

"Please take me away," Chris whispered, face twisting and forlorn. "Don't leave me here with Him. He's angry and hungry. Please don't leave me."

Scott looked around the room and saw them first. Dark stains seeping through the wallpaper and spreading down the walls. Jessica saw it, too. She slowly moved closer to Scott, watching the rotten walls as if something might burst through them at any moment.

As the stains continued to spread, a sour odor filled the room. Scott gagged as his stomach clenched.

He turned to Chris. "Who? Leave you here with who?"

Tears streamed down Chris's face. "*Him*. The Dark One. The Crawling One. He Who Walks."

Chris pointed a trembling hand to the room's farthest corner. "*It.*"

Scott followed Chris's gesture. Even as he looked, the walls shed ragged strips of wallpaper like old skin. Wood softened and peeled away, revealing a blackness which slithered in between the slats. Its slick, shiny skin glistened.

Jessica gasped. Knowingly, Scott thought. As if she recognized this shapeless, black void and had seen it before.

Chris whined, high and shrill. "Please! Don't leave me here! Don't leave me, take me away—!"

Jessica grasped Chris' shoulders and pulled the sobbing child-boy-teen into a crushing embrace, ignoring the twisting and coiling black thing in the walls.

Chris didn't resist. He buried his face into her shoulder and cried, sobbing over and over, "Please don't leave me! Please!"

"Shh. Shh." Jessica held Chris close. "It's going to be okay," she whispered.

She held Chris as the child-boy-teen poured out the guilt, shame, loathing and self-hate. It spilled everywhere, pouring into the room. The black thing wallowed in it. Feeding, gorging itself on misery, growing larger.

It spilled into Scott and he felt everything Chris's Daddy did to him down in the sweaty, dark basement. Every one of Daddy's touches and thrusts. He felt the stains and rot spreading inside him. The rot Chris tried to cut out of his own flesh. Scott felt every slashing and stinging blade, dreaming the same dreams Chris had every night his whole life.

Jessica must've felt it too, because she rocked and wept with Chris as the black thing lapped it all up and slithered under the bed, coiling and twining beneath them.

Looking around at walls which were seeping black, oily fluid, Scott whispered, "How do we stop this?"

Jessica swallowed a sob and looked up at the streaming ichor sloughing off the wallpaper and rock posters, pooling on the floor around them. She sensed it, just as Scott did.

There wasn't much time left.

Jessica composed herself and asked Chris, "Do you want to get out of here?"

Like a child, Chris hesitantly peeked out from under his hoodie. The child-boy-teen sniffed. "Yes. I've t-tried so hard, but the Dark won't let me. Can't do it by myself."

Jessica nodded. "I know. No one can do it by themselves, I don't think."

Chris looked doubtful. "Will it hurt?"

Jessica nodded gently. "A little. But after, not anymore."

Chris nodded and wiped his eyes with the heels of his palms.

"Give me your hands," Jessica whispered.

Chris reached out. She gently took his hands, and Chris gasped slightly. As Scott watched, the words EVIL and DIRTY slowly faded from his arms, one letter at a time. As the letters disappeared, the expression of pain which seemed etched into the very lines of Chris' face gradually smoothed into a look of peace. Contentment. Belonging. The fear in his eyes turned into a shining kind of hopeful love, as he looked at Jessica and slowly, tremulously, smiled.

The last of the letters vanished, replaced by fresh, unblemished skin. Impulsively, he threw himself into Jessica and hugged her, as if by clinging to her, he could remain there with them.

In Jessica' arms, Chris slowly became translucent, until he faded away completely.

Scott blinked, and then . . .

39.

SCOTT KENNSINGER STOLE HOME. Tentacles lashed at his face. He ducked and dove, his hands outstretched. His palms thudded against Its chest and his hands sunk up to their wrists in what felt like slick putty.

Something inside squirmed.

He grabbed, and twisted.

It screamed.

He gasped.

A brilliant flash of light blinded him. Shockwaves splashed outward from the Thing, battering his mind. His hands burned but he held on while a thousand guttural voices screamed in his head. Scott gritted his teeth and bit his tongue, swallowing thick saliva and blood.

A force threw him back. He smashed into the wall and crashed to the floor.

not your fault, Chris,

not your fault

thank you

Dimly, he heard Jessica scream. A great, high-pitched ringing filled his head. He clapped his hands to his ears and looked up.

It wasn't dead yet. Whatever darkness remained still towered above. A surging, pulsing mass of blackness. They may've healed part of Chris and released him, but all his rage, anger, and hatred still throbbed with terrifying life.

It flailed Jessica in the air, a tentacle still clutching her neck. She screamed again, clawing at the thing's black flesh, to no avail.

Scott felt it glowing, then.

In his pocket. It was time for one last pitch.

He stood and pulled the battered and blood-stained baseball from his pocket. He held it lightly. The ball's laces fit neatly in his grip, even after all this time. Power thrummed from his heart, into his shoulder, down his arm and into the ball. The power throbbed there, waiting. As it always had been.

It was the bottom of the ninth. Bases loaded. Two outs down, and once again, a *monster* stood at home plate. Scott coiled like a spring into the tightest wind-up of all time, then unspooled faster than he ever had, letting the ball fly.

His release was true.

He brought the heat, one last time.

The ball—encased in fire—screamed from Scott's hand and hit the Thing, center-mass.

A sonic *boom* quaked the house. Air rushed around him, forcing him to his knees as he stared, transfixed at the horrific beauty blossoming before him.

A pillar of white flames cascaded over the Thing. He couldn't make out details past vague flickers of tentacles thrashing within a burning white nimbus of fire. The tentacle holding Jessica dropped her to the floor.

Another piercing scream. This one weaker, somehow. Pitiful. Of surrender, not triumph. Another great rushing wind blasted through the room, followed by a teeth-shaking thunderclap obliterating all other thought.

The wind died.

So did the flames.

The Thing, parts falling off it and dissolving, crawled out of the room.

40.

OW. HOLY. SHIT.

Ow.

Jessica shifted, wincing at the small bruises which peppered her all over and flared into pain as she moved. Her muscles felt twisted and abused. Her joints ached. Her back felt stiff, her head was pounding. She wanted to curl up into a ball and go to sleep, right now. She knew she couldn't, however. Because everything had changed. A snippet from a poem—Robert Frost, she thought—came to her then, and seemed perfect.

I have promises to keep
and miles to go, before I sleep

She pushed herself up on her hands and knees. Slumped back into a sitting position against the wall. Clutched her head and pressed it, trying to squeeze the pain away.

What happened?

Her throat felt raw, from where that . . . *Thing* grabbed her and squeezed, with something thick and rubbery . . .

The house.

On the porch.

Down the hall.

The room, and the boy.

Chris.

An immense grief—a profound sadness mixed with joy—consumed her. She covered her face with her hands and wept at the fuzzy, half-memories swirling in her mind.

will it hurt?

a little

but then never again

Her sobs faded slowly. A sense of peace rushed in, but as she quieted and sniffled, the sound of something dragging itself across wood sparked her awareness.

She wiped her eyes. Blinked rapidly, scanned the room . . . and saw it.

Weak and diminished, limp and rubbery, dragging itself out the door, losing pieces which evaporated into a foul-smelling smog.

But still there.

The floorboards creaked as Scott crept towards her, staring at the Thing dragging itself away. When he spoke, his voice thrummed with a curious new confidence.

"I think it's done," he whispered, eyeing the flopping, dying thing.

She nodded, barely remembered images slowly fading already. "I know," she whispered, "but we have to make sure. Don't we?"

He nodded, lips pursed tight. "Yeah."

They got up and crept after it.

***

They followed it out the old house's front door, but stopped when they heard the throbbing a few feet away, in the old driveway.

A heavy, pulsing big block engine. One they recognized.

The Monte Carlo.

The car's headlights blazed alive, burning with a strange yellow light which didn't seem normal, somehow. It was a *different* kind of yellow. Burning with an intensity which made Scott and Jessica wince and hide their eyes. It also cast the burnt thing crawling toward it in stark relief.

It looked like a crude and sloppy caricature of a human, except for its four arms, which looked more like tentacles than anything else. Its skin was burnt to a crisp, oozing a thick black liquid. Instead of panting or wheezing, it gurgled, like an animal drowning in its own blood.

The Monte Carlo's door creaked open. Gravel crunched under boots as someone stepped out.

"Son of a bitch. I'm not going to lie, Scott. I didn't think you had it in you."

Scott shaded his eyes and tried to peer at the man standing behind the open driver-side door, but he couldn't see much past the headlight's glare. Someone tall, broad-shouldered, wearing an outback hat, jeans, boots, and a black duster. The hat threw shadows on the man's face. But where the eyes should be, Scott thought he saw two red embers glowing.

He recognized the voice, sure enough.

Tonight's the night!

"Yessir. You surprised the *hell* out of me, Scott boy. I knew you had the spark. Just figured you'd fold, honestly. And you, sweetheart," the man pointed a very normal and human finger at Jessica. "Well played. You snagged *another* one from me. BUT," the man's voice became hard as steel, "you need to step lightly, little miss. At some point, I will have to respond. We'll just have to see *when*. As for you . . . "

The man rounded the corner and approached the thing crawling toward him. Even though the headlights revealed more of his body, the hat still cast shadows over his face.

Scott tensed, but the man showed no interest in him at all. He reached down and grabbed the thing crawling on the ground and lifted it, squealing and writhing, into the air.

He shook it roughly. It whined piteously. "You were a *fucking* waste. Last time I invest in someone with Daddy issues, that's for sure. Suppose I can use you for *something*. Just don't know what."

The man spun on one heel and walked back around the Monte Carlo's open door. Casually, he flung the thing into the car's dark interior. Its squeal of pain and terror cut off sharply as it disappeared inside the car's depths.

The man paused. Scott could definitely see red pinpricks glowing in the shadow under his hat, and somehow, Scott knew the man was grinning.

"Happy Halloween, folks. See you next year." The man got into the Monte Carlo. The door swung shut, seemingly by itself. Gears thunked deep within the car. The engine revved, and it slowly backed down to the end of the driveway. Once there, it backed onto Haverton Road, pointed away from Clifton Heights, and drove off into the night. The shadows swallowed it whole.

Instinctively, Scott took Jessica's hand. She didn't resist, and held his tightly as they stood in the night, silent. Because they had no more words, nor did they need them.

OCTOBER. Sunsets of red-orange bleed into purple-bruised skies shot through with streaks of yellow. Crisp air playfully nips at noses and earlobes. Trees wave tapestries of red, orange, yellow and burnt umber, and rust-colored leaves crackle across sidewalks. Jack-o'-lanterns grin joyful fire from porches.

October.

My favorite time of year.

At least, it used to be.

I combed through the book Kevin gave me at least twice before I started searching the town archives to find connections to the stories I'd read. I found news articles about Evan Carrington's tragic accident. The autistic boy killed in a tragic hit-and-run. Peter Carrington's murder of Judd Kirsch (the man who hit his son Evan) and Peter's subsequent suicide. I didn't call Webb County Assisted Living because they wouldn't have been able to tell me if Evan Carrington was still a resident. That would've been a privacy violation. In some ways, I felt better because of that.

I found numerous sports articles about the day Scott Kennsiger inexplicably smashed Chris Testani's face with a fastball near the end of a sectional baseball game. He dropped off the map after that. I didn't find any reports about violent altercations at the Mobilmart on Haverton Road over the past ten years. Which, of course, didn't mean much. Those sorts of occurrences often go unreported in Clifton Heights. I did find a Jessica Hagarty listed in the phone book as living in The Commons Trailer Park. I had no intentions of calling her. There was no way, really, of knowing whether or not Evan Peters had been a bat boy for Clifton Heights' varsity baseball team.

I remember Micah Cassidy's basketball exploits from high school, especially because they so often came at the expense of the Clifton Heights varsity. I had moved away before the accident at Blackfoot Valley which destroyed his college basketball dreams, however, so I'd known nothing about that previously. I knew who the Longtrees were, of course. Everyone did. I also knew Deputy Tony Phelps. A good man. Hard to imagine him as . . . well, dead.

Blackfoot Valley Basketball Camp was torn down years ago.

A Google search for news articles in the York Township in Pennsylvania did turn up a small article in the York Daily News about the suicide of Lilly Ford, the assumed accidental death of her mother Beth several days later, and about Reverend Wesley Ford, presumed to have fled the scene. I found no local articles about anyone finding a man dead by a gunshot wound to the head, in a tent at the end of Boden Hill trail. This, however, wasn't surprising.

I could speak to Sheriff Baker and Father Ward when they get back into town. Confirm the story of Evan Carrington (which Father Ward had never told me, but I also assumed he had good reason), and ask Sheriff Baker about the legend of the 'reappearing skeleton.' I could ask them about these things, and I had no doubt they'd tell me the truth. Especially after all this time.

But as I sat on my cabin's deck, looking out over Clifton Lake as the sun set, I knew I wouldn't ask them. I didn't need to, did I? Nor did I need to believe the stories I'd read in that book were any more real than any other Halloween ghost story. This was my go-to. My sweet spot. Blurring the lines between fiction and reality, landing somewhere in the middle. I didn't need to think about it any deeper than that.

OCTOBER NIGHTS

And the fact that I'd passed a midnight black 1977 Monte Carlo parked in the turn-off next to Black Creek Bridge had nothing to do with my decision, at all.

Gavin Patchett
October, 2021
Clifton Heights, New York

BE LOST

It's all part of the show.
home
light
warmth:
they're a maze inside me,
& I'm blundering
toward
the heart.
where the night & my
true self
wait.

—Jessica McHugh

THE END?

Not if you want to dive into more of Crystal Lake Publishing's Tales from the Darkest Depths!

Check out our amazing website and online store.
https://www.crystallakepub.com

We always have great new projects and content on the website to dive into, as well as a newsletter, behind the scenes options, social media platforms, our own dark fiction shared-world series and our very own webstore. If you use the IGotMyCLPBook! coupon code in the store (at the checkout), you'll get a one-time-only 50% discount on your first eBook purchase!

Our webstore even has categories specifically for KU books, non-fiction, anthologies, more books by Kevin Lucia, and of course more novels and novellas.

ABOUT THE AUTHOR

Kevin Lucia is the Ebook/Trade Paperback editor at Cemetery Dance Publications. His short fiction has appeared in several anthologies, most notably with Neil Gaiman, Clive Barker, Bentley Little, Peter Straub and Robert McCammon.

His first short story collection, *Things Slip Through* was published November 2013, followed by *Devourer of Souls* in June 2014, *Through A Mirror, Darkly*, June 2015, his second short story collection, *Things You Need*, September 2018 and his novella *Mystery Road* from Cemetery Dance Publications, March, 2020.

Readers . . .

Thank you for reading *October Nights*. We hope you enjoyed this collection.

If you have a moment, please review *October Nights* at the store where you bought it.

Help other readers by telling them why you enjoyed this book. No need to write an in-depth discussion. Even a single sentence will be greatly appreciated. Reviews go a long way to helping a book sell, and is great for an author's career. It'll also help us to continue publishing quality books. You can also share a photo of yourself holding this book with the hashtag #IGotMyCLPBook!

Thank you again for taking the time to journey with Crystal Lake Publishing.

Visit our Linktree page for a list of our social media platforms. https://linktr.ee/CrystalLakePublishing

Our Mission Statement:

Since its founding in August 2012, Crystal Lake Publishing has quickly become one of the world's leading publishers of Dark Fiction and Horror books in print, eBook, and audio formats.

While we strive to present only the highest quality fiction and entertainment, we also endeavour to support authors along their writing journey. We offer our time and experience in non-fiction projects, as well as author mentoring and services, at competitive prices.

With several Bram Stoker Award wins and many other wins and nominations (including the HWA's Specialty Press Award), Crystal Lake Publishing puts integrity, honor, and respect at the forefront of our publishing operations.

We strive for each book and outreach program we spearhead to not only entertain and touch or comment on issues that affect our readers, but also to strengthen and support the Dark Fiction field and its authors.

Not only do we find and publish authors we believe are destined for greatness, but we strive to work with men and woman who endeavour to be decent human beings who care more for others than themselves, while still being hard working, driven, and passionate artists and storytellers.

Crystal Lake Publishing is and will always be a beacon of what passion and dedication, combined with overwhelming teamwork and respect, can accomplish. We endeavour to know each and every one of our readers, while building personal relationships with our authors, reviewers, bloggers, podcasters, bookstores, and libraries.

We will be as trustworthy, forthright, and transparent as any business can be, while also keeping most of the headaches away from our authors, since it's our job to solve the problems so they can stay in a creative mind. Which of course also means paying our authors.

We do not just publish books, we present to you worlds within your world, doors within your mind, from talented authors who sacrifice so much for a moment of your time.

There are some amazing small presses out there, and through collaboration and open forums we will continue to support other presses in the goal of helping authors and showing the world what quality small presses are capable of accomplishing. No one wins when a small press goes down, so we will always be there to support hardworking, legitimate presses and their authors. We don't see Crystal Lake as the best press out there, but we will always strive to be the best, strive to be the most interactive and grateful, and even blessed press around. No matter what happens over time, we will also take our mission very seriously while appreciating where we are and enjoying the journey.

What do we offer our authors that they can't do for themselves through self-publishing?

We are big supporters of self-publishing (especially hybrid publishing), if done with care, patience, and planning. However, not every author has the time or inclination to do market research, advertise, and set up book launch strategies. Although a lot of authors are successful in doing it all, strong small presses will always be there for the authors who just want to do what they do best: write.

What we offer is experience, industry knowledge, contacts and trust built up over years. And due to our strong brand and trusting fanbase, every Crystal Lake Publishing book comes with weight of respect. In time our fans begin to trust our judgment and will try a new author purely based on our support of said author.

With each launch we strive to fine-tune our approach, learn from our mistakes, and increase our reach. We continue to assure our authors that we're here for them and that we'll carry the weight of the launch and dealing with third parties while they focus on their strengths—be it writing, interviews, blogs, signings, etc.

We also offer several mentoring packages to

authors that include knowledge and skills they can use in both traditional and self-publishing endeavours.

We look forward to launching many new careers.

This is what we believe in. What we stand for. This will be our legacy.

**Welcome to Crystal Lake Publishing—
Tales from the Darkest Depths.**

Made in the USA
Las Vegas, NV
16 December 2021

38220391R00233